SILVER AND SMOKE

OTHER TITLES BY VAN HOANG

The Monstrous Misses Mai

SILVER AND SMOKE

VAN HOANG

47NORTH

Published by 47North, Seattle

www.apub.com

ISBN-13: 9781662517853 (paperback)
ISBN-13: 9781662517860 (digital)

Cover design by Kimberly Glyder
Cover image: © Dave Wall / ArcAngel; © Mariia Demchenko, © MoustacheGirl / Getty; © Mia Stendal / Shutterstock

Printed in the United States of America

For Mom.
Con viết một cuốn sách nữa!

Chapter One

Culver City, California, 1936

Issa Bui did not like mirrors, which was rather problematic for someone who dreamed of becoming a movie star.

It wasn't that she hated seeing herself, but rather that she would often see something else alongside her. Some*one* else, who most other people couldn't see.

Lately, that someone looked a lot like her grandmother, which didn't make sense because Bà Ngoại wasn't dead. Not yet, anyway.

She avoided looking at the reflective metal wall behind the panel of judges, even though she was fond of the waves she'd spent hours curling into her chin-length bob and the flattering maroon lipstick she'd applied and blotted so carefully. Instead, she focused on the casting directors for the movie she was auditioning for, but their faces looked so somber and serious that she wondered if any of them even liked moving pictures. Films were fun and entertaining, full of laughter and escapes into different worlds. The two men and one woman sitting behind the white Formica table in the small audition room looked like they'd never even heard of the concept.

The woman chewed on the cap of her pen and raised a brow at Issa. Her red cloche hat swept over her forehead, matching her lipstick almost perfectly.

"Shall I begin?" Issa held the script a young man had handed her before pushing her through the door. It only had about ten lines—most of it stage direction.

The man on the left scribbled something in his leather padfolio. He wore a brown suit with a matching bowler hat, which he'd set on the edge of the table. The one in the middle was in his shirtsleeves, bags under his eyes apparent even as he smiled and gave a slight nod that Issa chose to take as encouraging.

"I believe," Issa began, reading from the script, remembering a second too late to look up and actually *act*, "you have the wrong—"

Smoke swirled in the shiny wall behind them, like fog rolling in from the coast.

"The wrong—" Issa stammered. She blinked and shook her head. No, this couldn't be a visitation. Not here, of all places. Just a trick of the eyes. It wasn't even a mirror, just a shiny wall. A cloudy, dusty, somewhat shiny wall. She must be mistaking the smoke.

One of the men cleared his throat.

"The wrong file," Issa continued. The script shook in her hands. "Please, can I start over?"

The woman nodded while the man on the left dropped his pen loudly on the table.

"I believe you have the wrong file," Issa bit out quickly. The smoke thickened. It would clear soon, and once it did . . . well, she didn't want to be here. "The right one is in the center wing. We can go there together." That was it. She scanned the rest of the page, but she had no more lines. Relief washed over her, mixed with a heavy sense of dread and regret.

"Thank you," the friendlier man in the middle said before she could ask to try yet one more time.

All three of them bent over their notes.

Issa let out a breath, but already the smoke in the reflection had spread, clearing a bit to reveal the figure of someone she most definitely did not want to encounter. She hurried out of the room, wiping her sweaty palms down her hips.

Her skirt made it hard to walk as fast as she wanted, a long, fitted style that her best friend, Olivia Nong, had convinced her was perfect for the part. Olivia had been called into the audition room first, both of them technically auditioning for the same role though willing to take any part as long as they were cast. Issa felt a bit lost as she navigated the office building. She passed several people who kept their eyes fixed determinedly ahead.

Downstairs in the lobby, she sighed when she spotted Olivia by the door. With her long hair curled and carefully sculpted, Olivia already looked like a movie star. She'd chosen a simple white blouse, tailored perfectly to her body, paired with a midlength skirt that hit just below her knees. The outfit would have made Issa appear shorter and frumpier than she was, but on Olivia, it accentuated her height.

She noticed Issa and held out a hand. They looped their elbows and stepped outside the Lion Building toward the East Gate entrance of the MGM backlot. With only a temporary employee card allowing them inside for auditions, they weren't allowed to venture farther into the campus-like grounds of the studio. Issa craned her neck, trying to see past the concrete jungle of soundstages to the universes beyond, where whole worlds were created and filmed and made into movies viewed by millions. She longed to see more, but alas, she shuffled toward the exit under the careful attention of a security guard who made sure only stars and crew members went anywhere near the magic.

People gawked at Issa and Olivia, some turning as they passed to get better looks at them, but Issa felt instantly comforted now that she had someone to walk with. She was used to being stared at, being a young Asian woman in Culver City, but with Olivia, at least she wasn't the only one.

"How was it?" Olivia asked in her soft, low voice.

"It happened again," Issa said. "Smoke and such."

Olivia was quiet. Issa didn't have to explain much further, grateful that Olivia knew almost everything there was to know about her—including the family secret that wasn't that much of a secret, except that Issa's mom never allowed them to speak of it.

"Which ancestor do you think was trying to visit you?" Olivia asked.

"I didn't stay long enough to see who it was." Issa chewed on her lip as they walked to the Red Car stop a few blocks away. "But there's only one person it could be." It just didn't make sense because only spirits of people who'd died could visit, and besides, as far as Issa knew, *she* was the one who had to summon them. They couldn't just show up without her say-so. She was the shaman, after all.

Then again, she didn't know much about her shamanistic gift because Ma didn't see it as a gift, but rather as a curse. When Issa was six, her father passed away, and Ma packed up their belongings and moved out of Chinatown—away from Bà Ngoại, Auntie Yen, and Dead Auntie Phi. Once they were settled across town in Culver City, Ma expressly forbade Issa from contacting their family ever again, or having anything to do with summoning the dead or other clan business that Issa heard only vaguely about.

So it wasn't entirely Issa's fault that she didn't know much about what she could do or the strange occurrences becoming more frequent as of late. Perhaps she was conjuring the dead without meaning to.

"I wish we could talk to your aunt and find out," Olivia said as they joined the crowd at the streetcar station. It was just after noon, so most people must have been headed to lunch—men in suits and fedoras and women in business dresses and pinched heels, clutching purses.

"Ma would kill us if we did," Issa said, narrowly avoiding bumping shoulders with a woman who'd turned around abruptly as if she'd forgotten something. Issa stumbled into a man behind her instead, both grumbling pardons barely heard over the clanking of the approaching trolley.

Issa was grateful Olivia didn't point out the obvious—that they were both twenty now. Adults who could do what they wanted, technically.

"We'll go when she's at work," Olivia said. "She won't notice. We hardly see her."

"I feel guilty enough going to this audition," Issa said.

"One day, we'll make so much money that Ma won't care," Olivia said.

Issa smiled, daring to dream, just for a little bit. The trolley was crowded, people jostling each other for a seat, so it was nothing short of a miracle that she and Olivia found a vinyl-covered bench near the middle. With the clanging of the streetcar, the loud motors of passing cars, and the constant construction in the neighborhoods they passed, it was too loud to talk, so she imagined the life that she and Olivia dreamed of. The life of movie stars. A distant future, but one she wanted to believe in so much that it was impossible to picture anything else.

She loved the movies, loved the magic of stories, of being transported someplace different, to live someone else's life and lose herself for an hour or two knowing that no matter what happened, there would be a happy ending or, at least, some resolution. She found comfort in the certainty of a movie, of a story well told, found it all fascinating. She longed to be an actress. The art of pretending she was someone else, yes, but also the chance to be part of something bigger, something experienced and witnessed by millions of people. She wanted that life, knew she was destined for it—a long-lost home waiting for her in the distant future. She just had to find her way there.

When they got to their small two-bedroom apartment, they found Ma in the kitchen. Working the night shift at a downtown hotel meant she kept unusual hours, which, when added to the fact that she never slept much or regularly, amounted to Issa not knowing if or when she'd see her own mother. Her heart always warmed at the sight of Ma, now wearing a floral-print nightgown, her hair wet and curling in black ribbons about her shoulders, as she labored over the kitchen stove.

"That smells marvelous," Issa said, throwing her purse on the entrance table cluttered with mail and random knickknacks no one was willing to tidy. She gave Ma a peck on the cheek, noticing a new dark spot by her left eye. Ma had great cheekbones and an attractively strong chin, but the effect was ruined by the wrinkles and blemishes that she didn't care to get rid of. There were creams for that sort of thing, but Ma would never spend money on anything so frivolous when she had to pay the rent and feed the three of them on a launderess's pittance, Issa supplementing what she could from odd jobs she'd managed to get after school.

Issa leaned over her shoulder to sniff the broth in the pot. "Chicken soup?"

"It's for the church," Ma said. "But you can have some before I take it." She nodded at the cupboard where they kept small bowls and teacups.

Olivia was already there, setting the table with three places before anyone asked her.

"Where were you two?" Ma asked as she stirred the soup. She hadn't looked at them, but Issa heard a suspicious lilt in her tone.

Issa didn't like lying to her mother, mostly because Ma was incredibly shrewd and always detected it anyway. For the most part, Ma was an aloof sort of parent. She worked too much to pay attention to what Issa did and cared so little about much, but what she did care about, she did so with an intensity that was quite scary. Issa tried to never invoke her rage.

"We were out looking for jobs," Olivia answered for her. Not a lie.

Ma tapped the ladle against the edge of the pot before setting it down in an empty bowl. "Jobs? What jobs? Why do you need to search for jobs? I told you there's an opening at the hotel."

Ma had been trying to convince Issa for months to interview at the hotel basement laundry where she worked. She'd never liked the idea of them being in movies and scowled and lectured every time it came up, convinced that movies were the devil's work and that the girls were tainting their souls. Since deciding to shun her own mother and sisters, she had moved so far into the opposite realm of beliefs that Issa found it difficult to agree with her. But to Ma's credit, she'd never once forced Issa to go to the Catholic church where she spent most of her free time.

"I don't want to work in the laundry room," Issa said. "Not permanently." She sometimes helped when Ma brought in extra work from private clients.

Olivia took their bowls of soup to the dining table, giving Issa a look as if to say, *Be careful.* She never liked it when Issa and Ma bickered, which they did more often than not.

"So what kind of jobs were you searching for then?" Ma turned slowly, hands on her hips.

Issa sat down and blew on her bowl.

"Issa," Ma said.

"Acting jobs," Issa answered with a sigh.

It was a good thing Ma wasn't holding the ladle any longer, or she might have flung it across the room. Her wet hair practically steamed, her face growing red with heat.

"Acting pays well," Olivia said, probably trying to stop the scolding before it started.

"I'll give you everything I earn," Issa joined in.

Ma crossed her arms. "If you get a role."

"We will," Issa said.

"I'll give my pay to your church, Auntie," Olivia added with a sweet smile.

Ma's face softened. She'd always had a weak spot for Olivia. Most people did, when Olivia chose to bestow her charm on them. It wasn't just that she was pretty; she also had a magnetism that drew people to her and made people feel warm and happy and comforted and cared for. Or perhaps Issa only felt that way because they were best friends.

"You only need to give ten percent," Ma said.

"That's a horrible outlook," Issa teased, encouraged that Ma hadn't said anything about demons and movies yet. They might avoid an argument after all. "You're supposed to tell us to give it our all. One hundred percent. How else are we going to achieve our dreams?"

"I meant to the church," Ma said with exasperation. She had never understood sarcasm. Or humor, come to think of it. "A typical tithe is ten percent. Besides, I would never tell you to give it your all. There'd be nothing left of you."

Issa's motivation to stay cheerful waned as it often did around her mother. "It's just an adage, Ma."

"Well, it's a stupid one. Nothing is worth giving up everything. Not even this silly dream of yours."

"It's not silly."

"You want to be famous? A star? For what? Nothing wrong with your life now."

Issa took a deep breath, the muscles of her shoulders tensing in preparation for a fight. But she took a long look at Ma—her tired face, her hunched back as she reached down to retrieve a pot lid from a bottom drawer—and decided she didn't have it in her today.

"You're right, Ma." Issa got up to give Ma a hug. "Thank you for everything you do."

Ma leaned away, flabbergasted, but then she settled against Issa's arms.

"When I'm rich and famous," Issa said, "I'll buy us a house so big, we'll have to shout at each other to talk."

"What do I need a big house for? So much dusting."

Issa smiled and smoothed Ma's hair from her face. "I'll make sure you never have to dust anything ever again."

Ma rolled her eyes. "Dusting is not a bad thing. If you would just do it once in a while, you'd know."

Issa laughed. "Nothing will make you happy, huh?"

"I am happy!" Ma moved toward her bedroom, tossing her hands up. "Don't I look happy?"

Chapter Two

In the bedroom they shared, Issa threw herself face down on the twin-size bed.

"Issa, you'll dirty the sheets with your makeup," Olivia said. She went to the small dresser in the corner of the room and came back with a cloth. "Here."

Issa lifted her head awkwardly, inspecting the bedspread for stains before sitting upright. "She's so exasperating."

Olivia smiled and patted her back. "At least she loves you."

Issa didn't know what to say to that because of course Olivia was right—she and Ma were often at each other's throats, but she knew it was only because Ma cared about her. Many others weren't so fortunate. Olivia's parents died when she was very little, and she had been sent to live with an uncle who drank too much and worked too little.

Olivia never liked to talk much about her life at home—even less, now that she had left it behind—but Issa had gleaned what she could throughout their years of friendship. They met when they were six, the only Asian children in their entire school, and instantly became friends. When Issa asked her about her uncle, Olivia always changed the subject, not even bothering to make up a lie.

When they were schoolchildren, Olivia came over so often that Ma bought her a chest of drawers, and Issa cleaned out half her closet—though they shared so many things, it was hard to differentiate what was whose. Eventually, Olivia stopped going home altogether, and Ma didn't even ask why. Issa understood it to be some incident regarding Olivia's uncle, but her best friend didn't like to go into detail, so she left it alone. Ma even started bringing home clothes for Olivia as well. They couldn't afford nice dresses, but Ma understood the importance of appearance and kept Issa's things clean. Sometimes she found fancy outfits that had remained in the lost-and-found box of the hotel for too long—a tailored jacket she had fixed to fit Issa, a blue cotton dress that made Issa appear better off than she was so kids at school wouldn't pick on her—and without anyone mentioning it, Ma kept her eyes peeled for anything that might fit Olivia's taller, more coltish frame.

Never once had Ma made Olivia feel unwelcome, adopting her so seamlessly into their family that Olivia felt more like a sister than a friend. In fact, Ma never hid the fact that she sometimes wished Issa was more like Olivia—quick to obey, at least to Ma's face, and quiet and demure with her elders.

Issa might have been jealous and resentful of her best friend, except that she, too, had always pretended Olivia was her real sister. They'd done everything together since that fateful day in first grade when neither of them understood a word the teacher said, following each other like two dots of oil in a pot of water. Olivia had spent most afternoons with Issa in the two-bedroom Ma rented, coming over after school to finish their homework under Ma's strict instructions to never-not-ever unlock the door for anyone but her as she left for the evening shift at the hotel.

When they were old enough to walk home without Ma, they began making stops on the five-block walk from their school, scrounging any change they came across on the sidewalks to tuck away like magpies. Ma was too busy to worry, and Issa always assured her they went straight home to lock the doors, which gave Ma time to pick up more shifts and earn more money so that they could afford better things.

Strangers often mistook Issa and Olivia for sisters, though that was only because they were both young Vietnamese women. Really, they looked nothing alike—Issa's nose was flatter and wider, her face more moon-shaped, her complexion quick to blush and bordering on ruddy, with the peculiar ability to acquire and lose a dark tan practically overnight.

Even if she did resemble Olivia, her best friend always ended up drawing the curiosity of everyone they met. People looked at Olivia with enchantment, like she was some ethereal goddess from a different realm. Other girls had hated Olivia, resented the attention she drew. But Issa knew better than to envy her best friend, knew that Olivia's mannerisms were a result of a childhood lived in fear. The only thing that marred her features was a scar on her lip from the time her uncle had split it, though even that had healed in a way that distinguished her, giving her an impish, shy sort of smile.

Issa got up to change, not wanting to ruin the nicer clothes they reserved for auditions. Ma had yelled at Issa often enough about leaving things in her pockets, so she dug through them out of habit, surprised when her fingers brushed against the sharp corner of an envelope.

"Another one?" Olivia asked when Issa pulled out the note.

Like the others, it was plain, with a red wax seal bearing no stamp.

"How much did she give you this time?" Olivia asked.

Issa tore the edge of the envelope and reached inside. The note, a rectangular card, was simple. "I need to see you," she read out loud. It wasn't signed.

Issa should have known that the people bumping into her at the Red Car station were her grandmother's employees, their movements carefully orchestrated to keep watch on her. It had happened so many times before, starting when she was old enough to walk home from school without Ma. Bà Ngoại's network of aunties and uncles always found her. The notes had never come from Bà Ngoại directly, but just because Ma decided she didn't want Bà Ngoại in their lives anymore didn't mean Bà Ngoại respected her decision.

At first, Issa had done what Ma told her—stayed away from her grandmother and anything to do with her—and tossed the envelopes away. But one time when they were sixteen, Olivia was with her when a man handed her a note.

"Your mom never told me to stay away from your Bà Ngoại," Olivia had pointed out. So Issa shrugged and let Olivia pop the seal off. A piece of paper slid out of the opening, along with a one-dollar bill. Their mouths fell open. Issa imagined her eyes were just as wide as Olivia's.

"Wow," Olivia said, holding up the crisp note. Issa had never held a dollar bill before. They rarely had more than that in the tea can they kept as a coin bank, always dipping into it for groceries or some emergency. She took it from Olivia and rubbed the fibrous paper between her fingers.

"What should we do with it?" Issa asked.

"We can't give it to your ma," Olivia said, and Issa wanted to hug her for being the one to say it. "She'll know. Or ask questions. Then you'll have to spill about all the other notes from your grandma."

They debated this for some time before Issa remembered the note that came with the bill. She unfolded the piece of paper, expecting a lengthy lecture in the form of a letter, but there was only one line.

"Remember who loves you," she read out loud. "Is that . . . is this a threat?"

"I think it means she loves you."

"I don't know," Issa said, folding the note. "It doesn't sound very . . . loving."

Olivia shuddered. "Your grandma is terrifying. Even my uncle is afraid of her."

Issa held the dollar bill between her thumb and index finger, and then an idea came to her. "Let's go to the pictures."

"What?" But it was clear Olivia had heard her, a smile already brightening her face. "Really?"

"Yeah, whyever not?" Ma wouldn't be home until close to dawn.

"How? Where?" Olivia asked.

"We can take the streetcar to downtown," Issa said.

"Downtown?" Olivia's eyes widened. "But—"

"There's a theater there. Ma talks about it all the time. Complains about how crowded it gets on the sidewalk in front and makes her late to work."

"But she works downtown. What if she sees us?"

"She's too busy. It'll be aces." Issa held up the dollar bill. "When will we have the chance again?"

Olivia grinned. "All right, then, let's go."

They were so excited, they held each other's hands as they walked down the street, something they hadn't done in years. Issa had ridden the streetcar with Ma a few times, but Ma considered even that an extravagance and insisted they walk everywhere. As she sat on the bench with Olivia, a sensation she'd never experienced before washed over her.

Freedom. Why hadn't it occurred to her before? She could do whatever she wanted, really. She and Olivia were left to their own devices for hours every evening. Ma worked so much and trusted them to get home and feed themselves and go to bed, like good little girls. Issa had spent every afternoon and evening like this since she was a child, and it had never occurred to her not to obey. But right now, with the dollar in her pocket, she felt as if she could do anything.

"I wonder if the other envelopes you threw away had money in them," Olivia said.

Issa went hot and cold. "Let's not dwell on that." Though once Olivia said it, it was all she could think about, bringing on a mixture of emotions. Regret and guilt over literally throwing away money—though how could she have known? Then anger and resentment—but with whom, it was hard to tell at first. Herself for not once questioning why she obeyed so trustingly, but mostly Ma. Here was Bà Ngoại wanting to hand them money, and Ma was working her knuckles to the bone just to get by. And as far as Issa knew, Bà Ngoại had never done anything wrong except believe in something that Ma was afraid of.

That day Issa maintained a small flame of anger as they made their way through the crowded downtown sidewalk, construction clanging and whirring as the steel-framed buildings around them seemed to grow taller by the minute. They passed men in suits carrying briefcases and women in silk blouses, cinched waists, and flared skirts, looking like they were going somewhere important. Beggars lined the streets, some seeking shelter under the scaffolding in front of buildings or collecting their belongings as policemen blew on whistles for them to move along.

No matter who they saw or how fast they walked, everyone turned and stared at Issa and Olivia. Issa wasn't sure if it was because they looked too young to wander around on their own—being petite and chubby-faced, she was often mistaken for a child—or if it was because they were Asian. They weren't the only Asians in California, of course, but there were so few that they often attracted unwanted attention.

It used to bother Issa, but she'd learned that the only thing to do was to lift her head high and make tracks with her shoulders back as if she didn't care. Walking next to her, Olivia somehow looked like she relished the attention, assuming a carefree yet pleasant expression. One man even stopped midstride and took off his felt hat, turning his head blatantly when they passed.

They spotted the theater from half a block away, its arching roof with the marquee rising above the sidewalk and shading the people in line beneath as if they were in a protective cave. The blocky black letters announced several titles.

"What should we see?" Issa asked.

The theater was showing three movies: *Little Women*, *42nd Street*, and *Dinner at Eight*. Since neither of them had ever been to the pictures before, they both studied the options as if the answer would blink at them.

"Isn't *Little Women* a book?" Olivia asked.

Issa chewed on her lower lip. "If Ma asks, which she won't, but if she does, we could say it's for school."

"All right, then, that settles it."

Issa made sure to enunciate her words as they bought tickets at the front booth because even though she didn't have an accent, people often expected her to and, subconsciously or not, chose not to understand when she first spoke. The man wore what looked like a black porter's uniform with gold trimmings as if he worked at a hotel instead of a theater, and didn't bother to look up as he handed them two tickets.

Inside, the main lobby seemed bigger than possible from the exterior facade, the red patterned carpet extending to the beige walls, the ceiling stretching high. A grand staircase dominated the center, but it was roped off, and an attendant directed them to theater number three.

It was already dark in the cool space, but the silver glow of the screen lit their path. Most of the seats were filled, so Issa and Olivia had to sit near the front. With so many people behind her, she felt exposed, even though she knew, rationally, that they were paying attention to the screen, not her. It didn't matter anyway, because the movie started, and everything faded away.

Issa would always remember that first movie she saw, the way she lost herself in the story, the way the actress's face looked onscreen and the handsome actor who held her. Issa had read the book for school, but seeing it play out gave her a different sensation, the realization that other people thought similarly yet differently from what she imagined. It made her feel both other and as if she belonged. A confusing blend.

More than that, she was aware of everyone's reactions around her. When Olivia cried and took her hand, she gripped it right back. When a character said something funny, the entire theater laughed. Toward the end, she caught several women dabbing their eyes with handkerchiefs. All because of the movie, which she knew was fictional. And yet it had miraculously transported them all into the lives of other people for two hours.

When the screen went dark, she and Olivia remained seated while everyone else left. Neither of them said anything, a heaviness present between them as if they could sense the weight of what had just happened.

"That was amazing," Olivia spoke at last when they got home.

Ma was still at work, and Issa had forgotten to worry about getting in trouble, but it didn't matter. Ma was never home. And even though Issa knew she had to work hard to take care of them, the bitter resentment returned. Ma insisted on being free from Bà Ngoại when the lives they lived weren't exactly *free*, not if she was imprisoned in a hotel basement all day and night, working until her hands were raw. If Ma insisted that freedom from her own mother's control was the way she wanted to live, then how could she argue with Issa for wanting . . . the exact same?

"We could do that," Issa said as she and Olivia lay next to each other that night in Issa's twin-size bed, squeezed in shoulder to shoulder. "Act."

It was a profound statement. Neither of them knew the first thing about acting or how to get started.

"You think so?" Olivia asked. "You think we can?"

"Anna May Wong did it," Issa said. "She's doing it. Why can't we?" They'd never seen Anna May in theaters, but she was in the papers all the time, her beauty and talent always remarked upon.

"How?" Olivia asked.

Issa took her questioning as a positive sign. "We'll find out tomorrow."

And that was what they did, every day, for the next four years, researching all they could at the school library, then the public library in downtown, picking up newspapers and circling ads for extras in movies. The studios were not far. In fact, MGM and RKO were practically in their backyard, and Warner Bros. and Walt Disney were in Burbank, just a few streetcars away. They took trips to the studios after school, none of it amounting to anything, but it was still exciting to see the lots, even if it was just from the gates.

Once, they'd even snuck in after a tour group at MGM, Issa feeling slightly guilty when offered champagne and cubes of cheese during the midday break. It had been worth it to walk around the soundstages, which looked like concrete warehouses from the outside but revealed magical worlds inside the hangar-like doors. An entire building was dedicated to storing the archives of all the films ever made. Whole towns built for movies, facades designed so realistically she wanted to live there herself. Streets resembling famous areas in New York City or Chicago, or entire villages constructed to bring a historic era to life.

She found it fascinating that some actors and writers lived on the lot in adorable dressing rooms bigger than their entire apartment. She stared at the white-curtained windows with envy, imagining her life as a contracted star. What a dream—to know for certain that you were guaranteed five, six, seven movies.

The first step was to get a studio to sign them for just one movie—both her and Olivia. They were practically a package deal, going everywhere together, depending on and supporting one another.

Once they discovered that studios provided acting lessons and coaching to their actors, they realized their dream wasn't impossible. Stars weren't just born with natural talent, they were taught, which meant that Issa and Olivia could be taught.

They sought out group classes, but the only one that they could afford turned out to be a sham, the instructor an old white man whose knowledge of the industry came from books far out of date, and who groped the female students in almost every scene. Another coach laughed right in their faces when she saw them, making up gibberish words that Issa assumed the woman thought sounded like an Asian language. Another had seemed promising but cost way too much.

They had done well to keep the movie business a secret from Ma at first. Not a difficult task, until one day, Ma woke up earlier than usual before they left for the day.

"Now that you'll be done with school soon," Ma said before Issa closed the door, "you can work with me at the hotel. One of the maids is getting married, and the manager said she'll give you a chance first, because of me."

"What?" Issa wasn't sure she'd heard right. "But I don't want to work at the hotel."

"Want? What do you mean, 'want'? No one *wants* to work there."

"But, Ma—"

"What else are you going to do? Once you graduate, I can't have you sitting around all day. You need to start earning your keep."

Issa glanced at Olivia. They hadn't lied to Ma, not directly, but they'd never told her the truth either. If she cared to ask what they'd been up to, which was rare, they would vaguely say they spent their afternoons studying or at the library.

"We have auditions," Issa said. Half a lie. Aspiring actors gathered every morning outside the gates of MGM in the hopes of being chosen as extras, but Issa and Olivia had never been bold enough to ditch school to join the throng. Once they graduated, they'd be free to do so.

"Auditions?" Ma spit out the word like it tasted bad. "For what?"

"For movies, Ma."

"Movies?" It took Ma a moment to understand, the idea so preposterous that Issa didn't blame her. She had thought so, too, at first, and only by telling herself day after day that it was possible could she believe it would be. She needed it to be. "Ayah, you think you can be in the movies? Are you delusional?"

"Ma—" Issa started to argue.

"We're going to be late for school," Olivia interrupted before they could launch into a full fight. "I'm sorry, Auntie Linh, but we have an exam first thing."

That was a lie, but it was the only thing that would stop Ma from keeping Issa there until Issa admitted Ma was right, which would be never. Ma was wrong. Issa knew it deep in her bones, the way she knew Ma was wrong to keep her away from her grandmother. She wasn't meant for a life doing laundry in a hotel basement. She was destined for something bigger.

"We'll talk about this later," Ma said to Issa. "But you go to the hotel for a job interview next week."

Issa opened her mouth, but Olivia shut the front door and pulled her away.

That had been a year ago.

If Ma was wrong about acting, then what else was she wrong about? What else was she keeping Issa from? Issa knew that she was meant for greater things. The blood of shamans ran in her veins, after all. The life she wanted was just waiting for her. It must be, because she couldn't keep living like this. Yet here she was, four years after she began dreaming of acting, still sharing a small apartment with her mother, afraid to upset anyone but herself.

Issa folded the note neatly into squares, her grandmother's handwriting etched into her mind. *I need to see you*, she'd written.

"I think it's time to pay Bà Ngoại a visit," she said.

Chapter Three

But first, they had to find out the results of their audition.

Ma didn't make enough money to own a telephone, so they made the trek to the MGM lot the next day. Issa didn't mind—she loved visiting the studio, passing through the gate with their temporary employee cards, pretending for a second as she walked by the tall white pillars leading to the Lion Building that she belonged there, a contract actor, a star on her way to fame.

The casting department was a big room full of desks and heavy tables, stacks of paper cluttering every surface, people on telephones or talking to one another in hushed tones. They didn't see an official receptionist's desk, so they stood awkwardly until a harassed-looking young woman in sharp glasses rushed over to a pile of papers by the door.

"Name?" she asked them without any other greeting.

"Olivia Nong," Olivia said.

"And Issabel Bui." Issa had to spell out her name. She was used to it, but every time she did so, she got annoyed at Ma all over again for misspelling it on her birth certificate and dooming her to a lifetime of explaining every time she was introduced.

"Right." The woman ran a finger down a list of names. "Nothing. Sorry." She slapped the file down and ran off as someone waved her over.

"Nothing?" Issa repeated, not quite sure what had happened.

Olivia looked both shocked and indignant. "What do you mean, 'nothing'?" she shouted after the woman, but no one paid them any attention except for a man with a thick mustache eating a doughnut. A sprinkle got caught in his bristles as he leered at them.

"Extras?" he asked.

"We auditioned for small parts," Olivia said, listing her hip into an attractive pose.

It got his attention, because he flipped through the file the other girl had set down. "Right, they cast Collete Augustine for the lead."

"We didn't audition for leads," Issa said. "We were up for secretaries."

The man looked her up and down. "Darling, our secretaries don't look like, uh, you. Perhaps you should try a war piece or . . . something with a maid."

Issa's mouth fell open. She tried to come up with something equally rude to say back, but Olivia pulled on her arm and dragged her out of the room.

"Ridiculous," Olivia muttered. "We were wonderful. Perfect for the part."

They seethed as they stomped out of the building, but then Olivia suddenly stopped and threw her head back with a frustrated groan.

"It took us weeks to even hear about that audition," she said.

Issa nodded, furious. They'd lined up with the masses in front of the gate every morning when producers scouted the crowd for potential extras. Hundreds of people competed for attention, beautiful women dressed to the nines, men shouting and singing to be heard. It was like winning the lottery to be chosen, and it was only by luck that they had overheard a man tell another man about the open call, with the producers willing to see the first fifty applicants. After years of obsessing over movies, it had been their first lucky tip. Only to end in failure.

As Issa's heart rate calmed, she smoothed her palm over Olivia's back. "It's fine," she said. "We'll get another chance."

"How?" Olivia asked, her eyes glistening, her nose reddening.

"We'll go back to storming the gate."

Olivia laughed. "I suppose we don't have many other options."

Issa smiled, even though her heart sank just as heavily from the news. She waited a few more seconds for Olivia to compose herself. "Come along then," she said. "Let's go ask my grandmother for money."

⟡

Bà Ngoại owned a building in Chinatown with a redbrick facade and maroon steps. She lived in the large apartment that took up the entire top floor with Auntie Yen. When she died, half of the building would belong to Ma, though of course Ma would never accept it, even at the expense of starvation.

"Picture how rich we'd be," Issa complained as they walked through the darkly carpeted hallway. "Even if it is blood money."

"Blood money is still money," Olivia said.

It wasn't a luxury building by any means. Everything was a shade of brown, from the walls to the ceiling to the rows of mailboxes in the empty lobby. It smelled like mildew, sweat, and piss, and the stairs were likely haunted from the many fatal falls they had witnessed, but the family rented the rooms out cheap to other immigrants who had difficulty providing paperwork elsewhere, as well as to friends of friends of friends, and the income was substantial.

Issa didn't know much about the inner workings of Bà Ngoại and Auntie Yen's business. She'd only dared to visit a few times after Bà Ngoại demanded it in the notes she delivered to Issa through her network. Bà Ngoại never went into the details of the family operation. From what Issa gathered, she understood that Bà Ngo ại wasn't a bad person. She was a good person who sometimes did bad things, and who occasionally partnered with bad people to help the good.

At the door to apartment 3C, Issa took a deep breath before knocking, riddled with nervousness and guilt, and also a bit of irrational fear that Ma would find out.

There was no answer.

"Maybe she's out," Olivia said.

"It's Tuesday," Issa said, though that wouldn't mean anything at all. "We came all this way. We have no money to get home. I knew something like this would happen—"

"Hush, now. It'll be all right." Olivia reached into her bag for a pack of cigarettes. Issa hated when she smoked. Olivia only did it when she was nervous, and only because she thought it looked sophisticated, holding the cigarette between her index and middle fingers and letting ash fall everywhere.

Before she could light it, the door opened. A man in a black suit and matching hat shouldered past.

Inside, Auntie Yen waited in a gray silk robe, not surprised to see them.

"Come in, shut the door," she said. A kettle started whistling, then screaming, until she lifted it off the stove and poured it into a teapot. The tray was already set with three porcelain cups, which she carried over to the sofa and placed on the coffee table. In the corner, a record spun on the Victrola, the volume turned low on a Duke Ellington number.

Olivia lingered behind Issa, but followed her after a pause. They took off their jackets to hang on the coatrack and kicked their shoes off to place neatly on the shelf by the door. The space was decorated in bold jewel tones, gold trimming, and damask, an eyeful of decadence. The sofa was a bold red, uncluttered except for two gold throw pillows. Around the coffee table, floor cushions covered in thick, shiny blue-and-green brocade sat in neat stacks.

Auntie Yen took the seat on the sofa, spreading one arm over the back like a queen. She was older than Ma, but she didn't look it. One couldn't tell, actually—she could claim to be twenty or fifty, and people would believe her. It wasn't just that she'd smoothed her skin over with makeup, but that she always dressed well, carrying the air of someone who knew she was highly sought-after. People treated her with respect. Issa found her terrifying and awe-inspiring.

"Hi, Auntie," Issa said, bending down to kiss her on the cheek.

Auntie Yen smiled and kissed the air next to Issa's face, her lips barely pursed in a somewhat distant manner. "Sit," she commanded, gesturing toward the sofa.

Issa was relieved Auntie Yen didn't expect them to huddle on the floor like peasants. Usually Bà Ngoại sat alone on the large seat while everyone else had to kneel on the floor pillows. It was humbling for rich men in fancy suits without their shoes to lower themselves before the matriarch of the Left Tusks, the name she called their group. Since Auntie Yen sat in the middle of the sofa, the girls took the space on either side of her. Issa was used to not wearing shoes indoors, but something about it here made her feel vulnerable, like she wouldn't be able to run away as quickly as she wanted, if the occasion called for it. She hoped it wouldn't call for it. But this was her aunt, for goodness' sake. They had come here because they needed her. And Auntie Yen seemed to know they were coming.

"Where's Bà Ngoại?" Issa asked.

"What do you mean?" Yen asked.

Issa fought the urge to look at Olivia for reassurance. "She sent me a note. She said she needed to see me."

Auntie Yen let out a sigh, picked up a cigarette box, and gave it a hard tap, then a second one when she glanced at Olivia. "When did you get the note?"

"Just yesterday."

Yen lit a cigarette and handed it to Olivia before lighting the second one for herself. "Always playing games, that one."

Issa didn't know what to make of that.

"We brought a pork bun," Olivia said, handing over the white-wrapped package with both hands and a little dip of her head.

"Such sweet girls," Auntie Yen said. She smelled the package and smiled before placing it on the maroon-lacquered coffee table.

"What did Bà Ngoại want to see me about?" Issa asked.

Yen blew out a puff of smoke. "Only she has the answer to that."

"Right. So why isn't she here?"

"Because she's dead."

"What?" Issa jerked upright, sitting on the edge of the sofa. "What?" she repeated, unable to form any other words.

Yen leaned back. "She's been trying to get you here for weeks."

"Yes, but you know how Ma is."

At the mention of her youngest sister, Auntie Yen pursed her lips. "She doesn't know you're here, of course."

"No. But—what do you mean, Bà Ngoại is dead? She can't be—she was so . . . alive . . ."

What a stupid thing to say, but Issa couldn't seem to think straight, flooded with emotions. Confusion, mostly. Dread. Her grandmother's demise had always been a distant threat, a harbinger of things to come—what would happen to the clan? And where did Ma fit into its future? What about Issa? She'd always picked up on the unspoken expectation in her interactions with Bà Ngoại, brief as they were, that they expected Issa to come back, to join their gang once Ma could be convinced.

Issa had known her grandmother wouldn't live forever, but the old woman was so formidable, so tough and intimidating, that her death had barely seemed possible.

"You're sad?" Auntie Yen asked.

It took several seconds for Issa to truly consider the question. Was she sad? Well, surely—this was her grandmother, after all. But they hadn't been *close*. Bà Ngoại was, perhaps not loved, but revered by so many people that Issa could hardly edge in among the crowd. Her grandmother was a shaman who specialized in mediating between the breathing and the dead, and she was so famous that people traveled from Las Vegas and New York, even Vietnam, to see her. A year into her career, as the family lore went, she gained the attention of Mr. Song, a notorious crime boss who controlled most of the underground dealings in Chinatown Los Angeles, and rose to power within the echelons of the underground elite.

She was a frightening figure, a cautionary tale, an omen, a dark and scary presence who had made Issa feel both trapped and watched and cared for. Despite Bà Ngoại's attempts to stay in touch through the subterfuge, the notes, the secret meetings, there had never been many opportunities for a relationship.

Issa *was* sad, though. But she was sad in the way one was when one learned about a favorite celebrity passing away. And she also felt guilty for being sad, because she didn't deserve to grieve over someone she hardly knew. And then she felt guilty for not being *sadder*.

"Why didn't anyone tell me?" Issa asked.

"Bà Ngoại tried to," Auntie Yen pointed out. "She summoned you several times."

This was true, but Issa had been too obsessed with standing in line at the MGM gates and trying to nab an audition to pay attention. In Issa's defense, Bà Ngoại was perpetually asking her to visit, and even when Issa did, her grandmother always scolded her for not doing it often enough. Ignoring her requests became a constant source of guilt that she eventually found easy to live with.

"She had plenty of time to prepare," Yen continued. "She tied up everything nicely. Except she wanted one last chat with you."

"Was it cancer?" Issa asked. Bà Ngoại had been diagnosed with disease of the lung—not surprising, considering how much she smoked—but that had never stopped her from going about her business, and everyone sometimes forgot she was even sick.

Yen nodded and took a long pull of her cigarette. At the sight of the embers glowing red, something seemed to give away inside Issa, and tears filled her eyes. Bà Ngoại usually sat in this exact spot, smoking and studying Issa with an intense judgment that Issa didn't exactly miss, but now realized she would never experience again. She ducked her head, embarrassed at her reaction, especially in front of her domineering aunt.

"Stop your tears, now," Yen said, stubbing the cigarette butt on an ashtray on the coffee table. "You can speak to her if you want."

Olivia, who had been listening quietly, dug in her purse for a handkerchief, which she handed to Issa.

"I can?" Issa asked.

"Silly girl," Yen said. "You're a shaman, just like Bà Ngoại and me and your ma."

"Oh. Right." Issa had always known she could summon the dead, but she'd never once done it intentionally and had never had any desire to.

"Your ma never kept up the lessons?" Yen asked with a hopeful expression.

Issa shook her head.

"She was so good at it, you know. Even better than me. We would summon your Dead Auntie Phi together." Dead Auntie Phi was Ma's older sister but she was, well, dead, and had been so for as long as Issa could remember. "Shame she left the profession," Yen continued. "I'm too busy leading the Tusks to summon the dead, and with your grandmother gone, we're short of shamans. Had to turn away good money the other day because we didn't have anyone to conjure the dead for this poor widow."

"Do you really make a lot of money conjuring?" Issa asked. "How much?"

Auntie Yen lit another cigarette. "It's decent. It's how Bà Ngoại got her start."

Olivia had been quiet until now, smoking her cigarette with polite eagerness. "She built an empire by raising the dead," she whispered with deep reverence.

Issa glanced over, surprised by the respect in Olivia's voice.

Auntie Yen beamed. "What an eloquent way to put it."

"Well, Ma will never come back," Issa said. "No matter how much money she could earn if she did."

Auntie Yen sighed, then gestured at the tea tray on the coffee table. Issa hurried to pour for all three of them, handing Yen her cup first with both hands. "I could use her help getting the gang in line. Ever since your grandma died, there's been trouble."

"What sort of trouble?" Issa asked.

"You know your uncles. Uncle Quanh and Uncle Truong—they believe they should inherit the leadership. They didn't want your Bà Ngoại to leave it to me."

"But she did," Issa pointed out.

"She left it to her daughtersss," Auntie Yen continued, drawing out the plurality of the word. "The uncles are using that as a technicality to challenge my leadership. Since your ma isn't here to run things with me, they're saying I don't have the right to rule."

"But you're doing great," Olivia said softly. "I heard you helped sponsor the Huynhs, which must have cost a fortune, and the new buildings in Chinatown are all because of your investment."

Auntie Yen waved a hand, but she looked pleased. Issa raised her brows at Olivia, surprised that she knew so much. Olivia gave a sheepish sort of smile.

"Those old men call themselves the Right Horn," Auntie Yen said with a snicker. "Can you believe it? Because we're the Left Tusks." She gave a snort. "Ridiculous. We'll see how long their little gang lasts."

"Be careful, Auntie," Olivia said. "I heard they set fire to a hotel building on Fifth and Spring. Don't you own that plaza?"

"I do. It's not the worst they've done, and we've retaliated in kind. We have more people than them, and more money. I'm not worried." Her tone sounded a bit hollow, as if she had repeated this mantra many times in the hopes it would come true.

Issa wished she could help, but she had nothing to offer.

Auntie Yen sipped her tea, then set the cup down with a clink. "Enough about me," she said, standing up. "Let us conjure your dead grandma."

Chapter Four

Auntie Yen led them down the hall to a room dedicated to communing with the deceased, outfitted with floor-to-ceiling mirrors. Golden bowls formed a circle on the floor, each filled with dried rice grains to prop up incense sticks in varying lengths, ash curling at the ends.

"Here," Yen said, handing Issa her lighter. "I usually have help, but this is a private matter, so I've asked my assistant to leave us alone for the next hour."

Issa paused before she took the lighter from her aunt. She still couldn't shake that instinctive, nagging voice—which sounded a lot like Ma—telling her to stay away from this sort of thing.

"I'll do it," Olivia said, but Issa shook her head and stooped to light the incense.

She'd always felt detached from her family—her clan family, which no longer included Ma—but it seemed especially pronounced after seeing that Olivia knew more about the Left Tusks than she did. The least she could do was make herself useful. Lighting the incense gave her an excuse to hide her face as she examined why she felt both shame about her family and embarrassment for feeling so.

She wanted to blame her resistance to her shamanistic background on Ma, but she knew that was just an excuse. The truth was she didn't want any part of the family business—the drama and danger and violence—to affect her life in any way that would impede her from achieving her dreams. She knew that if she let them, the family would drag her down, would absorb her into *their* dreams. She knew how important a star's public image was. If she wanted to be a famous actress, she'd need to separate herself from the clan and their criminal dealings. And yet, she still needed Yen's help.

With the incense lit, she straightened to find that Auntie Yen and Olivia had settled in the middle of the circle. Issa sat down next to Olivia. Smoke clouded the air.

"We'll need a picture of the spirit," Yen said, gesturing to the frame she had propped up to face the mirrors.

In the photo, Bà Ngoại didn't look much younger than Issa remembered, dressed in a traditional Vietnamese áo dài made of thick brocade, the collar rising high on her neck, her chin lifted, her black hair piled on her head in a puffed updo. Jade earrings ornamented her lobes.

Wherever Issa turned, Bà Ngoại's reflection stared back, alongside Olivia, who looked excited. Issa's own face looked more nervous than anything, so she felt reassured when Olivia smiled and nodded at her.

Issa didn't know what to expect—when she'd lived here as a very young girl, she hadn't witnessed the summonings, and Bà Ngoại hadn't performed any during her recent visits. For some reason, she expected Yen to perform a proper chant, something dramatically ritualistic.

Instead, Yen just looked into the reflection and waved. "All right, Ma? Are you there? The girls made it."

Smoke thickened, swirling as if it might turn into words. When it cleared, Bà Ngoại was *there*. Well, not really there, but her picture was, and the reflection of her picture moved in fits and starts.

"Connection between the living and dead can be difficult to establish," Auntie Yen explained with a shrug. The mirror grew foggy, and Bà Ngoại's photograph kept freezing, but Yen didn't look concerned. "We can light more incense, but it's still draining for the spirit, and the shaman. Or we can offer some blood."

"Blood?" Issa gulped and clutched her finger, practically feeling a prick there. "No thank you."

"Since there's two of us here," Auntie Yen said, "we have some time before we need to resort to that."

Issa started to ask who the second shaman was, but then she realized it was her.

"Focus on your grandmother," Yen said, nodding at the picture.

Issa turned toward the mirror and studied Bà Ngoại's features, which looked so different from her own. Bà Ngoại had a large, prominent forehead, a square-shaped face, and a strong chin with a muscular jaw used to clenching in anger. Issa's face had always been round and soft and too chubby.

"Home at last!" Bà Ngoại called out in her raspy voice, her eyes shifting to take in the room. "I miss this place."

"You were just here last night," Yen said.

"Ayah, you don't know how long a day feels in the underworld. Wait till you're dead. You'll hate it."

"I thought you said you enjoy the afterlife," Yen said. "You have time to rest and gamble as much as you want now."

"Bah. Even that gets boring sometimes. If only I can find a worthy body to possess, I wouldn't be so helpless."

"You can do that?" Issa asked. "Possess bodies?" The hairs on the back of her neck rose.

"Didn't you listen to anything I taught you?" Bà Ngoại said. "Only the most powerful ghosts can, and they can only get stronger by spending more time in the mortal world, which they cannot do without the help of a shaman witch." She barely paused for breath. "*Which* they cannot do, because we are one of the few shaman families in existence, and the others are simply frauds."

Auntie Yen gave Issa a little shake of the head as if to tell her not to believe everything Bà Ngoại said, confusing her even more. Was any of this true or was her grandmother being dramatic or was her aunt just trying to assuage her fears?

"Should have never told you that," Bà Ngoại continued. "Now you'll be all like your mother, scared of every spirit that may haunt her doorway. As if anyone wants to visit her, the ingrate. Claims she doesn't believe this stuff, as if she didn't summon your worthless grandfather a hundred times after he died to complain about me. You know he tried to possess me! The imbecile. He forgot that I taught him everything he knows."

"Did he succeed?" Issa asked, becoming more horrified the more she learned about her family. Bà Ngoại and Auntie Yen always went out of their way to claim that spirits were harmless. That they were actually just lonely and wanted to help. But once in a while, they would let slip some scary detail like this that made Issa question everything they'd ever taught her, which wasn't much to begin with.

"Just barely," Bà Ngoại admitted. "Only a finger. I was tempted to cut it off, but I know a simple trick to ward off spirit possession. Burn their pictures. Anything that gives them a connection to this world. I was stupid enough to keep your grandfather in a locket. A moment of sentimental weakness. Well, don't you worry, I got rid of every single image that he snuck into the house, the self-centered coward."

That explained why they didn't have pictures of any men in the clan. All this time, she'd assumed Bà Ngoại just hated her uncles and any reminder or smallest hint that she might not be the best leader of the Left Tusks.

Bà Ngoại's face smoothed into a genuine and affectionate smile as she took in the sight of the girls as if noticing them for the first time. "Issa, look at you." She smiled wide, her face transforming into what Issa imagined other warm and welcoming grandmothers looked like. But then she said, "You've gained weight."

"Oh," Issa said, crestfallen. She couldn't help covering her belly with her arms.

"Of course I gained weight," Olivia said, nudging Issa playfully, even though they both knew Bà Ngoại had been talking about Issa. "Not much to do now that we're done with school except get fat." She guffawed, making her laugh deliberately obnoxious. Her real laugh was more of a pleasant tinkling.

"What are you talking about?" Bà Ngoại said with a tsk. "You look even skinnier than the last time I saw you. Like a twig. I was referring to my granddaughter."

Issa rolled her eyes. "It's nice to see you too."

"See me? When do you ever come to see me? For months I lay on my deathbed wondering when my only, precious granddaughter will come to visit. Finally I have my answer: When I'm dead."

"You know why I couldn't see you. Ma forbade it."

"Oh? Oh, she forbade it, did she? The same way she forbids you to smoke those cigarettes? And the same way she forbids you to go see those movies because she thinks they're the devil's work?"

"That's different . . ."

"Ack." Bà Ngoại cut her off, or perhaps she was just hacking up a lungful of smoke. The reflection clouded over. "You think you're so special? I don't want to talk to you either."

"Ma," Auntie Yen said with exasperation. "You called her here for a reason."

Bà Ngoại harrumphed and turned her chin up. The smoke stopped swirling for a moment.

"We're sorry we couldn't make it to you in time," Issa said.

"We tried, honestly, we did," Olivia joined in. Issa felt an enormous swell of gratitude for her best friend.

Bà Ngoại nodded at her in acknowledgment. Like Ma, she didn't miss a beat in accepting Olivia as if she were Issa's sister, including her in both praises and lectures. "Well, at least you summoned me correctly," Bà Ngoại said. "I thought your mother would have beaten it out of you."

Issa didn't point out that technically it was Auntie Yen who had done the summoning. "Ma never beats me. She used to sprinkle holy water on us, but you know that doesn't do anything."

"Except stink up the place." Bà Ngoại reached out as if to pinch their cheeks, but her fingers plinked against an invisible wall in her picture's reflection.

Issa gave her sweetest smile, her chest filling with strong emotions she knew better than to admit out loud. Things were not *said* in their family. Feelings were kept to oneself, never expressed. It was simply understood, because if you had to say it out loud, then surely you didn't feel strongly enough about it.

And because of that, Issa remembered that even though she was the shaman now that Bà Ngoại was simply a spirit, Issa was the one who'd actually been summoned.

"Why did you want to talk to me?" Issa asked.

Bà Ngoại's lips curved mischievously, which was a rather frightening sight, as Issa only ever saw her look so gleeful when she talked about revenge.

"As you may know, I'm dead now," her grandmother said with a grin. "And I have a substantial sum to leave behind."

Issa nodded calmly, while next to her, Olivia's knee bounced with excitement. Issa had always assumed that Auntie Yen would inherit everything. Yen was Bà's filial daughter, the one who naturally took leadership. She did the work and would receive the pay.

"I'm giving some to you," Bà Ngoại said.

Olivia took Issa's hand. "Oh wow," she said. She jostled Issa to say something.

"But I thought I was disinherited," Issa said.

Bà Ngoại made a funny sound. "How so?"

"Because Ma is disowned—so as her daughter, by extension . . ."

"Your Ma *left*!" Bà Ngoại shrieked. She'd never been able to maintain her temper for long when Ma was the topic of conversation. "She made a *choice*. And I have *never* abandoned her. In fact, you can have her money too."

"I can't do that," Issa said. "Ma would find out."

"No she wouldn't," Olivia said.

Yen had been staring off into the distance, but now she looked at Issa. "Take the money, Issa. Buy her a laundromat or something. She'd love it."

"She always talks about us owning one together," Issa said. Working there until they died, a morbid sort of dream, though Ma would call it realistic. "Wait, you're giving me enough to buy a laundromat?"

"You don't need to buy her a laundromat," Bà Ngoại said. "Give her the one on Fifth Street."

"We're using that one to field the drug ring," Auntie Yen whispered, as if the girls were too naive to understand or hear such things.

"Ayah, I forgot." Bà Ngoại shook her head. "No matter. That ingrate doesn't deserve it anyway. You can have everything I set aside for her, Issa. It's yours—don't even tell her. With one condition."

Issa bit back a groan, but she couldn't control her face.

"You have to return to us," Bà Ngoại continued, ignoring Issa's dismayed expression. "Leave your ma and come back here. It's more comfortable anyway. We have more space. You and Olivia can each have your own rooms. We'll even give you an apartment."

"But I'm here already," Issa said, acting deliberately jejune because even though what Bà offered was tempting, she did not want it.

Bà Ngoại gave Issa a blank stare with fire in her eyes that conveyed more than anything she could have shouted. Bà Ngoại was the one in charge here. Issa's role was to listen and obey. But Issa couldn't bring herself to agree, repulsed by this life they expected her to live. She was destined for other things. She'd already decided this, had made a deal with herself that she couldn't compromise, that she'd do what it took even if she had to turn down money. Ironic that she was more like her mother than she cared to admit.

"Who do you think you are?" Bà Ngoại asked finally, her voice soft but full of venom. When Issa looked down, shame making her skin tingle, Bà Ngoại spoke louder. "I'm asking you—what purpose do you serve in life, Issa Bui? Do you think you were placed here for the pleasure of your company? No—you were born into this family for a reason. You are our sole heir. Has that ever occurred to you?"

Issa glanced at Auntie Yen, who wore a stern expression and didn't come to her defense. After Ma abandoned the clan, she and Issa lived in isolation and Issa rarely thought about her auntie and grandma. It had seemed like Bà Ngoại was willing to let them go—but then they found out that Auntie Yen couldn't have children, and that was probably why they made contact again. It wasn't because they loved her. They simply needed her.

"Isn't there a cousin, or . . . There's got to be someone who would do a much better job than me. Someone who's not an uncle or one of us—someone in the middle? What about Ngoc Le?" Issa had met the woman—an older cousin, five times removed—when she was just a child, and remembered her as a frightening, loud bully of a girl. She would be perfect.

"I suppose she would be a neutral candidate—" Auntie Yen started to say.

"I will not entertain this line of thought," Bà Ngoại snapped. "It is out of the question. I built a legacy, and I will not leave it to rot and decay."

"But Auntie Yen is here," Issa said. "And she's doing a marvelous job. There's no way I can ever take over."

"Yen won't be around forever," Bà Ngoại said. "This is a dangerous profession. Look at Dead Phi. Shot during her rounds. It was an accident, but still."

Issa knew Phi had been picking up money from the local businesses in their network when she'd been caught in an altercation that didn't necessarily involve her.

"And you want me to be part of it?" Issa asked.

"There is no such thing as *want*," Bà Ngoại said, reminding Issa exactly of her mother. "Not in our family. You were born into it, whether you or I or anyone wants you to be—that's not the question."

"Apparently it is," Issa said.

Bà Ngoại breathed in and out, smoke thickening around her face. "What else do you have planned for your life?"

Issa stared at her hands, her shoulders curling in on herself. She wanted to disappear, to escape this conversation. Perhaps if she stayed quiet enough, Bà Ngoại would simply leave.

Something brushed her elbow, making her jump. It was only Olivia, nodding at her encouragingly.

"We're going to be movie stars," Olivia said when Issa couldn't bring herself to speak up. "We've already been to a few auditions."

"Movie stars?" Bà Ngoại's lips twitched, but at least her jovial tone was back, and a bit of tension eased from the room. "I know a dead star on this side, you know. She's not any happier than the rest of us."

"Who?" Olivia asked eagerly.

"Ava Lin Rang. Have you heard of her?"

"She was famous during the Silent Era," Yen said. "You're too young to remember her."

"She couldn't have been that famous then," Issa said.

Olivia shook her head. "But she's Asian?"

"Chinese," Yen said with a smile.

"That's wonderful. She'll know exactly what we need to do to get roles," Olivia said.

"But she's dead," Issa pointed out. "How can she help us?"

"She can give us advice," Olivia said. "She'll probably be more help than that useless coach we paid."

Issa didn't like the idea of asking a ghost for help. A shiver tickled her spine.

"What do you want to be famous for, anyway?" Bà Ngoại asked.

"Well, I . . ." Issa didn't want to explain the longing that she felt every time she thought about it, the irresistible pull that insisted she take part in this glamorous world. Once she became a star, once she'd really *made* it, she imagined it would feel like coming home after a long trip, everyone wondering where she'd been all this time. She couldn't admit this sentiment aloud, especially to someone like Bà Ngoại who had never cared what anyone else wanted. It felt too vulnerable.

"We want to help others." Olivia summed it up for her, though Issa wouldn't agree that that was the sole reason she wanted to act. "Imagine our faces"—she pulled Issa close—"on-screen. Imagine all the little girls like us who can start believing in themselves too."

Issa beamed, hiding the surprise she felt at Olivia's words. Her best friend had never hidden the fact that she wanted to be famous merely for the money. After how she'd grown up, one could hardly blame her.

Bà Ngoại studied Issa's face as if she could see right through her. "This is what you really want?"

Issa nodded, not daring to hope. Instead, she prepared to walk away from this the way she did when she argued with Ma—frustrated and sad and ready to prove everyone wrong.

"How about a compromise?" Auntie Yen suggested.

Bà Ngoại pursed her lips and waited.

"There's no reason you can't give it an honest try," Auntie Yen said. "You have time. I'm not going anywhere. So let her take the chance," she said to Bà Ngoại. "See if she can prove herself."

Smoke swirled in the reflection so thick that Issa thought Bà Ngoại was leaving, angry at the prospect of Issa being successful. But then the image cleared.

"If you fail," Bà Ngoại said, "then you belong to us."

"Goodness," Issa said. "That sounds ominous."

"Don't be a child," Bà Ngoại said.

"I don't want to belong to anyone."

"What we mean," Auntie Yen said, "is that you commit to us. The same way you'll commit to your acting career now—give it everything you've got. Don't make any excuses for yourself. Do everything you can to succeed. But if you stop or if you fail, you have to give us the same commitment. Move back here, learn from the business, train to take over should anything happen to me."

"Is that all?" Issa asked, unable to keep the sarcasm out of her voice.

"I think it's a rather fair compromise," Yen said. She raised her brows at Issa, and Issa knew that she was right. Making this compromise was better than continuing to argue with her family about what she should do with her own life.

"How long do we have?" Olivia asked.

Yen and Bà Ngoại looked at each other.

"A year," Yen said.

"That's hardly enough time," Issa protested. "We've been going to the MGM gates for months, and so far we've only had a small bit of luck that went nowhere." She regretted admitting this out loud, realizing that Yen and Bà could use it as fuel for their fight.

But to her surprise, Yen gave her a reassuring smile.

"Yes, but you didn't have us to help you," her aunt said.

"But don't you want me to fail?"

"Why would we want you to fail?" Bà Ngoại asked. Her voice seemed raspier, her reflection more staticky as she moved. Yen lit another incense stick.

"Because then you win," Issa said. "And I commit to the family and all that."

"This isn't about winning," Bà Ngoại said. "We're on the same side. And you're already committed to the family, Issa. That's what we've been trying to tell you."

Issa still didn't quite understand or believe her. Yen and Bà were used to getting their way; they hadn't gotten to where they were by being nice. Perhaps this compromise was just a trick to get her to depend on the clan so she'd have no choice but to return to them.

Still, she knew that they had a better chance of success with Yen's approval and money than without.

"If I succeed, who'll take over the clan then?" Issa asked.

"We'll consider other candidates," Yen said with a crooked smile. "Ngoc Le really isn't a terrible choice, but if we decide to go that route, then we'll have to invite other cousins to propose an heir."

"Like auditioning," Issa said.

Bà Ngoại must have seen the doubt on Issa's face. "If you're going to be a star, then be a *star*. Because if you fail, you failed because you were meant to. There can be no excuses. If you return to us, you will return to us fully. Committed. No second guessing or doubts."

Issa glanced at Olivia, whose eyes shone with such hope that Issa couldn't even think of refusing, even while a part of her knew that

Olivia had nothing to lose in this bargain. She wasn't the one signing her life away to criminal dealings and gang wars.

"I'm with you no matter what you decide," Olivia whispered. She took Issa's hand, her fingers warm as they wrapped around Issa's.

Issa could walk away from all of it, but she needed Yen's help if she wanted to be a star. The image of a boring life of obscurity flashed in her mind—and Issa felt so repulsed that she quickly shut it down.

She turned to the ghost in the mirror. "Let's make a deal, then."

Chapter Five

Issa collapsed on the sofa in Yen's living room, feeling suddenly exhausted. Olivia sat next to her with a comforting hand on her shoulder while they waited for Yen to finish talking to Bà Ngoại.

"What's wrong with me?" she mumbled when Yen came back.

"Communing with the dead is tiring work," Yen said, her own voice sounding distant and quiet.

Issa covered her face with a throw pillow. A small bell chimed, Yen whispered instructions in Vietnamese, and then, a second later, a teapot and cups rattled. Yen's maid had brought them another tray, this time laden with sandwiches, fried dumplings, and almond cookies.

"Oh, thank goodness." Issa wolfed down handfuls, not caring how she looked, and Yen did the same. Only Olivia nibbled daintily, holding her teacup in her slender fingers like a proper lady.

"Does it always feel like this?" Issa asked.

"It will get better the more you practice," Yen said. "But be careful at first, especially when you summon on your own. You won't feel the effects until after the ritual, and it may leave you more depleted than you realize."

"I don't plan on conjuring on my own," Issa said.

"You'll need to. You'll have to call on Bà Ngoại for monthly updates," Yen pointed out. It was part of the compromise they struck. "We provide you with the funds, as agreed. As a monthly allowance. So you must check in with her and brief her on your progress."

Issa ate another sandwich, mulling this over.

"I've never summoned on my own," she said.

"Well, you just saw how. It's not that hard. Just take a picture of her with you and some incense, and all you'll need is a mirror, which acts as a portal into our realm. Incense is the key to unlocking it, as well as the blood of a shaman witch."

"But we don't have to use blood, do we?" Issa asked.

"No one is saying you have to bleed," Yen said. "You simply must be present to establish a connection in the first place, and once done, nothing more is needed. Just be careful at first. In return, we'll help you in any way we can."

"Do you know anyone in the movie business?" Olivia asked.

"Not that I can think of at the moment," Auntie Yen said. "But our network is large."

Issa gave Olivia a skeptical look. Their network was large but full of criminals—surely no one in Hollywood.

"The best way to go about this," Yen continued, "is to seek that dead star for advice."

"I agree," Olivia said at the same time that Issa said, "No."

Olivia looked at her. "There's no harm in it."

"Bà said ghosts get stronger the more time they're in the mortal world," Issa pointed out.

"Stronger how?" Olivia asked.

They looked at Yen.

Yen sighed. "They develop powers. Supernatural gifts—the ability to seduce or convince mortals, for example, among other things. Each spirit is different, so it depends on the individual. And certainly there is the chance of possession—"

"Oh, all right, then," Issa said with a nervous laugh, even though her blood ran cold.

"But it's rare," Yen said, "and can only happen if the bond between the two is incredibly strong to begin with. It takes a lot of power to completely take control of someone."

"I feel so much better," Issa said dryly.

"We don't know this star," Olivia said. "So the chances of possession are pretty slim."

"Exactly," Issa said, surprised she had to argue the point at all. "We don't know if we can trust her."

"We'll keep the conjuring short," Olivia said. "I think we should at least meet her."

Issa covered her mouth. The idea of any sort of summoning made her stomach churn.

"All right, not now," Olivia said, patting her back.

"You can always decide later if you want to summon her," Yen said. Her face also looked slightly green. "In the meantime, you have the next best thing at your disposal."

"What's that?" Issa asked.

Yen smiled over her teacup. "Money."

Olivia had a plan. "There's this party on Catalina Island every year," she explained on the streetcar home. "I read about it in *Variety*. All the stars attend, it's practically required."

"Won't we need invitations for that sort of thing?" Issa asked.

"We'll bribe a waiter or something," Olivia said.

"I don't know, Olivia. What if we get caught?"

"And?"

"Won't they give us the boot?"

Olivia laughed. "We'll just go home. No one will care or remember us."

Issa groaned. The idea of it was so embarrassing.

"You aren't willing to try anything," Olivia said with a frustrated huff.

"That's not true," Issa said.

"You don't want to talk to the ghost—"

"With good reason," Issa hissed. There weren't many people on the streetcar, but she didn't want anyone overhearing.

"And now you don't want to go to a simple party."

"I just . . ." Issa wished she could explain—or rather that Olivia would understand—how debilitatingly embarrassing it felt. But Olivia had always been the brave one, bold enough to do what it took to get what she wanted. Sometimes Issa wanted to step into Olivia's body, to read her mind, to feel how Olivia must feel. Unencumbered by doubt and ready to take charge. Maybe that was why Issa wanted to be an actress so much. There was freedom and escape in pretending she wasn't who she was, a shy woman always worried about what other people thought.

Olivia sighed. "There will be so many celebrities and industry people there, I'm sure one of them will discover us. Maybe introduce us to a director, someone who could give us a start."

"If you're so sure it will work, why didn't you mention it before?"

"Because we never had so much money before."

It was true. When Auntie Yen handed Issa the envelope stuffed with her allowance for the month, they both nearly fainted. Issa clutched her purse now, scared she'd misplace or lose the money somehow. Of course, it had included Ma's portion, and Issa would set that aside. She couldn't steal from her own mother.

When the streetcar pulled up to their stop, Olivia got out first. With her longer legs, she always walked a bit faster than Issa, and Issa struggled to keep up, unable to shake the feeling that Olivia was deliberately leaving her behind. Even though Issa could have reached out and touched her shoulder, it felt like Olivia was miles away.

"Oh, all right. Let's go to this party," Issa said.

Olivia stopped walking and studied her face. "You're certain?"

Issa nodded even while she battled her inner turmoil of dread and anxiety. "We'll have to buy something to wear."

Olivia did a little dance in excitement. "That won't be a problem."

They spent the next few weeks getting ready. Issa read as many copies of *Variety* as she could find at the library to learn about this annual gathering of the stars. She dug up what she could on the actress Ava Lin Rang that Bà Ngoại mentioned, learning that she'd been rather famous before retiring several years ago. Or at least everyone assumed she had retired. Unlike most other stars, she hadn't made a public announcement, and had simply stopped making any more movies.

They told Ma they were going to attend a weekend-long class on the island, keeping the lie to a minimum. Ma had gotten huffy, but then Issa handed over a little bit of cash from what Yen had given her. She wanted to give her more, but knew that too much would look suspicious.

"From my acting job," she said, feeling slightly guilty for the lie, not just for telling it but because it was something she wanted so badly. If only they'd gotten the parts they'd auditioned for, she wouldn't have to crash some party and possibly make a fool of herself.

Ma's face went slack with surprise. "You got the job?"

Issa nodded, gulping. Ma took the money and couldn't seem to meet her eyes.

"When will the movie be out?" Ma asked.

"What?" Issa said, surprised. "You mean, you want to watch it?"

"Of course. I want to see you."

Issa's lower lip started quivering. She didn't think Ma cared. Ma had always made it seem like Issa was delusional for wanting something so far-fetched and impractical, for daring to have dreams outside of laboring for the rest of her life.

Issa resolved that she would use this event to get a role. If only so her lie to Ma wouldn't be a lie at all.

"Probably in a year," Issa said. "These things can take a long time."

Ma nodded but didn't say anything, only clutched Issa's hand. "Be careful." But whether she was just talking about the weekend or something else, Issa wasn't sure.

Chapter Six

Auntie Yen made arrangements for Issa and Olivia to stay at the Hotel Saint Catherine on Catalina, a famous attraction on the waterfront known for hosting stars. With more money in their pockets than they'd ever seen in their lives, they took the Catalina Steamer to the island, then transferred to a separate taxi boat. It dropped them off at a dock leading up to the multibuilding grounds surrounded by gardens and bougainvillea like a modern-day fairy-tale castle. Well-manicured hedges and rosebushes adorned the path up to the lobby.

As they approached the hotel, people stared, and Issa couldn't tell if it was because of the usual reason or because they appeared terribly rich in their fancy new clothes, carrying expensive luggage. She sweated profusely and itched to get out of the English country tweed suit Auntie Yen had lent her. It had looked so adorable when she dressed this morning, in a dark autumnal overcheck, paired with a cashmere scarf that she'd chosen on an impulse, thinking the ferry ride would be abysmally cold. Olivia wore a high-end number as if she lived in that sort of thing, a spring suit in black faille with white dots, the peplum flaring at the waist, creating a flirty flounce that contrasted with the wide shoulders of the top.

When they got to their room, Issa nearly choked. The bed was nice, yes, at least four times the size of the twin they shared, with a canopy and curtains out of some sort of gothic novel. But it was the view that caught her eye, the wide window showing off the hills of the island

and the water surrounding it, spreading forever across the horizon and disappearing into the blue, cloudless sky.

"Goodness," she said, but they were interrupted as the bellhop brought in their suitcases.

Issa waited while Olivia tipped the boy, taking the time to peel back a dollar from her stack. They'd been so careful not to show how much cash they had, so Issa knew Olivia was calculating something.

"What time is the party tonight, again?" Olivia asked the boy.

"Party, ma'am?" he asked. It was weird to see Olivia being addressed as *ma'am* when the boy was probably no older than them.

"We accidentally left our invitations at home, you see," she said. She slowly peeled back another dollar—probably more than what he made in a week. "And I promised Robert Taylor we'd be there on time. He's always berating us for being late." She gave a dazzling laugh.

The boy stared at the folded cash in her hands. His lips moved as if his mouth salivated. "They won't let you in without an invitation, ma'am. Is there someone you can call to have replacements sent over?"

Olivia pouted in disappointment. She folded the second dollar back into the stack.

"The Garden Ballroom is terribly exclusive," he explained quickly. "I don't have any say, of course. But you probably understand, esteemed ladies such as yourselves, how we need to protect our guests from . . . the general public."

"Of course, of course," Olivia said, unfolding the same dollar. "We know exactly what it's like to be bombarded by fans. It's only that we're from overseas—it won't be so easy to get replacement invitations. We left them in Vietnam, you see. We must have lost them at our last movie premiere."

The boy looked from her to Issa, who turned on her best smile as she wondered what Olivia was on about. Vietnam? Neither of them had ever been to Vietnam, both born in Los Angeles.

"My shift usually ends at eight," he said. He licked his lips as Olivia peeled back another dollar. "I can escort you to the party."

"Can you, really?" Olivia peeled back another dollar, about to hand him all four, but thought better of it. "Here's for helping us with our luggage." She gave him three. "And we'll have more tonight once we're at the party." A twinkle in her eye. Something like determination in his.

He nodded, taking the bills in his gloved hands. "Thank you, ma'am." He gave a little bow before leaving.

"What was all that about Vietnam?" Issa asked once he was gone.

"Who's to say that we're not famous there?" Olivia said.

"Well, we're not."

"But they don't know that, do they? Come on, we're always getting turned away because of this." Olivia gestured at her face. "We might as well use it to our advantage."

They waited until eight, but the bellhop never showed up. Impatient, Olivia insisted on going down to the Garden Ballroom, but they were too intimidated to walk past the men in suits standing sentry by the rosebush path leading up to it. Instead, they loitered in a small garden close by, pretending to enjoy the view of the oceanfront village, its pretty lights reflecting off the black ocean surface like an underworld city.

"It's like heaven for the wicked," Olivia said as they listened to laughter from somewhere in the distance, the sound of music playing, drunken flirting and cavorting. Or at least that was what Issa pictured—everyone having fun without them.

"Where is that boy?" Issa said, looking over her shoulders.

"He probably took the money and ran," Olivia said. "Three whole dollars. I should have offered him more."

"Nonsense, you were quite generous, all for a bit of nothing. We could have brought up our own suitcases. Look where we are. Sitting out here in the dark like peasants. Perhaps they'll get sleepy soon enough." Issa nodded toward the suited guards. "Or we can seduce one of them." She pulled at the folds of her neckline to reveal another inch of skin, feeling glamorous in the full-length sleeveless evening gown with a high neck and silk collar. Olivia's creamy dress was loose at the bodice and cinched by a belt at the waist before flaring into a flowy, pleated skirt. It looked very similar to one modeled by Jean Harlow in *Harper's Bazaar*. They were quite a becoming pair.

Olivia gave her a lascivious look. "I'm not above it."

A wave of impulsivity washed over Issa, as it often did when Olivia challenged her to do something. It might have been childish to act rashly or indulge in a moment of silliness, but Issa got up and did a little dance.

"What are you doing?" Olivia whispered.

Issa laughed and walked away. Before she could lose her nerve, she sauntered over to the security guard, relishing the way the man looked up and down her body.

"Excuse me, sir," she said in her sweetest voice, injecting a bit of an accent into her words. It was a horrendous attempt, as Issa grew up speaking English, and she inwardly cringed. "We lost our invitations to the party."

"S'that so?" the guard said, stepping forward to meet her.

"We've come all the way from Vietnam, you see," she continued, bolstered by Olivia's presence at her elbow. The guards looked to Olivia, who turned on her magnetism like switching on a light, batting her eyelashes in a seductive yet somehow shy manner that always brought out a protective urge in others, particularly older men.

"We must have dropped them somewhere," Olivia added. Like Issa, she also spoke with an accent, but she managed to make it sound sophisticated. Well traveled.

The first guard laughed. "That shouldn't be a problem."

Issa glanced at Olivia. Could this really work?

"Because we have a list," the second guard said, pulling out a clipboard from the podium. "What are your names?"

"Um," Issa stuttered, and because she couldn't come up with something fake fast enough, she blurted out their real names.

The guard laughed. "Your last name is Bui? Boo-y? And you want to be in showbiz?"

His companion joined him, both men snickering into their fists. Issa thought she saw one of them tug on the corner of his eye, wiping away a tear but lingering a bit too long to stretch the lid. Her veins flooded with hot, liquid anger, followed by a cold numbness. She was reminded of a time when she and Olivia were about fourteen, their first chance to go to the spring formal, and they'd scrimped and saved as much as they could for dresses. Issa had even done a few jobs with Ma, folding laundry for special clients at the hotel for pennies. Then Issa and Olivia went to a secondhand shop downtown, where they found only ball gowns two sizes too big for them and much too long.

Olivia tried on a purple taffeta thing that made her skin tone appear almost putrid. It was the first time Issa had ever seen anything unflattering on her.

"Purple certainly isn't your color," she said.

The sound of giggles distracted her from a few racks over, but she ignored them.

"The yellow one isn't so bad on you," Olivia said.

"It's way too big."

"You can ask Ma to take it in."

"Then we'll have to tell her about the dance."

More giggles, closer this time.

"I don't think we should hide it from her," Olivia said.

"She'll think it's silly."

"But she'll let you go."

"Yes, probably." Ma had never been the strict, overbearing type of parent. There was only one thing she forbade—Bà Ngoại and anything to do with her.

The giggles came even closer, followed by whispering. Issa spun around, freezing when she spotted three white girls from her school behind a rack, covering their mouths and glancing at Issa and Olivia.

"What?" Issa snapped, hands on her hips, not caring how she looked in the baggy dress.

The girls burst into laughter.

"Who would take you to the spring formal?" one of them said, her words barely coherent because she couldn't stop laughing. She'd turned to her friends and made the same gesture the security guards made now—tugging on the corner of her eye in a mocking imitation.

It wasn't the worst thing that ever happened to them. Boys and girls alike—sometimes grown people—called them horrible names. A boy who sat behind Issa in class stuck a pouch of pins on her chair once, right as she sat down, and she cried out as the sharp points pierced the bottoms of her thighs. The teacher sided with the boy, assuring Issa that it was a mere accident—as if it were normal for a boy to carry pins in a pouch and leave them around. But there was nothing Issa could do about it. When she told Ma, she seethed and muttered something about curses, but told Issa to leave it alone.

"Things will only get worse if you don't," Ma said.

But things would only get worse if she *did*. Because she *had* left it alone. All her life, she let things go. She stayed quiet, she accepted her role and her fate, and all it brought her was pain or invisibility. If she wasn't picked on or made fun of, she was ignored . . . made to apologize for her existence. Something had to change. She was not going to live in obscurity for the rest of her years.

Olivia was still arguing with the guards, who snickered the same way those teenage girls had all those years ago.

"Your names aren't on the list, sweethearts," the second guard said. The first guard couldn't stop laughing.

"You didn't even check," Olivia said.

"Don't have to. I know they wouldn't have invited you."

"What—why?" Olivia demanded.

Issa tugged on her arm. She knew where this was headed.

"But—" Olivia said.

"Let's just go," Issa said quietly.

The men leered at them as Issa pulled Olivia away.

"I don't understand," Olivia said through gritted teeth. "They didn't even look at the list."

"It's a good thing they didn't," Issa reminded her. "We're not on it."

"But we could have peeked at it—said one of the guests forgot to list us."

"That would have been a good plan," Issa said, just to encourage her, but she couldn't stop thinking about the way the guards had looked at each other. Issa and Olivia were easy prey for them, the casual targets of jokes and cheap laughs.

This was not new, yet it still stung. Issa had spent much of her childhood in Chinatown, but as soon as she set foot outside that neighborhood, she was barraged by messages of how she'd never belong. People spoke loudly to her as if she couldn't understand them, calling her names when they thought she couldn't hear, or treating her with hostility right to her face. The acting industry wouldn't be any different. In fact, the blatant discrimination was probably worse because so much of the job depended on looks, and while Issa and Olivia weren't *ugly*, they nevertheless looked different.

They wandered the hotel grounds, too on edge to do much else. Issa seethed every time she pictured the guards, imagining all the ways she could make them pay for their cruelty, imagining the curses she would invoke on their heads. They stirred up reminders of other times she'd faced similar disdain, rejection, mean laughter—it all rose to a deafening crescendo. When she became a successful actress, when she was rich and famous and powerful, she would grind these people beneath her heels.

"I'm so tired of this," she muttered to Olivia as they walked back to their room. "Being pushed aside, being stepped on, barely given the time of day when we have what it takes."

Olivia studied Issa's outraged face. "What are we going to do about it?"

Issa unlocked their door. "Show them exactly what we're capable of."

Chapter Seven

In their hotel room, Issa pulled the incense sticks from her bag and propped all the ritual items in front of the vanity. They had only one chair, so Olivia perched on the bed just behind her.

Issa sat back, feeling like she was forgetting something. Surely it was more complicated than this—conjuring the dead—but she couldn't remember anything else Yen had done differently.

"Bà Ngoại?" she asked.

Something tugged sharply in her chest, making her gasp and lurch forward. The reflection clouded over with smoke, even though the trails from the sticks on their side of the reflection swirled calmly.

Bà Ngoại's picture moved, but she bent over coughing so hard she couldn't talk for several seconds. Smoke thickened and cleared, thickened again. Something must have gone wrong. Issa wasn't doing this right.

"Ayah, can't breathe," Bà Ngoại said, wheezing.

"What can I do?" Issa asked.

"Nothing, just—wait for—to clear."

"It wasn't like this last time."

"You had Yen—last time."

"Do I have to give you my blood?"

"No. It would help—"

Issa's stomach turned over with dread.

"—but no."

Issa leaned forward with relief. "Bà Ngoại, we need your help."

"Of course you do," Bà Ngoại said. The reflection cleared, and she straightened.

"We're at Catalina Island," Issa said, "but they won't let us into the party." She described briefly what had happened with the security guards.

Bà Ngoại pursed her lips in anger. "We shall rain curses on everyone who steps in your path."

"Of course I agree with you," Issa said, "but perhaps we should try a few other things before we resort to such means. You mentioned a dead actress."

"Yes. Ava Lin Rang. She's always talking about her famous days, as if the dead care about such things."

"I looked her up at the library," Issa said. "I do remember seeing her in some movies, but hadn't realized that she'd died."

"I thought she bought a farm or something and retired," Olivia added from behind her.

"You think I know about every dead person's life?" Bà Ngoại snapped. "She's here—I can talk to her, means she's dead. Good enough for me."

"All right, sorry," Issa said. "We were just surprised. If she was so famous, we thought we would've heard more about her."

"Exactly my point. Being famous is not what it's cut out to be." Bà Ngoại's reflection froze, then resumed moving. "I'm getting tired." Her voice sounded even raspier than before. "Do you want to talk to her or not?"

"Yes," Issa said as Olivia added, "Of course."

"Great. Now." Bà Ngoại smiled, and it was quite frightening, for she had a devious look in her eye, which Issa imagined she normally reserved for her enemies. "Don't be frightened. I'm going to briefly let her use my image to talk to you."

In Issa's experience, when an older person in her family told her not to be frightened, they were about to do something incredibly terrifying indeed.

The mirror flickered, smoke swirling in the reflection. Bà Ngoại's picture froze. Only her lips shifted in staggering movements. Then, she went still, though it was clear she was there, a light in her eyes indicating a presence.

Her expression was different, though. Possessed. Bà Ngoại was letting the spirit speak through her image.

"Hello?" Olivia asked. Issa was grateful her friend took the initiative. Communing with her grandmother was one thing, but this entity who looked out at them with Bà Ngoại's face was another matter.

As her eyes fixed on the two girls, she smiled. It looked different from Bà Ngoại's smile. More elegant and sophisticated. This spirit held her chin high, her shoulders pushed back, a strange sight on the body of her grandmother, who, while intimidating, was not snobbish and had lived a life of hard work with the slumped shoulders to prove it.

"Hi," she said. Bà Ngoại's voice sounded throaty, as if she were a singer. "My, my, look at you two. Just as beautiful as your grandmother said you were."

"Thank you," Olivia said. "You're Ava?"

"That's correct. Ava Lin Rang. You've probably seen me in *The Kid*, *The Blue Brick*, and *Yellow Drapery*. I'm sure you've seen all these movies."

"The silents," Issa said.

"Yes, some of them."

"To be honest, we haven't seen many silent movies," Issa said.

"Except Charlie Chaplin," Olivia said.

"Oh yes, he's the best," Issa said.

"Were you in anything with him?" Olivia asked.

"No, though Charlie and I were good friends." Ava's lips turned downward. "We always talked about doing something together, but sadly that never happened."

Olivia got up from the bed and leaned over Issa to peer closer in the mirror. "Will you help us? We want to be like you."

"That depends," the spirit of Ava Lin Rang said, her eyes taking on a mischievous twinkle. Olivia smiled at her and took Issa's hand, the way she usually did when they were about to embark on something adventurous.

"Is there something that you want?" Issa asked. "Perhaps unfinished business we can take care of for you?"

Ava laughed with Bà Ngoại's raspy chuckle. "Oh, I don't know. I lived quite a fulfilling life. Besides, what can you two girls possibly do for me? You look like you're barely out of school."

"We're twenty," Issa said, trying to sound adult. "We're just . . . ageless."

"With your help, we could be stars," Olivia said. "And once we are, we'll have the power to do anything you need us to. I bet you can tell us how to break into the business. Stars are made, they say. So make us stars. Tell us which producers and directors will help us. Who we need to talk to . . . you know, the right people."

"Hmm," Ava Lin said. "I can, yes. What studio are you auditioning at?"

"We don't have auditions yet, but we're hoping to get in at MGM."

"MGM." The ghost beamed. "That's where I was. Not a bad place to start at all." The ghost looked away briefly, then her eyes widened, her face showing such an innocent moment of vulnerability that immediately endeared her to Issa. "I suppose there is something you can do for me."

"What is it?" Olivia asked, leaning forward.

"I won an Academy Award a few years ago, perhaps you'd heard."

"Yes, of course," Olivia said quickly.

"Well, it should have been mine," Ava continued. "Technically, they gave it to the director, but I was the one who stole that show. Everyone knew. Even *Variety* published an exposé about it, how that trophy should have been mine. But the director took it home in the end, traitorous thief. I've never been able to stop thinking about it, even though it's such a small, childish thing to obsess over a meaningless object."

"It's not childish at all," Olivia said. "It's yours, like you said. You deserve it."

"Do you," Issa asked, "want us to steal it for you?"

Ava smiled. "Yes!" She laughed. "I would love that! Imagine that cretin's face if he knew that I ended up with it after all."

Issa found Ava's joy quite contagious. "Which director is this?"

Ava's face twisted. "Weston Redrick. He's with MGM as well. He practically lives on the studio lot. It must be in his office, or his house in Beverly Hills."

Olivia clapped her hands. "Splendid. We'll get you the trophy, Ava."

"Of course, you won't be able to get anywhere near him until you're rich and famous enough that he can't ignore you," Ava added, tapping her chin. "Which makes this quite an even bargain. I shall help you become stars so that you can take back my trophy."

"That's a marvelous plan," Issa said, smiling. Ava returned her smile. She had quite a magnetic pull herself—that star quality that made her irresistible—but the effect was at odds with Bà Ngoại's cunning face.

"What sort of holiday are you on?" Ava asked. She spoke with such elegance that Issa couldn't help sitting up taller in a bid to impress her.

"We're at the annual celebrity gathering on Catalina Island," Olivia explained.

At that, Ava's eyes lit up. "Oh my! I know all about that. You'll have to talk to—" Her image started freezing, then moving, then freezing in the mirror, her words cut off.

"No," Olivia whispered. "What's happening?"

The incense was still burning.

Bà Ngoại's raspy cough told them it was their grandmother back in her body—or at least in the image of her body. "Can't stay much longer girls—"

"Wait, bring Ava back," Olivia said. "Who do we need to talk to?"

"Summon us again. Not before midnight. Issa will pay the—"

"Bà Ngoại, we need to talk to her now," Olivia said. *"Please."*

Bà Ngoại's eyes rounded on Olivia. "All right, all right. Give me a bit of your blood."

"Blood?" Issa took hold of Olivia's wrist. The eager girl was already about to take a bite out of her finger. "But you said we don't need it. Blood is too strong, what if—"

"*Your* blood is too strong," Bà Ngoại interrupted. "But Olivia's should be fine. It will help you, Issa," Bà Ngoại added, her tone so uncharacteristically soft that Issa quieted and listened. "This will tire you out. Trust me. We don't want you to be ill."

"Yes, we still have to go to the party after this," Olivia pointed out. "It's fine." She tugged her wrist out of Issa's grasp. "What's she going to do? She's just a ghost."

"She could possess you," Issa whispered.

Bà Ngoại made an indignant sound. "She's not strong enough. We will stop her if she tries." When Issa scoffed in horror, she added, "It's very rare for possession to happen. She'd need to form an unbreakable bond with a living person, and that will take much more than a drop of blood."

Issa sighed and let go. She didn't like this one bit. Yet, Olivia was determined, and she was outnumbered.

Olivia bit her knuckle, hard, squeezing a drop of blood through the broken skin. She held it up to the mirror.

"Not to me, silly girl," Bà Ngoại said. "The incense. The smoke will carry it here."

"Right." Olivia positioned the bead of blood over the incense stick, almost touching her hand to the ashy stump. Smoke drifted from it and seemed to absorb into her wound. Her skin sealed together, forming a silver scar that looked like it had healed weeks ago. She studied her hand in fascination.

"Good job." Bà Ngoại coughed again as the mirror glazed over with smoke. It grew thicker and thicker until it flowed through the mirror, tendrils curling toward them like seductive fingers.

Issa leaned back, bumping into Olivia, who pulled her into a hug. Neither of them had known what to expect. The whole room grew foggy so that they could barely see a few feet in front of them.

It could have been minutes or hours, but eventually the smoke cleared. Standing in front of them, outside the mirror, on this side of the mortal world, was the spirit of Ava Lin Rang.

"Hello, girls," she said with a smile.

Chapter Eight

Issa slapped a hand over her lips. Her heart hammered at the sight of the actress before them. She looked only a few years older than Issa, with a smooth alabaster complexion and hair styled in an old-fashioned updo, dressed in dark jewels and what looked like a costume from a period piece.

Her image had a muted, gray quality. A veil of silver wrapped over her head and framed her face in fringes. She must have played the part of a princess or courtesan, her costume draping over her skin in loose yet sexy layers, revealing just the right amounts of curves and smooth skin.

Bà Ngoại coughed and coughed. "This is wearing me out too much. The three of you talk. And don't summon me again until the next full moon. I mean it!" But she smiled and twitched her lips in a crude imitation of a kiss before her image stilled into the photograph.

Ava remained, gasping when she caught herself in the mirror. "Oh goodness, I'm a ghost!" She laughed demurely. "I didn't expect to appear so gray."

"You're not like this on the Other Side?" Issa asked.

"No, but you are. It's astonishing to see you in color—so alive." She took notice of Olivia, and began walking around her in circles, studying her from head to toe. "You are gorgeous."

"Thank you," Olivia said, standing there calmly as the ghost finished her inspection.

Issa sat down, not sure she wanted that kind of attention. Thankfully, Ava only looked at her face and smiled.

"Well?" Ava said. "Don't we have a party to get to?"

It was late by then, and the celebration was in full swing judging from the shouting and laughing inside the Garden Ballroom, almost drowned out by the loud saxophone and cymbals and other instruments playing jazzy tunes.

"Can other people see you?" Issa asked as they approached the guards.

Ava walked with her hands on her hips, a determined but amused expression on her face. "We'll find out."

The security guards didn't seem to notice her, though, their eyes fixing on Issa and Olivia with mirth.

"Back so soon?" the first one asked.

"Have a different name this time?" the second one said, whipping out his clipboard. "Because all of them have been claimed, you know."

Ava wrapped an arm around the guard—or tried to—and she nearly tumbled forward into the grass as she went right through him. It took all of Issa's control not to rush forward to help her up.

"Oh dear," Ava said, gathering her composure and dusting herself off.

The second guard looked at the ground, but he was only following Issa's gaze. "Whatchu staring at?" he snapped.

"These are famous actresses," Ava whispered in the first one's ear. "You'll let them into the party, of course."

"What was that?" The guard wiggled a finger in his ear.

"What was what?" the second man said.

"This is Issa Bui and Olivia Nong," Ava whispered to the second guard. "They're stars in their country, and soon to be stars here. All the celebrities know them. All the directors want them in their movies. All the producers are searching for their exact talents. You best let them in before you get blamed for insulting someone important."

The second guard stood there dazed, his mouth hanging open.

"Unless you want to lose your jobs," Ava said to the first man. "Do what's right, darling. Their friends are waiting."

The first man cleared his throat and stepped aside. "Come on through, ladies," he said with a slight bow. His manner changed abruptly, no longer leering and jeering, but showing a nervous respect. Perhaps he really was afraid they'd get him fired.

The other man only stared at them as Issa and Olivia walked by. Ava blew them a kiss that they couldn't see, but as they disappeared from view, Issa thought she saw the first man shiver.

The ballroom was decorated in a gold-and-green color scheme, the ceilings high and lit with chandeliers. Issa walked into what smelled like a wall of alcohol. The odor wafted from everyone in the crowd, mixing with musky cologne, floral perfume, and sour sweat. A jazz band played a swingy tune, making it impossible not to bounce and sway to the rhythm.

Already, she recognized a few famous faces. She could hardly believe they were real—Joan Bennett, Katharine Hepburn, the platinum-blond hair of an actress she thought she recognized before the woman turned away and the rest of the names slipped from her mind. The whole night felt like a fever dream—from conjuring her grandmother, something she never thought she would willingly do, to the ghost now following them around a ballroom full of stars.

Olivia went to the refreshments and took two glasses, her small purse dangling from her wrist. Issa accepted one gratefully, letting the cloying taste of alcohol singe its way down her throat and take the edge off her nervousness. Her skin prickled as if everyone were staring at her, and her knees wobbled as if she'd eaten an entire cake on her own and now suffered the consequences.

No one paid her and Olivia much attention, and when anyone did notice them, they glanced away quickly with disdain, like they couldn't believe they'd been tricked into meeting the eyes of mere nobodies.

"Goodness it's been forever," Ava whispered to them, standing close to Olivia. "We never have parties like this on my side of the world."

"You would think that's all you would do," Olivia said.

Ava laughed. "Those ninnies will all think it's an ackamarackus."

"What do we do now?" Issa asked.

"We'll mingle," Olivia said. "Make conversation. Fish around for someone looking for some beautiful, exotic actresses such as ourselves."

"Find a director," Ava said. "They're easy to spot. Not as attractive as the actors, but their egos are just as big."

"Is that one?" Issa asked, half joking, as she pointed to an older man in a stuffy sweater-vest.

"Goodness gracious, he's still alive," Ava said.

"You know him?" Issa asked.

"Why yes, that's Eric Goldman. He's directed so many films, I can hardly count. We worked on a few together, in fact. He's one of the few who are quite amenable to women of our . . . flavor."

Issa resisted making a repulsed face at Ava's analogy. "Do you think he'll be willing to cast us in anything?"

"Let's find out," Olivia said. She threw back the rest of her drink and grabbed another before heading Goldman's way.

Issa hurried after her with Ava practically floating in the evening dress she had magically transformed into when they'd joined the party. Whether she glided because she was simply that graceful or because she was a ghost, Issa wasn't sure, but she suddenly had a strong desire to walk the exact same way, her head held high, her shoulders pushed back, neck long, and a serene, confident expression on her face as if she never once doubted her right to be at the party.

"Mr. Goldman!" Olivia announced, arms stretched wide as she approached the director, who stood by himself with a plate of cheese and crackers and a glass of wine balanced in the same hand. "It's so lovely to make your acquaintance."

Mr. Goldman blinked at her from behind his wide-framed glasses. "I'm sorry, Miss . . ."

"Olivia Nong." Olivia held out a hand.

At the same time, Ava draped herself over Goldman's shoulders and gave him a slow smooch on his cheek that he of course couldn't feel. He frowned and swatted at his face as if shooing away a fly.

"Issa Bui," Issa introduced herself as well, though she took pity on Goldman's confused expression and lack of free hands and did a little curtsy that she immediately regretted.

"We wrote to you," Olivia lied. "From Vietnam. We're visiting and hope to be in your next film. We heard you're looking for actresses like us." Olivia stepped back and propped her hands on her waist with her hip to the side.

"Look at them, Eric," Ava whispered in his ear. "Such lovely girls."

Issa sipped her drink, easing into the discomfort of his scrutiny. To her surprise, Goldman really did take a long look at them.

"They're perfect," Ava said in her sultry voice, making Issa's heart swell with warmth. "For your next project."

Goldman dug a finger into the ear closest to Ava, even looking directly at her face, though probably seeing nothing but air. Ava kissed him on his nose, and he blinked, turning back to Olivia and Issa as if just remembering they were there.

"I say, you do have the perfect look for what I'm searching for," he said. "Two small roles, nothing major, mind you. Taiwan, you said?"

"Vietnam," Olivia said. "We're quite famous over there."

Goldman stuffed a cube of cheese in his mouth. "So you have experience?"

"Oh, tons," Olivia said.

Issa smiled and downed her drink.

"Any films you can send my way?" Goldman asked.

Olivia glanced at Issa.

"We already sent some," Issa said, feeling the need to take on some of the lies.

"You saw them," Ava whispered. "They were wonderful. Absolutely perfect."

Goldman focused on Issa's and Olivia's faces. "I can't hire you on the spot. The execs would lambaste me."

"We'll audition," Olivia said, quick with an answer.

"No," Goldman muttered, rubbing a hand over his face. "Then we'll have to audition everyone. We're already behind schedule. If only the two original girls hadn't gotten so . . ." He let his voice trail off.

"You know they're the girls for the part," Ava whispered, hanging on to his shoulders. "What more do you need, Eric? Book them now before it's too late."

He looked over his shoulder, and Issa noticed a man hovering behind him, wearing a pressed suit with a thin tie, blinking from behind thick glasses, though unlike everyone else there, he had the appearance of being at work rather than at a party. "Get them in for a screen test." Goldman turned back to Issa and Olivia. "Next week."

He walked away as the other man stepped forward, reaching into his pocket for a business card.

"Call my secretary and set an appointment," he said. His name read *Emmett Tratee.*

Olivia opened her mouth to ask a million questions, but he'd followed after Goldman before they'd even finished reading his card.

They didn't stay at the party long after that—Issa was too nervous about getting in trouble for crashing and oh, also, lying about being famous actresses.

"No one's going to find out," Olivia said with a laugh as they let themselves into their hotel room.

"Yes, darling," Ava said. "Learn to live a little."

"It still doesn't feel right," Issa said. "What if they take one look at the screen test and realize it?"

"The screen test is just to see what we look like on-screen," Olivia said.

"Yes, I gathered that," Issa said with a laugh.

"Oh, it's wonderful," Ava said, draping herself over the lounge chair by the window. "It's even better than an audition."

Olivia beamed. "And it was all thanks to you, Ava!" she said with more enthusiasm than Issa expected. It was odd to see Olivia so friendly toward this stranger. At school, they had stuck to themselves, more out of self-preservation and habit than because they were actually unfriendly. They'd put up with so many bullies in their younger years, snobby girls who never gave them any attention and mean boys who gave them too much of the unwanted kind, so they'd learned to neutralize their expressions and remain aloof. Olivia's face looked so openly inviting to Ava that Issa tried to paste a similar look on her own.

"Think nothing of it. It's what you called on me for, isn't it?" Ava waved a hand, her fingers slender and long.

Next to each other, Issa saw clearly how similar Ava and Olivia were, both tall and thin and elegant. They even had similarly long, sleek black hair, while Issa kept hers bobbed and bouncy. Issa curled her fingers toward her palms, aware of how completely opposite she was—shorter and . . . well, stubby overall, not just her fingers.

Then Ava smiled at her with such kindness that Issa brushed aside her insecurities.

"Do you have any advice for us?" Issa asked. "Did you ever do a screen test?"

"A few," Ava said. "Perhaps they're picturing you for a large role, but they want to make sure you don't look ghastly on camera. Some people are naturally beautiful, but put them onscreen and . . ." She shuddered.

"What can we do to increase our chances?" Olivia asked.

"There's nothing you can do if you're ugly," Ava said in a voice that suggested they were silly for thinking otherwise.

"But we're not ugly," Olivia pointed out.

Ava smiled, her mouth stretching slowly. "No, of course not."

Which made Issa wonder if she felt the exact opposite. Still, Issa wouldn't get perturbed. She was used to people staring and judging. She was used to ignoring what others thought.

"Anyone can be a star," Issa pointed out. "With the right makeup, lighting, marketing. So teach us . . . make us into stars."

"It takes a whole team to do that, darling," Ava said.

"We've tried acting coaches," Issa said. "But they're incredibly expensive."

"That one cockamamie coach was such a scam," Olivia added with a sigh. "He kept trying to feel us up as he corrected our posture."

Issa felt suddenly drained, as if she might faint. It came on so fast that she sat down, the smile dropping from her face.

"What's the matter?" Olivia asked, sitting next to Issa on the bed.

"I don't know," Issa said. "I feel absolutely lousy."

"Poor thing," Olivia said.

"As do I," Ava said. "I think these visits take a toll." She closed her eyes briefly as if fighting back a pang of nausea.

"We've done enough today, anyway," Olivia said. "Thank you so much, Ava."

Ava could only manage a nod. Her throat rippled as she swallowed, and then smoke clouded over her, consuming her image as it dispersed into the air.

Issa lay back on the bed. The world spun as she fought back her gag reflex. Thankfully, they hadn't eaten much all day, but her stomach threatened to turn if she dared even move an inch.

"We should have been more careful," Olivia said, feeling Issa's forehead with the back of her hand. "Auntie Yen told us that these conjurings affect the shaman the most. I should have paid attention—I'm so sorry, Issa."

"It's not your fault," Issa muttered, but talking made her dizzier, so she could only hope Olivia didn't feel too guilty.

"Do you need anything?" Olivia asked.

"No, just . . ." Issa swallowed. "Maybe close the curtains? And . . . don't talk to me." She added a soft chuckle to take the sting out of her words, but even that made her want to hurl, so she rolled over and pulled a pillow over her head. A second later, the room darkened, and Olivia put a hand on her shoulder with a comforting squeeze before leaving her alone.

Chapter Nine

Issa was so sick, she hardly remembered the return trip from Catalina. Only that Olivia took care of everything, buying their fares, making sure they got to the right dock, and guiding her onto the ferry and then onto the streetcar, where Issa shut her eyes and endured the clanky ride. She finally collapsed onto their bed at home, where she slept for what felt like weeks. She recalled vague images, blurry along the edges, of Ma and Olivia checking on her, and even though she felt horrible, she was glad to have an excuse not to join Ma at the hotel to fold laundry for a few extra dollars.

When she finally felt well enough to get out of bed one afternoon, Ma was already at work, and Olivia was reading a newspaper in the kitchen. A pot of some savory-smelling broth gave off steam on the stovetop.

"You're alive," Olivia said with an exaggerated sigh. "I was beginning to worry."

"I don't feel alive," Issa said. Her stomach growled loudly.

"That's a good sign," Olivia said, setting a bowl in front of Issa. She waited for Issa to take several sips before giving her that smile that meant she had a plan.

"What is it?" Issa asked.

"How do you feel, first. Are you well enough?"

"Well enough for what?"

Olivia leaned forward and grabbed Issa's hands. "For our screen test."

"Is that really happening?" Issa asked. "Part of me thought it was all a dream."

"I called Goldman's office like he said, and the studio wants us to come in this week."

"Goodness! That's quite soon."

"But we're ready, aren't we?"

"Of course. We've been ready."

Olivia beamed. But then her smile drooped.

"What's the matter?" Issa asked.

"Do you think?" Olivia started to ask, then shook her head.

"What is it?"

"It's just . . . do you think it's right? The way Ava manipulated those guards."

"They deserved it." Issa's blood boiled at the memory of the guards' laughter.

"And what about Eric Goldman? He seems like such a nice avuncular sort."

Issa got up to make tea. "If he's anything like the uncles in my family, then he deserves it too."

"I don't know." Olivia brought her nails to her mouth, then remembered that she wasn't supposed to bite them. She studied her knuckle instead, and Issa noticed the silver scar from when she'd bitten herself during the ritual. "This was all safe, right? The blood and all that."

Issa swallowed as the kettle began to whistle. "Bà Ngoại said it was fine." Guilt flowed through her as she busied herself with making the tea. "I'm sorry you had to be the one to offer your blood. It should have been me."

"Nonsense, your grandma said your blood is too strong." Olivia smiled reassuringly. "Besides, I'm happy to help in any way I can."

"If you feel anything . . . anything out of the ordinary, tell me," Issa said. Even though she had no idea what she'd do about it. She could run to her aunt for help. Of course. They weren't in this alone. Not anymore.

"Do you think perhaps we can call on Ava again, then?" Olivia asked. "Once you're completely better, of course. Just to make sure we have everything we need."

Issa gulped, thinking of the horrible last few days.

"It's too soon," Olivia said right away. "No, don't even think of it. I shouldn't have asked."

"I think it will be all right," Issa said. "As long as we keep it short. We kept her around the entire night last weekend. No wonder I got sick. Yen's conjurings have always only lasted minutes."

"That's true. We'll be more careful."

When Ma asked her to help at the laundry room the next day, Issa didn't mind riding with her on the streetcar to downtown LA, so bolstered from the successful weekend that nothing bothered her. Ma spoke little, but she occasionally looked at Issa with concern before patting her hand.

"I'm fine, Ma," Issa said, trying to keep the exasperation out of her voice as they walked down the basement hallway of the hotel.

"You're so pale," Ma said.

"Don't you like that? You're always telling me to stay out of the sun."

"Ayah, you have something to say for everything, don't you?"

Issa smiled to herself.

After a grueling few hours folding clothes, Issa's shoulders ached, and she longed for daylight, realizing how much time Ma spent in darkness. No wonder she was always grouchy. Yet Ma seemed to enjoy it, or rather, didn't prefer anything else; she was always so energetic after an evening of hard labor.

When they got home, the apartment was sparkly clean, and Olivia was snoring softly. Issa bathed and fell asleep to the rising sun, waking a short time later when Olivia got up.

"I hope you're not miffed," Olivia said, "but while you were with your Ma, I paid Auntie Yen a visit."

"You did? By yourself?" Issa put the kettle on the stove. "Whatever for?"

"I wanted to see what would help you recover faster from the conjurings. I hated seeing you so ill. She gave me some special gunpowder tea. It's not real gunpowder—that's just what it's called, but it's delicious, and it will help you get your strength back up, she said."

"Of course, there's nothing that tea can't fix, is there?" Issa brewed a pot for them both. There wasn't much by way of breakfast, so they shared some rice crackers. "I think I can try summoning Ava later today."

"Are you sure?" There was a hopeful light in Olivia's eyes. "I don't want you getting so sick again."

"We need all the help we can get before our screen test," Issa said.

Olivia held her teacup daintily in both her hands. "What did you think of Ava?"

Issa studied Olivia's face, but it remained neutral, giving nothing away. "She's fantastic, isn't she? You could tell she was quite the star in her heyday. And she's so beautiful."

Olivia smiled in agreement. "You think we can trust her?"

"Absolutely," Issa said. But when Olivia didn't respond right away, she tilted her head. "Don't you?"

"I do if you do," Olivia said. "I did give her some of my blood, so it's a bit late to change our minds, isn't it?" She laughed. Issa listened for a hint of nervousness, but Olivia seemed so sure of herself.

"We don't have to call on her anymore if you have any doubts," Issa said. "Any at all."

"Oh, I don't." Olivia touched Issa's hand in reassurance. "As long as we're in this together. I think she'll do wonders for our careers."

So once Ma left again for work that night, they lit incense in their room and held hands and called on Ava. Even though they had no photograph, Issa couldn't help looking in the mirrors. Smoke clouded in little spots about the room. They spun this way and that, and several times, it seemed as if Ava's face would form in a puff of smoke, only for it to dissipate.

The incense snuffed out, though there was plenty left to burn. Issa's muscles turned to liquid. She slumped over, sapped of the strength to sit upright. Saliva pooled at the base of her mouth, and she fought the urge to gag.

"There there," Olivia said, rubbing circles on her back affectionately.

Issa swallowed and tried to talk, but all she could do was close her eyes as the room spun.

"It was much too soon. I'm so sorry, darling."

Issa tried to shake her head, but that caused a wave of nausea, so she let Olivia help her get to bed, racked with guilt that she couldn't do the one task that she was supposed to be good at.

Their screen test was on the MGM lot, in an office building staffed by unfriendly, attractive people in beautiful dresses or tailored suits. She and Olivia waited in a lobby that felt very much like a dentist's waiting room, the walls stark white but smudged with dust, the seats cushioned but uncomfortable, and the receptionist ignoring them as she checked names off a list. Several other actors and actresses waited in the lobby, but no one talked to or even looked at one another.

Eventually, the door opened and a woman with a clipboard called out Olivia's name.

"Good luck," Issa said. Olivia squeezed her hand before she disappeared behind the door. There must have been another exit, because no one ever came back out.

It felt like hours before the door opened again and the woman called Issa in. She followed her through a gray hallway and down to a room with a large camera dominating the center.

"Stand there," the woman said, pointing to an X on the floor. She gave Issa a sheet of paper that turned out to be a very short script, a few lines of dialogue that didn't seem related to each other at all.

"Look into the camera," the woman instructed as she pressed a button on the contraption. It whirred noisily, and a light above the lens shone directly into Issa's eyes. Issa resisted the urge to cover her face. "And read the first line when you're ready."

"Oh." Issa looked about the room nervously. She'd expected some sort of audience. A casting director or producer—someone to perform to, but the woman left her alone in the room and closed the door.

Issa stared down at the script, taking several deep breaths, knowing that the camera was recording every single second that she took to compose herself. Finally, she looked into the lens. It loomed bigger in her vision, like a deep, cavernous eyeball. Her words stuck in her throat. The lines swam in her vision, not making any sense. What sort of story was this? How was she supposed to know how to act when the dialogue was so out of context?

Eventually, she just stared into the black glass lens of the camera and did her best to pretend that Olivia sat behind it, smiling encouragingly at her. That helped a bit, and she said the lines as best she could.

Glancing over her shoulder, she realized that the woman hadn't come back in yet, so she shrugged her shoulders to loosen them, and then said the lines again, trying them in several different ways. She was practically enjoying herself when a knock came at the door.

"All done?" the woman asked.

Issa nodded, handing over the single-page script.

The woman fiddled with the camera, and the light turned off. The silence seemed unwelcomingly loud after the whirring.

"Check back next week," the woman said, handing Issa another instruction sheet. She led Issa down the hall to the exit.

Chapter Ten

The days dragged on, blurring into one another. Without anything better to do now that they weren't in school and because Issa had recovered from her illness, Ma expected Issa to join her in the laundry room almost every day. Thankfully, Olivia sometimes went with them, making the loads easier to fold and get through, though no matter how much they worked, more kept coming. After a few days, the same items popped up again, as if they were in an endless loop of laborious torture.

Issa didn't know how Ma did it. It wasn't just the lack of sunshine, it was the monotony and repetition with no hope in sight. And Ma did it day in and out, had so for years. Issa couldn't imagine ever learning to love it; she could barely tolerate it after a week. She didn't want to live this way. But Ma made it clear: now that they were adults, they needed to work. Even though they had money from Auntie Yen, they couldn't admit that to Ma without explaining why, so they had no choice but to join Ma in the laundry.

The only thing that helped Issa endure such grueling hours was thinking about the results of their screen test, hoping against hope that they had a chance.

When they finally returned to MGM, she and Olivia were directed to an office building near the front gate. A receptionist sat in a small room behind a window in the wall.

"Name?" she asked as soon as they walked in.

Olivia told her, and the woman looked through a stack of papers.

"Here you are," she said, handing over two packets.

At first, neither Olivia nor Issa reached for them, too shocked at what they resembled.

"Scripts?" Issa asked. "Are those scripts?"

The woman smiled at them, but in a rather condescending way, as if she found their excitement juvenile. "It looks like it, doesn't it?"

"Thank you," Olivia said, snatching them.

Olivia and Issa rushed outside to look through the cast list. They eyed the script intently, searching for their names.

It took them a while to find, but there they were. A smile spread over Issa's lips. Her name was on a script. She was going to be in a movie.

"Wait," Olivia said, sounding oddly sad. "We're just Asian maid number one and two."

"Well." Issa wasn't sure why Olivia wasn't happier. She flipped through the pages. "At least yours has a speaking role. I just stand there."

Olivia's mouth twisted unhappily. "I suppose Goldman did say they were very small roles."

"And we got in," Issa said. "We got parts, Olivia."

Olivia glared into the distance at first, but then she couldn't seem to help it, her expression breaking into a smile as well. "We're in a movie!" she shrieked.

Ma wasn't exactly ecstatic about the news when they told her at dinner that night. "You're sure you want to do this, Issa?" she asked. "Your face . . . it will be on-screen. The first movie was just a small part, right? This sounds bigger. Are you sure you want so many people to know you and . . . and see you?"

"Well, that's the point of being famous," Issa said quickly, having forgotten that she'd lied to Ma about the role before this. "Think of the money we'll bring in." Even without Yen supplementing their income, they'd make more for a few weeks of work on one movie than months at the hotel laundry.

"I've never cared about that," Ma said, digging her chopsticks into her mound of rice a bit aggressively for someone who wasn't eating much of it.

"But I do," Issa said.

"You should be happy for us, Auntie," Olivia said. "We've been working so hard for this."

At that, Ma gave a defeated little smile. "Yes, of course. Congratulations." She rested her chopsticks on the top of her rice bowl. "I have a bit of news as well. Actually, I've been meaning to tell you for some time, but I've . . . found it difficult."

Issa sat up straighter, unaccustomed to her mother's hesitance. "What is it?"

Ma looked between Olivia and Issa. She opened her mouth several times, the silence growing thicker with each second that she struggled.

"It's all right, Auntie," Olivia said. But she looked just as alarmed as Issa felt.

Ma took in a deep breath. "Your grandmother is dead."

She proclaimed it with such a dramatic sense of doom that Issa sat there for several seconds, waiting for the second shoe to drop. Underneath the table, Olivia's foot nudged her ankle.

"Aaah," Issa burst out, trying to come up with something sad to say. "That's . . . horrible."

Ma picked at her food, not meeting Issa's eyes. "I know you didn't have the chance to know her, and that's my fault. And I don't regret my decision, but you have a right to know."

Issa nodded, trying to look surprised by the news and also show an appropriate amount of sadness for someone who supposedly wouldn't remember much about the deceased.

"You need to be careful from now on, Issa," Ma added.

"What? Why?"

"With Bà gone, Auntie Yen and her clan may seek you out. They'll try to coerce you into the gang. You must promise me." Ma reached for Issa's hand and gripped her wrist so tightly that Issa almost dropped her chopsticks. "Promise me you won't join them. You won't go back there."

"I, uh," Issa said.

"It's dangerous," Ma continued. "When my sister Phi died, your father . . ." Ma stopped and swallowed, blinking rapidly. She rarely spoke of Issa's dad, always broke down in a similar fashion each time she'd tried. "Your grandmother wanted to retaliate—said a lesson needed to be taught, even if Phi had been caught in a misunderstanding. Bà made several men in our clan join the attack. Your father felt obligated to go. I begged her not to make him, to order him to stay, but in the end, he insisted. And . . . well . . ."

Ma's lips quivered. Issa stared, not knowing what to say. She knew her father had died in some sort of gang-related altercation, but she'd never learned the details, only that it drove Ma to pack up and leave her family.

"You must promise, Issa," Ma said, tightening her grip on her wrist.

Issa's chopsticks clattered across the table. Ma jumped and let Issa go.

Olivia scrambled to pick them up, giving Issa a wide-eyed look that Issa couldn't read. What was she supposed to do? Was a promise really a promise if she broke it before she'd even made it? Besides, she'd already made a deal with Auntie Yen—who was she supposed to obey? The family matriarch or her own mother?

"I—" she stammered.

But Ma seemed to have been startled out of a trance. She stood and hurried to clear the plates.

"Ma," Issa said. "I'm sorry . . ." Her words felt inadequate, the losses Ma had endured too great for a formulaic platitude.

"No no," Ma said dismissively, her back to them as she went to the sink. "I'm sorry for bringing it up when this should be a night of celebration. With your new jobs and all. Forget I said it. Please."

"Ma," Issa tried again.

"You girls run along. I'll clean up."

Later that night, after Ma left for work, Issa sat on the floor clipping her nails while Olivia flipped through a magazine on the bed, occasionally showing Issa a particularly stylish dress, when a movement in the vanity mirror caught Issa's eye. Smoke swirled in the glass, and when it cleared, Bà Ngoại's eyes roamed the space.

"Bà Ngoại!" Issa exclaimed, sitting on the chair. "What are you doing here?"

"I sensed you talking about me earlier."

"You what—you can sense that?"

"Of course I can. All ghosts can. That's why people are so afraid to talk about them, because doing so invites them into one's life."

"I thought that was just superstition."

"Ayah, all superstition is based on fact, to a degree. But don't worry, only the stronger spirits like me can actually show up without a proper conjuring. And it's very taxing. Why don't you find my photograph and light some incense while you're at it?"

Bà doubled over coughing as Olivia handed Issa her purse where they kept all their ritualistic items, and Issa did as she was told.

"What were you two saying about me?" Bà Ngoại asked once the smoke cleared.

Issa glanced at Olivia, who stood behind her. "It wasn't us, not really. It was Ma. She knows you're dead and felt like she should tell me."

"What took her so long? She was notified months ago, that disgraceful child. I shouldn't have left her so much money. If I'd known she wouldn't accept it . . ." Bà Ngoại trailed off and muttered to herself, smoke thickening around her.

Issa twisted her fingers together, wishing Ma and Bà Ngoại and Auntie Yen would just talk out their differences. She felt pulled in three different directions, wanting to make each woman happy while still trying to pursue her own dreams.

"We got the parts!" she exclaimed, hoping the news would make Bà Ngoại happy, or at least distract her from insulting Ma.

Fortunately, it worked. Bà Ngoại's wrinkles smoothed back as she smiled. "Of course you got the parts. Didn't I tell you that you could do anything? See what happens when you let us help you?"

Issa leaned forward. "Thank you, Bà Ngoại. We really couldn't have done it without you." She knew she was laying it on quite thick, but it was true. She and Olivia had tried so hard for years just to get through the gates of MGM. As soon as Bà Ngoại got involved, it seemed like everything got much easier. "If I'd known, I wouldn't have stayed away for so long."

"Does this mean you'll commit to the clan once and for all?" Bà Ngoại asked.

Issa's chest clenched. She still reeled from Ma's warning on the dangers of the gang, but she knew better than to bring that up with her grandmother. "You said we had a year to try our hands at acting."

Bà Ngoại raised her eyes heavenward. "Yes, yes. You still have the year."

"What else can you do?" Issa asked. "What other powers do we have?"

Bà Ngoại's laughter echoed in the small room. "Calling on the dead isn't enough for you, is it?" She smirked. "I get it, I get it. You're hungry for power now that you've gotten a taste of it. But you must master being a medium before you learn the rest. And then we'll talk, hah?"

Chapter Eleven

Issa had no reason to attend the table read the next day, and she suspected that Olivia didn't need to be there, either, especially when the man with a clipboard gave Olivia an uncomfortable look, like he was gathering the courage to say something unpleasant. Olivia did that thing where she breezed right by, her strong chin raised in a way that left no question as to how important she was. Issa always marveled at how Olivia could be so demure and soft spoken around her elders but change into a totally different person when she was determined to get what she wanted.

They were one of the first ones to arrive at Soundstage 4, which looked like a large warehouse building, square with a gray exterior and large hangar-like doors. Inside, a crew was busy building the beginnings of a living room set—a tall wall with built-in shelves, markings on the hardwood floor, furniture set to the side.

Within the huge open area, black folding tables were arranged in a U formation, with about fifteen chairs and nameplates designating the seats. Eric Goldman's name was located at the head of the arrangement, producers on each side of him, including Emmett Tratee, the bespectacled man they'd met briefly at the party at the Hotel Saint Catherine. Each person's role or title was typed in a smaller font beneath their bold names. Olivia quickly moved several nameplates around, found a couple of blank ones to scribble their names on, and plunked them next to Emmett's.

"Sit here," Olivia said to Issa, gesturing to the chair next to her. People started to arrive; some joined the crew, others went to get a drink at the refreshments table, and no one paid them any mind.

"I don't think I'm supposed to be here," Issa said. "I'll just stand over there and observe."

"Nonsense, you need to study the script with us and be prepared if there's a chance you can step in."

"They'll just kick me out, Olivia," Issa said, embarrassed at the thought of it.

Aside from moments of chaotic impulsivity brought on by alcohol or Olivia's energy, Issa didn't find it as easy as Olivia to blatantly go after what she wanted without any regard to the rules or to what people would think. She wanted to be in the pictures just as much as her best friend did, but she didn't want to upset anyone on her climb to the top. She wanted the reputation of the Nice Star, the One Who Was Pleasant to Work With.

Olivia laughed as if she could read Issa's mind. "Just sit," Olivia said. "You won't be a bother."

Issa sighed and obeyed as people started to approach the table, scripts in hand. A man smiled at them but didn't say anything and looked away before Issa could smile back. Olivia ignored them all, studying the few lines she had, so Issa pretended to look busy reading the script, too, even though she really had nothing to memorize. Her part was so small, it was barely mentioned.

When Eric Goldman showed up, he looked exactly as he had at the party, an older man with peppered hair and a knitted grandfatherly vest. He gave one loud clap but seemed to lose his focus as everyone turned to him. He whispered something to Emmett Tratee, who hovered perpetually behind him. It sounded suspiciously like, "Which one is this?"

Tratee answered in a low voice, showing Goldman the front of the script. Goldman took his glasses off to squint at the title.

"All right," Goldman said to the group, his voice flat and unenthusiastic. "Welcome to *Our Dangerous Love*. Table read today, rehearsals tomorrow, so on and so forth. Shooting starts next month. Any questions? Good. Emmett." He said it all without any pauses, taking the seat next to Tratee, who had turned his attention to the screenplay along with everyone else.

"We'll start with the leads," Emmett Tratee said.

Everyone went around the table introducing themselves, stating their parts. Issa felt awkward, dreading the moment someone would turn to her and demand to know what role she played and why she was sitting at the table, but no one seemed to notice, not even when Olivia named herself as Asian Maid Number One.

"Right," Tratee said. He gave his own introduction, gesturing to the two empty seats of the remaining producers. "I manage what the production needs. We will stay on budget. Everything must be cleared through me, or else the film could get canceled, are we clear?" He peered over his spectacles at no one in particular, but all the actors nodded. "Let's begin."

Pages rustled.

"Act One," the director Goldman said, "scene one, exterior . . ."

Issa sat back and listened as the screenplay opened with the main actress, who read as if she were already playing her role. That was the point of a table read, Issa knew, but she was still shocked that no one held back, acting their hearts out. Elation buoyed her for a second as she imagined herself with a lead role, proving her talent to everyone. Her heart pumped faster and her hands grew sweaty at the anticipation, even while she knew that she wouldn't be reading today.

When it came to Olivia's lines, Issa watched her best friend proudly. Olivia sat tall and practically shouted her dialogue in a theatrical voice, pronouncing each word clearly. "Would you like me to burn the documents, Mr. Inglewood?" she belted out. "It will be less—"

Eric Goldman cleared his throat as giggles erupted, instantly hushed by a look from Emmett Tratee.

"Perhaps," Goldman said, "you may want to speak as if you were a maid, and not . . ." He gestured vaguely in the air.

"Oh," Olivia said, but she wasn't discouraged, and tried again, sounding very much the same, only not as loud.

"Close," Goldman said. "Try it again. More demure. Quiet, like you're afraid to speak up."

Olivia frowned. She repeated her lines, quieter.

"Hmm," Goldman said. "We'll work on it."

Olivia said nothing, but next to her, Issa felt her friend seething, a heat practically radiating off her skin in shimmering waves.

"I thought you were aces," Issa said as they walked from the studio to their streetcar station. Olivia stomped on the pavement like it had personally offended her, not caring that she was sweating through her dress.

"Stop being so angry, you'll ruin your heels," Issa scolded her.

"Did you see the way he looked at me?" Olivia hissed as the clang of the trolley sounded. Olivia turned around and paced in front of Issa. "Like I was a child. And *demure*! I know why he gave that note, oh, trust you me. He didn't stop anyone else, not even that dumb tart Jenna what's-her-name. She sounded like an absolute machine. Artistic choice, my nose."

"Olivia," Issa said with a nervous chuckle as people glanced their way.

They had left the studio during rush hour, men in suits holding briefcases and women in uniforms clutching handbags hurrying home from the long workday. The seats on the streetcar were taken so they had to stand, something Issa loathed because she couldn't quite reach the straps hanging from the ceiling. When they got to their empty apartment, Olivia stomped down the hall. In their bedroom, she yanked incense sticks out of the package so fast that several sprang from the box to land on the floor. She ignored them and plucked out three more to plunk into the bowl of dried rice.

Olivia lit the incense and went back into the hallway, to the wall mirror built into the space next to the shared bathroom. Ma usually draped it with a spare sheet, a habit she'd formed from growing up in a household of shamans, but Olivia yanked it down.

"Ava?" she called out. "Are you there?"

Issa stopped short. Olivia seemed so angry that she hesitated to interrupt whatever it was she planned to do.

But then her best friend looked at her imploringly. "I need her help, Issa. Please."

Issa looked into the mirror. "Ava? Can you hear us?"

A tug pulled at the center of her chest, and smoke formed in the hallway. Unlike the last failed attempt, Issa knew instinctively that this one would work, the pang and nausea returning in her belly.

Olivia spoke before the spirit fully materialized. "It went terribly today. Goldman barely looked at us, and if he even remembers us, it won't be fondly. We need your help."

Ava's form solidified a few seconds later, her muted gray figure standing next to Olivia. She wore silky black robes and a heavy gold headdress made of miles of fabric wrapped into a thick turban-like crown.

"You look gorgeous," Olivia said. "Is that from one of your pictures?"

"My favorite, *The Emperor*," Ava said, placing her hands elegantly on her hips, studying her reflection. "It feels as if I'm in a movie, whenever I see myself like this. How I miss it. Now, start over."

Olivia recounted the events in such excruciating detail that eventually the apartment grew dark, and Issa had to go around turning on all the lights.

"Tomorrow is the first rehearsal," Olivia said. "What do I do?"

"Well, isn't it obvious?" Ava asked. "You can't do anything. No matter what, you're going to be a blight on their production."

"That can't be it. I'm not going to give in just like that."

Olivia looked at Issa for support, but Issa was starting to feel exhausted from the summoning. She sat down cross-legged on the floor, letting her shoulders slump even though it was terrible for her posture.

Ava traced an elegant finger along her jawline. "I'll need to observe what's really going on. I don't see any other option. Summon me at rehearsals, and I'll tell you exactly what to do."

"All right," Olivia said at the same time that Issa made a funny noise, thinking it was a joke. "What?" Olivia asked her. "It'll be like having an acting coach. Other stars do it."

"B-but," Issa sputtered. She wanted to remind Olivia that Ava would grow more powerful the more time she spent in the mortal world, but Ava was staring right at her, and it seemed rude to, well, not want her to grow more powerful, somehow, or admit so out loud. Then there was the fact that Issa would tire out so much from the conjuring that she wouldn't last the day. When they'd kept Ava on for hours on Catalina Island, she had slept for days to recover.

Olivia made a sympathetic noise. "Oh dear, I'm sorry, Issa. I know this takes a toll on you. We'll ask Yen if there's a better way so you won't get so ill next time."

Ava smiled down at Issa, and Issa wished she hadn't sat on the floor. There was something about the actress, especially when she stood next to Olivia, that made her feel like a little girl. She longed to impress her somehow, to prove that she deserved Ava's admiration as much as Ava had hers.

Chapter Twelve

Rehearsals started the next day, but since they had small roles and their scenes weren't on the call list, Issa and Olivia used the time to visit Yen in Chinatown.

Her aunt wasn't expecting them, and they found her apartment bursting with activity. Men and women gathered inside in small groups, working on every available surface. They shielded their work from Issa and Olivia as they walked in. Issa only caught a glimpse of what they were doing—counting money, mostly, and having heated discussions over ledgers—before Yen ushered them down the hall to the mirrored room.

"What are you two doing here?" Auntie Yen asked once she'd closed the door. "You need to give me more of a notice."

"We don't have a telephone," Olivia pointed out.

Yen's mouth pursed, but there was nothing she could do. Even if she paid to install a phone in their home, they'd have to tell Ma why and how.

"I thought you wanted me to visit more," Issa said, prickling with hurt at the rejection. Auntie Yen was usually so put together, but now her hair threatened to fall from its loose bun, wisps floating around her face. She wore a dress suit, her skirt tapered to fit her curves, the jacket accentuating her broad shoulders. "You said monthly reports and all that."

"Yes, yes, I did, but . . . today is a busy day. Has it been a month?"

"Almost," Issa said.

Yen's face softened. "Did you come for something? Need anything? How is the spirit?"

At that, the mirrors started fogging over.

"What's happening?" Issa asked, looking about the room. None of the incense sticks had been lit.

"Ayah, it's your Dead Auntie Phi. She must be bored." Auntie Yen went to a small cabinet in the corner of the room and opened it to reveal several picture frames. "Where are you? Which one are you using today?"

"What?" Issa asked, but she realized Auntie Yen wasn't talking to her when a voice responded from inside the cabinets.

"This one! No, not that one—over here! I keep telling you it's my favorite."

"You think I don't have better things to do than keep track of your vanity?" Auntie Yen rummaged through several frames before pulling one out. "All right, here you are." She propped the photo on top of the cabinet, facing it toward the mirror so that the reflection of Dead Auntie Phi could peer out at them.

Dead Auntie Phi was nicknamed that because she was, obviously, dead, but she'd died so long ago that Issa couldn't remember a time she wasn't, and so that had simply become part of her identity.

"Hi, Auntie Phi," Issa said. She hadn't seen her in several years, but she remembered her fondly as the plump and happy one who was always trying to pinch her cheeks.

Olivia waved at the black-and-white reflection. "Hi!"

"This is my best friend, Olivia." Issa introduced them.

"I've heard so much about you," Olivia and Dead Auntie Phi said at the same time, then beamed.

"You look so skinny, Issa!" Phi added. "Are you eating enough? Your ma's not feeding you or something?"

Someone knocked on the door. "Ayah, it never ends—" Auntie Yen said.

"Go, go!" Phi urged her. "Handle your business. I want some time with the girls anyway."

Auntie Yen gestured at the cabinets. "She can visit on her own for a short time, but you still need to light the incense. All supplies are in there."

After Yen left, closing the door behind her, Olivia helped Issa find the matches and put some incense into a few bowls of rice.

"So Bà Ngoại tells me that you're acting now," Auntie Phi said, smiling her dimpled smile. "Such ambitious girls. You think you'll really make it big?"

"That's what we're hoping," Issa muttered. She was tired of this line of conversation because most who asked thought she was delusional.

"Ava Lin Rang has been helping us," Olivia added. "So we know exactly who to talk to."

"That's great," Auntie Phi said. "Good for you! I'm so glad you're back in the family, Issa. We missed you. Always talking about how to bring you back. I know you want to act, though, so don't let Yen drag you into the family business if you don't want to. She has enough people for that."

"Thank you," Issa said, surprised at Phi's show of support. She wondered if Phi had had similar dreams of leaving the clan before the business literally killed her. "Did you ever want to do something like that?"

"What do you mean?"

"Did you ever want to be a star or . . . just something else . . ."

"Hah?" Auntie Phi had the most confused expression on her face, like she'd never imagined such a thing. "No. Of course not. I had my place with my family. Helping my sisters and mother. There wasn't much time to do anything else. We were always so busy. And I'm not even Yen! Look at her, always running around, people harassing her all day about this or that. No thank you."

"But she's in charge," Olivia said. "She has power."

"What good is power when you're too busy to enjoy it? Except when you're dead." Phi guffawed, but then cut herself off, her face falling. "Actually, that's not funny. Your aunt is under a lot of stress right now. She acts calm, but this war with the Uncles—I refuse to call them the Right Horn—it's got her down. She's losing money, losing business." Phi shook her head.

"I've been reading about it," Olivia said. "It sounds serious."

"Reading about it?" Issa asked. "Where?"

"It's in the dailies," Olivia said. "There's been fires, thefts, explosions."

"You should pay more attention, Issa," Phi said. "One day, this will be yours."

Issa made a strangled face. "Even if I don't want it."

Phi shook her head. "Neither did I. I don't envy Yen. You should pray that she gets through this, so that you don't get pulled in."

But it was too late for that. Issa was the sole heir to this underground empire, after all. "Why can't we just give it all to the Uncles?" she muttered. "Or remember Ngoc Le? Auntie Yen seemed to like the idea, and I still think we should consider her. What's the point in fighting when Yen is so distraught, and I don't want it?"

"Even if Bà Ngoại allows that to happen, Auntie Yen would rather die before she gives up control to the Uncles. But look!" Phi grinned again. "Nothing bad about being dead! I don't have to worry about it anymore, for one thing. Now I get to do whatever I want all day. No one to bug me."

"What do you do all day?" Issa asked, genuinely curious.

Phi's voice became distorted as she answered, smoke gathering over her reflection. Issa caught the words *mah-jongg* and *tea* but not much else.

"Who's that—what are you doing—conspiring without me?" another raspy voice demanded.

Phi looked to her right. "Your Bà Ngoại wants to talk to you, Issa ơi. Find her picture in the cabinet, will you?"

Issa rummaged through the stacks of frames and found the same one of Bà Ngoại they had used last time, her frowning eyes peering out at them as Issa propped up the picture to face the mirror.

"There you are, your face looks puffy," Bà Ngoại said. "Have you been eating too much salt?"

"No." Issa patted her cheeks. Olivia shook her head in reassurance. "We came because we have some questions."

"How is the stardom going? Famous yet?" Bà Ngoại smirked.

Issa ignored her. "I get exhausted every time we summon the spirit for long, but we need her to help us at rehearsals."

"Why?"

"Like an acting coach," Olivia said simply, as if that was sufficient.

Bà Ngoại didn't say anything, just waited for Issa to explain.

"We like having her around," Issa said with a shrug. "She gives us advice. And she's . . . nice."

"Nice?" Bà Ngoại shrieked as if Issa had said a terrible word. Issa covered her ears. Olivia cringed. Even Dead Auntie Phi froze in her picture. "Nice? You think any of us got anywhere by being nice?"

"No—I'm not saying *we* want to be nice," Issa stammered. "But Ava helps us. Isn't that what you wanted? You're the one who suggested it."

"I suggested she give you tips, not to follow you around like a monkey." Bà Ngoại's lips moved like she was cussing at them silently, but Issa couldn't make out the words. "In that case, I should shadow you—since you need someone to hold your hand so terribly."

"That's not it," Issa said.

"So you don't want me around?" Bà Ngoại demanded. "You'd rather have this *star*?" She said the word like she didn't believe Ava had truly been as famous as she claimed.

"Of course not, Bà," Olivia said. "We want you around always. Your wisdom has brought us so far. We wouldn't be here without you."

"You know how to flatter with your words, don't you, pretty girl," Bà Ngoại snapped, but the scrunched folds of her face loosened.

"I get so ill with each summoning," Issa said. Already, she felt the effects of summoning two spirits without Yen there to help her. "If you want me to call on you more, maybe just tell me how to not get ill every time."

"You get ill?" Bà Ngoại seemed concerned.

"She was in bed for days after Catalina," Olivia said.

"That just means that your connection isn't strong," Bà said. "The more you practice it and call on the spirit, the stronger the connection will get."

"But Olivia gave her some blood last time," Issa pointed out. "I thought that would have established a good enough bond."

"It was a mere drop, you fool. And Olivia's not even a shaman. Of course it won't last."

"So there's nothing I can do?" Issa asked.

"Drink more tea," Bà Ngoại snapped. "Now stop bothering me. I'm tired too." With that, her image froze and she was gone. Issa breathed in deeply, trying to contain her exasperation with her family.

Chapter Thirteen

Issa and Olivia were both expected to be on set the next week, along with the rest of the cast, even if they weren't filming. The producer Emmett Tratee wanted the entire crew present, just in case they decided to pivot and film a different scene than the one scheduled.

"It's important for us to show our faces," Olivia said as they stood on the soundstage—constantly getting in the way as stage designers moved around them. Issa's instinct was to scurry to a corner and make herself as inconspicuous as possible, but Olivia liked to be in the center. She wanted to be remembered, not caring whether it was for something good or bad. "What if someone dies or gets into an accident or something," Olivia continued. "We need to be available to step in. That's how ninety percent of actors get their lucky break."

"At the expense of someone else?" Issa asked.

"Issa." Olivia lit a cigarette, ignoring Issa's gesture for her to put it out. Issa supposed it didn't matter in the end. The air above their heads was already cloudy, and the producers' corner where they hunched over papers and frowned and looked important was a vortex of cigarette smoke. "This is how the world works. There's only so much good to go around, you have to take it for yourself."

"You really believe that?"

"That's what Bà Ngoại taught us. Auntie Yen would say the same."

"But they're . . . you know, gangsters." Issa whispered the last word, though no one came near them to overhear it.

Olivia smiled and pulled her into half a hug. "Yes, rich gangsters. We should learn a thing or two from them. Besides, I have a good feeling about today. Especially because Ava will be here."

"I hope it won't make me sick." Issa said.

"Remember what Auntie Phi taught us," Olivia said. Issa had been too annoyed with Bà Ngoại to pay much attention to the rest of her aunt's visitation. "She even said we can get rid of the incense, as long as we keep a mirror around. Just keep drinking your tea every morning, and you should be fine." Olivia had explained some of the things Phi said when they'd gotten home from Yen's house, but Issa wasn't sure that Phi was the best shaman in the family to learn from, considering that she hadn't survived long in the family business to begin with.

A man behind Olivia snapped his fingers in their direction. "You there."

Issa looked behind her, not sure the man was talking to her, and at the same time, fighting the indignation starting to churn in the bottom of her belly at being treated like a dog. Since no one else responded to the man, she pointed a finger at her chest, while Olivia looked him up and down.

He didn't notice, or didn't care about, her expression of loathing. "You're up. Asian Maid."

Olivia blew a stream of smoke in his direction. He stood too far away for it to hit his face, but his eyes narrowed, registering the insult.

"Number one or number two?" Olivia asked.

The man looked at the sheets of paper in his hand, then let his arm swing at his side. "Does it matter?" He snapped his fingers at Issa again. "You then, let's go."

"Oh, but," Issa started to say. She was quite sure he had meant to call Olivia, whose role had an actual line, while all Issa's character did was move things around for the main characters to interact with.

"Just go," Olivia said. "I have to take care of a certain someone anyway."

Issa wanted to ask Olivia how she planned to do that if she had to be on set, but the man tapped his wrist. Even though he was rude, he was still a white producer-looking person, someone who could easily cut them out of the film, so Issa moved to follow him.

"About time," he muttered as he led her to a different section of the soundstage. They were surrounded by cameras and lights that weren't turned on yet. Issa didn't know anything about the equipment, except that she shouldn't touch it. Stage crew busily fixed things, tinkering with tape on the floor, while others constructed a fake wall and brought in fancy-looking furniture.

"We're ready," the man said as they walked up to a group of actors Issa recognized from the table read, as well as Emmett Tratee, who stood surveying something in the distance.

"Right," Tratee said, giving Issa a cursory glance. "Now remember what the director said. Not too . . . dramatic. Tone it down a bit."

"Oh, actually . . ." Issa was about to remind them that she was Asian Maid Number Two, who had no lines, and point out that Olivia was the real Asian Maid Number One, but the man who had escorted her there grabbed her elbow, not too roughly, and pulled her over to what she realized would be the background of the scene just out of the spotlight. Her character was practically invisible, which was, sadly, not far from reality, considering that no one noticed that she wasn't even the right actor.

The others read their lines, performing them with gusto, while Tratee watched with his hands on his hips, the oddly angled lights in the studio reflecting harshly off his glasses and casting shadows on his expression. The seed of dread in Issa's stomach grew.

It was only then that Issa noticed Ava. The actress had blended so well into the set, her gray pallor merging with the dark shadows. She stood with a group of actresses, gazing at the soundstage around her, her eyes moist, her hands clasped over her chest in such a wholesome gesture that she looked like she was performing in a film herself—a small-town girl in the big city on the cusp of something big and life-changing.

No one else could see Ava, or if they could, they were rather good at pretending not to notice a mysterious, slightly smoky presence. The air around her was blurry, and her physical presence was still cast in a dull black-and-white tone, so bleak compared to everyone's bold makeup and carefully designed outfits.

Ava smiled when she spotted Issa, gliding over to stand next to her. Issa thought she could feel tendrils of hair brush her skin, but it was her imagination because when she eased closer to the ghost, her arm passed through her like smoke.

How was it possible? Issa hadn't called on Ava, and Olivia couldn't conjure her on her own before. She hadn't felt a telltale tug in her heart.

"I'm here, I'm here," Olivia said, rushing onto the set as well.

Emmett Tratee fixed his domineering stare on her. "And?"

"I'm Asian Maid Number One." Olivia held out her hands as if this were obvious.

Tratee looked directly at Issa, whose face immediately grew hot. To his credit, he had the decency to sputter with embarrassment.

"I'm Asian Maid Number Two," Issa explained quietly.

"It's all right, she was just standing in for me," Olivia said, entering the circle to join Issa.

"Oh, who cares," one of the actresses said. "Let's just get on with production."

Tratee snapped his fingers at Issa. "Fine. Leave."

Issa hurried out of the circle as quickly as she could. Something like shame made her want to disappear into herself, a numbing coldness that spread over her skin. Which was silly because she'd done nothing wrong.

She didn't know where else to go, so she stood near the vanity mirrors, watching as the actors found their spots to take the scene from the top.

"It's their fault for mistaking the two of you," Ava assured her. Issa was grateful for the comment, even though she couldn't respond without looking like she was talking to herself. "What horrid treatment."

Someone yelled "Action!" and the scene unfolded.

"Goodness, this is exciting, being back on set," Ava said. "It looks like Olivia's about to speak."

Olivia shifted, her face showing eagerness as her cue approached. She spoke with as much dramatic flair as she had at the table read, and Ava barked with laughter, shrieking so loud that her voice echoed in the warehouse. Or at least, in Issa's and Olivia's hearing.

"Oh dear, I'm sorry." Ava covered her mouth. "I couldn't help it. That was . . . well, that was something."

Tratee didn't stop the scene, though he wrote something down on his clipboard.

"Oh, I see why now," Ava said. "I see." She didn't elaborate on what her big revelation was, and Issa couldn't ask her.

Olivia looked crestfallen, though she remained professionally blank-faced. Issa could tell she was upset from the rounding of her shoulders, the barely there lines bracketing her nose and mouth.

The rehearsal ended, and Tratee told them all to take fifteen minutes while he conferred with the other producers. Olivia joined Issa by the vanity mirrors. Her attention fixed on Ava.

"Well, you certainly do a good job of stealing the show, don't you?" Ava remarked.

With Tratee and two other men standing nearby, Olivia couldn't respond, but her expression was furious.

"You're trying to be the star," Ava continued. "But you need to pay your dues. You need to be the maid. You need to live it. Not just pretend. You are the maid. So act like it."

"That's very helpful," Olivia said, unable to keep the sullen tone out of her voice.

"You're the one who conjured me for my advice," Ava said. "Or perhaps you already know what to do. In that case, my presence isn't needed." She started to fade away, her edges becoming smoky.

"No, don't go," Olivia said. She gave a heavy sigh. "What am I doing wrong?"

Ava took a deep breath and stood taller, and after a second, her form resolidified. "It's clear you're a fan of films from a decade ago. That acting style is more dramatic, but actors had to compensate for the lack of other things. Things that movies can do better now. So actors are allowed to be more authentic today. Like I said, don't just pretend. Live it! Make it real."

Olivia nodded. Issa smiled at her with sympathy, and Olivia's eyes grew shiny.

"And stop looking at your friend," Ava added. "You two are not the same person."

"I know we're not," Olivia snapped. It was the first time she'd spoken sharply to Ava. "I'm looking at you. You're supposed to be coaching me."

Ava pushed her shoulders back. "Of course, my dear. You certainly need it."

Issa pulled Olivia aside. "How did you do it?" she asked. "How did you summon her on your own?"

Olivia was clearly agitated, both from her poor performance and from Ava's criticism, avoiding Issa's eyes as her complexion grew ruddy. "Don't you remember?" she said, lighting a cigarette absentmindedly. "Phi told me a trick."

"What trick?"

"A bit of a pain sacrifice, kind of like with the blood."

"Sacrifice?" Issa whispered. She glanced at Ava, who watched the set with a dreamy, hopeful expression, lost in her own memories. "Pain? Olivia, that sounds dangerous." She enjoyed Ava's company as much as Olivia did and could see value in having Ava coach them, even if she'd been rather harsh. But was it worth it?

Olivia blew smoke out in a puff. "Honestly, with these heels, it's hardly a change from before."

Chapter Fourteen

They spent most of the rehearsals with Ava observing them and instructing them—or rather, Olivia—on how to act. Issa made mental notes of all Ava's tips to keep in mind when she landed a bigger role. Even though she had such a small part, she relished being on the set, imagining herself as a lead actress one day, shining and being praised, standing in the spotlight.

Ava didn't limit her comments to Olivia's acting. "Good God, what sort of face is that?" She laughed at the lead actress's attempt at crying in a particularly fearful scene. "She looks like she's trying to let out a fart without anyone noticing." The ghost caught Issa's eye as she tried not to snort out loud. "Darling," she said to Issa, and Issa braced herself for some mean criticism of her own appearance, but Ava surprised her. "You do look pretty in that light."

Issa had to admit that Ava didn't look so bad herself. The more they summoned her to help them, the more solid her form appeared, not so smoky around the edges, and with a bit more color in her cheeks. Not that she hadn't been radiant before, but all spirits, including her grandmother, had always looked a bit washed out, so Issa couldn't help but notice that Ava started to appear more vivid.

Finally, rehearsals were finished—the director had figured out the technicalities of the set, where to place the lights, where the actors should stand, how loudly they should speak, where they should look—and filming began.

Even though Issa had a small part, she looked forward to seeing herself in the movie, pictured the moment every day, and was filled with elation that success was on the horizon. If it felt this good playing a small role, she couldn't imagine what playing a much more important one would feel like.

With Ava's help and Eric Goldman's constant reminders, Olivia managed to say her line exactly how she was supposed to—demurely and without calling attention to herself. But she complained about it every day on the streetcar. Issa wished she could help Olivia, help her understand how to be content with what they'd already accomplished. Months ago, they would have died for this sort of chance, but Olivia seemed only hungry for something bigger, something better.

By the end of the few months it took to make the movie, Issa earned more in one check than she'd made her whole life helping Ma in the laundry room. She gave all of it to her mother, flooded with satisfaction at the surprise on her face.

"I hope that means I won't have to join you in the laundry room for at least a year," Issa said, kissing Ma on the cheek.

Ma wiped it away with the back of her hand. "As long as you keep out of trouble," she mumbled, but gave Issa a sly look. Even though she didn't say it out loud, Issa knew Ma was proud of her, or at least proud of the money she'd made.

After the wrap-up, Issa was surprised to get invited to a cast party at Eric Goldman's house.

"I expect you all to be there," he said to everyone. Already, the stage crew was breaking down the set, scrounging parts for the next film. "Even the extras. No small parts, I tell you. My assistant will give you the address and details."

Olivia grabbed Issa's hand in excitement. "A cast party. Isn't that marvelous?"

Issa smiled, but her stomach churned with nervousness. She'd spent weeks around these people with hardly a word exchanged except the polite *excuse me* and *hello*. What would she say to anyone at a cast party?

"You have to go," Ava said, though why she felt the need to give this advice when Olivia practically jumped out of her skin with excitement, Issa wasn't sure. Issa liked Ava, but she wondered why Ava stuck around when filming had ended and Olivia didn't need to be coached anymore. Of course, she'd never say this out loud. Olivia could summon Ava just as easily as Issa could now, which meant the dead actress was often around. And even though Issa enjoyed Ava's company, part of her felt a weird twinge of discomfort each time she appeared. Sometimes, she just wanted to be alone—well, alone with Olivia, since they shared a bedroom—only to have Olivia summon the dead actress casually, as if Ava had always been part of their group. It felt like an intrusion into their friendship, which Issa had considered exclusive, and thought Olivia did too.

"Emmett Tratee will definitely be there," Ava said. "The producers and everyone important are required to be at the after-party. You need to get on his radar. Make sure he notices you."

"We know, we know," Olivia said, waving her away.

"And ask around for Weston Redrick," Ava added. "It's about time you start searching for my trophy."

"Don't you think it's early for that?" Issa asked. "We only had small roles in this film—they'll think it's presumptuous if we start sniffing after a director, even if we have different motives entirely."

"You said you'd get my trophy if I helped you," Ava said with a pout. "So far I've done everything you asked. Can you say the same? Have you even tried?"

Issa deflated. "You're right, Ava. Of course, we'll ask around for him."

Ava smiled even as she faded into smoke.

Issa studied Olivia as they sat at the vanity tables while Olivia wiped off excess makeup with a cloth, revealing her slightly tanner though still beautiful complexion. Olivia wasn't a shaman, as far as they knew, but she'd been around so many of the rituals that Issa wondered if it was somehow seeping into her veins. She glanced around to make sure no one paid attention. "You're not giving her your blood, still, are you? That was just to establish a bond."

"Oh, darling, I know." She smiled reassuringly when Issa gave her a pointed look. "You don't have to worry about me. Anyway, what are you going to wear to the party?"

Issa thought about begging not to go, but after the way Ava had stressed the importance of attending, she doubted Olivia would let her stay home.

"Probably the red dress," Issa said.

The soundstage was already half-empty. The lead actors had their own dressing room, one of the dorm-like apartments on the backlot, but Olivia, Issa, and the actors who had small roles made do with the makeshift vanities on the set. When the lights suddenly shut off without warning, Olivia snapped her compact mirror closed, threw it in her purse, and got up.

"Why don't we celebrate with new outfits?" Olivia suggested as they made their way out of the building. "It's not every day we can say we finished filming a movie. And we just got paid."

"I already gave Ma my pay," Issa said. "And we spent most of Yen's allowance on new dresses last month." They'd also been splurging on taxis to and from the lot, dessert after dinner, and other random items they'd never indulged in before, like a silly book on the importance of charm that Olivia insisted they needed but left gathering dust on their side table every night.

"Then it's my treat. I owe you so much, let me buy you a ball gown." Olivia widened her eyes and batted her lashes. "Like the black glittery one we saw—imagine showing up dressed like Jean Harlow. Without the platinum-blond hair, of course."

"Oh, all right," Issa said, picturing the admiring faces.

Olivia squealed with delight.

Chapter Fifteen

The party was in full swing by the time they arrived, sweat beading on top of their makeup from the walk up the driveway. Issa hated being late, but Olivia never minded.

"We can make an entrance this way," she panted, forcing them to stop before they got too sweaty.

"You look ridiculous," Issa said as Olivia flapped her hands under her armpits in an attempt to dry them.

"We need to look gorgeous, Issa, don't you understand? Ugh, now I know why your mom carries around those folding fans. Aren't you worried your makeup's going to be ruined?" Olivia asked when Issa made no attempt to fix herself as they reached an open wrought-iron gate at the top of the hill that let in a line of cars.

"Why? It's not like we're auditioning for a role right now."

"We're *always* auditioning, Issa. The sooner you understand that, the better your chances of becoming a star."

Several cast members they recognized from the studio stood in front of the mansion, a huge house that Issa imagined could accommodate ten families comfortably. She didn't notice much about it except that light gleamed from the windows, reflecting off the shiny waxed paint jobs of the cars parked in front. Guests talked to each other in little clusters, not looking at them, sipping drinks from dainty glasses. Ladies in swaying fringed dresses and men in perfectly tailored suits over starched shirts. Even the stage crew wore their best outfits.

No one acknowledged them. Issa felt oddly exposed yet simultaneously invisible, as if she were naked but no one cared. Perhaps she had traded places with Ava, and she was the spirit watching the party behind a looking glass, leaving a trail of smoke that no one noticed.

Olivia didn't bother with being self-conscious. She exuded an air of mystique, going straight for the refreshments. Frosted cold martini glasses lined the table, and Olivia grabbed one for each of them.

Issa hated the taste of vodka. She much preferred something sweet, but Olivia finished her glass in two gulps.

"Drink it," Olivia urged. "It'll make you feel better. Besides." She put her empty glass down and immediately grabbed another one. "This is expensive."

"If you say so," Issa said, holding her breath to take a large swallow, fighting her gag reflex.

"I bet there's a shrimp platter here somewhere," Olivia muttered, scanning the crowd. "At least we can eat our worth, if we don't get to speak to a director. Do you think Eric Goldman's around?"

"This is his house, isn't it?"

"So they say." Olivia finished her second glass, her eyes moving quickly, her expression determined and scheming.

"Olivia," Issa said, already knowing that she was probably too late. "Don't you dare leave me."

"Issa," Olivia said with the same resigned tone Issa had. "I know you don't really want to go kiss up to some producer. You should get drunk and enjoy the party."

And with that, she disappeared into the crowd.

Issa tried to navigate the party without Olivia, even attempting to join a circle of small-role actors she recognized from the cast. She hung on the outer edges hoping to wedge herself in, but no one even looked at her, and after several excruciating seconds, she rushed away, hoping no one had witnessed her failure.

The embarrassment, short as it was, made her face flame, and she escaped through a glass-paned door onto a patio that was thankfully empty. It was a disgusting night, the air so humid that it left a constant layer of moisture on her skin, with no breeze to speak of. The patio could have easily fit their apartment living room, the railing a white European design with tiny pillar-like columns holding up a ledge that was the perfect height to set her drink on.

Issa breathed in the freedom of being outside, the relief and joy of solitude, right before a heavy loneliness settled over her, growing larger as the sound of music from inside drifted through the crack of the slightly open door. A low hum of conversation buzzed from the house, punctuated now and then by uproarious laughter. She wanted to be part of that conversation, but she didn't know how.

Not for the first time, she wished she could be like Olivia, ignoring anything that made her feel small and insignificant and amplifying the things that made her feel confident. Olivia had simply charged into the party with a purpose, and at that very moment, was probably grabbing for everything she'd ever wanted. Why couldn't Issa do the same? If Olivia could do it, she told herself, then so could she. She would go back inside and demand to be included. If it all went wrong and everyone thought she was eccentric, well . . . at least the film was wrapped.

Issa took a deep breath and steeled herself to make another entrance, but just as she reached the door, it opened and a man stepped out, almost barreling into her. She stepped back quickly to avoid a crash. He didn't notice, his head bent over cupped hands as he flicked a lighter, a cigarette balanced between his lips.

Only when he took a deep inhale and blew out a stream of smoke did he finally look up and meet Issa's eyes. She was too stunned to move, frozen like a squirrel in the middle of a path waiting for some sort of treat.

"Oh, hello," he said. "Sorry, you don't mind, do you?" He flicked ash into the air.

Issa couldn't imagine why he would need her permission. "Oh, uh, no. Of course not."

He smiled. He didn't seem like an actor—they were always meticulously dressed and groomed. His suit looked a little rumpled, his tie loosened, and he had stubble on his jaw. That and he was actually being nice to her.

"Are you an actress?" he asked.

"Yes, I had a small role in the film."

"In that case, I'll actually watch it." He smiled kindly, an easy sort of smile that created deep lines on his face, as if he smiled often and wasn't self-conscious about it.

"Are you?" she asked, aware that she was supposed to contribute politely to the conversation and afraid that she might ruin her chance. Finally, someone was talking to her. "An actor?"

"Me?" He chuckled. "No, no, never."

"Why not?"

He shook his head and laughed to himself. An unpleasant sensation twisted in Issa's chest, as if the man were laughing at her. At her own ridiculous dream. She squished it down. How could that possibly be true? He didn't even know her. But perhaps her dream *was* ridiculous, and everyone knew it but her.

"I'm a writer," he said. He must have read something in her expression because his face softened, and he held out a hand almost as an act of contrition. "Jem Meier."

Issa took it, feeling the weathered quality of rough skin, the palm of someone who was used to working.

"I have the bump to prove it," he added. "See?" He pointed at the middle finger on his right hand. Cigarette smoke drifted up between them.

"Bump?" It was difficult to make out anything even with the light from the windows.

"Here."

He grabbed her thumb and ran it over the knuckle of his middle finger, and Issa was so surprised at the warm tingling sensation that traveled up her arm and deep into her belly that she didn't register how strange the situation was.

"It's the writer's bump, a little callus you get from holding a pen for too long."

There was a pause in the music as the song ended, and the embers at the end of his cigarette lit with a glow, emphasizing the lull in their conversation. They both realized that he still held on to her thumb and stepped apart at the same time.

"Did you write this film?" Issa asked.

"With Eric? No. Nothing I've done has been made. Yet."

"I'm sure that you'll be famous one day."

"Writers don't get famous. That's not why I do it."

"Why do you do it then?"

He shrugged. "To be remembered in a way. Or to have my stories live on. To leave something behind. Morbid thought, really, but most of us are. Morbid. That's why we do what we do, right? To be immortalized in some way."

Issa stared at him, at a loss for words, mostly because it so accurately described how she felt, even if she'd never found the right phrase for it. She wanted her life to be different, to mean something, to impact someone somehow. Jem Meier laughed it off casually, and Issa felt silly because it was a desire that consumed her, and gave her a reason for living, and here she thought that she had such a profound purpose when apparently many people like Jem found it a common, banal characteristic of their profession.

Luckily, she didn't have to think of anything to say because through the windowpanes of the door, Olivia appeared. She glanced around and saw Issa, then strode outside.

"Issa, there you are." Olivia spotted Jem. "Oh, hi. Are you a producer?"

"No," Jem said good-naturedly. "Writer."

Olivia turned from him and grabbed Issa's hand. "I need you."

Issa waved an apologetic goodbye to the man as Olivia pulled her inside. "What is it?" she asked once they were surrounded by people and loud music.

"Why were you talking to a writer?" Olivia asked, grabbing an hors d'oeuvre from a uniformed server walking around with a tray. "You know they never get a say in anything, and Ava said we need to cozy up to the producers."

"I didn't seek him out," Issa said. "He came out for a smoke. And it's not like you left me with instructions before you abandoned me."

Olivia laughed and nudged her with an elbow. "Don't be dramatic. I couldn't find Weston Redrick, but I did hunt down Emmett Tratee, and we had a little chat by the pool."

"There's a pool?"

"We got another role."

"What, you're serious?" It couldn't be that easy, not after the lengths they'd gone to get the small parts in the film they'd just been in.

"It's not a big role, obviously," Olivia said. "In fact, it's kind of similar."

"Asian maids?"

"Asian nurses. It's a war movie. But he did hint that if we do well, there's a chance the studio would hire us as contract actors, instead of just extras. Isn't that exciting?"

Olivia didn't look excited, her eyes darting all over like she was scheming even more now that she'd successfully managed a step in her plan.

"Yes, that's amazing," Issa said, bouncing a little and jostling Olivia on purpose to get her to snap out of it.

But even though she smiled at Issa reassuringly, that gleam remained in her eye.

Chapter Sixteen

Olivia slept in for most of the following day, and while Issa was just as exhausted after weeks of being on set, she found herself the only one awake during the midmorning hours. It was frustratingly difficult to keep quiet trying not to wake the others, so she hopped on the streetcar for an impulsive trip to her aunt's house.

Luckily, when Yen's associate opened the door, things weren't as chaotic as they'd been during her last visit. Auntie Yen held court on the sofa dominating the middle of the living room, conferring with a few people while a number of staff prepared food in the kitchen, the smell of beef broth and basil greeting her.

"Issa, come on in," Yen said as the associate stepped aside to let Issa through. She got up to give Issa a hug.

"Is everything all right?" Issa asked.

Yen had bags under her eyes and looked paler than usual. "Of course, dear. Bà Ngoại has been expecting a visit from you. We both felt like things ended a bit abruptly last time you came."

Issa followed Yen to the mirror room, where the ritualistic objects were already set up. Yen didn't waste time as she lit the incense and called out for Bà to join them.

"Well?" Bà demanded without preamble. Issa stood tall under her grandmother's black-and-white inspection. "What have you to report? Are you stars yet?"

"We've only been in one movie, as extras," Issa admitted.

"Long way to go, then." Bà Ngoại sniffled loudly. "But it's something."

"It's better than we would have hoped for a few months ago. Thanks to Ava's help. And yours," she added with a wide-eyed smile.

"Are you still getting violently ill every time you conjure her?"

"I was never violently ill—no." Issa didn't feel like arguing with Bà Ngoại the same way she bickered with Ma, mostly because Bà, like Yen, still scared her a little, and there was none of the unspoken love and mirth that usually lay beneath her arguments with Ma. "Olivia learned to conjure her on her own now. Something about a pain sacrifice?"

Bà Ngoại nodded. "Pain is known to work, yes, outside of blood. It's not unheard of that once a shaman establishes a bond, those who don't have the gift can commune with the dead, as long as they have a good relationship. It seems like this spirit likes the two of you. She's always bragging about her time among the living again."

"So Olivia doesn't need to keep giving her actual blood, does she?" Issa asked.

"She very well should not," Bà Ngoại snapped. "That would be of the utmost foolishness."

"Why? What will happen?"

"It will create an incredibly strong bond. Which is not dangerous in and of itself, but . . . would be hard to break, should you need to. One drop, initially, was harmless. Two, perhaps not so terrible. But continuous offerings should be avoided. And you, Issa, should never, under any circumstances, offer your own blood to a spirit you don't trust."

Issa nodded. "I would never do that even if I did trust them."

"Good. Some useful things come from being a bit of a coward, hah?" She had a teasing twinkle in her eye, but the insult stung.

"I don't want to do anything . . . wrong," Issa said.

"There's nothing wrong you can do, girl," Bà Ngoại said. "Ghosts aren't here to harm you. Your mother has silly ideas in her head about evil and such nonsense, but there's no such thing. There is only want. You want something and the spirit wants something, and you've made a trade to each help each other. Besides, you and Olivia seem to get on well with this ghost. If you think she's trustworthy, then you have nothing to worry about.

"You're lucky," Bà continued. "People have their own desires, and sometimes that goes against other people's desires. The same way the Uncles want control of the gang that I left to your aunt. And now look what's happening. War! After all the work I did to instill power in my clan."

"Is there anything I can do?" Issa asked.

"No," Yen said with a sigh. "Ma, I told you not to involve Issa in these matters. She has enough of her own troubles right now, what with you bribing her to talk to you. And you are not very nice when she does visit."

"Nice!" Bà Ngoại shrieked. Issa was starting to realize that this word did not sit well with her. "You want me to be nice?"

"No, no, I don't," Issa said. "I like you just the way you are."

"So you're saying I'm not nice, are you?"

Issa took in a deep breath. "You don't have to bribe me to talk to you. I'm here because I want to be."

"But the money doesn't hurt, does it?" Bà Ngoại burst out laughing, her mouth open so wide Issa could see her molars. She couldn't help smiling as well. Even Yen chuckled. Her grandmother's laughter ended in a hacking, wheezing cough. "All right, then. This is exhausting. Take your cash and go."

Issa and Olivia were expected at the studio the next week to jump into the middle of the film, a musical ridiculously titled *Banana Cakes*. This time, Issa had a speaking part, and she spent most of the day reading the script even though her lines were very short. Olivia had a slightly larger role. After all, her last part had been a bit bigger than Issa's, so she technically already had more experience. Plus, she'd done the legwork of actually getting the job.

Issa felt equally anxious and excited to say her lines on camera. She worried about the response, especially that of the director—a domineering man who stopped the filming every five seconds because the pronunciation wasn't correct or the actor hadn't put enough emphasis on a word he liked. Issa was terrified of him and, unlike Olivia, did her best to stay out of his way. Yet she was eager to test her skills. She practiced her short lines every night, in front of the mirror. Sometimes Ava appeared to give her notes, though she was there more on Olivia's request than Issa's.

At first, Olivia had responded with enthusiasm and encouragement as Issa ran through her lines, but after a week or so, she looked bored and clapped listlessly.

"You'll do fine, Issa," Olivia said when Issa wanted to rehearse for the hundredth time.

Olivia had downplayed the part she'd gotten in the film. She had more than a few lines. Issa watched her with no small bit of envy as Olivia became increasingly natural in front of the camera. A quick study, she took the notes the director had given her in the last film and continued improving her skills. She no longer spoke in that overly dramatic way. Not that she ever completed a scene in one take—no one did with this new director, not even the veteran stars.

Issa liked having Ava around on set and listened closely as Ava whispered advice to Olivia. Issa tried to keep Ava's pointers in mind in her own acting.

"She's getting much better," Ava said. "You both are."

Issa beamed.

"Olivia reminds me of me," Ava said. "So full of potential."

Issa agreed, watching Olivia as she moved in front of the camera as if it weren't there.

"You'll get your moment," Ava said.

Issa let out a soft breath. "I hope so," she said as quietly as she could.

"One day, maybe fifteen movies in, you'll be surprised at your sudden fame. Some notorious critic will recognize your talent and call you an overnight success, as if you hadn't been working for years and years. It might take a lifetime, even, but if you keep going at it, it'll be worth it."

Issa smiled at Ava. "Thank you. I hope that's true."

"Me, too, darling."

On the day of filming Issa's speaking part, she spent more time than necessary at the vanity table. The makeup artists transformed her with each stroke of their brushes. In the mirror, she looked nothing like herself, her skin caked with makeup, her eyelashes thick and darkened. It gave her the confidence she needed to step into the role, to be someone else. She wasn't Issa Bui—she was Asian Nurse Number Four, ready to tell that soldier what to do when he insisted on ripping off his bandages.

The lights were much brighter than she'd expected, and her eyes burned from resisting the urge to squint. In a way, that was good because it prevented her from seeing the cameras, and she was forced to focus on the actor playing the soldier in the film. With the bandages over his face, made up to look bruised and broken, she could also forget that he was a famous star.

"You can't get up, sir," she said, her voice wobbling slightly from nervousness. For a second, she expected the director to stop the scene. Olivia was probably watching somewhere in the studio, biting her knuckle the way she did when she was anxious. "You can't look yet."

The actor mumbled beneath his bandages. She leaned forward to pretend to listen to what he said, speaking the lines in her head so she knew how long to pause for.

"I'm sorry," she whispered, the subtext being, *Your friend is dead.* A crack in her voice she couldn't hold back. It was a truly sad moment. "I'm so sorry."

"Cut!" someone shouted from the other side of the lights.

It seemed as if the whole stage gave a collective sigh. The actor sat up and lifted his bandages off carefully from his mouth.

"Someone get me some water," he demanded. Several footsteps pattered as the entire crew responded to the request.

Issa looked around. Olivia's silhouette went from black to color as she appeared in front of the lights.

"Careful with the makeup!" one of the crew shouted at the actor as Olivia pulled Issa off the set.

"That was amazing," Olivia said. "You were wonderful."

"Was I? My voice was shaky—I was so nervous."

"It was totally believable. I think they loved it." Olivia squealed and gripped Issa's hands tightly. "I'm so proud of you!"

Issa grinned back. She was suddenly exhausted, but it was in a relieved, fulfilled sort of way. She had done her part, and it felt exhilarating being someone else, pretending for a few minutes that she lived in a different era, a different place, with different problems. Someone important. Someone . . . not herself.

She frowned at the thought, but after a few seconds, she decided that it wasn't really a bad thing. She didn't hate who she was, nor her life, and she didn't want to escape *from* it, so much as she wanted to escape *toward* something else. Fame and fortune, perhaps, or more likely, a sense of competence. Accomplishment. She rarely felt like this. In a way it was like a game, but unlike the few she'd played in her childhood, she was actually good at it. And she loved it.

Chapter Seventeen

Filming wrapped up a few weeks later, ending with another cast party that was a fun, drunken, yet forgettable blur. The day after, Issa woke up with a headache and cottonmouth, feeling like she'd been wrung out.

She found Olivia in the kitchen with Ma, drinking steaming cups of tea and talking in low voices. The air smelled of sweet vanilla and a hint of jasmine.

"Hi," she said as she turned the stove on to make her own cup. "What's the score?" she asked to lighten the mood, which felt too heavy for so early a morning.

"I was just telling your mom about that laundromat that was robbed a few days ago," Olivia said. "The one on Spring and Fourth."

"What laundromat?" Issa asked. She didn't wait for the kettle to whistle before taking it off the stove to pour into a small cast-iron pot. Tea leaves swirled around in it, floating to the top before Issa placed the lid on it and brought the pot and her cup to the kitchen table next to Olivia.

"Where did you get gunpowder tea, anyway?" Ma asked. "It's very medicinal, that blend. It's known to have healing properties. Did I buy that?"

Issa met Olivia's eyes, unable to think of a lie. "Olivia got it," she blurted out, flushing with guilt even though she hadn't actually said anything wrong. "Why would anyone rob a laundromat?" she asked quickly. "They can't make that much money, can they?"

"Of course they can," Olivia said. "Everyone needs to wash their clothes."

"Exactly," Ma said with a nod. "Laundry is one of the most important, overlooked jobs."

"I just can't imagine it making enough to warrant thievery," Issa said.

"Well, you're kind of right as well," Olivia said. "Since they don't generate a lot of money on a daily basis, the funds aren't collected that often. So the money just piles up."

Issa sipped her tea. "How do you know so much about laundry?"

"It's in the article." Olivia reached behind her to a storage cabinet that was so untidy, stacked with papers and unread mail, pamphlets, and dusty books that Issa hardly ever noticed what was on top of it. Ma lectured her to go through the shelves once in a while, but since they all contributed to the junk, Issa felt neither accountable nor justified in cleaning it off. What if she threw away an important bill they forgot to pay?

Olivia dug through the top few layers and pulled out a newspaper that was still pristinely folded. It was one of those free dailies that no one bothered to read, except for Olivia apparently.

Issa skimmed the article, which did have an alarming amount of information on how a laundry business was run. "Golly. Maybe we should quit acting and open a laundromat instead."

"A perfectly reasonable and honorable profession," Ma said. "I already have the experience." Her face brightened, and Issa's heart sank as she realized Ma thought she was being completely serious. "We could run it together, the three of us—and then you'll have something to do once I'm gone."

"Once you're gone?" Issa said. "Is there something you need to tell us? Are you sick?"

"No." Ma frowned. "But you can't expect me to live forever. And take care of you for the rest of your life, hah?"

"No, of course not." Issa sighed. "I'm the one who's going to take care of you, remember? That's why we're both going to hit it big, so you don't have to worry about that."

"You should come work at the hotel with me, get something with more security."

"I'd have to fold a million sheets to make enough just for rent every month."

"But at least you know it's possible! Better to quit your silly dreams and open a laundry instead."

"It's *not* possible, Ma," Issa said, gesturing to the newspaper. "We don't have the upfront capital for it. We'd need about five thousand dollars at least."

"Maybe once we land our first big roles, we can give you the money," Olivia said with a wink.

"It says here that the thieves didn't even take that much," Issa said. "They barely broke into a few machines when they could have taken more. The cops showed up long after they were gone, according to witnesses."

"Exactly," Olivia said. "If they didn't take that much, what was the point?"

"You think it was the Uncles?" Issa asked before she thought better of bringing them up in front of Ma.

Ma sat up straighter. "What do you know about the Uncles?"

"Apparently they've been making things really hard for your sis—" Olivia cut herself off at Ma's narrowed eyes.

"For certain groups," Issa said. "Who own laundromats and businesses in Chinatown."

"Ayah." Ma got up, her chair scraping noisily on the tiled floor. "I don't want to get mixed up in that business." Her hackles raised, she looked like she was ready to launch into full-scolding mode, though Issa had heard this one many times. How evil Bà Ngoại was, how the clan was no good, how their dealings were cursed, destined to invoke misery on anyone who dared to enter their lives.

"We're not," Issa said. "I didn't even know about the laundry attack until Olivia told me right this moment."

Ma considered this and, to Issa's relief, seemed to believe her. "I don't want you reading any more about it either. The more you learn about the clan, the more danger you'll be in."

Chapter Eighteen

Despite finishing an entire teapot by herself, Issa still felt tired and groggy and hoped for at least an afternoon to rest, but Olivia had plans for the day.

"We should visit the studio," Olivia said. "Find Eric Goldman."

"Whatever for?" Issa asked.

"He's the only one who actually liked us," Olivia pointed out. The last director had barely noticed them, and Issa hadn't found his style pleasant, constantly shouting at the actors or throwing things when he was upset. "We should capitalize on his willingness to cast people like us. Ava thinks he's our best chance. Plus, she seemed to have a strong effect on him, probably because they used to work together when she was alive. Do you think she'll do that whispering trick?"

"Of course, if we ask her," Issa said, burying her head into her pillow. "But can't we just rest? For one day? I think I drank too much last night." She yawned. "Do you think Ava felt sad to be left out of the party, especially when she helps us so much on the set? It makes me feel guilty that she doesn't get to enjoy the celebrations."

"She was there last night," Olivia said. "You don't remember?"

Issa blinked. "I don't remember much, to be honest."

"It was just as well—she can't eat or drink anything, so she hardly has any fun, I suspect." Olivia dug around in their shared closet. "Can I borrow this?"

"Of course." Like most things, the dress Olivia held up was something Ma had salvaged from the hotel's lost and found, a light-blue A-line with a high neckline that always made Issa extremely aware of her ample bust because it attracted more stares than she was comfortable receiving. On Olivia's frame, it was much more flattering.

"Say, you don't have to come if you don't want to," Olivia said.

"What? Why?" Issa had just been complaining about having to go back out so soon, but she didn't think Olivia would let her off so easily. "It'll be much harder by yourself."

"I won't be by myself, not really," Olivia said, wiggling her hips to help the dress settle down her body. It ended below her knees, but instead of looking dumpy like it would have on Issa, it lengthened her figure and accentuated her long legs. "I'll have Ava."

Issa's throat tightened. "But Ava's not really there."

"Of course she is. People won't see her, but I know she's there, and she's the one we really need to do the work. The persuading."

"Are you really going to have her seduce Goldman into giving us another role? Hasn't the poor man been . . . persuaded . . . enough?"

"It's not like she's physically going to touch him. She can barely touch us."

"She can't touch us," Issa said.

Olivia laughed. "Exactly! You never had a problem with it before." Olivia sat down happily, bouncing the mattress. "Honestly, I think it's a neat trick, especially on men who always get what they want. What's left for the rest of us? They walk around acting like the whole world owes them a favor, and we're always expected to bow and nod and say please and thank you like good little girls. I'm so sick of it."

"I mean, we *should* say please and thank you . . ."

"That's not what I mean, Issa. Doesn't it bother you how some people just . . . get things? But we don't? We have to work three times as hard?"

Issa didn't dwell on such things. What was the point? She'd learned early on that she was different from most other people. Perhaps when she still lived with Bà Ngoại before her father died and Ma took her away, she had felt like she belonged to the clan. But once it was just Ma and her in their new neighborhood, she was suddenly aware of how . . . alone they were.

Until then she had looked at Ma as infallible, a superior being who could do no wrong, who was capable of anything. But for the first months after they left the clan, Ma couldn't find work, and they were forced to leave the apartment. Luckily, someone had taken pity on them and told Ma about the church shelter, so Ma had bundled Issa up in as many clothes as she could wear so they'd have to carry fewer belongings, and they walked the ten blocks to the church, hungry and tired and soaking in sweat by the time they reached the steepled building.

The cots in the church gymnasium were uncomfortable, and the broth served for dinner had no flavor. As Issa sat alone waiting for Ma to ask one of the sisters for work prospects, she smelled something faintly sour and salty and, after some investigation, discovered it was her own armpits. She hadn't bathed in days because the water at their old apartment had shut off, and when she looked up, hot and ashamed, she no longer saw the perfectly composed mother who could do anything and everything, but an exhausted, lonely woman who could barely stand. An exhausted, lonely woman who didn't have any answers when Issa asked . . . so eventually she learned to stop asking. Stop asking about her father, stop asking about Bà Ngoại, stop asking about the aunties and uncles. Start obeying. Just listen. Be a filial daughter. Nod and smile at the white people. Speak clearly. Don't mumble or chew with your mouth open or slurp your soup or cough more than twice or clear your throat too loudly.

Then school started, and she knew she was . . . other. From the way the teachers spoke to her loudly and slowly, their impatience, the quick way they snapped at her when she had a question, assuming she asked out of stupidity rather than curiosity—the world and society taught her that she was from an entirely separate universe. This wasn't her home, but perhaps, one day she would find it. A place in which she'd be treated like a normal person, one who belonged, who didn't have to apologize or justify her existence.

Maybe that was why she loved movies so much. Because in movies, anyone could have a story. In pretending to be someone else, she could escape the fact that she had no idea who she truly was or where she came from, much less where she belonged. The script had the answer for her. She didn't have to search it out. She wouldn't even know where to begin.

"That's just how things are, I suppose," Issa said when Olivia raised her brows, still expecting an answer. She didn't want to point out that she used to feel sorry for herself, a poor little Asian girl who didn't have as many nice clothes or things, until she met Olivia. A poorer little Asian girl who didn't even have a mother who loved her.

When they were seven, Issa learned that Olivia didn't own more than two shirts. Issa's own wardrobe came from the hotel lost and found, but she knew she had more than Olivia. It took her months to design some subterfuge to share her clothes with her best friend without making it obvious she felt sorry for her. She made up a story about how they could swap outfits, knowing Olivia had nothing to swap in return. From the way Olivia's face froze, Issa knew that Olivia hadn't fallen for it. She'd smiled and gone along, as if in turn, she was the one providing Issa with charity, humoring her by allowing her to help.

It was then that Issa understood that she couldn't change much about the situation. She couldn't save Olivia, she couldn't bring Olivia's parents back, couldn't take her away from her uncle. She could barely convince Olivia to accept something as simple as clothing that Issa technically got for free in the first place.

So she'd understood also not to ask Ma for impossible things. She'd had to accept that there were some things she just couldn't do. Some things she simply couldn't have.

"But it doesn't need to be that way," Olivia said, still smiling brightly. "We can change things. We don't have to work three times as hard. We have Ava on our side now. Isn't that right, Ava?"

Issa sat up as the ghost appeared in front of the mirror, tilting her head this way and that at her own reflection.

"What is it, darlings?" she asked. "Have you gotten your next scripts yet?"

"No, we're going to find Goldman today," Olivia said. "You'll still join us? Do your little parlor trick?"

Ava laughed, a throaty sound that gave Issa goose bumps. "I wouldn't miss it. Being dead has its perks. You know, men fell at my feet before I died, but now it's even more delicious."

Issa smiled. "If only I had your confidence."

"But you can," Ava pointed out. "You just have to pretend to be me. Walk like me, act like me, talk like me. And it will happen."

"Anything can happen, as long as you believe in it," Olivia said. She threw on a silk scarf and admired herself in the mirror next to Ava. "What's stopping us?" she asked Issa. "We have money. We have power." She pretended to peck Ava on the cheek, sending up a trail of smoke from the ghost's face. "We can do anything we want."

"We only have a little money," Issa reminded her. They couldn't stop themselves from buying frivolous new dresses for parties and treats to eat on their way home from the studio. It was so hard to say no after a grueling workday.

"And there will be more to come," Olivia said. "We'll make it happen. We just need to work for it, and our dreams will come true."

"You really believe that?"

"Yes. I believe that everything we've ever wanted will happen for us." Olivia pulled Issa to her feet. "Now go put on something pretty, darling. And let us chase our dreams!"

Chapter Nineteen

They walked to the Lion Building and found Eric Goldman's office on a floor with low ceilings and dimly lit hallways. It wasn't a nice building by any means, and peering through the doors they passed, they saw unsightly old desks, mismatched chairs, and boxes stacked full of reels, paper, and other items that were probably props—old hats and jackets, fancy-looking jewelry, tangled wigs strewn about.

An older lady sat outside Goldman's office, squinting at her typewriter through half-framed spectacles held on by a chain around her neck. She wore a deep-purple dress suit that was a size or two too big.

Olivia knocked on the door, but she didn't look up.

"Hello?" Olivia asked, stepping inside. "We're looking for Eric Goldman." They hung back near the door.

"Eric?" the woman repeated. "He's not here."

"Can you tell us where to find him?" Olivia asked.

"He's directing!" she screeched, as if that were obvious. "He's on the lot somewhere."

Olivia smiled and clasped her hands in front of her, the innocent look she projected when she wanted something. "Which one?"

"How should I know?"

"Can you tell us which titles he's working on at the moment?" Issa asked. "Perhaps he has a list? We can try to narrow down which stage he's at that way."

The woman didn't seem to hear or care what Issa had asked, turning her back on them to reach for a cabinet on the floor. She whipped out a piece of paper.

"*Love in the Afternoon*," she read out loud, "*Still Green Waters*, and *Avocado Sunset*." Olivia didn't miss a beat, snatching the sheet out of the woman's hand and spinning toward the door.

⁂

They tried Soundstage 4 first, an enormous building blending in with the rest of the concrete jungle, which was where *Love in the Afternoon* was being filmed according to the schedule Goldman's secretary gave them. Outside, everything seemed sterile and clean, nothing but rectangular gray shapes. You'd never guess that whole stories and universes were constructed within each one.

He wasn't on the set, and the producer wouldn't even look at them as he shooed them out.

"Who even makes up these titles?" Issa said, smarting at being turned away so rudely. "They're ridiculous. What is an avocado sunset?"

"Who knows?" Olivia mumbled as they hurried to Soundstage 7, which was even farther away on Lot One than they anticipated. When they got there, no one knew where Goldman was. A trackless trolley almost ran them over, and Issa was tempted to hop on the back of it like she'd seen in action pictures. Outside the soundstages, crew members prepared other sets, full-size house facades and storefronts decorated to look realistic, held up by the flimsiest scaffolding, or in one production, several men.

Olivia consulted the schedule. "*Avocado Sunset* is filming at Joppa Square and Castle Finckenstein. Where is that?"

Issa frowned. "It's on Lot Two. I remember a producer talking about it."

"How far is it?"

"We could walk, I think, but it might be quite a hike."

Olivia cursed. "We just can't catch a break today."

A truck honked at them from behind, and Olivia and Issa scrambled to move out of the way. Instead of driving past, it slowed to a stop, a man poking his head out the passenger window.

"Hello there," he said.

Issa waited for Olivia to approach all sultry and flirty, but when Olivia turned to her instead, Issa peered closer at the man.

"Oh, Jem!" she said. It was the writer she had met at the wrap party for their first film, which felt so long ago that it took her a moment to remember him. He'd been the only person who was nice to her back then. "Hi! What are you doing?"

Jem gestured to the back of the truck. "Borrowing some props for creative inspiration." A tarp covered the items, and he didn't elaborate. "What are you doing?" He smiled politely at Olivia, but kept his focus on Issa, for which her respect for him grew immensely.

"We're looking for—" Issa started to say, but Olivia cut her off.

"We're supposed to be filming a scene today," she said. "But no one told us it was at Joppa Square."

Jem sucked air in through his teeth and grimaced in sympathy. "That's not the first time that's happened." He looked at the driver, a smallish man in shirtsleeves and suspenders. He nodded toward them. "Can we give them a lift?"

"That'll cut into our writing time," his friend said. "Boss won't be happy."

"They probably won't use anything we come up with today, and we're not getting paid, anyway," Jem said.

"We're on spec," his friend explained, leaning over him. "That means we'll only get paid if they end up liking what we write."

"We know what *on spec* means," Olivia snapped. She raised her brows when Issa shot her an admonishing look.

"Are you a writer as well?" Issa asked his friend.

"Peter Grenwald," he said, smiling at her.

Issa gave a dainty wave, then widened her eyes at Olivia, who sauntered over to the driver's side. The men both watched as she took her time going around the front of the truck. She peered through Peter's window.

"I always thought writers were the real backbone of the movies," Olivia said. "Without you guys, films would never get made."

Peter's face grew red, but he couldn't seem to think of a response.

Jem propped one elbow against the door to speak to Issa. "It won't take us any time to get you to Joppa Square. Do you have big roles today?"

"Oh yes," Olivia answered for her. "Big roles."

"All right, then," Peter said. "But you'll have to hang out the back."

Olivia straightened. Issa thought she'd complain or protest, but she walked to the truck bed without a word.

"I'm sure we can squeeze them in," Jem said.

"No space," Peter said.

Jem gave Issa an apologetic look, which she appreciated, but she was distracted by the sight of Olivia climbing the mountain of props. She sat on top of the tarp, balancing on some odd-shaped object beneath, grinning down at Issa.

"The view's amazing from up here," she said, patting the lump next to her.

Chapter Twenty

The ride was bumpy, and they slid around the tarp so much that Jem kept hollering out the window to see if they were okay, to which Issa always shouted back, *Of course*, even though by the time they drove down Overland Avenue and on through the Lot Two entrance, her hips were bruised in several spots.

She was too distracted by the outdoor sets they passed to care—whole neighborhoods of constructed housefronts to represent New York Street, a whimsical suburban town square, and even a cemetery. Film crews were busy setting up lighting and microphones, while cameras whirred on other sets. Issa craned her neck to catch glimpses of shots. Lot Two was where most of the exterior scenes were filmed, but Issa had never been called here. Driving through it was a bit of a thrill, like traveling the world on the back of a truck. She even spotted a lake in the distance, while tall European buildings and modern houses alike loomed around them.

Olivia didn't seem as awed by the surroundings. "Thank God that's over," she said when they stopped just up the hill from a castle—an actual castle! It had several towers, with turrets and everything!

Issa must have looked like a naive schoolgirl, but she couldn't help ogling everything around her as she stumbled off the truck. The set was oddly empty, however. No cameras or crew in sight.

"Thank you, gentlemen. You've saved our lives," Olivia said to Jem and Peter.

Peter sputtered, attempting to make a smooth remark. "Well—you bet—we'll be—one of these days—"

Olivia smiled at him, waved, and started down the hill toward the castle.

Issa felt like she owed Jem more of a thank-you, but she couldn't stay long as Olivia walked off. "I'm sorry we're always hurrying off," she said.

"It's pretty standard around here," he said with an easy grin.

"I'll make it up to you, I promise," she said to be polite as she followed after Olivia.

To her surprise, he stuck his torso out the window. "How about dinner?"

"What?" She laughed.

"Dinner!"

Issa was so astounded, she couldn't think of an answer, still walking, half turned back to look at him.

"You better say yes," Olivia said so only Issa could hear.

"You think so?" Issa asked.

"He did us a huge favor. We wouldn't want word getting around that we're ungrateful."

Issa waved at Jem. They were too far for her to shout an answer now, so she hoped he took it as a positive.

His door opened, and he stirred up a cloud of dust as he jogged after her. Olivia gave a knowing smile and kept walking, leaving Issa alone to wait for Jem.

"Was that a yes?" he asked breathlessly. He smelled faintly of sweat, like he had been busy all day. It was pleasantly mixed with the scent of fresh soap.

Issa laughed again. "You ran all the way here for that? Your friend is probably incredibly annoyed."

"He's not a friend, just an officemate. And it's fine. They never use anything he writes, so he's as productive out here as he is on the typewriter."

"That sounds horrible. All that work, and there's no gratification?"

Jem shrugged, the seams of his shirt smoothing out over his round shoulders. He was taller than her by a foot, and he'd stood at a considerate angle that blocked the sun from her face. "That's the writer's life."

"But you love it, I bet," Issa said.

"I do." That easy smile again. "So what was your answer?"

"To what?"

He laughed. "Dinner."

"Oh. That. Well, I suppose there's no other way to thank you for your help."

"There isn't."

"Then it's a yes."

"Yes?"

Issa nodded, hoping she wasn't growing too red as he also grinned wide with delight.

"Do you have a card?" he asked. "A phone number?"

"No."

"Issa!" Olivia called. Her patience must have run out.

"I should go," Issa said.

"Wait, how will I find you?" Jem asked.

She held her arms out in a shrug as she raced down the hill.

Castle Finckenstein was not real. Issa knew that most of the streets and villages on the lot were just fronts—but for some reason, she expected the doors to open so she could explore the interior. Instead, they were not only locked out, but they couldn't find anyone who knew anything about the film.

Olivia finally waved down a man walking by, carrying a prop rifle.

"Must have moved locations for the day," he said. "They were filming a different one earlier here. *Speed*, or some such. Double bookings happen all the time."

"Thank you," Olivia said as the man kept walking. "What now?" she asked Issa.

"We can keep looking?" It was a sun-drenched day, and neither of them were dressed for anything too physically demanding, both in cotton day dresses and heels that were only two inches high but still not suitable for walking.

"What else is there to do?" Olivia said with a sigh. She pulled off her scarf and fanned her face with her fingers.

They were sweating by the time they made it out of Joppa Square and into an area under construction that had scaffolding erected above a white European-style building with arched walkthroughs and tall colonnades.

"This must be an important feature," Issa said.

"Who cares, we're not in it," Olivia mumbled.

Issa had never seen her friend so forlorn. Olivia's face was splotchy and red and a bit dusty. The wind picked up, and they had to squint to keep debris out of their eyes.

"We should have asked your friend James if he knew where Eric Goldman is," Olivia said. "Instead of lying to him."

"You mean Jem." Issa was surprised to hear Olivia admit she'd done something wrong. "I doubt he would have known. He said he was contracted to Paramount or some such. I wonder what he's doing here."

"Perhaps he got lent out. Studios do it to stars all the time. In any case, we could have asked him to hang around and give us a ride back."

"We would have owed him another favor," Issa said.

"I know what kind of favor he would appreciate." Olivia gave Issa a playful glance and nudged her with an elbow.

"I already owe him dinner for the ride."

"I thought you don't believe in love."

It wasn't that Issa didn't believe in love, but simply that all the men in her family had never fared well. The Uncles were constantly trying to overthrow Auntie Yen, her grandmother hated her grandfather as much when he was dead as when he was alive, and her father had died at such a young age that Issa couldn't help concluding that life was much better without male distraction.

"I believe in a free meal," she said.

Olivia laughed. "Hardly sounds like work."

Issa smiled. "He's a contract writer."

"I heard they're paid well."

"Really? Perhaps we should consider writing."

Olivia grinned. "Have you ever heard of a famous screenwriter?"

Issa thought about it. "No, I suppose not, but that might be because we never cared to look."

"Exactly. No one does." Olivia held a hand over her forehead. "No, I want to be a star. I want it more than anything. I want to be famous and known. I want to act in the movies. I want people to look at my face, to look again not because of"—she gestured between the both of them—"but because I'm famous. Because they could have sworn they saw me in something amazing."

Issa imagined the same scenario. It was quite shallow, but neither of them had shied away from their desire—the loyalty, the adoration. And a small bit inside Issa wanted to spite all those people who had ever given her a dirty look. All the small interactions she had every day—when people looked down on her, or when they treated her mother badly because they thought she was worthless just because of how she looked. Issa wanted to show those people that she was superior, that her life amounted to more than what they presumed after giving her just a single glance. She'd do more with her life than they could ever imagine.

"There's nothing else for me," Olivia added so quietly that Issa thought she'd misheard.

"What do you mean?" Issa asked.

Olivia turned her face away. "I can't do anything else. I have no other talents. Where would I go, if this doesn't work out?"

"Why do you need to go anywhere?"

"I can't stay with you and your ma for the rest of my life."

"Why not?"

"Issa," Olivia said. There was no humor in it.

"You're right," Issa said. "I mean, of course you can stay—you're practically my sister. But I don't want to live with Ma forever either."

"Exactly. And if we don't do this, you'll have to keep your promise to your grandma and auntie. And I . . . Well, I don't know what I'd do."

"Please, I don't want to think about that. Not right now. We still have time."

"Don't you see, though? We have to do this. *I* have to do this. I don't have any other option. I'm not good at anything else. I mean, I don't want to be. Nothing in life is easy, and if I'm going to work hard at something, this is it. I know it."

Issa knew Olivia was determined to be in the movies, but she'd never considered what would happen to Olivia if they didn't make it. Not because she was delusional—or at least, she hoped not—but because Issa knew that Ma would be there for her, and of course there was always Auntie Yen, if she was desperate. But Olivia . . . well, Issa had always assumed Olivia would just come along with her, that they would follow each other, wherever they ended up.

"There's always laundry work," Issa teased.

Olivia laughed.

"We'll get there," Issa reassured her. "With or without anyone's help."

"It'll be easier with someone's help, though," Olivia said. "We have Ava anyway."

"Right," Issa said, caught off guard because it hadn't occurred to her that Ava could be the answer, which was rather silly, since she was the reason they had made it as far as they had. "Let's get out of this lot and go home."

They walked with slow, dragging steps to the next set, going down a street of Spanish-style building fronts with stucco walls and red-clay roof tiles. Issa kept her eyes peeled for any trucks that could take them back to Lot One.

Olivia grabbed Issa's elbow, her grip tightening.

Issa turned, and Olivia gestured at someone behind the truck. It was a producer that Issa recognized. He had his name on almost every project, and the man next to him was Eric Goldman.

"Eric!" Issa shouted out before she could stop herself.

The producer snapped his folder closed and headed to the truck. Eric tucked a pen into his shirt pocket and gave them a curious look.

"Yes?" he asked. He must not recognize them.

"Your secretary sent us here," Olivia said, her face brightening. "We're wondering if we could have a word with you."

He waved them off dismissively and walked off around the back of a fake storefront. Olivia followed, taking Issa with her.

"We were in your movie," Olivia said. "And we were hoping that you could cast us in your next one."

He gave a huge sigh. "Unfortunately, I don't always make those decisions."

"But you're the director," Issa said. "Shouldn't you get a say?"

"That would make sense, wouldn't it?"

A car waited for him—a beige sedan that blended into the surroundings. Goldman got into the front seat and slammed the door, starting the engine without another word. There was nothing they could do but stand there and watch as he drove away. Olivia gave Issa a forlorn look. They looped their elbows together, holding each other up as well as they could.

Goldman's car had moved just a few feet when the brake lights came on.

His window rolled down, and he stuck his head out. "I suppose you both want rides back to the East Gate," he said gruffly.

They ran forward.

"Yes, that would be lovely," Olivia said. "If it's not too much trouble."

"Only if you stop hounding me about the film," Goldman said.

Olivia boldly got into the front passenger seat, while Issa slipped in the back, claiming the middle so she could lean forward and insert herself into the conversation.

"Of course," Olivia said. "Forget about the film." She closed the door. "How about a contract with the studio instead?"

Goldman laughed.

In the rearview mirror, Olivia gave Issa a conspiratorial look. Issa leaned back, out of view, turned her head to the side, and whispered Ava's name.

"Contracts?" Goldman asked. "For what?"

"Acting, of course," Olivia said. "Don't you remember how well we did? Even Emmett Tratee said we were rising stars. He said we could get contracts if we did well enough, and we certainly have."

"Honey, I direct five movies a year, and that's just on average. What makes you think I remember every young talented potential who steps in front of the camera?" Goldman glanced at Olivia. "I suppose you're rather easy to remember, though. Are you two sisters?"

Issa tried not to roll her eyes. As she leaned forward to answer, she caught a reflection in the rearview mirror of someone sitting next to her and almost yelped in fright, immediately feeling silly. Ava had shown up, dressed in a day dress, looking more casual than Issa had ever seen her. She winked.

"Do you want us to be?" Olivia asked.

Goldman frowned, not falling for her baby-voiced drawl. "It might help, but there can't be two of you. It'll confuse the masses."

"But we are two different people," Issa said.

"I know that," Goldman said. "But will the audience know that?"

"I think people are smarter than you give them credit for," Olivia said.

Ava leaned forward, her face appearing right behind Goldman's in the mirror, though of course he couldn't see her.

"Oh, what will it hurt, Eric?" she whispered. There was a fantastical quality to her voice that Issa had never heard before, a hissing, echoing sound that created a sharp sensation in her ears. "Give the girls a contract. You know they'll be amazing."

Goldman swatted the air as if chasing away a mosquito. "It's not up to me."

Ava wasn't finished. "But look at them. They're gorgeous. So exotic. So talented. They'll be stars, you know they'll be. They have that quality about them. You can tell. I know you can."

Goldman dug a pinkie finger into his ear. "I can't make them stars." He turned sharply to Olivia. "I can't make you stars," he repeated.

"But you know who can," Ava whispered. Her voice seemed made of gossamer, airy cotton candy floating in smoky tendrils. "And everyone will praise you, the director who discovered them."

Goldman's hands tightened on the steering wheel, and he shook his head. "A terrible idea."

Ava didn't seem perturbed, smiling gently. "Give them a chance. You'll see that you were right all along."

"A chance," Goldman repeated.

"Just a chance," Ava repeated.

"Just a chance," Olivia whispered as well, like she couldn't help herself.

"A small role, even," Ava added.

"Yes," Goldman muttered.

Issa was so surprised that she jerked forward in her seat. "Really? You'll give us another movie?"

"Not too small a role," Ava said. "Something worthy. Something that will get them noticed."

"Secondary," Goldman said. "Supporting."

"Exactly. With an opportunity for contracts."

Goldman nodded. Olivia met Issa's eyes in the mirror. Issa was too nervous to let herself hope.

"There's a project," Goldman said. "Several, I'm working on. You two would make great supporting actresses."

"That's wonderful," Olivia said. "And you'll give us contracts if we do well?"

"Yes. If." Goldman pulled into Lot One, parking close to the Lion Building. "Come find me at Soundstage 3." He turned off the engine and looked a little dazed, peering back at Issa with consternation as if just noticing he had passengers. "You can audition for one of them."

"Auditions?" Olivia asked. "I thought you said we had the roles."

"You did," Ava said. "You gave them the parts."

"You'll still have to meet the other execs," he said. "But the producer will take a shine to you. He wanted an exotic element."

"And you'll be bringing two," Ava whispered.

"Yes," Goldman said.

Ava smiled, and then her reflection disappeared.

"Wonderful, then." Olivia opened the door.

Issa got out as well, and they leaned down to peer through the window at Goldman together.

"We'll see you soon," Olivia said.

Chapter Twenty-One

Issa was slightly nervous when they made their way to Soundstage 3 a few days later, expecting the producer and director to turn them away like they were beggars back for second helpings.

She wasn't even sure what this movie was about, but every other film they'd been in involved some romance or other. It had never mattered to her before because she knew she would never be cast in an important role.

But this was different. Eric Goldman had promised them—with Ava's persuading—that they would get secondary parts. Not leads, obviously, but something that might get enough attention for them to get bigger roles. A contract. That was all she wanted. Assurance that she would continue getting cast. And a paycheck would be nice, because ever since she offered Ma the pay from her last films, Ma had stopped pressuring her to work at the hotel laundry.

It was obvious that the movie was some sort of historical period piece from the way the actresses were dressed. They scanned the crew for Goldman, but there was no sight of his brown sweater-vest.

Thankfully, one of the producers seemed to be expecting them—a man in a white button-up shirt and black slacks, holding a clipboard.

"You the Nongs?" he asked.

"I'm Olivia Nong," Olivia said. "She's Issa Bui."

"Right, right." He glanced down at his clipboard. "We'll get you in dress and makeup and then shoot your first scene today."

They were so startled that neither moved. The man had already walked off, then stopped and glanced back at them with exasperation.

"Coming?" he asked.

"But we don't even know what parts we're playing," Issa said as she and Olivia caught up to him. "Don't we have to audition?" They walked through the dark soundstage, lit only by a lamp that shone the way to a walled-off, makeshift dressing area.

"We don't have time for all that. The script isn't finalized. The writers quit—don't worry, they're searching for replacements. So did the two actresses you're replacing. The movie was two meetings away from getting canceled, but apparently the studio received some funding for it, and the backers insisted on replacing the two roles you're up for. Goldman said you'd be perfect for the parts. Good thing the execs already liked your screen test."

"They did?" Olivia gushed.

"The director will tell you what's happening in the scene," the man continued, "and you'll do your best to come up with the lines."

"What?" Issa asked. "That's . . . that happens?" The idea set her stomach churning. How was she supposed to know what to say? She barely had the right words to offer strangers on a normal basis, and here she was expected to make up lines for someone else's story.

"It happens when the writers quit midproduction, yes," the man said. "The new ones will start next week, but meanwhile, we can't fall behind schedule if we've any hope of saving the picture. Elsa, these are the girls—get them ready, will you?"

A curly-haired woman wearing an apron with a million pockets, filled to the brim with hairbrushes and makeup tools, rushed over to them.

"All right, you," she said to Olivia, "costumes first. You"—she pulled Issa to her by the elbow—"makeup."

Olivia gave Issa an excited, raised-eyebrow expression before they were separated.

Elsa plunked Issa down on a chair that was too high for her, so she perched precariously on the edge of the seat. Her toes barely skimmed the floor. Elsa began wiping Issa's face with an unpleasantly wet cloth. Issa tried not to think about how many other faces it had touched before the woman applied a cold compress over her eyes.

"You're so puffy," Elsa muttered as she worked. "Lean back."

Issa frowned at the comment, but Elsa started tugging on her hair, roughly gathering it into a small bun at the nape of her neck.

"Keep your eyes closed, please," the woman said as she removed the cold compress. Then followed a series of things touching Issa's face—not all of them pleasant or bad, but all happening so fast that she couldn't quite keep up. Cream, then a brush, then some sort of powder, then more dusting, then a pen stabbing at her eyelids. Finally, Elsa revealed Issa's reflection in the vanity before her.

She looked transformed. She'd been made up before for other films, but never so extensively. She was a completely different person. Her eyes were defined, her cheekbones accentuated. The effect was only ruined by her flattened hair, which Elsa had plastered against her head.

It was clear why when she returned with a big blond wig, which she placed carefully over Issa's head.

"They'll have trouble working around this in costumes, but they'll have to make do," Elsa said, applying some sort of adhesive with a brush over Issa's hairline. "Try not to sweat too much, but if you do, come back here so I can fix it. Don't wait too long, or else it will fall off and ruin everything. Understand?"

"Yes. Thank you."

Elsa patted her on the shoulder. "To costumes with you. That way."

Issa's head felt heavy, and she was afraid to bend her neck too far in any direction in case the wig fell off. It was piled at least a foot high with twisted braids and flattering tendrils framing the sides of her face.

She passed someone in a long blue gown, almost not recognizing Olivia until they were right in front of each other.

"Oh my goodness, Issa?" Olivia said. "You look marvelous!"

"So do you!" Issa said.

"This is so exciting. I got a run-through of the storyline—"

"Chop-chop, ladies!" Elsa shouted from behind Issa.

"I'll tell you about it later," Olivia whispered. "It's a royal court drama, and it sounds absolutely addicting."

"Ahem!" Elsa's voice came again.

Issa grinned and hurried to another walled-off area, where a similar ball gown had been laid out for her, though this one was in a cream color with gold trimmings. After she changed into the slip provided, three assistants had to help her get into the gown, tightening the bodice strings so securely that she only had an inch of breathing room, her lungs constricting every time she took a breath.

"Hurry, they're about to start shooting," said a producer whose name she hadn't learned—they never introduced themselves, anyway, assuming she was another extra or one-shot wonder, probably. The man put his hand against the middle of her back and pushed her gently but urgently down the dark makeshift corridor.

A spotlight lit up the set, a velvet-covered room furnished with heavy furniture and jewel-tone cushions. Several girls dressed exactly like Issa and Olivia lounged around on the luxuriously decorated chairs, sipping tea and pretending to nibble on the prop cookies set up on the tea tray.

Eric Goldman sat in his director's chair next to the camera. Whether he recognized her or not, he gave no indication, instead snapping his fingers at her and pointing to a taped X on the floor.

"We've been waiting," he said.

Emmett Tratee stood close by with a clipboard. She was too focused on not tripping in her heavy, layered skirts to be bothered by everyone's stares. Girls shifted around her to make space, though not in an unfriendly manner, which was quite a change from what she was used to. It must have been the makeup.

Olivia stood on the other side of the room, sandwiched between two girls on the chaise. She met Issa's eyes with a conspiratorial wink.

Goldman surveyed the scene and smiled. She thought she heard a small sigh escape his lips, and then someone called, "Action."

Issa didn't have any lines in the first few scenes. She was merely a background character, along with the other girls, part of a court for the two leads.

They had only gotten through three short sequences in the story before Issa felt her wig start to melt and slip down her face. She wasn't the first girl this had happened to, and she followed the others down the corridor to Elsa for repairs.

When she got back to the set, the others stood to the side, watching the two main actors in the next scene. The characters were about to declare their undying love for one another, but their dialogue was stilted and stiff, and Goldman kept shouting at them to stop so he could give them notes.

Olivia leaned over her shoulder. "I think I have it. You and I are ladies-in-waiting to the princess." She gestured with her chin at the lead actress, dressed in the most puffed-up ball gown of them all, the skirt so wide that the actor could barely get close enough to kiss her. He had to wedge himself into a small opening in the hidden birdcage beneath, and the actress had to surreptitiously push away the layers of fabric right before he did so, though she was so adept at it that you could hardly tell unless you knew what to look out for.

"Are we going to have an actual speaking scene?" Issa asked, lowering her voice so the other actors wouldn't hear.

"Yes, soon. We're supposed to try to discourage the princess from the match and tell our own sob stories about why we hate love."

"That shouldn't be hard."

Olivia gave a soft laugh. "For you, maybe. I still believe in love. The kind that will earn me a million dollars."

"Well, that love, I do believe in."

A producer shot them a mean look, so they quieted down.

"Anyway," Olivia whispered once his focus returned to the filming. "We'll shoot that if we ever get around to it, and then they'll fill in the beginning scenes depending on how we do or what we say."

Issa nodded, filled with nervous excitement. Her mind whirred with what she could possibly say, whether she should give her authentic opinion or make up something more poetic. This might be the time she showed everyone what she could accomplish, a potentially life-changing moment, and she was determined to get it right.

Chapter Twenty-Two

They took a dinner break, though Goldman refused to dismiss them for the day. "We haven't finished the list," he snapped at anyone who asked.

At least the studio had more food delivered to the set. The costumes made it impossible to eat her fill, but Issa was starving so she grabbed a sandwich.

"Do you know what you're going to say?" Olivia asked her as they found a corner to themselves.

"About love? That's easy." Issa took a swallow of water. "I don't think it really lasts. Not romantic love anyway. It's short and fun, but then it's over and you move on. What else can you do if you don't? Because it will end. It always does, in my experience."

"In your experience?" Olivia asked playfully. "Have you fallen in love with someone and forgotten to tell me about it?"

"No, you know what I mean. Look at Bà Ngoại and Ong Ngoại. She hated my grandfather. She's always talking about how she burned his pictures so he wouldn't come visit her after he died."

"Hmm," Olivia said. "In his defense, your grandmother is quite an unconventional woman."

"Are you saying she was difficult to love?" Issa asked with a grin.

"Do you love her?"

Issa had to think about that. "I love her in the obligatory sense. Because she's my grandmother. But I barely knew her."

"But she loves you."

Issa breathed in deep. If Bà Ngoại loved her, it was in the same sense and for the same reason that Issa did—because she had to.

"See, family love—that means something," Issa said. "You have to love your family. You don't really have a choice, or else they come back to haunt you. Mine do anyway. But even Auntie Yen—she can do what she wants. Everyone listens to her. She can probably get whoever she wants as well, but she chooses not to, so what does that say?"

"That she's too busy to think about love right now?"

"Exactly. There's much too much to do. The last thing I need right now is a distraction. How would a man fit into our goals?"

Olivia smiled. "And what about your mom? She loved your dad very much. She gets that starry-eyed look whenever she talks about him."

That was true. Issa remembered her father as a scholarly sort of man, short and skinny with rectangular glasses, who had never been too busy to play with her or teach her some small lesson. Over time, her mental image of him faded and blurred, though his presence in her memory remained warm and happy.

"But he's dead," she pointed out.

Olivia nibbled daintily on her sandwich. "Men just don't have any luck in your clan, do they?"

After the break, Olivia called on Ava to join them, even though there wasn't much she could do to coach them.

"This is just how it is," Ava said when Issa complained about standing around waiting. "Sometimes you get all dolled up for nothing."

"I wouldn't want to be anywhere else," Olivia said, twirling in her dress.

Issa supposed she had a point, but it was still aggravating. She was antsy and itchy for actual work, a chance to feel useful. The sun had set, and she caught several of the cast members fighting back yawns.

She was heading to the refreshments for more water when a producer snapped his fingers in her direction.

"You're up next," he said. "Go back to Elsa and get touched up."

"Oh," Issa said, so surprised that she looked around to make sure he was talking to her and not another actor.

"Hurry," he said, slapping his clipboard and rushing off.

Issa did as she was told, wondering where Olivia and Ava had disappeared to as Elsa applied a fresh pat of powder on her nose and made sure her hairline was up to par.

When she got back to the set, Olivia still wasn't there. Several producers gestured for Issa to stand on her blocking while others prepared the princess character.

"Wait, there's supposed to be another of us here," she said.

Goldman waved at her. "We'll add her in later."

Issa knew not to argue, but her heart clenched with worry over where Olivia could be, and what it would mean if Issa did the scene without her. She tried to convince herself it would be fine; they had acted in different scenes in the other two movies. But this felt different because it was a bigger, more important role than what they'd had before, and it could launch them into even bigger roles. She couldn't charge forward without Olivia. She wouldn't be here without her. And yet, there was nothing she could do about it as someone shouted, "Action!"

The princess character turned on the waterworks. Issa went over to her, gently taking her arms.

"What's the matter, Your Majesty?" she asked.

"Cut!" Goldman shouted. "'Your Majesty' is something you call the king and queen. Call her *Your Highness* or *Your Grace*."

"Oh, sorry."

"From the top," Goldman said.

"What's the matter, Your Highness?" Issa asked this time.

"The duke has just asked for my hand in marriage," the princess sobbed.

"But . . . then why are you crying?" Issa manipulated her face into an expression of clear confusion.

"Because I'm not sure that I love him . . . oh, but I do. But is that enough?"

Issa turned her face toward the camera, affecting an expression of dismayed longing. For a second, she couldn't speak. She was aware of the seconds ticking by, of the camera lens watching like a giant black eyeball. Finally, the words poured out: "I thought it was enough once. But I've learned that it can't be. It doesn't last. Life is too hard, and love isn't strong—"

"I'm here!" Olivia called out, running onto the scene as fast as her dress would allow her. She panted as she waved at the camera. "Sorry, I was—"

"Cut, cut!" Goldman heaved an exhale and pinched the bridge of his nose. "It would have been perfect," he muttered. Or at least, that was what Issa thought he said. A small fire churned inside her as she glared at Olivia. She'd been doing well, she knew she had—everyone was enraptured, and she actually *felt* what her character must have felt.

But when Olivia turned and smiled at her, both apologetic and cheerful, Issa's anger melted, and she smiled back in reassurance.

"All right, then," Goldman said. "From the top."

Though there was no script, Issa and Olivia's characters were supposed to do the scene together, each of them giving their own spiel on love. Now when the princess repeated her line, Olivia and Issa both moved forward to comfort her.

"Cut!" the director shouted at them. "Only one of you—both overwhelms the character."

"And you're blocking my face," the princess actress said. "You're supposed to stand there." She pointed at practically invisible marks on the floor.

Issa glanced at Olivia. So far, she was the one who had bigger roles, but Issa had gotten a taste of what it was like to be in the scene on her own and wanted it to remain that way. But she couldn't say so. It wasn't up to her, and it would be a great betrayal.

"You can go first," Olivia whispered at her as they reset their blocking.

Issa immediately felt guilty. Olivia had always looked out for her, always fought for both of them to become stars. And here all Issa felt was resentment without any evidence that Olivia was attempting to steal the limelight. Perhaps Issa only thought Olivia did so because she herself was subconsciously doing so.

"No, that's all right," Issa said. "You go."

She watched as Olivia went first to comfort the princess, remaining in the background while also showing her face to the camera. Part of her hoped Goldman would cut the scene and direct her to move forward, but he didn't, observing the current take with an unreadable expression.

Olivia stepped toward the camera as she prepared to make her speech. "I used to believe in love," she said, her voice sad. "But now I've learned that it's not enough. Love always fades. It always ends, and all you can do is move on." She grabbed the princess's hands, turning her so that Olivia's face was in the camera's frame. "You must follow your heart, but make sure that it's strong enough to withstand whatever love throws at you. Make sure that it will heal from the break."

There was a moment of silence. No one called "Cut," but it was the end of the scene, as far as Issa could tell. And she hadn't said a word.

Eventually, Goldman stirred. He motioned for the camera to stop. Next to him, Emmett Tratee scribbled notes furiously on his clipboard. Olivia and Issa both waited with bated breath for feedback, but Goldman just got up from his chair and stretched his back with a few pops.

"That's it for the day, folks," he said.

The crew let out collective sighs and disassembled. Issa stood on the set for a second, knowing her face would sweat her makeup off if she stood under the spotlight for too long, but not caring. Olivia didn't notice, joining a crowd of girls dressed in similar ball gowns and wigs as they congratulated her on the scene.

With a loud thunk, the spotlight above her turned off, and Issa's vision went completely black. She was grateful that no one could see her, because no matter how much she tried to control her face, after all that practice in front of the mirror, she couldn't stop her lower lip from quivering.

Chapter Twenty-Three

They did the take a few more times that week, and thankfully Goldman did ask Issa to step forward more in the scene. She tried her best, but her heart wasn't in it; she constantly replayed the first take in her mind and felt quite confused about why she was so upset about it. It wasn't as if Olivia had stolen anything from her. She had told her to move into the scene first . . . And the words . . . Issa couldn't quite remember how she'd phrased it when they talked about it, but Olivia couldn't have repeated them verbatim.

And if she had . . . surely Olivia didn't do it on purpose. Perhaps she'd liked what Issa said and subconsciously applied it to her own dialogue. Olivia would never steal anything deliberately from Issa. They were just so close, knew each other better than anyone else, so of course it was reasonable if she felt the same way about love as Issa, expressed it in similar lines.

On Thursday, the new writers showed up on set, to the relief of all the cast, who no longer had to improvise their lines. Issa returned from having her makeup done to find two familiar men at the tables by the vanities. One glanced up, did a double take, and smiled at her.

"Well, what do you know," Jem Meier said. His friend Peter whatever-his-name-was nodded at her, but kept reading his script.

"You're going to be working on this film?" She felt ridiculous for asking when the answer was obvious, but Jem smiled as if it was the best news.

"It appears so," he said. "You look different."

Issa touched the lustrous wig piled atop her head. "I needed a change."

He grinned and leaned back in his seat, loose pages in one hand and a fountain pen in the other. "I've just reviewed the scenes you've written on your own."

"Written? Oh, when we had to make up our own lines."

"They're quite impressive."

Issa's face grew warm. "Oh, it was nothing, really."

"Don't sell yourself short," he said. "They've asked me to rewrite some things, but I think your lines were perfect."

Issa opened and closed her mouth, saved from coming up with a clever response when Olivia approached. She nodded at Jem in surprise but didn't have much to say to him.

"They're ready for us," she told Issa.

Issa gave Jem yet another apologetic smile as she followed the other cast members to the cameras.

As the production went on, she didn't know what she found more distracting—her insecurity over her performance compared to Olivia's or her awareness of Jem on the set. Not that he ever did anything to fluster her, but her skin always prickled when he was nearby, and she found herself searching for him in the crowd, or disappointed if he didn't show up that day. Sometimes, the writers were called to different films to address an emergency edit, and Jem told her that he was on loan from Paramount, which meant he went wherever the studio needed him.

"You still owe me dinner," he reminded her one day as they both grabbed a snack from the refreshments table.

"Oh," she said with a thrill. "I thought you'd forgotten."

"Very funny," he said. "I know you're busy now, but perhaps after this film wraps?"

She was so nervous, she could barely answer, only nodding while Peter called Jem back to work. The rest of the day became a happy, blissful blur.

By the end of the following week, she was confident that she and Olivia had an equal number of lines in the film, and there were still the subsequent scenes to finish. There would be opportunities for both of them to succeed. And what did it matter in the end, so long as they both got contracts?

"Some of the girls invited us out for drinks after we're done for the day," Olivia said as they headed toward the dressing rooms to have their costumes and makeup removed.

"Do we have to?" Issa asked. "I'm feeling quite . . . pooped."

"Oh, come along, they've never invited us before. It'll be a chance to vent and make more connections."

Issa considered turning down the invitation, but she imagined how she'd feel when Olivia came home, happy from her outing and with plenty of new friends. Probably miserable and left out and ten times worse than she did now.

"All right, then."

"We can splurge on a taxi for the way home," Olivia said.

"Heavens, that seems premature. We haven't got contracts yet."

Olivia took her hand and shook it with enthusiasm. "Oh, but we were so good, Issa. This is the beginning of something. I just know it."

They followed the group of about ten girls to a local bar, the dimly lit golden wall sconces, tufted leather seats, and deep-brown walls making

Issa feel like she was in some sort of high-end speakeasy. Olivia kept looking at Issa to make sure she was okay, and tired of reassuring her friend that she felt completely fine, that of course she was up for coming along, Issa ordered one drink after another, which did well to quiet her obsessive thoughts.

She normally didn't drink that much, but the other girls seemed to, and soon they were all laughing, recounting the events of the day, congratulating Olivia and Issa on a successful scene, and attracting so much attention that men kept buying them rounds.

"Get used to it," Maggie Laken said. She was a boisterous brunette with a voice and laugh that carried. "There are perks to being an actress, even if we never become stars."

"Isn't that the point, though?" Issa asked. They were sitting in a corner booth, a jazz song flitting over from the jukebox. "To be so famous that everyone knows who you are and treats you like royalty?"

"As long as I get steady work and get to be in movies, I don't have to be super famous. It's just fun to be part of something, don't you think?" Maggie said.

"Oh, we're aiming for the high beam," Olivia said, throwing an arm around Issa's shoulder. In Issa's state of resentment, she couldn't help feeling like Olivia was being overly possessive of her, as if she didn't want Issa making any other friends. "We're going to be so famous that they'll be using our names to draw people to box offices."

"I want to be so famous, I never have to buy my own meal again," another girl said.

"I want to be so famous that I never have to wait in line for anything," another said.

"Or have to worry about where to live."

"I'd own five different houses—all mansions—and never clean a single toilet."

"I want all the magazines to fight over interviewing me."

"Or have me wear their clothes."

"And the free jewelry!"

"Fur coats!"

Issa took a long pull of her drink, no longer grimacing at the cloying taste. "I suppose it would be nice to be as content as you are," she told Maggie, who had fallen wistfully quiet as she listened to the other girls' far-fetched dreams.

"That's the trick," Maggie said. "To stop wanting so much, and then you'll always be happy."

"That's really deep," Olivia said, her voice slurred as she laughed in Issa's ear.

Issa fought the urge to shrug off Olivia's arm, bearing it until Olivia thankfully moved away to joke with another girl.

To Issa's disappointment, the writers finished their script treatment and were no longer required on set, so she had no reason or way to get in touch with Jem. It happened so abruptly, she was surprised and dismayed that Jem hadn't bothered to explain it himself.

The next week, the cast shot a few more scenes to establish their characters as the ladies-in-waiting to the princess so that their big scene would make more sense. A few more days of filming followed, but these were easy in comparison to the grueling first days, and Issa found her good mood again. It was difficult to stay mad at Olivia when they saw each other almost every moment of every day, and Olivia was constantly doing little things for her—saving her a cookie from the refreshments table, covering her streetcar fare even when it was Issa's turn to pay, and being so kind and generous and supportive and selfless and cheerful, Issa felt like a grump in comparison. Olivia's buoyant mood grew each day that she did well on set, and Issa tried to focus on her own accomplishments as well, basking in the attention that the crew gave her. Even Goldman, not known for his praise, told them both how much they'd improved.

By the time the film wrapped, Issa no longer cared about that big dialogue scene, and all was well between them.

They conjured Ava most nights when they got home, giving her a recap on how the day went. Olivia sometimes stayed up into the small hours of the night as they went over the director's notes and Ava's advice.

"Oh, this is wonderful news," Ava said when Issa told her about nearly finishing the filming. "When your movie releases, and you become instant stars, the directors will all clamor to get ahold of you. Try your best to ask to work for Weston Redrick, and then you'll have ample opportunities to get into his office to get my trophy back."

"What do you mean, 'ample opportunities'?" Issa asked. "Does he invite a lot of actresses into his office?"

"If they're interested in being contract players, yes."

Issa glanced at Olivia, who was filing her nails as she sat on the bed. Today Ava wore a traditional cheongsam, buttoned high on her neck, her hair loose around her shoulders, giving her a wholesome, naive look at odds with the mischievous gleam in her eyes.

"We'll get your trophy as soon as we can, Ava," Olivia said. "We're working on it. But who knows when the movie will release—they say it could take months. We might not see it until next year."

Ava scrunched her nose in annoyance, but she immediately smoothed out her features, as if even in death, she was wary of developing wrinkles. "Well. It's not as if I'm going anywhere."

Chapter Twenty-Four

As requested, Issa summoned Bà Ngoại every few weeks to give her a summary of their progress. During each visit, Bà Ngoại would imply that Issa was running out of time since, despite how much they'd achieved, they were nowhere close to her definition of "stars."

"The year's not even halfway over," Issa said when Bà Ngoại demanded to know when she would visit Auntie Yen to learn more about the family trade.

"Fine," Bà Ngoại huffed. "But the ghost keeps bragging about how much time she gets to spend on set with you."

If Issa didn't know better, she might have thought her grandmother's lower lip jutting out resembled a pout. She smiled, letting a bit of teasing show in her expression. "Do you want to be there too?"

"Ha!" The effect of her sarcastic laugh was ruined as Bà Ngoại doubled over with coughs. "You think I don't have better things to do?"

Issa waited for her to pull herself together. "I want to learn more from you, too, Bà Ngoại. This shaman thing is quite the bee's knees, isn't it? I never realized it before."

"It's about time!" Bà Ngoại said.

When the movie wrapped, Issa needed a distraction from wondering if she'd ever have that dinner with Jem Meier. She couldn't very well wait around for him to show up, but she had no way of contacting him either.

Instead, she busied herself learning everything that she had missed out on after Ma took her from the clan. Olivia sometimes joined her and Bà Ngoại, taking as many notes as possible, but Bà Ngoại was an eccentric instructor. She often showed up without warning, setting the girls into a whirlwind of panic to light incense before her image disappeared—it was always more difficult to conjure her back if they didn't act quickly enough, as if appearing unsummoned cost more energy than she cared to admit. Her lessons had no structure, her knowledge dished out at her whim. Sometimes her visits consisted of lengthy lectures on the history of spirits, segueing into meandering tangents on all the people she once knew, interspersed with the occasional compelling tidbit that was often more horrifying than helpful.

"People come to shamans because we can speak to other realms," Bà Ngoại said during a rare afternoon when Issa was alone in her bedroom. Olivia had to run some errand that she'd acted deliberately vague about, so Issa hadn't pushed. "They always assume that the only realm we can enter is that of the dead."

"Are there other realms, then?" Issa asked. She attempted to take notes, but there was always a risk that Bà would lose interest in the topic as soon as Issa put pen to paper.

"Of course, girl. Our realities are not finite or singular."

"Are you saying we can commune with other . . . dimensions?"

Bà smiled secretively. "Only if you concentrate."

"How?" Issa leaned closer to the mirror.

"By listening, very carefully," Bà said, "to your elders."

Issa let out an exasperated breath.

"And obeying everything we tell you," Bà added with a cackle.

"Bà," Issa said, setting down her pen.

"All right, all right. There's something you can practice, even in your sleep. Deep breaths and transcendence, so that you can be awake when you dream."

"That sounds like a contradiction."

"Don't talk back to me, girl, and listen. If you can master your dreams, then you can master your mind and spirit, and travel into the dreams of others."

"Isn't that a terrible invasion of privacy?"

"Yes, but think of all the secrets you'll learn. The truths you'll uncover. But it must be done with caution, because in order to enter the minds of others, you must abandon your corporeal body, and temporarily leave it vulnerable to attack or possession."

"I . . . don't . . . know about that," Issa said, trying not to sound too terrified. In her experience, Bà Ngoại did not respond positively to fear. She was like a predator, able to sense it even from the Other Side.

"Ayah, how am I supposed to teach someone so thickheaded?" Bà Ngoại exclaimed. After that she didn't talk to Issa for a full week, even when Issa tried to summon her.

Unfortunately, this was often how their lessons would end. At first, Issa had been excited to learn about her powers, even practicing the deep breath exercises that Bà Ngoại taught her to get into a trance state, as terrified as the idea made her. She was no good at it, though, her thoughts interrupted by lines she'd memorized or what she needed to do the next day, and Bà Ngoại could somehow always tell.

"You're not focusing hard enough!" she would shriek, and no matter how hard Issa tried after that, it was impossible to quiet her mind.

Over time, the novelty of learning this nebulous new skill wore off, and with Bà Ngoại frequently getting angry at her for not catching on quickly, she found it more and more difficult to care.

For lack of anything better to do, one day Issa and Olivia decided to visit the studio to find out any news about their success in the film, even though it was probably too early to tell.

"We should get a telephone," Olivia said as they grabbed their purses on their way out. "It would be much easier for people to reach us, and we wouldn't have to worry that we're missing out on anything important if we can't make it into the studio."

"We don't have enough money for that," Issa responded more out of habit than reason.

"What are you talking about? We made more money than we ever had in the last film."

"Ma would say that it's an expense we don't need."

"But we do need it. And you can tell her that it's my phone. I'll cover the cost."

"That's too much."

"Let me," Olivia said with a pout. They walked to their streetcar stop. "I want one, and I don't have enough money to move out yet."

"You're thinking of moving out?" The idea horrified Issa so much that she reached for Olivia's hand. "I didn't know you were thinking about it."

"No, of course not." Olivia smiled and rubbed Issa's shoulder. "I wouldn't do that—I love living with you both. I'm just saying . . . it would be nice to have a phone."

"All right, then, we'll get one," Issa said. But she felt an unbearable tension between them, and when they finally got to their stop, she couldn't keep it in any longer. "But you are thinking about it, aren't you?" Olivia wouldn't have brought it up if it wasn't on her mind.

Olivia looked down the tracks to see if the Red Car was on its way, but there was no telltale rattle. "I mean, when we get contracts, we might have to move into those dressing rooms we saw on the studio tour," she said distractedly.

Issa saw it for the diversion that it was. Olivia was trying to let Issa down easy.

"That's optional though," she said.

"Oh, but who would turn one of those dressing rooms down?" Olivia laughed, lightening the mood. "They're fully outfitted—probably bigger than your ma's place. Did you know Marion Davies had an entire bungalow as her dressing room? Doesn't it sound lovely?"

They'd always talked about those rooms like some distant, unrealistic dream. Small little apartments they'd have all to themselves. So much space after living in the cramped room they shared. But this was the first time Issa seriously considered the possibility.

"We could probably share one to start," Olivia said. "I'm sure they'll let us." She smiled so warmly that the tension eased from Issa's shoulders.

"That does sound lovely. Oh, but Ma will be so lonely."

"As if you wouldn't visit her every weekend. Besides, that apartment is too small for all three of us. Our stuff is piling up. Maybe when we were little girls, it was fine, but your ma probably wants her own space as well. We're not young anymore."

Issa smiled wistfully. "I suppose you're right."

They went to Goldman's office when they got to the lot, not expecting to find him. When the secretary saw them poking their heads through the doorway, she got up so fast that she almost fell over.

"Oh, it's you two," she said. "He'll want to talk to you." She held her arms out as if to hug them, thought better of it, dug through her piles of paper, and found a manila folder. "Come along, come along. He said to interrupt him as soon as you arrived. Almost threw a conniption when he realized he couldn't reach you—no phone number, no address."

Olivia gave Issa a look as if to say, *I told you so*, and Issa gave an expression back conceding that she was right.

They followed the secretary to the front of the building to a small truck used for transporting set pieces. When they arrived at the soundstage where Goldman was directing, the doors were closed, the red light above them turned on, so they had to loiter outside.

"I thought you said he wanted to be interrupted as soon as we arrived," Olivia said.

"Well, not in the middle of *filming*," the secretary retorted.

"Can you tell us why he wants to see us so much?" Issa asked, hopeful for good news but not wanting to let herself wish for too much.

The secretary shook her finger, but she was smiling. "Of course I can't. How should I know what's on his mind?"

With that she got back in the truck and drove slowly away.

As soon as the secretary left, the doors burst open and several staff rushed out, heading in the direction of the commissary.

"Thank God," Olivia said, slipping through the door.

Spotting Goldman climbing down from his director's chair by the camera, they hurried over.

"Eric—" Olivia said breathlessly. "I mean, Mr. Goldman. Your secretary said—"

"Yes, yes, there you are," he said, waving off the rest of her words. "The execs saw the shots we took. They loved you. They want to meet you."

"Oh my goodness." Olivia touched her chest and closed her eyes, her lips quivering into a half smile. "Oh my goodness."

"But what does that mean?" Issa asked. "Do they want to sign us to the studio?"

"I don't know," Goldman said. "I don't make the decisions. Come along, I'll take you to the office." He went through the back exit of the soundstage, mumbling as he went. "Tried to call you, but don't have your number and couldn't find any way to get ahold of you. Once these men make up their minds, suddenly it's the end of the world and my fault for it. Get in, get in. I only gave everyone fifteen." He ushered them into his sedan.

"We're going to get a phone," Olivia said. "We should be able to afford it now."

"Don't worry about it," Goldman said. "The studio should provide you with one."

"Oh, wow." Olivia clapped her hands.

"Don't get too excited. They'll call you at all hours of the night." Goldman sped through the streets behind the buildings and slammed on his horn at a bicyclist towing a cart, cursing at the boy as he passed.

Inside the Lion Building, they followed Goldman into the elevator. When the doors opened, Issa knew they were headed somewhere important. The carpet was clean and plush, muffling the sounds of their heels. The walls were wallpapered in green floral prints, accented here and there by black-and-white pictures of men such as Irving Thalberg and Louis B. Mayer, a cast holding up trophies, famous actresses she recognized from her favorite movies. It was nothing like Goldman's office, or any of the other buildings they'd seen on the lot.

"This way," he said, leading them down a hall to a lobby area where a young woman sat outside an office door at a mahogany desk facing them, as if barricading a fortress wall.

She greeted Goldman with a measured look. "Are you here to see Mr. Grenier?" she asked.

"Unless he's switched offices lately," Goldman grumbled back in annoyance. "Tell him I've got the Nong girls."

"One Nong girl," Olivia corrected him. "And a Bui."

Goldman waved at her dismissively while the secretary spoke into the phone.

"Eric Goldman here to see you with two actresses," she said. Despite her frosty demeanor, Issa was grateful that she didn't feel the need to label them, at least not yet. "He'll see you."

Goldman went to the double doors and pushed his way through.

Issa had expected a nice office, but she was surprised by how extravagant it really was: more like a suite, with a conference table and seating area at one end and a shiny brown desk at the other. Behind it sat a broad man in a suit, talking on the phone and completely oblivious to their presence.

Goldman gestured to the couch and some love seats with side tables in each corner. Issa and Olivia sat down while Goldman paced back and forth, eager to get back to his film.

Mr. Grenier kept them waiting. He eyed them a few times, so he obviously knew they were there, but he chuckled into the phone and continued his conversation without any rush. Olivia looked at the rolling cart crowded with glass bottles full of amber liquid and sparkly tumblers, but Goldman didn't make a move for the drinks, and Issa would never have dared.

Finally, Mr. Grenier hung up and wrote something down in his padfolio before he walked over to the bar.

"Anyone care for a drink?" he asked, holding up a decanter.

"Yes, please," Olivia said.

He poured four glasses even though no one else answered him and handed them out one by one. Finally he sat down in the love seat next to the couch, leaning back to stare at them through half-closed eyes. Issa thought perhaps he had simply fallen asleep like that.

"Mr. Gre—" Olivia started, but he held up a hand, and she closed her mouth, hands in her lap.

After several seconds, he sucked in a deep breath as if just waking from an accidental nap. "I can see it," he said.

Neither Olivia nor Issa knew what to make of this, but apparently Goldman did.

"I knew it," he said, standing behind Issa. "I just knew it. Didn't I tell you?"

"Didn't believe you. Had to see the scenes." Grenier reached into his pocket and pulled out a cigarette. He didn't offer any to them, thankfully. "All right. You two look good on camera. You win."

"We win?" Olivia asked.

"What do we win?"

Grenier lit his cigarette, inhaled, and let out a puff of smoke. "What every actor and actress would die for. Contracts."

Grenier offered a salary of $200 a week each, which was more than what they'd earned for all of their pictures combined.

As soon as Issa and Olivia walked out the door, they locked arms and smiled, managing to contain themselves when they realized Grenier's secretary was watching them with unadulterated judgment.

Once they were in the elevator and the doors closed, they screamed with excitement, not caring if anyone heard.

Chapter Twenty-Five

They discussed it all weekend and decided to tell Ma about moving onto the MGM studio lot, though Issa still wasn't sure about it. Every time she decided she did indeed want to move into one of the rooms—according to their contract, MGM would provide Issa and Olivia a shared unit—she thought of how strange it would be not to see her mother every day. The truth was, however, that she sometimes didn't see Ma for days at a time.

"It won't be much different," Olivia said. She wanted to move as soon as possible. "In fact, you might see her more often than you see her now, since you'll make time to visit her."

"Let's see what she says," Issa said, unable to think about it anymore. She had changed her mind so often she was becoming sick of herself.

They made a point to get home early enough to see Ma before she left. She was cooking in the kitchen.

"Hi there," Issa said, spontaneously giving her mom a peck on the cheek.

Ma stiffened slightly, side-eyeing Issa with lowered lashes. "What was that for?"

Issa didn't blame her. It was rare for anyone in their family to show that they cared for each other, but . . . what if Ma was so angry after this that she never wanted to see Issa again? Things were changing—she and

Olivia were finally ready to start their lives. Their *destiny*. And while she was eager for it all, part of her clung to a semblance of the past, longed for some sign that her mother would still love her, even while she pulled away and went against her wishes.

"I just wanted to remind you that I love you." Issa wrapped her arms around her mom's shoulders. "Can't I do that once in a while?"

"I know you want something." Ma wiggled a bit so Issa loosened her grip, but she still hung on even as her mother pulled out a drawer to grab a spatula. "Spit it out, don't make me beg for it."

Issa hugged her mom tighter. "I don't want anything but your love."

Ma snorted but stayed still and leaned back. She took in a deep breath, almost like she was relishing the comfort of their hug, and warmth spread through Issa, followed by a slight swelling in her chest as if her heart were expanding.

Then Ma patted her arm. "All right, all right, enough. I want to finish cooking this so I can take it to the church."

Issa released her, feeling like a popped balloon. Olivia pursed her lips and pointed her chin back at Ma when Issa tried to walk away. They had to do this.

"Great news, Ma," she started. Olivia nodded for her to keep going. "We got contracts!"

"Contracts? What contracts?" Ma pulled a pan from a bottom cabinet and placed it on the stove, lighting the burner with a match.

"For acting," Olivia explained. "It's a really big deal. Not everyone gets one, but the studio wants to hire us for eight movies."

Ma didn't say anything as she spread oil on the pan. Her face remained unreadable in its usual tense frown.

"We'll each earn two hundred dollars a week," Issa added.

"That's good," Ma said. "What's the bad news?"

"Who said there'd be bad news?"

"You said 'great news' first, which is always followed by something bad. What is it? You need a down payment first? They need you to pay them for lessons or what?"

"We will be taking lessons, but we don't need to pay them," Issa said. The next words clogged in her throat. "But we're going to move."

"Move? Dance classes?"

Issa didn't know if Ma was joking or being deliberately obtuse, but then she remembered that her mother had no sense of humor, had been born without the ability to understand laughter.

"They have dressing rooms at the studio," Olivia explained when Issa couldn't manage the words. "They're practically apartments. Actors and writers and staff live there when they're on production, so they can cut the costs of traveling and save time. And we'll be easier for the directors to reach since we don't have a telephone here."

"We could get a telephone," Ma said.

Issa's heart melted. She had begged Ma for a telephone once when they were teenagers, but Ma had been adamant about it costing too much. This was the only sign her mother would give that she didn't want them to move out, Issa knew, because her mother's dignity would never allow her to beg.

"It's too expensive," Issa said.

"You make more money now," Ma said. She placed a slab of chicken on the pan and it sizzled, the aroma making Issa's stomach growl. "I have enough for rent, for several months at least. Now we can get a telephone, you won't have to worry so much."

"The rooms are paid for by the studio," Olivia went on, pretending not to hear her. "We'll be so busy filming that we'll be getting home too late anyway." More sizzling as Ma added vegetables to the pan, not saying a word in response. "It'll be safer for us. We won't need to take the streetcars or taxis to get home every day."

"And we'll visit," Issa said. "Every weekend."

Ma stirred the food. Steam created a slight sheen on her face, and she wiped at it with her sleeve. "All right. I don't want you on the streetcars in the dark. It will be safer this way."

Issa was so relieved, she wanted to jump up and hug Ma again, but her mother's shoulders were stiff, her back straight. She had given her consent, but she wasn't happy about it, and she still hadn't looked at Issa once.

"I'll still help with the rent," Issa said. "But you'll have so much more space. You could do something different with our room. Change it into a library."

"What do I need with that?" Ma snapped. "I'm happy how I am. I don't need anything different."

Olivia shook her head slightly, discouraging Issa from engaging in another argument.

"I'm just saying"—Issa couldn't help herself—"that you can do anything you want with the extra room."

Ma finally met Issa's gaze. Her eyes were slightly red, though from the flames as she cooked or from something else, Issa tried not to think about it. Her expression was sad, and she didn't say anything else. But she didn't need to. Issa knew the words without having to hear them. All Ma had ever wanted was her little family unit, all together.

Issa went back to her room with Olivia to pack, feeling equal amounts guilt, relief, and excitement. Ma always said that she was happy with her life as a laundress, but Issa had never believed that to be true. Her mother never seemed happy. Her smiles were hard to come by, laced with fear and anxiety. Neither had Ma ever allowed Issa to be content with her own existence, always pressuring Issa to work harder, study more, to become better, though better in only the ways that Ma deemed fit.

Issa *would* become better, she knew she would, but in her own way, which didn't mean that she was abandoning Ma. This wasn't a complete goodbye or an ending. Just a different path that she knew, or at least hoped, would still lead her home.

Chapter Twenty-Six

"We're here!" Olivia shouted as they burst open the door to their new home—Dressing Room B22, a lucky number, Issa decided. An auspicious omen. They'd learned that most actresses were assigned smaller rooms and had to share the communal bathroom in the dorm-like building next door, but since they were willing to share, they had a suite to themselves.

They stopped just inside the door, observing the space with trepidation and a sense of something Issa had trouble defining. Elation and freedom mixed with fear and anxiety.

The accommodations seemed enormous compared to what they were used to. The living room was equipped with a long couch and two armchairs facing a glass cabinet. Amber bottles, glass tumblers, and decanters filled the shelves, a bottle of wine cooling in the metal ice bucket with a note propped up next to it proclaiming, *Welcome!*

"Goodness," Olivia said. "How sweet." She picked up the card to read the inside. "'Ms. Nong and Ms. Bui—you're part of the family now.'"

"Where would you like this?" asked the page who had helped them cart their things through the studio lot. He held up the two heavy bags of their clothes.

"Oh, we need to decide on rooms," Olivia said.

"Just put it on the floor," Issa said. "We can unpack them later."

"It's no trouble, miss," he said with a smile.

"Oh, all right, then."

Olivia and Issa went to each of the rooms, but they were practically identical with queen-size beds. As they passed from one bedroom to the next, they peeked inside the bathroom at the claw-foot bathtub and double sinks. Issa felt almost like royalty, unsure what to do with this sort of luxury after a lifetime of sharing a smaller space.

"Can I have the one with the window facing the street?" Olivia asked. "I want to watch the little people as they walk by. If you don't mind the other one."

Issa pulled back the drapes in the second bedroom. It had a view of the small grassy walkway between the other buildings. "Are you sure? This one is much nicer."

"I like the street view. Imagine the uproar I'll cause when I change with the windows open."

"Olivia," Issa said with a laugh as the page placed the bags in their rooms. He went back to his truck to bring in the rest of their things.

"We're actresses now, we're expected to be scandalous," Olivia said. "It's in our contract."

"No, it's not."

"It's what they don't say that's important. Although that clause about how we're not supposed to gain more than ten pounds is a bit ridiculous."

"That's easy, we never have enough to eat to gain that much."

"We'll have to be careful now, though. We'll have more money."

Issa squealed. "Two hundred dollars a week!"

Olivia grinned. "A fortune!"

The page brought in their other bags, then hovered by the door. Issa didn't understand why until Olivia bounded over to her purse, pulled out a five-dollar bill, and handed it to him.

"Thanks for the help," she said.

He grinned, tipped his hat, and practically skipped out the door.

"Olivia," Issa admonished, starting to feel like she'd replaced Ma. "That was way too extravagant. He probably earns that much in a week."

"Exactly," Olivia said. "Poor thing needs a raise."

They opened the bottle of wine and conjured Ava as soon as they could to show off their new space, but the dead star didn't seem impressed.

"I don't know why you're so excited about this dollhouse," she said. "It's so tiny."

"It's a suite," Olivia said. "The other actresses just get a single room and have to share the bathroom. At least we have a kitchen and everything here."

"You should have negotiated for a real apartment or a house." It was clear Ava was in a terrible mood. She didn't twirl and admire her own reflection, and the lines around her mouth were deeply set, as if she was fighting back a sneer.

"Everything all right, Ava?" Issa asked.

She pouted. "I'm fine, thank you."

"We're not big enough to make demands yet," Olivia said. "Be happy for us. We have rooms to ourselves! And we don't have to walk up millions of stairs every night."

"Those stairs kept you trim," Ava said with her hands on her hips. There were mirrors everywhere, which made sense considering that the rooms were for actors and actresses. Ava flitted from one reflection to the other, gazing at herself as if inspecting her aging signs. She looked as flawless as usual, her color muted in her ghostly way. "Trust me, once your movie comes out and you start earning a fortune for the studio, you can ask for a mansion. Something with a pool. And start asking for endorsements now. Free clothes and jewelry that you can help 'promote.'"

"We have to go to a party later," Olivia said. "What should we wear?"

"Obviously something expensive," Ava said. "Establish your dominance now before anyone gets any stupid ideas."

"What sort of ideas?" Issa asked.

"Other actors will see you as a threat," Ava said. "Young and beautiful and exotic? You'll be like fresh meat in a lake of sharks."

"Sharks don't go to lakes," Issa pointed out.

"Oh, you know what I mean," Ava snapped. "That's beside the point. Now, this party of yours—will Weston be there?"

"We don't know," Olivia said.

"What's taking you so long to find him? I've done everything for you—I got you into the party in Catalina, I gave you notes on your acting, I told you who to talk to, I convinced Goldman to cast you, and what have you done for me in return?"

Issa and Olivia both sat up straighter, alarmed at her flare of temper. Neither of them had ever seen Ava like this. She was usually so sweet and kind.

"Ava, we're doing the best we can," Issa said.

"It's not good enough!" Ava took a deep breath. "You haven't been thinking about me at all, while all I've done is help you get everything you wanted. Acting contracts, this suite, more films, more money! What's in it for me? The one thing I asked you to do—the one thing—"

"All right, all right." Olivia held up her hands to stop Ava's voice from getting any shriller. "We'll ask around for Weston Redrick tonight."

Ava's chest heaved up and down, her nostrils flaring. "You promise?" she asked, thankfully in a calmer voice.

"Of course. We'll do our best."

"Good." Ava lifted her chin, shaking her head slightly to get her hair out of her face. "I expect good news tomorrow."

Olivia and Issa both nodded, speechless. Issa's heart pounded, though she tried telling herself that Ava meant no harm. Yet her behavior had come out of nowhere and with an intensity Issa hadn't expected. She reminded Issa of a boiling pot of soup, simmering one moment only to overfill with scum the next.

With a plume of smoke, Ava disappeared. A smell lingered, like incense, but with a rancid aftertaste. Issa sniffed, but Olivia didn't seem to notice it.

"She's right, we haven't done anything for her at all," Olivia said. She looked more sad than scared.

"She didn't have to yell like that, though," Issa said.

Olivia sighed. "She deserves to be angry. I would be, if the roles were reversed. We need to try harder for her sake." She finished her wine and got up. "Let's go pick out what to wear."

The party was held in a famous actor's home, but he was surrounded by so many people that they couldn't thank him for his hospitality. And they didn't know him very well, so Issa would have felt like an overzealous fan pushing through the crowd, just to say a polite thank-you.

They asked around for Weston Redrick, but most people were too drunk or merry to answer, or they didn't know who that was, or they hadn't seen him.

"Maybe Goldman knows," Issa said. "Let's ask him instead."

"Goldman is probably sick of doing favors for us," Olivia said.

They'd chosen sheath dresses that hugged their curves and flared at the knees in playful fringes, catching the eyes of those around them. Olivia elongated her neck, relishing the attention.

"That's true, we should probably space out the favors we request from people," Issa said.

"We need to find Redrick before we conjure Ava back," Olivia said. "I never want to see her like that again."

"Yeah, angry like a banshee."

"No," Olivia said, giving Issa a funny frown. "Upset. She's our friend. She's our friend, and we shouldn't make fun of her for quite a reasonable reaction to something that's our fault."

"Oh. Right." But when Olivia turned to look across the crowd—as if she'd know who Weston Redrick was just by looking at him—Issa let her face fall. She felt thoroughly reprimanded. Ma could scold her all she wanted. But her best friend? It didn't feel right, and she was confused and ashamed.

Yet, she understood that Olivia was right—they hadn't tried very hard to fulfill their end of the bargain. Issa had gotten so used to Ava being around, and Ava was so friendly that she'd had no trouble accepting her into their little circle. She sometimes forgot that it was supposed to be a mutually beneficial deal.

She focused on finding Weston Redrick, but she could tell people were starting to get annoyed with her.

One man looked her up and down. "Sweetheart, if you're trying to get a role on Weston's films, these parties are not the right way to go about it."

"What?" Issa said. "Oh, I'm not—unless I get assigned to one, of course. I'm a contract actress at MGM." It was the first time she'd said it out loud to a stranger, and it felt quite satisfying to see the man's expression change from snobbish indifference to unwanted interest.

After that, Issa gave up and tried to enjoy the party. She loved telling people that she was an actress on salary at the studio, and she loved how impressed they looked, which contrasted so much with the dismissive looks they had just sported that it was comical. She mingled, bringing up her contract at every opportunity, and she had a much better time than she'd anticipated. Usually she hated these sorts of gatherings, but she discovered that they were much more fun once you were somebody. Somebody important. Someone worth listening to, worth watching.

The next morning, two manila envelopes arrived at their dressing room. Olivia's door was still closed—it was unusual yet pleasant having rooms to themselves—so Issa made her usual cup of tea as she opened the envelope marked for her.

"A script?" she nearly shouted. Already?

She tucked the thick envelopes under her arm as she hovered outside Olivia's door and knocked gently.

Olivia opened it a second later. "What is it?" she asked groggily.

Aware she was mildly obnoxious for being so cheerful in the morning, Issa waved the envelopes in Olivia's face. "Just arrived."

"What?" Olivia took the one with her name. "Two films at once?" she asked as she compared the title pages of her and Issa's copies. One was for *Mighty in Love* and the second was for *Clear Horizons.*

"They sure like love and horizons," Issa said. "Or sunsets or sunrises." She took one of the scripts and flipped to the casting page. She found Olivia's name as a supporting character but her name wasn't listed. "I don't have a role in this."

"Me neither," Olivia said, reading through the cast list for the other script.

They switched packages, somewhat perplexed.

"Wait," Issa said, finding her name next to a secondary character. "We're in different movies?"

Olivia took a moment to answer. "It would seem so."

For a few moments, neither of them knew what to say. They'd been in three movies together—their only movies. And while Issa knew it would happen eventually, she didn't expect to be separated so soon.

She met Olivia's eyes, comforted by Olivia's sad expression. She must have felt the same dismay.

"It's just one movie," Olivia said. "Maybe we'll be cast together again after this one."

"Maybe."

"We'll put that in our contract next time," Olivia said. "That we prefer to work together."

"Eight movies from now?"

Olivia smiled. "Not a bad problem to have, right?" She ran a hand through her hair. "I better find some coffee."

Issa grinned. "Yes. We've got work to do."

Chapter Twenty-Seven

A few weeks later, Issa attended her first speaking-role table read. Most of the other actors were new or up-and-coming, so they were much friendlier than the actors on her previous films. Her seat had her name printed on a little card, and when she introduced herself, everyone clapped as if she were already a star. The director had a few notes for her as she read her lines, but no more than what he gave to everyone else, and all in all, it was a wonderful start.

She missed Olivia, though. It was bizarre not having her best friend in the same soundstage. She kept turning to see Olivia's reaction when something funny happened. She felt oddly alone; not even Ava was there to keep her company. Ava usually went with Olivia, perhaps because Olivia always asked for more notes or feedback on her acting, while Issa preferred to let things play out or hear what the director said.

She and Olivia had talked about meeting for lunch at the commissary, but breaks depended on the director's whims, so they couldn't schedule anything.

Issa headed to the cafeteria anyway when the director called for fifteen, hoping to run into Olivia. The walk through the studio lot seemed much farther without company, the multiple buildings looming around her larger than before.

Inside the commissary, round tables were fitted with white tablecloths and gleaming chairs. Issa stood at the entrance, perusing the scene for a friendly face, hardly expecting the man in front of her to turn around and beam at her with a welcoming smile.

It was Jem Meier. He wore charcoal slacks and a maroon sweater over a white shirt that hugged the curves of his shoulders, and he smelled like subtly sweet coffee and something woodsy, perhaps sandalwood.

"I've been hoping to run into you," he said. "I've come here every day since *Lost in the Queen's Love* wrapped."

"Oh, hi," Issa said, affecting a casual manner she hoped came off as breezy yet still romantic.

"You still owe me dinner, don't forget."

"I haven't forgotten, but there was no way to get in touch," Issa said.

"Whose fault is that?" He grinned good-naturedly, and Issa allowed herself to smile back.

"I have to be back on set," he explained after they ordered. "What are your plans for the day?"

"It's our first table read."

"Already? Seems so fast after the last movie."

"I could say the same for you. You're always running around from one job to another."

"I enjoy staying busy."

"So do I."

His eyes roamed her features, taking his time in careful observation. Issa blinked, standing taller.

"What is it?" she asked, touching under her eyes to swipe away any smudged makeup. "Do I have something on my face?"

Jem shook his head. "How about Saturday night?"

"For what?"

"Dinner. I can pick you up at six."

"That sounds wonderful."

As he left, he placed a hand gently on her shoulder, sending warmth down her arm and leaving behind a hint of his cologne and a disturbance in the air. She was so distracted that a cook at the counter had to shout out her order several times before she remembered that she'd asked for soup.

Issa hoped Olivia would be there when she got home, but the windows were dark, and the rooms were empty when she let herself in. It had been a short walk from the soundstage, but she was used to a much longer commute, so after she hung up her keys and took off her jacket, she wasn't sure what to do with herself. She could study her lines some more, but her brain was mush from the long day on set. She went to her bedroom, but even with the lamps on, the corners felt dark and lonely.

When she went back to the living room, she almost screamed.

Ava stood by herself.

She was slumped over, resembling a marionette doll. At Issa's presence, she straightened slowly. Her appearance seemed more muted than usual. Sometimes she had almost a pink tinge beneath the gray of her skin, but now it was absent, and a staticky film seemed to cling to her. She stared at Issa for several seconds, her expression rather harsh.

"Goodness, you scared me," Issa said, hand over her heart.

For a moment, Ava continued staring, and Issa grew numb with fright, filled with an inexplicable urge to run.

But it was just Ava—just their spirit friend who'd been helping them, although she couldn't do much from the Other Side other than whisper in people's ears seductively. Issa studied her closely, trying to read what she was thinking about behind her blank exterior. They hadn't spoken alone since Ava had thrown her temper tantrum about the trophy, though Issa often heard Olivia talking to her in her bedroom.

Then Ava smiled, the beautiful smile that had captured the hearts of many, and Issa's fear melted away, and she felt rather childish.

"Sorry, darling," Ava said. "Sometimes, it takes a moment to remember where I am. Jarring, you see, flitting between this world and the other."

"I can imagine," Issa said with a polite laugh.

"How was your first day on your new film?" Ava asked.

"It was tiring." Issa yawned and perched one butt cheek on the back of the couch. She felt the need to lighten the mood somehow after that tense interlude. "How was your—um, whatever you do in the underworld?"

"Underworld?" Ava laughed. "Why do you assume I'm in hell?"

"I don't, I'm just—"

"Relax, darling, I'm just teasing you."

"I'm afraid we couldn't find Weston Redrick," Issa said. "Olivia was really upset about it. We tried all night at that bash, spent the whole party asking everyone about him, probably annoyed a lot of people."

"Of course, I forget sometimes that you're still nobodies." Ava waved a hand. "I mean, not nobodies. Just . . . not stars yet. People aren't going to fall over themselves to do your bidding. Yet."

Issa smiled to reassure her that she didn't find Ava's slipup offensive. Perhaps Olivia would have—Olivia wanted bigger and better things at a faster rate, but Issa was more realistic.

"I'm sorry I lost my temper," Ava continued. "I'm just getting . . . impatient. But it won't be long now. And you promised to try."

"Yes, we will."

Ava gave Issa an almost coquettish look. "You're the real medium among the two of you, aren't you?"

A tingle went up Issa's spine. "Yes. Olivia's not really a shaman. She's just . . . closely involved. But I've never been properly trained. I come from a line of witches, but my mom renounced the clan's ways and left before I was of an age to receive instruction."

"But you can conjure your grandmother, and me. It's in your blood."

"Yes," Issa answered, even though Ava wasn't asking a question.

"I . . . feel stronger when I'm with you. When I'm just with Olivia, the connection is . . . like a badly tuned radio."

"Doesn't it get better the more you visit us?"

"With you, yes. With Olivia . . . it's a struggle. It wears on one. I followed her to rehearsals, but without you there, it's not the same."

Issa smiled, her heart warming at Ava's kind look.

"It's only with the blood connection that our bond remains intact," Ava continued.

Issa suppressed a shudder. She had never liked the idea of Olivia offering her blood in the first place.

"Not that I mind it, truly," Ava added quickly. "She gets nervous about her acting, needs extra coaching."

Issa nodded, but a small twinge tugged in her chest. Was it . . . was she jealous? Of Olivia and Ava? The two had been spending more time together, but it wasn't any of their fault that Olivia and Issa had been cast in different movies. Besides, they were grown women now, they could talk to other people.

"Imagine if you give me some of your blood," Ava said, her eyes distant, dreaming. "I would feel much better, I think. Livelier."

Issa stiffened. "But you already had some of Olivia's blood." Cold fingers seemed to trace up and down her back. "Wasn't that enough?"

"It is. But sometimes, I just feel so . . . so far away." Ava held her hand up, as if reaching for Issa, even though she always passed right through whatever she tried to touch. "I don't fit in on the Other Side—those women are all so . . . so *happy*. As if they relish being dead."

"I'm sorry, Ava," Issa said. "I know what it's like to feel so alone."

"You're not like anyone else."

"Well, no," Issa said. "Other girls always seem so sure of themselves. They've always known what they wanted. Who they wanted to be."

"It's easy to achieve your dreams when they're mediocre and small. But you and Olivia have never had such lackluster goals."

Issa smiled wryly.

"That's why I love being with the two of you," Ava went on. "You remind me so much of myself. You remind me what it was like." Ava looked down at her hands. "I miss being alive so much. I miss people, I miss being loved. And the fame, if I'm honest. You must understand, now that you've had a taste."

Flattered that Ava would think so, Issa smiled. "Of course you miss it. You were so successful."

"I miss touch. I miss hugs."

Issa got up from the back of the couch and approached Ava. "The spirits there don't hug you?"

"It's not the same."

Ava still had her hand in the air. Impulsively, Issa held hers up as well and slowly, hesitantly, she pressed her fingers against Ava's. She expected to touch nothing but air.

Yet Issa felt Ava's hand move, palm against palm, and she almost jerked back. She could *feel* it. Flesh on flesh, skin sliding with hers—cold and hardened, but real. Before she could pull away, Ava grabbed her. Not roughly, but it was horrifying all the same. Ava was a spirit. She was supposed to be on the *Other Side*, the realm Issa's family had always been able to communicate with but never enter or touch . . . before.

"How—" Issa swallowed. The place where their hands connected was difficult to look at, like trying to look through a dark pool of water, and her eyes hurt when she tried to focus on it. Her skin grew numb. Ava's touch was shockingly cold.

Issa stepped back, but Ava's grip tightened on hers like steel, freezing and unbreakable.

"Don't go," Ava implored, eyes pleading. They were shiny from unshed tears, full of anguish and vulnerability. "Please. This feels . . . you don't know how warm you are, how much I've missed this. It's so cold over on my side, always so cold and distant."

"H-how is this possible?" Issa stammered.

"I grow stronger when I'm near you. Your blood, it calls to me—to us. The other spirits. That's why it's so easy for us to respond to your summons."

Issa breathed heavily, unwilling to come to terms with that. Her family had power she was just starting to understand, but this was something too bizarre for her to grasp, and her fascination was vastly eclipsed by repulsion.

Keys jangled at the front door, and the distraction made Ava loosen her grip. Issa yanked her hand away, walking backward until she hit the back of the couch. Her fingers were cold where Ava had touched her, warmth flooding back into them so fast that her flesh stung.

When the door opened, Olivia stumbled in, clutching the doorknob to keep from tripping. The waft of alcohol was a clear indication that she was drunk.

"Are you all right?" Issa asked, rushing to her side.

"Long," Olivia mumbled, the word slurred, "day."

She would have collapsed, but Issa held her up.

"I want to lay down," Olivia said, so Issa helped her to her room. "Couldn't say no."

"No to what?" Issa asked, concerned.

Olivia flopped onto the bed, fully clothed, eyes closed. "Tell you later." She was out cold the next second, her legs dangling off the side of the bed, one hand flopped over her pillow, the other bent awkwardly underneath her. Her hair, which she usually braided at night, fanned in long strands across her face.

Issa stood by the bed, wringing her hands. She needed to tell someone about what happened with Ava, but even if she tried to keep Olivia awake, Olivia wasn't clear-headed enough to discuss it.

Instead, Issa went back to the front door to close it, her heart hammering when she passed the large mirror. But Ava was gone.

Chapter Twenty-Eight

"Everyone wanted to go drinking after," Olivia explained the next morning. "I tried to decline, but they kept insisting, and it felt like bad form to be such a downer."

They sat at the dining table next to the modest kitchenette with steaming mugs of tea.

"Was it a good day, at least?" Issa asked.

"I don't know." Olivia had bags under her eyes, her lids puffy, her skin dull from a night of terrible sleep. Despite getting in so late, she had been up before Issa. "I had to do a take fifteen times, and it wasn't even complicated. Only two lines."

"Was it just you?"

"No, every scene was like that. One of the producers said that if this keeps up, they'll be behind schedule, which will reflect badly on any other project lined up after this."

"They can't expect us to keep working back-to-back. Sure, we did it before because our roles were so minor, but we'll need to have a break between movies now."

"Not if we want to be stars. This is normal. Greta Garbo does about ten movies a year."

"Goodness."

"Quantity over quality until we have more power to choose our projects." Olivia sipped her tea.

Issa's skin went numb as she remembered her encounter with Ava last night. "There's something I should tell you," she said and recounted how she and Ava had been able to touch. She waited for Olivia's reaction, expecting surprise or concern, or at the very least, confirmation of Issa's fears, but Olivia just sipped her tea calmly.

"It makes sense that she'd be drawn to you," Olivia said.

"But she actually touched me. I didn't know spirits could do that."

"There's a lot you don't know, though."

This was absolutely true, but it hurt nonetheless. Issa sat back in her seat, feeling defeated. Why was Olivia dismissing it as if it wasn't a big problem?

"I don't mean that as an insult," Olivia said, touching her hand. It was comfortingly warm from being wrapped around her mug of tea. "I mean, you're so smart, of course—but you never got the training from Bà Ngoại you might have had if you lived with her."

Issa took a deep breath and looked away.

"Please don't be mad," Olivia said. "I'm sorry." She wrapped her warm fingers around Issa's, a stark contrast from how Ava had gripped her last night. "That came out wrong. I know you don't want to get involved with all that, and you already did us a huge favor by agreeing to conjure Bà Ngoại and Ava in the first place. If you hadn't, we wouldn't be here." She squeezed Issa's hand and gave such a bright smile that Issa's resentment melted. "But imagine what more you could do. What if you're able to get us even better roles down the line?"

Olivia made a good argument. They'd only gotten their start because she'd finally given in to her shaman abilities.

"I'll talk to Auntie Yen," Issa said. "Learn what I can from her. If she has time, anyway."

"You could conjure Bà Ngoại also," Olivia said. "Isn't it about time you gave her your monthly report?"

"She hardly cares," Issa said. Last month, Bà Ngoại had been so distracted, eager to return to her gambling, that she barely listened to what Issa said. "I don't see why she wants me to summon her so much when she always makes excuses to leave as soon as possible."

Olivia took up her mug again. "Have you been practicing those breathing exercises she gave you?"

Issa shook her head. "The idea of leaving my body is terrifying."

"I don't know . . . It sounds like an incredibly useful tool. Being able to learn everyone else's secrets. You could figure out what the execs want, when the casting directors are meeting, all the roles we'd be perfect for. Imagine that kind of power."

"I didn't think about it that way."

Olivia winked. "That's why you keep me around."

Bolstered by Olivia's encouragement, Issa sat down cross-legged on her bed that night and took in several deep breaths, hitching more air into her lungs when she felt she couldn't take any more, the way Bà Ngoại had screamed at her to do during one of their fruitless sessions. She imagined an orb of light moving from the top of her head down through her body, but before it reached her arms, she'd drifted off into sleep.

She snapped out of it as soon as her head dropped, looking around a brightly lit studio and blinking at the sudden vividness of the scene. Colors appeared deep and saturated, as if the film crew had tinkered with different filters for the lighting. A blinding flash followed by the pop of a bulb made her cover her eyes. She was on a velvet sofa—lounging across it, and she was dressed in costume—a silky cheongsam, her head heavy with some sort of hat.

"Hands down, please!" someone shouted at her from beyond the glare of stage lights.

"How do you expect me to work under these conditions!" she screeched back. But it wasn't her voice. It sounded familiar, laced with an affected accent somewhere between British and Asian.

Someone else spoke to the first voice. "What will these pictures accomplish, anyhow? We can't publish them when the audience wants a wholesome girl. Not . . . her."

"I can hear you!" Issa said against her will. "You promised you would market this film the same way you've done for the others. I'll not be blamed for it failing because you haven't done your part."

"Please stay as instructed, Ms. Rang," the other voice said as figures moved to fix the camera.

Of course . . . It was Ava's voice. But . . . did that mean . . .

Issa tried to move, but her body didn't respond. Instead, her arm shifted without her control, and her legs stretched seductively along the plump cushions. She felt it all—the soft texture of the fabric on her skin, the sticky sweat of her thighs rubbing together in the sweltering heat of the lights. But she couldn't do much. Her body was not hers, as if she had possessed someone else's . . . though perhaps that wasn't the right term, for it didn't feel as if she occupied another's body so much as she was trapped—

The thought brought on a panic. How long would this last? What if she couldn't break out of this . . . whatever this was? Vision? Dream? Issa struggled to move. She fought against the constraints of Ava's limbs, urged them to lift, tried to claw her way out, to find her own physical body somehow. But all it did was trigger a growing pressure along her flesh, as if the air were pressing in on her from everywhere at once. Her breath constricted. She gasped and gasped, or at least tried to, but it did nothing except stir an emptiness inside her. It felt like the ground had been ripped from her feet. Something was dragging her into a dark abyss, something heavy and unrelenting—

"Issa! Issa!" Hands gripped her shoulders, and Issa sucked in air. She sat upright. Back in her own bed. Olivia's face scrunched in worry above hers. "You were screaming. Are you all right? Was it a terrible nightmare?"

Issa clutched her chest. She could move. She was no longer trapped in Ava's body. Tears sprang to her eyes in relief. "Yes," she said. "It was a horrible dream. I think. I don't know." She couldn't articulate what had happened because she barely knew what it was. Surely this wasn't what Bà Ngoại meant when she'd said Issa could enter someone else's mind. Did that someone include a ghost?

Olivia sat next to Issa and pulled her into a hug. She didn't say anything, just rubbed Issa's shoulders until her breath returned to normal. The bed was much bigger and so different from the one they used to share, but she found it comforting nonetheless to have Olivia there, as if things hadn't changed. Issa was afraid to fall back asleep, scared to repeat the suffocating experience, but eventually Olivia's weight settled against the pillows. She started snoring, which she only did when she was extremely tired. Guilt made Issa's heart swell, as did gratefulness. Olivia must have had a long day at work.

Carefully, Issa extricated herself from Olivia's arms and made her way to the living room. She switched on all the lamps, spinning to look over her shoulders at the reflection of her own movements in the mirror. She was so jumpy, she could barely light the match.

Bà Ngoại didn't take long to appear.

"Something happened," Issa said, explaining the dream. "It didn't feel . . . normal. Is this what you meant? That I can enter different realms?"

"It sounds like a memory," Bà Ngoại said. "You've been spending so much time with the spirit, it makes sense you might have channeled yourself into her past."

"I can do that?"

"The mind is a powerful thing, and you've created a strong bond with Ava."

Issa rubbed her temples. "How do I never do that again?"

"Scared off already?" Thankfully, Bà Ngoại seemed to take her concerns seriously and didn't tease the way she maliciously did when she thought Issa was being a coward. "Well, how did you get there?"

"I did the breathing exercises like you taught me."

"Ah. So you've mastered it at last."

"I wouldn't call this mastery."

"It's a start. It's always frightening at first. But think, Issa girl. Did anything truly terrible happen? Were you harmed?"

Issa wrung her hands together. Other than the panic and suffocating sensation, inability to breathe, and a dragging downward? That was all it was. A feeling. "No, I suppose not."

"And I see that you made it back safely into your body. So from what I can tell, I'd say that this was quite an accomplishment."

Issa hugged herself. Her stomach felt empty, as if something had been torn from deep within. She certainly did not feel accomplished.

"To be quite honest," Bà Ngoại said, "I did not think you had it in you. Only the strongest shaman witches ever develop this ability. Which gives me such high hopes for you, my dearest granddaughter. Imagine what you can do with this power. How do you think I've managed to win against my enemies? By uncovering their plans and secrets without their knowledge. But I see that you will need even more training. More focus."

"Please," Issa begged, though she wasn't sure what she was asking for. "Not right now. Perhaps . . . later . . . after . . ." She trailed off.

Bà Ngoại smiled and nodded. "Oh, not to worry. We'll have plenty of time."

But that didn't make Issa feel any better either.

Issa put it out of her mind and focused on her new movie. By the time she woke up late on Saturday, she was grateful for the chance to bask in the laziness of the afternoon, until she realized with undue anxiety that she had her first date with Jem Meier later that evening. She had plenty of time to prepare, but that didn't stop her from rushing around the apartment, trying on different outfits and discarding each for being too fancy or dull or uncomfortable. Olivia laughed as she watched.

"My, I didn't know you had such a thing for this Jem fella," Olivia said.

"I don't," Issa said. "I mean, I don't know. I don't really know him, but it is kind of nice, to be asked out."

"Liar. I see you blush every time you talk about him."

Issa grew hot from that, the idea of anyone finding her attractive. She knew on some intellectual level that she had a pretty face; otherwise, why would she be cast for anything? Yet she'd never gotten much male attention before—that she was aware of, at any rate, and that wasn't unwanted. This nervousness was new, the excitement as well, and she tried to savor the thrumming in her veins as she put on her makeup and went down to meet him in front of her building.

Jem wore a deep-blue sweater over his shirt and tie, a more casual look compared to the suited men on the lot, which immediately endeared him to Issa. As she got into his car, she was glad she'd chosen one of her more comfortable outfits: a burnt-orange boxy sheath dress that fit her just right.

To her surprise, he drove to a local diner down the street.

"I know you're probably used to fancy meals and four-course dinners," he said as he opened the door for her. "But they have the best milkshakes here."

"Oh, this is perfect," she said. "Although I've yet to eat a four-course dinner."

"Never? I refuse to believe no one's taken you out for one yet."

Jem led her to a booth with cushioned benches covered in red vinyl. Outside the window, past the parking lot, the view of the city punctuated the night, white lights shining in buildings that rose high in the darkness.

"Are you from Los Angeles?" she asked.

"I was born in the Philippines," he said. "In Cebu."

"Really?" She didn't mean to sound so shocked. "I'm sorry—you just don't look . . ."

"I get it all the time. My father is Caucasian, my mother was Filipina. She died before we came here. That's the only reason we moved back. Dad didn't really speak the language—had depended on my mom for everything and just decided it was time."

"How old were you?"

"Six or seven. I remember little things about it. How hot and humid it always was. How green. California's a desert, but we forget because of the palm trees."

"I've never been anywhere else."

"Oh, you will," he said with a knowing smile. "You'll travel the world one day, you'll see. Where do you want to go?"

"I don't know. I suppose I've never thought much about it."

The waitress came to take their orders, and then there was a little lull in the conversation.

"Is it hard, being a writer?" she asked.

"I can't complain." He shrugged. He had such an easygoing manner, unlike the intense people she was usually surrounded by—cast who were so focused on their careers, directors who wanted things done exactly how they imagined, or producers who only deigned to speak to Issa when they needed something from her. It was refreshing but bizarre to be with Jem, and she wasn't sure how to navigate the interaction.

"I get paid to do what I love," Jem went on. "Many people would kill to be in my position, so I wouldn't want to do anything else."

"Is there some . . . some goal that you're aiming for?" she asked.

"Like what, an Oscar?" Jem asked. "No, not really."

"Oh." The concept of being simply content with what you had seemed strange to her. She was so used to aiming for the next step in her career.

"Writers never get much credit, anyway," Jem explained. "By the time the script gets made into a movie, it's been rewritten by so many different people, it's hard to tell who's the real creator. I suppose the goal is to simply . . . work." He smiled. "I'm never happier than when I've managed to put the puzzle pieces of a story together."

"I see writers credited all the time."

"Those are the big shots. It's like hoping you'll win the lottery."

"Will you be credited for *Lost in the Queen's Love*?"

"No." He laughed. "The original writer who was contracted for that story remains on the credits."

"Didn't he quit? Midproduction?"

He nodded good-naturedly.

"I don't know how you're not more upset," Issa said. "I'd be devastated."

"Like I said, I do this because I enjoy it." He toyed with his fork. "You seem to as well. Your lines on love were very . . . authentic."

"I suppose they were."

"You really don't believe that love lasts?"

She paused, wondering if this was some sort of test, if her answer might push him away. "I don't know—I've never fallen in love."

"Surely you've had men seek your attention."

Her cheeks must have been bright pink, which only made her grow hotter. "I've always had bigger ambitions."

"And love isn't one of them?"

She wasn't sure how to answer that. It wasn't that simple, was it? "No one in my family has placed much importance on it. My parents loved each other, but my father died when I was young, and my mother was never interested in romance after that."

"Shouldn't that prove that romance is worth pursuing?"

"Maybe. But she's never taught me one way or another, other than through her own example. She can't really talk about him. I think maybe she loved him too much to be able to, but as a child, I used to think it must hurt a lot—her love for him—and that was why. I suppose it's not a bad thing, that kind of pain. And my aunt"—she paused, thinking it probably wasn't wise to mention her gangster family—"isn't focused on pursuing a relationship either. Neither was my grandmother. And, well, I have so many goals that love never crossed my mind."

Jem's smile spread across his entire face, crinkling his eyes and forehead in a way that Issa's male costars never would have allowed. It was refreshing, but at the same time, hard to read. Did he agree with her? If so, what did that mean for them? What did she want it to mean for them? She liked him, but she also meant what she said. She had too much to do, her own dreams and goals, and a man had never factored into them. If she did marry, that would complicate everything she'd ever wanted for her life.

"So you just like to have fun," he said.

Issa wished she hadn't been so deeply open about her stance and tried to lighten the mood. "Outside of work, what else is there?"

After Jem parked the car, he walked with Issa across the lot to the dressing rooms. As they reached the buildings, Jem held out an arm as if to protect her.

"What's going on?" Issa asked.

There was a crowd gathered in front, and shouting. A man's voice. Jem took her hand, easing her body behind his as they approached. People gasped as someone stumbled in the center of the crowd.

"I'm only going to ask you once," a security guard said, grabbing a man under the arm and dragging him toward a gray car parked a distance away. "You're not to come back, hear?"

The man was dressed sloppily in a khaki shirt and dark pants, and as he passed, alcohol wafted off him, mixed with sour sweat. He leered at Issa, who startled, recognizing him. She clamped her teeth together to hide that she knew him, but he smirked knowingly.

"I'm glad I was here," Jem said, guiding Issa safely away from the commotion. The crowd had started to disperse, leaving a clear path to her front door.

He paused as she turned toward him. She knew this was supposed to be a romantic moment, but she was too upset at the sight of the man and wasn't sure how to proceed.

"Thank you for the lovely evening," she said.

He seemed to understand without her having to explain, glancing toward the East Gate, where the security guard had taken the man. "We'll do it again?" he asked with a casual smile.

She nodded. "Promise."

Inside, Olivia huddled on the corner of the sofa, clutching a handkerchief to her face, her shoulders jerking with silent sobs.

"Olivia." Issa threw her purse and coat down and rushed to her side. "What happened? Was that—was that your uncle?"

Olivia heaved in several deep breaths, only managing a nod in the end.

"What was he doing here?"

"M-money," Olivia choked out.

Of course. What else could he want?

"H-he thought I'd m-made it b-big," Olivia said through halting gasps.

"Goodness." Issa rubbed her back. "Don't worry, the security guard escorted him out."

"H-he'll be back." Olivia's breath hitched. "Wh-what will I d-do then?"

Issa looked around as if the answer would present itself. "We'll deal with it together. I bet I can ask Auntie Yen to pay him off."

"No." Olivia grasped her forearm. "Then he'll just keep asking for more."

Issa didn't know what else to say. "We'll get rid of him. We will."

Olivia could only cry some more, clinging on to Issa like a person drowning.

Luckily, the next few weeks showed no signs of Olivia's uncle, though Issa knew that he was just biding his time. She kept looking over her shoulder, wondering if he was following them, and walked back home each night with caution. She could only imagine how much more strained Olivia must have felt, but they rarely saw each other. If Olivia's work finished early, then Issa had to stay late, or one of them would get invited out with the rest of the crew. They shared brief moments in the morning when they would drink tea and talk, but even those times became shorter and more rushed, as they had to arrive on set earlier to catch up on the schedule.

Somehow, they managed to survive, and Issa's production wrapped on time. Unfortunately, Olivia's ran behind schedule, so she couldn't join the cast party. Issa went by herself, dressed in a gown the studio sent over. It was glittery pink, a bit more eye-catching than what they usually put her in, but she was already accustomed to people staring at her.

It felt peculiar walking into the house in Beverly Hills without Olivia, but Issa was getting used to going alone now that they had to work separately. Besides, since she played a bigger role in this film, the cast was friendlier to her, and people greeted her warmly as she arrived. Someone handed her a drink, and soon she was enveloped in the crowd.

As usual, Issa found the party loud and overwhelming, but it helped a bit that she was comfortable with the cast. End-of-production celebrations were hardly ever exclusive to the people who worked on the projects, however, and as the hours fell away, the partygoers who remained were strangers. She escaped to the backyard, a green oasis of a garden lit by flickering candles. Feeling lonely, she searched the crowd, hoping for a delusional moment that she'd run into Jem there. She hadn't heard from him after their date, but she'd been too busy to worry about it. She wished he was there now, not just to have someone to talk to, but because they'd probably have had a grand old time.

Instead, she nabbed a lounge chair and settled back, taking sips of her drink while she looked up at the stars. She would stay for a few more minutes—long enough that no one could accuse her of being a downer, but not so long that she'd get too drunk to walk—and then go home.

People talked in low voices nearby, sparking the sensation that someone was looking at her. She sat up slightly to see a man in aviator glasses, wearing a sweater and slacks, unlike the actors who usually wore tailored suits to these parties. He noticed her notice him and walked over.

"Issa Bui," he said.

Issa sat up, swinging her legs to the side so she could place her feet on the ground, and he took the spot next to her on the lounge chair.

"I'm sorry," she said, "do I know you?"

"I should hope so, considering you've been asking about me." He had a thick mustache that quivered when he talked.

"Are you Weston Redrick?" she asked.

His mouth quirked up at the corners. "Why, yes."

"Oh my goodness." She looked around as if Olivia would magically appear at the party.

"So why have you been searching for me?" he asked.

Issa couldn't read his expression, but she was already wary when it came to male attention, and something about him sent warning signals through her body, causing her shoulders to tense. Perhaps it was just that Ava hadn't spoken too fondly of him.

"I heard you won an Oscar," she said, hoping he would talk about his trophy. Or rather, Ava's trophy that she wanted them to steal.

"I've won several," Redrick said, clinking ice around in his glass tumbler. "Why? Is that what you're after? An Oscar?"

A very specific Oscar, but Issa said, "Isn't everyone?"

He chuckled and downed his drink. "You're only just signed, aren't you? What kind of a name is Issa Bui, anyway?"

"The one I have," Issa said.

"It's real? You were born with it?"

"As far as I know." She frowned at his smirk. "Why?"

"Here I thought someone had just made up something ridiculous because they thought it sounded exotic."

Issa narrowed her eyes at him. "What name was I supposed to use?"

He shrugged. "Usually the producers insist on something more appealing."

Issa raised her eyebrows and decided that the man was utterly idiotic and probably deserved to have the statue stolen. "Where's your office, Mr. Redrick? Is it in the Lion Building?"

He studied her from head to toe, and Issa suppressed a shudder. "Of course it is, right above Thalberg's." Which implied that he was more important than the producer, or at least thought he was. "I could put you in my next movie," he added.

Whether it was his thick, lascivious-looking mustache or the fact that Ava had described him as a lecherous thief, Issa's dislike for him grew. He gave off an oily sort of air, like he might try to slip something into her drink. Issa would much prefer not to accept his offer, or even give him the satisfaction of thinking she was interested, but it would be the best way to get into his office and steal the trophy for Ava.

"In a lead role?" she asked.

"I don't know about that," Redrick said. His drink was empty, but he threw a chunk of ice into his mouth and crunched on it. "What with your . . ." He gestured at the vicinity of her eyes. Issa wanted to smack his drink out of his hand. Why was it always the eyes? "We'll have to see your screen test first."

"What's this movie about?"

"I have a few different ones I'm thinking of. Why don't you pay me a visit in the morning, and we'll discuss it more?"

Issa got up, smoothing her hands down her dress. The look Redrick gave her left a rancid taste in her mouth. "I'll see you tomorrow, then."

Chapter Twenty-Nine

When Issa got back to their rooms, she was surprised that the lights were on so late. Inside, Olivia sat on the sofa, Ava next to her.

Issa closed the door with care, debating how to act. She hadn't seen Ava since that night when the spirit had . . . grabbed her. And then there was the dream that Issa had had when she'd been stuck inside Ava's body. She hadn't attempted to use her powers since, felt too terrified to even think upon it, plagued with the underlying fear that doing so would induce it to happen again.

"Hi there," Olivia said, propping her elbow on the back of the couch, holding a glass of wine.

Issa watched Ava as she moved closer, but the ghost only smiled and waved at Issa like she usually did, showing no signs that she remembered their last interaction.

"Hello, darling," Ava said.

"Hi," Issa said, dropping onto the couch with an exhale.

"How was the party?" Olivia asked.

"It was great. I met Weston Redrick."

At that, Ava brightened. "You did? What did he say? Did he talk about my trophy?"

"I asked him about it, but he didn't seem keen to speak on it."

"Of course not, considering how he got the thing." Ava crossed her arms. "What happened?"

"I'm supposed to meet him at his office tomorrow to talk about being in his next film. Maybe I'll see the trophy there, or if I'm cast, I can find out where it is."

"Do not," Ava said, "under any circumstances, go alone."

"Why?" Issa asked. "Ava, did he do something to you?"

"No, not to me," Ava said. "He simply doesn't have the best reputation."

Olivia took Issa's hand. "We'll go together."

"But you're still filming," Issa said.

"Most of my scenes are done, and the other stars are late all the time. This is more important."

Issa wanted to protest, but she was tired of being alone, and she missed her days with Olivia. If Ava thought she shouldn't go alone, then something about Weston Redrick was clearly dangerous.

"What should we say to him?" she asked Ava.

"Go to the meeting, pretend you want to be in his movie, and butter him up," Ava said. "Same as with any man. They just want to feel important."

"Where do you think he keeps the trophy?"

"It'll be in his office on display," Ava said. "Or it could be at his house."

"What's the story behind this trophy, anyhow?" Issa asked.

Ava heaved a big sigh. "The truth is that the cast won it for Best Picture, but he took all the credit. All the ideas that made the movie great were mine, and some of the other actors' as well, I suppose. But the director always gets all the praise, don't they. Not only that, but I should have won Best Actress, only he cut a scene at the last minute—the scene that would have made me a star, my best performance. I cried buckets for that take, tastefully, of course, but he was jealous of my stardom. Cut it without telling me, so the ending of the movie made no sense—it was a disaster. Later he claimed it made the movie better, but it did no such thing and lost me an Oscar to boot."

"That's horrible, Ava," Olivia said. "Things like that need to stop happening. Men stealing women's limelight because they're intimidated by us."

"Exactly. So I said the trophy belongs with me, and Redrick agreed."

"So why does he have it now?" Issa asked.

"That's the thing. He stole it back. Came over to a party I threw, and we had a big argument about the movie. He was never able to let it go. Why? He has so many awards he doesn't deserve, for credit he didn't earn. What does he want with mine? To spite me. I said no, obviously. But he took it anyway, and there was nothing I could do. It has his name on it after all."

"How petty of him," Olivia said.

"Most of these directors are simply toddlers in men's bodies." Ava flicked her hair from her shoulder. "I just want it back. I want to see it and know that it's safe in the hands of people I trust." She smiled at them. "You're my most wonderful friends, I hope you know. I've never really had friends, not before I became a star, and even fewer after. You must know what it's like, growing up so different. I was either vilified for my looks, or other girls were too resentful to ever want to be my friends. At least the two of you are lucky enough to have each other."

"Well now we have you, too, Ava," Olivia said, beaming. "And you have us."

For a moment, Ava looked down, her eyes growing glossy with tears.

"What's the matter?" Olivia asked.

Ava dabbed at her eyes. Issa felt like a stonehearted goblin as she sat there stiffly, feeling nothing in response, all while Olivia looked so concerned. She immediately grew guilty over it. But something about Ava's gesture seemed almost . . . performative.

"I just can't imagine what life would have been like if I had you as friends," Ava said. "I mean, when I was still . . . alive."

"Oh, darling," Olivia said, reaching out as if to hug Ava. Issa almost expected them to touch, but Olivia's hand passed through the ghost, and she had to settle for an air-pat.

Issa leaned forward, willing herself to be nicer. Here Ava was practically sobbing, and all Issa could think about was herself, when Ava needed comforting. She needed friends. She'd poured her heart out about the loneliness of being dead, and Issa had just stood there.

"We're your friends now, Ava," Issa said.

"I can't even remember when you weren't with us," Olivia added.

Issa frowned and tried not to lean back to look at Olivia. Surely she was just being nice to Ava but . . . how . . . insulting. Did Issa's friendship mean nothing to Olivia before Ava showed up?

Ava caught Issa's eye. "I'm glad we have each other," she said with a teary smile.

As Issa and Olivia walked through the MGM lot together the next morning, the silence between them seemed charged with a tension that Issa didn't recognize. They were always so comfortable with each other, talking about and sharing everything, but lately they hadn't had much time together, and what little time they had often included Ava.

Issa was relieved Ava wasn't with them, for once, though she couldn't bring herself to discuss it with Olivia. Olivia was loyal to a fault, had never let anyone say a bad word against Issa. There was no way Olivia would allow Issa to say anything negative about Ava, even if it was to just discuss what Ava's ability to touch her that night could possibly mean.

"Have you heard from your uncle?" Issa asked, loath as she was to bring up the topic.

Olivia's shoulders stiffened. She looked around as if afraid he might show up. "No. I don't know what to do. What if he comes back? The security guards know not to let him in, but what if he manages to find a different entrance?"

"I still think we should ask Auntie Yen to help us pay him to leave you alone."

"It will never be enough."

"So what should we do—"

"I don't know, Issa," Olivia said with a harshness that she never used with Issa. Issa would have felt hurt and angry, except Olivia's face crumpled. She covered her mouth with a hand, schooling her features into a semblance of composure. "I'm sorry," she said, her voice thick. "I just . . . I really don't know. I can't dwell on it right now. I've told Ava about him, and she says she'll help."

"How would Ava help?"

"She says she'll try."

But how? Issa knew not to press, yet her mind was racked with questions, imagining all the ways that a ghost might scare off an abusive drunk.

"What do you think happened between Ava and Redrick?" Issa asked, simply because she couldn't stand the silence between them anymore.

Olivia didn't respond right away, lost in thought. "Hmm?" she asked a few seconds too late.

"Ava and Weston Redrick," Issa said. "Do you think they had an affair or something?"

"Just because a powerful man was interested in her doesn't mean she slept with him," Olivia said, her tone surprisingly harsh again.

Issa's footsteps faltered. "That's not what I meant."

Olivia took in a deep breath. "I'm sorry. I don't know where that came from. I'm just hungry and tired." She smiled apologetically and looped their arms. "Oh, do forgive me. I don't know—maybe they did have an affair. But I think it's unfair how sometimes men give women unwanted attention, and everyone else thinks that of course she must have seduced him to get ahead."

"Oh. I don't . . . I wasn't thinking about that. Perhaps you're right."

Olivia sighed. "I just . . . Ava's told me some things about her career. And . . . I feel terrible for her and other women in her time. Probably in our time too."

"Has anything like that happened with you?"

Olivia was quiet for too long. "Not with anyone lately. Not in the studio."

"Olivia," Issa said. "You know you can tell me anything. I won't think differently of you."

Olivia pressed her lips together. She pulled Issa into half a hug. "I know, doll. You're my best friend."

For the rest of the walk, things felt more normal than they had in weeks. The irony was not lost on Issa that acting in movies was what they had worked so hard for together, and yet now that they'd finally gotten what they wanted, they hardly had time to see each other. Issa reassured herself it wasn't unusual. Friends grew apart. Even sisters—look at Ma and Yen.

Issa and Olivia were closer than that, though. Their friendship had withstood too much to disintegrate over time spent apart. She had to accept that they just couldn't be together all the time, what with their ambitions.

Redrick's office wasn't large. It had a standard wooden desk with a domineering leather chair, and two seats on the other side. There was no conference table or lounging area, and no bar cart. Redrick stood when the secretary showed them in, throwing aside a stack of papers and gesturing for them to sit.

"You're in that new one with Eamon Blackwood," he said, pointing a finger at Olivia.

She smiled prettily. "Why yes, I am."

"They're editing your previous movie now," he said. "The one you were both in together. I've seen bits of it."

"And what did you think?" Olivia asked.

"Oh, it will be a hit, I know it will. That's why I want to snatch you up before anyone else."

Issa looked sideways at Olivia, confused. Redrick had asked her here at the party last night, but he seemed more focused on her best friend than her.

Olivia reached over to take her hand. "Of course anyone would want to snatch Issa up. She's so talented and smart."

Issa squeezed her fingers. Olivia took surreptitious glances around the room, and Issa followed her example, spotting a cabinet of trophies on the wall behind them, the glass panels revealing a few Academy Awards inside.

"Oh yes, my accolades," Redrick said. "Look at them if you like." He opened an envelope as if he had nothing better to do than wait, so Issa and Olivia got up to peer inside.

"What was Ava's movie called?" Olivia muttered. "*Rooted to Your Love* or something."

"Yes, I think that was the one." The trophies had small plaques on the base labeled with what Redrick had won them for. She couldn't find anything for Ava's movie.

When they went back to his desk, he was still perusing the papers he had pulled out from the packet.

"See anything you liked?" he asked with a quirk of his mustache.

"Your awards are very impressive," Olivia said. "It's a wonder you don't have more."

"Those are just the ones I'm especially proud of. I don't have enough space in this office, so I keep the rest at home." He folded his fingers together. "In fact, I'm throwing a dinner party soon. You can see them there."

Olivia leaned forward. "We have so many invitations," she said. "I'm afraid it would have to be worth our while to give up our plans."

Redrick studied her face for a moment, the little muscles in his jaw and forehead twitching as if he couldn't decide how to react. But then he grinned. "I know for a fact that Jonathan Graylick has been working on a script about two . . . sisters. No promises, of course."

"But Jonathan Graylick." Olivia sat back in her chair. "Isn't he at Warner Bros.?"

Redrick raised his brows. "Yes, he is."

"We're contracted to MGM."

"It's not uncommon for studios to lend their actresses to one another. I can work it out."

"And we'll be in the same movie together?" Issa asked. She missed working with Olivia.

"We wouldn't want to separate the two of you, would we?" Redrick said. His tongue darted out; whether subtly hinting at something or simply a habit he had, Issa was repulsed. It took all her acting talent not to let it show on her face.

"We'll think about it," Olivia said.

Redrick laughed, but he scribbled down an address anyway and handed it to her. "Don't think too hard, sweetheart. We wouldn't want you getting wrinkles."

Chapter Thirty

"Ugh, what a vulgar, disgusting man," Issa said as soon as they were in the elevator.

"Shh," Olivia said. "Anyone can hear us."

"I think they'd agree." Issa choked on a gag.

"Me too. But we don't want to ruin any chances. We have to go to his stupid party. If the trophy is at his house, I can keep him distracted while you search for it."

"There's no way I'm leaving you alone with that pervert."

"I can handle it. We'll have Ava."

"What can Ava do?" Issa asked.

"She's getting stronger. From what you described, maybe . . . maybe she can do more." Olivia adjusted her purse over her shoulder. "We'll ask her what she thinks."

The elevator slowed as it reached the lobby. "Are you headed to the soundstage?" Issa asked.

"Yes. Where are you going? You have the whole day free, right? Doesn't it feel nice?"

"It feels odd," Issa said. "I don't think I like free time."

"Oh, honey, just go home and relax. Read a book or something, or go eat at the commissary." Olivia nudged her playfully. "Maybe you'll run into your writer friend."

Issa willed herself not to blush. She hadn't heard from Jem. Maybe her unconventional stance on love had scared him off.

They parted ways at a fork in the path, and on a whim, Issa decided to visit her aunt.

In Chinatown, the air smelled of grilled beef and jasmine rice. She passed a tea shop, the drapes pulled back from the storefront window to reveal a traditional low tea table with floor mats, small porcelain cups set around a cast-iron teapot. It made her want to sit still and rest for a bit. She missed the days when she and Olivia would roam the neighborhood after school, going on little adventures.

Auntie Yen's building was securely locked, but just as Issa stepped back, a figure appeared behind the smudged windowpane above the knob. A second later, a man in a black suit and fedora hat opened the door, standing aside to let her in. He said nothing but greeted her with a nod.

Issa walked down the hall, looking over her shoulder, but the man had already disappeared. Yen must have known that she was coming to visit.

She knocked on the apartment door, and Yen opened it a second later in a red dress suit with a tight pencil skirt.

"You're here," she said as a greeting.

Issa bowed with her arms crossed. "Are you busy?"

"No, of course it's fine. I've made tea."

"Thank you." Issa took off her shoes and placed them on the shelving unit by the door. The apartment was quiet; the only person there was a man wiping the glass windows at the back of the living room.

"Do you want to talk to Bà Ngoại today?" Auntie Yen asked, going to the sofa where she had a tea tray set up with a pot and cups and a plate of rolled wafer cookies.

"I'd like to talk to you alone first," Issa said, joining her. "I mean, we can talk to Bà Ngoại, too, if you want to conjure her, but I just thought it'd be nice to chat. I should have called first."

"It wouldn't have mattered. We've had trouble with the phone lines lately," Auntie Yen said, handing Issa a cup, which Issa accepted with both hands. She waited for Yen to pick up her own cup and sip before she did the same.

"Does it involve the Uncles?" Issa asked.

Yen sighed and closed her eyes. Except for the tight wrinkles around her eyes, her expression might have been mistaken for pleasure. "Yes. But I don't want to talk about that right now. All I do is talk about that with everyone here."

There was a knock at the door. As the man cleaning the window went to open it, Auntie Yen said to him in Vietnamese, "I don't want to be disturbed."

"Yes, madame," he responded. He whispered to someone at the door, then glanced over his shoulder; when Yen ignored him determinedly, he shook his head at the visitor, closed the door, and went back to his cleaning.

"What's troubling you?" Auntie Yen asked.

"Oh, nothing," Issa said.

"Tell me. You only visit when you need help with something."

"That's not . . ." Issa couldn't even finish protesting because it was indeed true. She sought out Auntie Yen only when she needed help or when she had to, as stipulated by her deal with Bà Ngoại, to get her monthly allowance.

"Oh, don't feel bad about it, we've been through this," Auntie Yen said. "I only meant that I'm here to help, so whatever it is you need, I'll see what I can do." Then, as her way of lightening the mood, she added, "Any actresses you want me to . . ." She jerked a thumb across her neck and clicked her tongue.

Issa laughed. "No, not yet anyway."

"Just say the word. It'll be easy."

"You're the first person I'll ask."

"And expect nothing but the best." Yen smiled at her, and Issa found herself wondering, not for the first time, if this was how it would have been had Ma allowed her to stay in touch with the clan. This easy way of being around family.

With Ma, things were always stiff and a bit tense. They loved each other, but Ma was not a mushy, feely, hugging type. She was more of a scolding, teach-the-values-of-hard-work-and-sacrifice type. Her words of affection, rare as they were, usually preluded an argument that had been brewing for days. Not that Auntie Yen struck her as incredibly affectionate either. Issa never realized she even wanted something like that, but suddenly it sounded very comforting.

"Speaking of uncles, Olivia's paid us an uninvited visit," Issa said. "Apparently he came asking for money."

"Don't give him a penny. That type will never be satisfied, and you'll be essentially keeping him on your payroll."

"That's what Olivia said. Well, not exactly. But."

"Do you want me to take care of it?" Auntie Yen asked.

"No. Olivia said no. But I don't know. He scares me. Mostly because he scares her."

"I can have our men watch over you two."

"That won't be necessary. Or even possible with the security at the studio."

"Clearly it's not that effective, if Olivia's uncle got through."

"Oh, I don't know . . ." Issa's teacup shook, so she set it down before she spilled any. "I wish everything would just . . . I thought life would be easy once I got into the movies. It was all I wanted for so long, but it seems as if it's just the same, but more . . . complicated."

She felt silly for complaining when, truly, everything she'd ever wanted was happening exactly as she wanted it, while Auntie Yen had much bigger troubles of her own. Yet Yen listened to her, calmly and without judgment.

"What else is troubling you?" Yen asked.

"Bà Ngoại has been teaching me more . . . powers," Issa said. "Well, 'teaching' is putting it diplomatically."

Yen's lips twitched, as if she knew what Issa was really saying. "I thought you were never interested in this sort of thing before."

"Only because Ma forbade it."

"Stop using that as an excuse. I'm tired of hearing it. You're a grown woman now, and even before that, you did what you wanted. You take after your grandmother—steadfast and stubborn. So don't blame it on your ma. You were scared of it. Even when you visited against your mother's wishes, you wanted nothing to do with it. You once asked me to cover up all the mirrors and turn the photographs face down, do you remember that?"

Issa nodded, stopping herself from explaining that it had been more out of habit than fear, since at home, Ma draped a sheet over the wall mirror in the hallway, and she turned pictures of people to face away from her wherever she went.

Auntie Yen might have lectured more, but she seemed to take pity on Issa.

"I had a weird dream a few weeks ago," Issa said, describing how she'd channeled herself into Ava's memory. "I asked Bà about it, but she doesn't seem concerned. In fact, she was impressed that I managed to do it at all, but it was so terrifying, Auntie. I don't want it to happen again. And before that night, I was able to touch Ava. I didn't think that was possible."

"Hmm," Auntie Yen said. "Yes, that is odd."

"Should I be worried? Maybe we should stop conjuring Ava. But Olivia trusts her so much, and she relies on her for her acting. I don't see how she'd want to stop. And Ava is so unhappy."

"Some people don't adjust well to death."

"You should see how sad she is. She's so lonely. I wouldn't want that . . . I should hope someone would still want to be my friend once I pass."

"If Bà Ngoại isn't concerned, then there's nothing you should be worried about. But it's still a good idea to learn more about what you're getting into." Auntie Yen took a deep breath. "About the dream, I've never been able to do it myself. I can see why Bà is impressed with you."

Issa was surprised to hear this. "It can't be that important a skill, then. If you never needed it, then why should I?"

Yen nodded with understanding. "We each have our separate gifts. I've always been able to see a bit into the future—nothing life-changing. Just the occasional vision, and only with lots of practice. If you don't want to develop this skill, then certainly no one will make you. But at least learn more about it so that you can prevent it from happening again, if nothing else."

"I suppose that's not a bad plan. Would you be able to teach me?"

"I'll need some time to gather the training materials. It's been a while since we've needed them, and I'll have to consult with Bà Ngoại on where to get started. Come back in a few days, and we can begin your lessons."

"Thank you so much, Auntie Yen," Issa said, bowing.

"You're my heir," said Auntie Yen. "This would have happened sooner or later. But I'm glad you're the one who wants it."

The words sent a jolt through Issa. She hated being reminded of the fact, and knew she'd never be prepared to take over. But that, she decided, was a problem—and an argument—for the future.

Chapter Thirty-One

Auntie Yen ordered food and made Issa eat while she made phone call after phone call, talking in such angry, rapid-fire Vietnamese—sprinkled occasionally with Chinese—that Issa couldn't follow even if she cared to. When she left, she thought of paying Ma a visit, but it would be too late by the time she made it back to Culver City—Ma would have left for work.

The dressing room was empty and dark, and for a second she debated going to the commissary for a hot drink, the image of Jem Meier popping into her mind, which she shook out immediately. It was only because Olivia had mentioned him, not because Issa actually cared to run into him. If he wasn't interested in calling her, then she wasn't going to chase after him.

It had been a breezy day, and the wind picked up speed, howling and rattling the windows. The building made eerie creaking sounds. Issa turned on every single light in the apartment, even going into Olivia's room to flick on the lamps. Something in the mirror caught Issa's eye. It wasn't a reflection that startled her, it was how filthy the glass was. Rusty spots, brown globs, and other gross markings of indeterminate origin covered the surface.

Odd. Olivia had never been messy. In fact, Issa was the one Ma usually scolded for not tidying up, while Olivia always cleaned up after herself, perhaps because she had never felt like their place was hers.

The rest of the room was clean, not so much as a sock in sight. Everything in its place. Unlike Issa's room, which was cluttered with half the contents of her closet.

Issa brushed it aside. Olivia was her own person and could do what she wanted in the privacy of her own room.

After a relaxing bath, Issa went to the living room to read a book, wondering when Olivia would come home. They didn't have any plans, but she missed having her around.

No matter how much Issa tried to pay attention to her book, she was too aware of the mirror behind her, and even though it remained clear and empty, she couldn't stop looking over her shoulder every few seconds, expecting someone to show up.

"Ava?" she whispered, unable to help herself. But nothing happened. Ava was probably with Olivia.

She must have fallen asleep on the couch because voices and giggles woke her, though Issa was too groggy to fully open her eyes.

"Shhh," she heard Olivia say. "Issa is sleeping, the poor thing, she must be exhausted." Her footsteps pattered to the bar cart, where Issa heard her pour herself a drink.

"You've both been working so hard," Ava purred back.

Issa wanted to open her eyes and tell them she was awake, but her lids felt so heavy and she was so cozy on the couch. A second later, something enveloped her—one of the throw blankets usually draped over the back. Olivia must have covered Issa with it.

"You two take such good care of each other," Ava said.

"We have to. We have no one else."

"What do you mean? Issa has her mother and aunt and grandmother."

"All right, then, *I* have no one else. Issa saved me. If it hadn't been for her, I . . . I'd probably be on the streets or something. One of those girls parents are always warning their daughters not to become."

Ava laughed. "Oh, you're serious," she said, cutting herself off. "Darling, it couldn't have been that bad for you."

Olivia's voice sounded like she had taken a seat on the armchair to the left of the couch. "My parents died a long time ago. I was told it was a car accident, but later I learned it was a drug overdose. At least they were together. Romantic."

Ava laughed but made a sound of sympathy. "You poor darling. How you must have struggled to move up in life."

Olivia didn't say anything for a long time. Issa finally managed to pry her eyelids apart, but neither woman paid attention to her.

"Everyone in my neighborhood said I was lucky my uncle was willing to take me in." Olivia stared down at her wine glass. She looked so small, curled up on the armchair, her legs tucked beneath her. "Lucky," she whispered, her voice breaking at the end.

"Oh dear," Ava said. Her arms lifted, like she wanted to give Olivia a hug. "Well, there's no more of that. He's gone from your life now. You never have to see him again."

Olivia's throat moved as if she could barely manage to swallow her tears. "You're right." She gave a watery smile into the mirror at Ava's reflection. Then she noticed Issa was awake.

"Olivia," Issa started to say. Olivia had never opened up like that before, never explained how her parents had died or what living with her uncle was like. When Issa asked, she would wave it away, or change the topic, or refuse to answer altogether. Listening to her confide so much to Ava—whom they'd only known for a short time—made her throat clog up with anger and sympathy all at once. Why had Olivia never wanted to talk about it with her?

Even now, Olivia morphed her expression into pleasant surprise. "You're up!" she shouted, leaping from the chair to the couch, giggling maniacally as she threw herself on Issa in a hug.

"Yes, I am." Issa laughed along, even though she wanted to return to the conversation. Olivia's arm pressed against her shoulder as she eased off her.

"Oh, we've had the best night." It was clear that Olivia was drunk from her breath and glazed eyes. "What are you doing sleeping out here when you have a room, silly?"

"She was waiting for you like a mother hen," Ava said.

Issa sat up, pushing Olivia gently aside. Ava danced about, dressed in one of her historical costumes.

"How sweet," Ava said. "I wish I had someone to wait up for me."

"Issa," Olivia said in an excited whisper, taking Issa's hands. "We found something out. Look what Ava can do."

"What?" Issa asked.

"Show her, Ava."

Ava stopped dancing and smiled with delight. She reached out a hand, and for a second, Issa thought Ava was about to lunge forward and grab her throat. A flash of an image—angry black eyes, dark veins beneath translucent gray skin—but then it was gone. Issa blinked and shook her head.

A glass tumbler with melting ice sitting on the side table beside the couch rose into the air as if someone held it. As if Ava held it.

Issa covered her mouth. "How?" she whispered. It came out so small that she didn't hear her own voice.

"I'm getting stronger!" Ava said with glee. But her concentration must have slipped because the tumbler dropped and shattered on the hard floor.

The girls screamed. Olivia covered her head and ducked, a rather overdramatic reaction, but Issa could see that her expression of fright was genuine.

"Are you all right?" Issa asked.

Olivia took a few deep breaths, blinking back tears. She looked at Issa as if just remembering she was there, though her eyes still seemed distant and unfocused, and not because of the alcohol.

"I'm sorry, darlings," Ava said. "It seems my control just isn't there yet. With more practice, I'm sure I'll get better."

"Olivia?" Issa asked, still worried about her friend's absent look.

"I'll clean it up," Olivia said, standing.

"It's all right, I can do it," Issa said.

"No, really. You're not even wearing shoes, just stay on the sofa."

Olivia hadn't bothered to take off her heels, and she went to the broom closet to get a dustpan, then swept up the chunks of glass and ice. Once most of it was cleared, Issa went to the kitchen for a dishrag to wipe up the remaining mess. Ava continued dancing in the mirror, but after a while she must have gotten bored when no one joined in her merriment because she waved goodbye and disappeared.

Issa wanted to tell Olivia about her day with Auntie Yen, but Olivia yawned loudly.

"Well, good night," Olivia said, not waiting for an answer before she shut her door and went to bed.

Olivia's film was quite behind schedule, which meant the producers forced the cast to work longer hours in the hopes of making up time.

While Issa waited for her next script, she busied herself by taking lessons with Auntie Yen, learning other ways to conjure ghosts, though the incense and mirror were the easiest and least messy.

"Statues work as well," Yen explained. "Or any sort of likeness. The more sentimental, the stronger the connection."

Auntie Yen didn't seem alarmed when Issa told her what Ava could do—lift the tumbler without needing to touch it.

"There are many different types of spirits," Auntie Yen said. "The more they're loved, the stronger they'll be, the stronger their connection to the living world as well. That doesn't just mean that they're able to speak to the living, but that they can sometimes affect the living world in corporeal ways. Ava was a loved star—her fans and admirers probably make her even stronger."

"And there must be a lot of her pictures out there," Issa said.

"And movies," Auntie Yen said.

"Movies count?"

"Any likeness does. Anything connecting their spirit to the memories of the living."

"No wonder she's developing all this strength." Issa felt better knowing there was an explanation for it, consoling herself with the fact that Ava didn't mean them any harm. How could she? She was their friend.

Issa wished they had more time to talk, but whenever she visited Yen, the apartment was always bustling with people, and Yen seemed distracted, constantly interrupted by her workers, so Issa felt like she was imposing and usually rushed to leave as fast as she could.

She visited Ma at home as well. Ma led such a different life from Auntie Yen as well as Issa and Olivia, and she never asked at all about the studio or what Issa's work felt like. They drank tea at the kitchen table while she updated Issa on people at her church whom Issa barely remembered. When Issa tried to bring up her movies, Ma would mumble something noncommittal in response but never ask further about it. Issa supposed she simply didn't care, and in fact went out of her way to make sure Issa knew she didn't want to hear about it.

Issa couldn't help the painful jerk in her heart, but she wasn't surprised. After all, her mother had never wanted her to go into show business, believing films were products of the devil. She must have felt like movies had stolen her daughter from her. But at least Ma had stopped lecturing her about it.

The day finally came when Issa and Olivia's movie together, *Lost in the Queen's Love*, premiered. Invitations arrived, their names embossed on thick cardstock like a wedding invitation. The studio sent dresses. Olivia wore a flowy lavender number and Issa a deep yellow that looked surprisingly flattering against her tan skin tone. Makeup artists and hair stylists arrived to make them presentable, and the studio sent a car to escort them to Grauman's Chinese Theatre on Hollywood Boulevard.

When they stepped out of the car, a camera flashed with a loud pop. They posed with the other supporting cast, feeling rather glam in front of all those bright lights.

Maggie Laken, one of the cast, grabbed Issa's hand and shook it excitedly.

"This is all so fancy, isn't it?" she asked as they walked into the darkened theater together.

Issa could only nod back, aware that the photographers never stopped snapping. Her skin prickled with awareness—everyone was watching, eyes peeled for any sign of discomfort, awkwardness, or, God forbid, ugliness. She kept a smile pasted on her face, tried to ignore the sweat beading on her upper lip, and focused her efforts on keeping her brows relaxed and happy.

When they took their seats and the theater went dark, Issa finally let out a breath, feeling as if she were still a little girl, sneaking around town with her best friend and spending their only dollar on a movie they technically weren't allowed to see.

But then the silver screen lit up, and the opening credits played, and, goodness, there was her name, right below Olivia's, and tears flooded her eyes before she could stop them.

She took Olivia's hand, and Olivia squeezed.

It was the first time they'd watched the movie from start to finish. Because everything had been shot nonsequentially, Issa had never fully grasped the story. Now as it played out, she had an innate sense that it was, perhaps not a masterpiece, but . . . it was good. She was in a good movie. She had a speaking role in something that was going to be a success, she could feel it.

When Olivia's monologue scene came on, she steeled herself for that old resentment that had bubbled up during production, but Olivia was so beautiful, so talented, so wonderful as she said the right words and tilted her head and cried sad, pretty tears that Issa didn't care. She was just as moved as the rest of the audience.

And when it was Issa's character's turn to speak, Olivia started crying, threw her arms around Issa, and kept pressing her lips to Issa's forehead like she had never been so proud.

When the movie ended, there was a brief moment of shocked silence. Then everyone clapped. The cast hugged and congratulated each other, and then they all filed out, heading to a bar at a nearby hotel where the rest of the night became a blur of clinking ice and glittery glass, and everyone smiling at her and wanting to hug her or shake her hand or buy her a drink or kiss her cheek. Men handed her their business cards—producers and writers and even a few directors, and then Eric Goldman appeared, his arm around her shoulder like an overprotective father in his sweater-vest.

"I told you it would happen, didn't I?" he said, squeezing and giving her a little shake. Emmett Tratee stood just behind him, smiling at Issa proudly as if he, too, had had a hand in making her a success. Staring at Goldman's face, Issa felt a flash of dread in the pit of her stomach. Guilt, perhaps, that they had used him—she and Olivia and Ava playing at their ghostly seduction—when he was quite innocent.

But like a spot of water in a heated pan, her unease disappeared in a puff of steam, and an overwhelming gratitude took its place. Who cared how they'd got here? So what if they had cheated? She was quite sure many other actresses did the same, in some way or another. She was grateful that Goldman entered their lives when he did, along with Ava. Because it was thanks to the two of them that Issa was finally where she wanted to be.

"You sure did," Issa said. In a moment of impulsivity, she leaned forward and gave him a hug. "Thank you so much, Mr. Goldman."

"Come along, now. After two movies, I think it's high time you call me Eric, don't you think."

She kissed his surprisingly soft cheek. "Thanks, Eric."

One of the producers pulled him away, and Issa sipped her drink in a brief awkward moment when she had no one to talk to. Olivia was surrounded by the cast, and Issa was about to make her way over when she felt someone behind her and breathed in the familiar sandalwood cologne.

"Jem," she said, filled with a bubbly excitement at the sight of him in his pressed suit.

"Hi." He leaned down and gave her one of those air-kisses, pressing his cheek to hers in almost chaste mockery.

"I wasn't sure you'd be here."

"I decided only at the last minute to come," he said. "The film was wonderful. *You* were wonderful. Congratulations."

"Thank you." Neither of them said anything for a moment, both waiting for the other to steer the conversation. They hadn't seen each other since their first and only date, which might have ended in a kiss had Olivia's uncle not been screaming in front of Issa's dressing room. But it felt presumptuous to assume he would have. She found the situation entirely confusing, and wished she had a script to follow.

"Why haven't you—" she blurted out, but, thankfully, he spoke at the same time.

"Have you been—" He stopped and grinned. "You first."

She shook her head, not wanting to ruin this moment, whatever this was. The wine was starting to heat her veins, making her feel bolder than if she were clearheaded. "Would you have kissed me? That night we went to dinner?"

She wasn't sure who was more surprised at the question—her or Jem. His eyebrows rose, and a slow smile played on his lips.

"I honestly don't know," he said, which made her flush hot and cold. What was this? What did he want? Didn't he like her? Why would he ask her out if he didn't? But why wouldn't he try to kiss her if he did? And why seek her out in these settings if he wanted nothing from her?

"Oh." She didn't like these games. She longed for a clear-cut answer, directions on how to act. Wishing to escape, she searched the crowd instinctively for Olivia.

Jem's touch on her forearm pulled her back. "I meant, I wasn't sure if that was what you wanted," he said. "What with your stance on love . . . and ambition."

"Oh," Issa repeated.

"Of course, I respect all your goals and dreams and such," he added. "But the truth is, I can't. I mean—I can't stop thinking about you. But I also want to wish you all the best . . . in your . . . endeavors." He was nervous, dropping his gaze, then meeting hers, his lips moving as though at a loss for words, which she found captivating in a man who should have been proficient with them.

She took his hand, and his expression registered surprise at her touch. "I don't have much experience in these matters," she said slowly. "But I believe it's quite possible for me to have dreams and kiss you at the same time."

He leaned down, as if he was about to do exactly that, in the middle of the party. "Right now?" he whispered.

Issa giggled. She would have done it—who cared what anyone said—but someone bumped into her from behind. It was Maggie Laken, laughing hysterically, yanking on Issa's arm.

"Come, darling, they want to photograph all the ladies-in-waiting. You can have her back." Maggie winked at Jem as she pried Issa's hand off his. "After."

"Call me," she told him over his shoulder, practically floating as she joined her friends.

Chapter Thirty-Two

The night of Weston Redrick's dinner party, Issa and Olivia took a taxi across the city to West Hollywood where the director's three-story house was squeezed between identical three-story houses, the long driveway gated by a fence where they stood waiting for five minutes in the dark before he bothered to let them in.

They hadn't known what to expect, having never been to a dinner party before, but it seemed socially acceptable for actresses to dress as fancy as they wished. Issa wore one of her favorites from the studio, a dainty thing with a Peter Pan collar around the neck. Olivia, on the other hand, wore a formfitting dress accentuating her slim curves and tall height, paired with a light jacket.

Inside Redrick's house, a sterile quality permeated the air. The minimalist decor looked like it was designed by a professional—the walls were papered with a classic geometric pattern, the carpet a plush beige topped with brown leather couches and dark-wood furniture. Lamps were placed strategically in all the corners so that the whole place was cast in dim lighting and an inviting glow.

"Come in, come in," Redrick said, opening the door wide. His mustache must have been trimmed recently, cut bluntly above his smirking mouth.

Olivia slipped out of her jacket. It wasn't a cold evening—she'd worn it for the effect of that very moment, her shoulders appearing sensuously, bare and tan and toned. Redrick took the jacket and handed it to a man who draped it over an arm and disappeared, like they were in some historical drama.

"Let me give you a tour," he offered. They passed a group of men and women sitting in the living room with drinks in their hands, as he led them straight to the trophy case. "I remember you two admiring these in my office."

"You've had such an interesting career," Issa breathed, leaning down to scan the titles on the plaques. But none of them were from Ava's movie.

"Those aren't even all of them," he boasted. "I haven't finished unpacking yet. Just bought this place last month."

"And it's gorgeous," Olivia said, hanging on to his arm.

He smiled at her, like a puffed-up rooster.

The doorbell rang then. Redrick looked momentarily confused as his staff answered the door, even more so when a group of semifamous actors walked into the house, shouting greetings at Redrick and the other guests.

"Heard you were having a party, Weston!" one handsome actor said, clapping him on the back. "Glad we finally get a chance to see the place."

Redrick looked poised to kick him and his friends out, but the bell rang again and even more people arrived. Olivia smiled knowingly at Issa, tilting her head toward the hallway. Issa hesitated, watching Olivia walk up to another actress and greet her with a casual kiss on the cheek. When had Olivia become the type of person who could do that so easily? She seemed to know everyone who arrived, though it only made sense since she had, after all, invited them here to distract Redrick.

And distracted he was. His face turned red and he looked flustered, but he couldn't turn so many actors away without seeming rude, so he spent the next few minutes ordering his staff to open more wine and bring out more food.

"Issa Bui," a man called out. He was big and stout, with gray hair and whiskers, practically shoving his way between two guests to get to her. "Issa Bui," he repeated, breathing heavily. He declared her name like a fun word he'd just learned. "I saw you in *Lost in the Queen's Love*. You were wonderful. So beautiful. In fact, I couldn't tell you were Oriental for most of the movie, except in certain angles. Almost didn't recognize you when you showed up here, but Weston told us to expect you."

Issa wasn't sure how to respond to that, so she just smiled and took a sip of wine.

This pleased the man, who kept going. "I've been hoping to cast a girl like yourself. Weston probably told you about my next project. A poor homely girl wants to move to America from her provincial country and seeks the help of a rich man in order to do so. You can't imagine the number of people this happens to in real life. It will be a smashing hit, I'm sure."

"And I'll be the poor provincial ugly girl?" Issa asked.

"The role would suit you perfectly," the man proclaimed, oblivious to the irony in her tone.

Issa looked across the crowd, spotting Olivia with Redrick.

"It's a sad role," the man continued. "But you'll find that the audiences clamor for that sort of thing. It will win you an award, I'm sure of it. A nomination, at least. All sad stories do."

Issa swirled her wine, watching the red liquid cling to the glass and drip slowly down. "What does that say about the award-givers, I wonder."

"That life is sad. After all, movies are supposed to reflect life, and we can't all have happy endings."

"No, especially not girls like me," Issa said, giving him a beautiful smile to hide the sarcasm.

He blinked, though whether dazzled by her smile or wondering if she'd just insulted him, she couldn't tell. Luckily, a waiter came by with a tray of food, and the man turned away to reach for a deviled egg. In the distraction, Issa wove her way through the guests and down the empty hallway.

Slipping farther from the party, Issa tried all the doors in the hopes of finding the one where Redrick kept his unpacked trophies. The first room was locked, the second a small office that only had a desk, the drawers still empty. Finally, after a dusty closet full of mops and cleaning supplies, she discovered a small room full of boxes.

She shut the door, and the noise from the party dulled to a muffle. The tape had been removed from most of the boxes, as if Redrick had been called away in the middle of the job. The first two she looked in were full of movie reels, labeled with titles she'd never heard of.

After opening ten or so—full of a random assortment of scripts, books, and films—she sat back and sighed at the remaining boxes in the room. There had to be a hundred. How would she look through them all?

As she spotted her reflection in the dark window, an idea occurred to her.

"Ava?" she whispered, not sure the spirit would show. Things hadn't exactly been tense between them lately, but Issa hadn't called on her at all since that moment when they'd touched. Ava often visited with Olivia, and she was all too aware that Ava now preferred Olivia's company over her own.

To Issa's relief, Ava appeared a second later, looking around curiously. "Where are we?" She wore a red flapper dress, as if she'd prepared for the party.

"Weston Redrick's home," Issa said, getting up off the floor. "The trophy might be here somewhere. Olivia's distracting him, and we don't have much time."

Ava pouted as she surveyed the mess. "What can I do?"

"You can move things now, can't you? Can you help look through a few boxes?"

"I can try." Ava reached out and mimed opening a box. One popped open next to Issa. "It's not that hard." Her face brightened. "I think the trophy is here somewhere. I feel stronger. Like it's giving me power."

"Do you feel strong toward any particular box?" Issa asked.

"Hmm." She closed her eyes and twirled, a gentle smile on her face. "It's over here. I can sense it. In that corner box."

Of course, it was a box in the very back, behind several stacks, and it was on the bottom. Issa struggled to get to it, choking on a plume of dust as she finally got it open.

"There it is!" Ava shouted, pointing at a sharp golden shiny thing.

Issa reached in and extracted a gold-man trophy, the classic symbol of the Oscars. All this work for such a small thing.

She held it toward Ava, who raised her hand to cup the statue, tracing over the face affectionately as if it were a real person. They both forgot that she couldn't hold anything when she tried to grab on to it and Issa let go.

It clattered to the floor.

"Don't break it!" Ava shouted.

"Sorry," Issa said, picking it up. She'd brought a big purse specifically for this purpose, and she hid the trophy inside it. The room was a mess, and she tried to stack the boxes back as neatly as she could.

"Go check on Olivia, could you?" Issa asked. "There's a party going on, but you never know . . ."

Ava grinned. "There's always a party." She disappeared through the walls. Issa continued moving boxes back where she thought they belonged until she was sweating and covered in dust. She was so on edge, worried about getting caught, that she jumped a foot in the air when Ava reappeared a minute later.

"She's fine," Ava said. "Redrick is talking to her about some movies that might suit the two of you, together."

"Really?" Despite her panic, Issa stopped and held a hand over her heart.

"Oh, darling, you don't want to do a film with this man."

"But if they're lead roles—"

"Issa, dear, you need to hurry. Go clean yourself up."

Right. Issa slipped through the door, Ava following at a distance.

"How ugly," Ava commented, running a finger along the wallpaper. "He's always had terrible taste."

Issa went to the bathroom and wiped off smudges of dirt from her face. Her hair was a lost cause, so she tied it up instead.

When she emerged, the party was in full swing, the conversation such a loud buzz that she could hardly hear herself think. Some people recognized her, waving and reaching out for hugs. Issa pushed through the crowd as politely as she could until she spotted Redrick and Olivia in the corner in the living room.

"Where were you?" Redrick asked her suspiciously.

"I got caught up in the party," she said, waving behind her.

"Mager was looking for you," Redrick said.

"Who?"

"The producer—he said he spoke to you about his melodrama." Redrick sneered as if he didn't think much of Mager's movie either.

"But I like Graylick's idea much better," Olivia said. "The one with the sisters."

Redrick looked between the two of them. There was something lascivious in his expression that sent shivers down Issa's spine.

Ava caught up to them at that second—Issa had assumed she'd just disappeared. When she spotted Redrick, Ava's face scrunched up in repulsion. She went up to him and slapped him across the face. Her hand went straight through his head and out the other side. Issa's eyes widened and she curled her fingers into fists in order not to cover her mouth, but whether she wanted to laugh or scream, she wasn't sure.

"Horrible man," Ava hissed.

Issa could tell that Olivia also struggled not to respond, gritting her teeth to keep from laughing. Issa focused on Redrick instead, registering his suspicion. He knew she'd been up to something, even if he couldn't figure out what.

"Oh, I'm sorry," Issa said, covering her mouth. "But Olivia, darling, I don't feel well. I think we better call it a night."

"Yes, we'll flag a taxi," Olivia said.

"Nonsense, I'll drive you myself," Redrick said.

"Don't you girls dare," Ava said.

"You can't leave your own party," Olivia said.

"'Course I can. I don't know half these people. No idea how word even got out about this—it was supposed to be a small gathering." He dug in his pockets for his keys.

"I've already called for a cab," Issa blurted.

Redrick glanced down the hall. "How?"

"Yes—well, I asked one of your waitstaff to call for me."

He seemed mildly disappointed but didn't know how to make them stay, and Issa and Olivia were already rushing toward the door.

"Thank you for the party," Olivia said.

"It was a wonderful evening," Issa added.

"You lying son of a bitch," Ava hissed, unheard.

Chapter Thirty-Three

They walked for almost an hour before they reached a main street busy enough to hail a cab home, and by then they were in hysterical laughter. Ava stayed with them the entire time, her gray pallor occasionally fading to smoke in the dark night only to appear solidly a few seconds later, especially when she got close to her trophy, which rested safely inside Issa's purse.

Issa took it out as they walked, showing it to Olivia.

"An Oscar," Olivia said, holding it with reverence. "What a beauty."

Indeed, it did say *Best Picture*, not *Director*. When they got to their dressing room, they poured themselves well-deserved drinks after the long night and fell across the sofa. Issa placed the trophy in the armchair so that Ava could curl her ghostly form around it and cradle it like an infant.

"I've missed you," she said, stroking the face of the statue.

"I'm glad to see you so happy," Olivia said. "We should have gotten it much sooner, I'm sorry." Olivia watched Ava with a motherly expression, and Issa felt a small unease tug in her chest, but she dismissed it as a silly reaction, tinged with petty, childlike jealousy.

"Was Redrick annoyed that people crashed his party?" Issa asked Olivia instead.

"He didn't seem too surprised," Olivia said. "This kind of stuff seems to happen a lot."

"He seemed suspicious of us, in the end."

"He's not a stupid man," Ava said. "But don't worry. There's nothing he can do to you."

Olivia looked mildly worried, staring down at her wine. "He really wants to cast me in his next movie."

"That's what they all say, darling," Ava said.

"I told him I would do it as long as you and I get to be in it together," Olivia said to Issa.

"And what did he say?" Not that Issa wanted to be in Redrick's movie, but he had seemed more interested in Olivia than in her, and she couldn't help smarting a bit from that.

"Well, the producer Jonathan Graylick overheard us, and said he's been wanting to do something with two sisters for a while—a musical."

"How exciting," Issa said, leaning forward.

"You two can't sing," Ava said.

"But we can learn," Issa pointed out. "They give free lessons at the studio."

"Redrick seemed hesitant to agree," Olivia said. "He said we shouldn't be too attached to each other. That we'd get nowhere if we weren't willing to work alone. Why can't they just let us stick together?"

Issa felt better after that, reassured that Olivia was still as dedicated to their friendship as she was. Eventually she went to bed, leaving Olivia to stay up and keep Ava company. The gray actress remained curled on the armchair, still cuddling her trophy as Issa closed her bedroom door.

One afternoon, the phone rang while Issa lounged on the sofa reading a book, debating whether to make some tea or head to the commissary. She sprang forward to answer it, hoping it was news about her next role.

"I understand if you've forgotten about me completely by now"—Jem's voice sounded gravelly over the phone—"but it took me a while to track down your number."

"Jem?" She clutched the phone. "Actually, I feel rather silly because I realized that I'd never given it to you."

"I managed to trick the operator into connecting with your dressing room."

"How resourceful." She grinned, waiting eagerly for his next words.

"How about lunch soon, if you're not busy?"

"I'm in between films right now. I suppose I can make time for you."

He chuckled and made plans to pick her up the following day. Issa couldn't sit still after that and spent most of the next few hours trying on all the things in her closet, hoping to strike a balance between sexy and casual. When Olivia came home, she watched Issa with amusement, but she retreated to her room with Ava after Issa rejected her third outfit suggestion.

When it was finally time for their date, Issa was so nervous that she almost left without her shoes, padding several steps into the hallway in her socks before she realized why it felt so odd. Jem waited outside in his car. He talked excitedly about his next script as he drove her quite a distance to an Italian restaurant in Signal Hill. They chatted about nonsense, Issa surprised at how easy it was to be with him. After lunch he drove them to a hilltop park so they could enjoy the sweeping views of the city and watch the sun cast a golden glow over the oil derricks lining the coast in the distance.

Finally, when she couldn't stand it anymore, Issa turned to Jem. They sat side-by-side on a bench in the dusk. People were leaving, and crickets started chirping along the bushes around them.

"Well?" she demanded.

Jem smiled, draping an arm behind her. He leaned close and then paused as if for effect, smiling like he knew a delightful secret, and Issa couldn't stand it any longer. She grabbed the back of his head and kissed him herself. The moment their lips met, she sighed and practically melted against him, grateful when he wrapped his arms around her and pulled her against his chest. They stayed on the bench long after the sun had set.

A couple of weeks later, a package showed up at the door. Issa had gone more than a month without working, filling her hours with classes offered on the studio lot between occasional dates with Jem, and she hoped it was news that she'd finally have a new role. She found two documents inside—a script and a contract, this one much shorter than the one she signed in Grenier's office. It was an agreement between MGM and Warner Bros. . . . to lend her out.

For a moment, she thought it was for Jonathan Graylick's movie. He was with Warner Bros., and she would get to work with Olivia. She was even excited to take singing lessons, to learn something new.

But as she read the opening lines, she knew immediately it was not Graylick but that toady producer man who had cornered her at the party and insisted she'd be perfect for the role of a poor homely girl who needed a man to save her.

Her abhorrence for the story only grew the more she read. The main character—her, of course—was mistreated in every aspect of her life, and yet she accepted it as her lot, and in the end, she was abandoned and left for dead and had to make her way in a world that had proven time and again to hate her. Issa didn't want anything to do with the movie, even if it meant giving up a leading role.

When she showed it to Jem during lunch at the commissary, he scanned through the pages. "I don't think it's horrible," he said. "But I can see why you wouldn't relate to the character. She's quite weak, but only at first. I think you can turn it into a worthwhile project."

Instead of reassuring her, his words only made her feel more conflicted.

Olivia came home early that night—filming finally wrapped on her current project—followed closely by Ava, who looked just as gray and pale as the night before, but even more ghostly, like she didn't belong in the glowing light of the setting sun. Issa was so used to her vibrant costumes that the grayness reminded her more of death than the smoke ever had.

"It's not that bad," Olivia said as she skimmed through the script. Issa had given her an earful about how gross the whole thing was. Ava sat on her armchair and listened, keeping her trophy close on the side table next to her, her fingers reaching for it even though she couldn't touch it. "The producer is right. People love sad stories. They always win the awards. The more torturous the suffering, the higher the accolades."

"But . . . but it has . . ." Issa didn't know how to voice her objection to the role. The idea that people like her only deserved to play tragic roles for everyone to dump their guilt on . . . It left a bitter taste in her mouth. Why couldn't she have a happy role? Something with singing and dancing and laughter. "What about Jonathan Graylick's movie?"

"I haven't heard anything," Olivia said. "And there's no way to ask him without going through Redrick."

"Do you think Redrick's behind this?" Issa waved the contract listlessly in her lap.

No one said anything. Ava avoided their eyes, studying her trophy.

Olivia made a sympathetic face. "He must have felt like we snubbed him. I'm sorry, honey. But you can't turn this down. You're on contract with MGM for eight movies, whether they're bad or not, and they're allowed to lend you out to other studios if they wish."

Issa buried her face in her hands, rubbing her temples as a headache began to form. Olivia wrapped an arm around her shoulder.

"Cheer up, Issa. It's only a few weeks of work, and then you'll be right back on this lot."

"And milk the tears for all they're worth," Ava added, speaking for the first time since she'd arrived. "You never know if you'll get an Oscar out of it." She stroked her prized trophy and smiled.

Issa signed the contract, and a few days later, the toady producer Larry Mager called. He came by a few weeks after to personally escort her to the Warner Bros. lot.

"Anything you need while you're filming, you can ask me," he said eagerly. "We can put you up in a dressing room. It's quite up to snuff, I assure you. Perhaps even your own bungalow?"

"I don't think that will be necessary," Issa said.

"You'll change your mind. All the actresses stay on the lot. It makes it much easier when filming runs late. You won't have to make the trek across town at one in the morning."

"I can manage."

"Really it's no trouble. I'll have one set up, and you can choose whether to use it."

"All right, then," Issa said because she didn't want to discuss it any more. She had no intention of setting foot in the bungalow, even if she was bone tired from a day of filming.

She hadn't expected the Warner Bros. studio to be as large as MGM, and she was surprised that it, too, was almost like its own city, equipped with soundstages, houses, and streets with facades. She was enchanted when they passed New York Street with trees covered in tinsel and ornaments for what must have been a holiday movie.

"This is us," Mager said. He was a short, stout man who walked with something of a waddle as he led her into a room with tables arranged in a square so the cast could face each other.

To her surprise, when she entered the room, everyone applauded like she was already the biggest star. She held a hand to her chest in genuine modesty.

"Oh my goodness," she said. "What a welcome. Are you sure you're not waiting for someone else?" She glanced behind her, which caused uproarious laughter even though she was quite serious.

"Brains, talent, and humor," Mager said. "We won't regret making this trade."

"What trade?" Issa asked as he led her to her seat where her nameplate listed her as the lead.

"We lend an actress to MGM, they lend one back," he said.

"Like we're players," said a man next to Issa's seat. He held out a hand. "James Thornton. I play your love interest." A charming smile followed, complete with a twinkle in his deep-blue eyes. Issa's knees wobbled a little as she lowered herself into her chair and took his hand after a pause long enough to be borderline rude.

"Not your real love interest," Thornton continued. "That's not allowed, on account of you being." He gestured to her face, particularly her eyes.

Issa wanted to squeeze them shut. "I see."

"He has that effect on everyone," another man said on his other side with a knowing sort of smile, as if he'd read her speechlessness as awe. "I'm Bill Walker. I play your best friend."

"Nice to meet you," she said, nodding to the rest of the cast.

"We loved your work in *Lost in the Queen's Love*," a woman said. "And your sister's."

"Oh, Olivia—she's not my sister."

"You two look exactly alike."

"Thank you," Issa said, deciding to take it as a compliment and leave it at that.

"All right everyone, time to get started," Mager said. To her surprise, he stayed for the table read after introducing their director. They were stopped a few times to receive notes but got through the script without any major hiccups.

Afterward, Mager escorted her outside. "You must be starving."

"I'm all right." Actually, Issa's stomach growled painfully, but she was determined to lose the pudge growing on her midsection. It would be absolutely embarrassing to have to send all the dresses she'd received from MGM back because she couldn't keep her figure in check.

"I must admit, it's nice to work with a rising star like yourself," Mager said, showing her to his car. "You're not like the other divas who make this work so dreadful sometimes."

"I'm not a diva yet," she pointed out.

He chuckled as he closed the door. He drove her deeper into the backlot, making it obvious they weren't returning to MGM.

"I said I wasn't hungry," Issa said, grumpier than usual because she was, in fact, quite hungry.

"I thought you might want to see your room," Mager said. "Then you can go home and pack, if you choose."

Issa sighed but pressed her lips together. Better to get this over with.

She was even more surprised when they pulled up to a complex of small apartment buildings and little houses. In front was a pond bubbling with spraying water and lily pads floating on the surface. Several actresses walked around, some in costume and some in bathrobes with their hair and makeup done. They smiled at her as Mager put the car in park.

"All the other actresses stay here when they're in the middle of a production," Mager explained. He led her through the entrance, which opened into a courtyard.

"You're in 40B," he said. They walked up the stairs to a dressing room much smaller than the one she shared with Olivia but well equipped and comfortable. Still, all this space, just for her? It was too extravagant by far, and she felt like a stray speck of dirt in the pristine room with its floral wallpaper and old, heavy mahogany furniture like something out of a *Variety* feature on a star in their own home. "Here's the key." He dropped it into her palm. "Of course, you don't have to stay if you don't want to. But you see it's only a five-minute drive from the soundstages, and you can walk safely through the lot. Some actresses like to bicycle around."

"How charming," Issa said. He seemed eager to impress her, to want to keep her happy and in his movie. "Thank you, Mr. Mager."

"Oh, it's Larry, if you please. Come along, then. I'll take you back to MGM."

Chapter Thirty-Four

She found Larry Mager difficult to look at—there was something about his pockmarked skin that made her shudder, his puffy and wide lips reminding her of a bloated frog, his short stumpiness grating on her patience—and yet, he grew on her. He was nice and friendly, incapable of being insulted even during her worse moods. Not that Issa was a prima donna by any means, nor was she openly rude, but sometimes he would talk and talk and she could not gather enough energy to muster an ounce of a response. He seemed used to worse treatment and never cared.

Her affection for him solidified when she arrived early on set one morning. Only the crew were there, working on the fake furniture, and she overheard Mager speaking with the director, Tony Ireland, by the camera equipment.

"She's not right," Ireland was saying. "Her face—it won't work."

"Find better lighting," Mager said. "Work your magic. You've done it before."

They couldn't be talking about her, could they? Issa lingered in the shadows.

"Are you quite sure about this, Larry? That other one was so perfect. She has that charming . . . complexion . . . and her eyes . . . so expressive. She'll draw in crowds, surely."

"It won't be authentic. I like Issa. She's got something about her . . . something that will make this work."

Issa backed away, not wanting them to know she'd heard. She had no doubt about it now—Ireland wanted to replace her. If the director didn't want her in his film, what hope would she have of surviving? Mager was only a producer. He would fight for her—had fought for her—but how much power did he hold? How long would she last?

She was filled with self-doubt after that, overanalyzing every little twitch of the director's face or the fleeting glances of the other crew during rehearsals. This was her first leading role, and she hadn't even wanted it at first. Yet now that she was in danger of losing it, she wanted more than ever to be good enough to keep it.

At first, Issa insisted on being driven back to MGM each night, longing for some familiarity. She started to wonder why after the first weeks. Olivia was never home—production had started on her next film—and even when she was around, Ava was usually there in her gray, smoky form, always with her trophy nearby, distracting Olivia. They laughed and giggled together in such a private manner that Issa felt excluded from the fun, even when they tried to explain the source of a joke or include her in a story.

Ava grew more solid by the day. She hadn't been quite transparent before, but now she was more . . . *there*, a hint of color appearing in her cheeks.

Some nights, Issa and Olivia would both be so exhausted after the long workday that they didn't talk much, heading straight to bed. In the morning, they'd still be lethargic and rather cranky, and once, they had one of their rare arguments when Olivia used up the last of the tea and hadn't bothered to send out for more.

That day Issa had a headache by the time she reached Warner Bros., desperate for some sort of hot drink, which Mager immediately fetched for her. She decided to spend that night in her dressing room instead of going back to MGM. It turned out to be so comfortable and convenient that she went home the next day to pack up her favorite things and the book she was in the middle of reading.

Olivia came home right as she was leaving. Ava was with her, as usual.

"You're moving?" Olivia asked, spotting Issa's weekend bag in her hand. Her mouth fell open like she might cry.

Issa hadn't expected to see her, intending to scribble a short note. "Only for a couple of nights," she said. "I've been staying on set later and later, and this week it will only get worse."

But Olivia took several heavy breaths. "Is this about the tea? I'm sorry—I won't do it again. It was a legitimate mistake. Look, I bought a ton more." She went to the kitchen to show Issa the fifteen boxes barely fitting in the cabinet.

"No, of course not, I'm over that. Ooh, black assam?" Issa picked up a box.

"I know, it's so creamy, I've already tried it."

"Wow, I can't wait."

"Why, have some now!" Olivia scrambled to put the kettle on.

"I don't want to be up too late."

"You're not really going, are you?" Olivia asked.

Ava lowered herself to the armchair, watching the two of them. As always, her trophy sat on the side table. The part of her face closer to the award seemed to glow with an inner light, though it might have been the effect of the lamps from the window.

"I'm not living there, it's more of a hotel," Issa said. "I'll be back this weekend." When Olivia still looked skeptical, she handed her bag over. "Feel how light that is. I'd take a lot more if I was really moving out."

"You could always send for your things." Olivia pouted as she gave the bag back.

"We'll have dinner on Friday," Issa said. "We'll go out—somewhere fancy like we always said we would."

Olivia considered this. "It's a date, then." She opened her arms. Issa leaned in for a hug, relishing the warm moment, which seemed rarer these past few weeks.

"Girls," Ava said from the armchair. "Look at this."

They broke apart. Ava's gray hand wrapped around the trophy, the color of her flesh immediately growing warmer, her wrist and forearm darkening to a lively tan. Even more horrifying, at least to Issa, though it didn't seem to alarm Olivia, Ava picked up the statue and held it triumphantly in the air. It didn't drop, didn't waver, didn't fall through her spiritual form.

"You've been practicing!" Olivia said, clapping her hands as if Ava were a toddler. "Wonderful progress!"

Issa wanted to speak, but she wasn't sure what to say. Ava smiled so wide, she practically glowed, and Issa didn't want to ruin the fun, so she swallowed the million questions forming in her mind and tried to act just as happy.

For the first night in several lonely weeks, Issa was grateful to be alone in her own dressing room after a grueling day at work. She hadn't seen Jem in a while either—he was as busy as always, flitting between different projects at different studios. Exhausted, the idea of performing a conjuring on her own didn't appeal to her, but she couldn't stop thinking about Ava's growing strength.

So she set up her incense and Bà Ngoại's picture and waited for her grandmother to appear in the reflection.

"What's this?" Bà said, looking around the room. The bed and open closet filled with Issa's regular dresses and some costumes from the current movie were visible in the reflection. "This is sooner than our monthly visits. Something the matter?"

Issa told her about Ava. "She can grab things now. Is that normal, Bà Ngoại? I didn't know ghosts could do that."

"They get stronger the more they visit, and you say she's there all the time."

"Yes, with Olivia."

Bà Ngoại grew thoughtful. "Has your friend given her more blood?"

"She's never said . . ." Issa couldn't imagine how else Ava had gotten so strong, how she could spend hours and days with them without Issa feeling a thing. Olivia had simply said that Dead Auntie Phi taught her a trick. "Perhaps . . ." Then she remembered the globs of brown stuff on Olivia's mirror. It was so alarming because Olivia was so fastidious . . . but maybe that was actually blood. "Is it harmful?"

"If she's offering it willingly, then that's her choice," Bà said.

"What if . . . something happens? Something bad?"

But what sort of something? Issa couldn't picture it. A dreadful sensation grew like goose bumps over her skin.

"Then you burn all of Ava's images," Bà said. "Take away her trophy."

But the trophy made Ava so happy. Ava was forever caressing or hugging the thing, and Issa couldn't imagine taking it away. Ava was her friend too. She'd helped them get so far, and really, she'd never done them any wrong. Perhaps it was just Issa, projecting her own fears where they didn't belong . . . that old resistance she had to the shamanistic part of her life and family history.

"Should I be worried?" she asked Bà Ngoại.

"You're a witch, Issa," Bà said. "The reason she's there is because of you."

"I know." Issa couldn't keep the guilt out of her voice. "That's why I'm trying to fix things before they get any worse."

"You're missing the point," Bà snapped. "What is there to fix? You have all the power, is what I'm saying. The moment you don't want her around anymore, you can get rid of her. *You* are in control. You just have to take responsibility for it, and the power is yours."

"You're right," Issa said. "I can do what I want. I can learn more about Ava. Search her memories, even."

Bà Ngoại smiled, and Issa thought she saw triumph in her face before she grew serious and studied Issa more closely. "I thought you were too scared."

Issa remembered when she'd unwittingly projected herself into Ava's body; she had felt suffocated, as if her soul were drowning. But perhaps it had only been the shock of it. If she tried it now, she might be more prepared.

Issa lowered herself onto her bed. Last time, Olivia had been around to wake her up. What if she didn't wake up while doing this on her own? What if she remained trapped in Ava's body forever, leaving her own exposed . . . susceptible to possession?

"Can you come with me?" she asked.

"I wish it were so easy. But I can watch over you," Bà Ngoại assured her.

Issa nodded and closed her eyes. She took in a deep breath, and then an even deeper one. This time, the orb of light was easier to picture, and she felt it move through her body in a calming, massage-like sensation. She fell asleep again, aware that she was dreaming, but unable to tell if it was her dream or a projection of someone else's.

Usually, Issa's dreams had a dark quality to them, figures moving in the shadows. This time the vision was colorful and bright, almost painfully so. She found herself walking between racks of clothes, but the scene did not feel familiar, nor did it resemble the vivid saturation of the memory she'd entered last time. Was she in some sort of store? She didn't recognize it, but she couldn't seem to focus, her vision blurry beyond a few feet right in front of her.

"I worry it's too much," a familiar voice spoke, sounding distant as if Issa were underwater. It was Olivia.

"You're afraid of me, is that it?" Ava asked, her accent easy to distinguish.

The two figures were blurry shapes. When Issa tried to get closer, their image wavered, their voices became more garbled. So she stepped back, aware that she didn't have a physical body in this space, just a sensation of clinging, knowing instinctively not to hang on too tight, yet cognizant that her presence was tenuous.

"No, of course not," Olivia said.

"I would never hurt you."

"I know . . . I'm just . . . I fear there won't be much of me in the work. I want to prove myself."

"And you will, darling. But nothing is done alone. You forget that I know what it's like. I've been exactly where you are, and I can help you move beyond the same mistakes I made. Imagine what we would do together."

"Yes. I deserve it. After all this time."

"You certainly do."

"I could be just as successful as that tart." Olivia glared in a direction that Issa couldn't follow, her voice more venomous than Issa was used to hearing, though she knew that Olivia had a mean streak inside her that she only revealed when she was angry.

"And with my help, you'll be even more so," Ava said.

Issa wished she could see Olivia's reaction, but she couldn't make out her face.

"What about Issa?" Olivia asked.

"We'll help her, too, of course. But it takes a strong bond, which I already share with you. I know you better than anyone—we're so alike. I see you, Olivia. Remember our conversation?"

Conversation? Ava and Olivia must have discussed this before. But what, exactly? And how could Ava claim that she knew Olivia better than anyone—better than Issa?

"But Issa—" Olivia said.

"She doesn't understand you the way I do. She doesn't understand *me* the way *you* do."

A zing of alarm shot through Issa's belly—what was Ava talking about? What conversation?

The thoughts jolted the image, dislodging her grip on the vision. "No," she whispered, feeling herself slip upward, the dream or memory or whatever this was growing blurry. She tried to grasp tight, but it was too late. It all disintegrated, and when she next took in a breath, she was in her bed, staring up at the ceiling.

"You're back," Bà Ngoại said from the mirror.

Issa felt so exhausted, she could only blink at her.

"What did you uncover?"

"I hardly know," Issa said.

"Anything you should be alarmed about?"

Issa's eyes filled with tears. She felt silly for the turmoil brewing inside her, because really, what had she overheard? That Olivia and Ava were closer than she wanted them to be? Jealousy. Was that what it was? Yes. Issa was jealous. Of both women. Ava wanted to help Olivia, was more willing to help Olivia than Issa, *liked* Olivia more than Issa. And why wouldn't she? Olivia was more talented, more beautiful, more deserving. And Olivia wanted to be a star so badly, Issa was certain she would choose Ava over Issa. And the worst part was, Issa couldn't blame her because she understood completely. They shared the same dream. If Issa were in her shoes . . . perhaps . . . she might make the same choice.

"Oh, Issa girl," Bà Ngoại said. "It can't be so bad. Come, now."

Issa bit her lip. "Was it real? What I saw?" It was unreasonable to expect Bà Ngoại to know, since her grandmother hadn't come with her, but Issa felt frazzled and wanted some explanation that would soothe her twisting thoughts.

Bà Ngoại nodded. "You were in the right state. But do well not to misconstrue whatever you heard. Use your own understanding to interpret it. That's what we do, as shamans."

Issa's mind was too boggled to make sense of it all.

Bà Ngoại lingered for several moments, but when Issa said no more, she bade her farewell, and her picture went still, the incense letting out a plume of smoke before the ends charred to black.

Haunted by what she'd overheard, as well as feeling guilty for intruding on a private moment between her two friends, Issa performed poorly on set the next day. Self-doubt plagued her every move. Each line she spoke was stilted, and she questioned her movements, overanalyzed every muscle twitch. The director yelled "Cut!" so many times that she came close to tears, and she could tell she wasn't the only one. The cast shot her equally nervous and scathing looks.

"What am I doing wrong?" she asked Ireland outright.

"Your face . . . ," he said with a groan. He pinched the bridge of his nose. "It's not right. Not right. Try again."

But she'd barely read two of her lines before he cut it short. Suppressed groans echoed on the stage.

"Let's take an hour for dinner," the director said.

Issa had never wanted a cigarette before in her life, but suddenly she wished she smoked along with everyone who filed out of the building to light up. She went anyway, hoping that the fresh air would do her good, but the sunset only made her more forlorn, the burnt-orange glow casting the sky in a romantic backdrop, pushing her downward into a nostalgia for a time and place that she may never see.

When she was a child, she'd been overcome with these floods of emotion, an overwhelming melancholia, a longing for some distant memory that she was sure she didn't possess. The world often took on a hazy edge as if she were in some dream, except if that were so, then she'd been in that dream all her life. These flashes often left her questioning her reality, wondering if it were all a fantasy—her existence a feverish sequence.

Watching movies usually cured her of these fugues, because the moments between one playing and one ending were so well defined that she could visibly distinguish between fake and real. But now that she was acting, she suddenly found it difficult to see the distinction.

She walked around the building, and as she leaned against the sun-baked wall of the studio building, a heavy loneliness flowed through her veins.

"Ava?" she asked, mostly out of desperation, not knowing who else to call on, regretting it immediately as she remembered the conversation she'd overheard between Ava and Olivia.

She was surprised when Ava materialized in front of her with a warm smile that brought inexplicable tears to her eyes. Ava's face furrowed in concern, and without saying a word, she leaned over and pulled Issa into a hug. Issa gasped at the touch of her cold skin. She knew Ava could touch things now—her trophy giving her strength—but they hadn't had any physical contact since that first day that Ava had grabbed her fingers. She almost pulled away, but managed to remain still, knowing it would be unseemly and rude, especially when she had been the one to summon Ava.

"What's wrong, doll?" Ava asked, breaking the hug and thankfully letting go of Issa's arms.

"I'm just having a bit of trouble today," Issa said, dabbing at her eyes so as not to ruin her makeup. "I just thought . . . you might . . . understand." Oh, she was pathetic, really. Begging for affection? Just because she thought Olivia was growing closer to Ava? This was all so silly.

"Would you like some help?" Ava asked. She tilted her head with a compassionate expression on her face. "It's quite easy, you know."

"Not for me," Issa said with a huff. "The director's notes are no help. Maybe I just don't have the talent."

"Nonsense. You're capable of anything." Ava touched her hand, her fingers like sticks of ice. "We both are. Just give me the word."

Issa looked into Ava's eyes—deep, dark pools of black ink. "Will you observe and give me advice, like you do with Olivia?"

"I can. But I can help even more than that."

A cold sensation crawled up Issa's spine, stemming from where Ava still held her. "What do you mean?"

"Oh, don't be alarmed. Olivia does it all the time. It's how she's improved so much."

"Yes, but what do you mean?" Issa repeated. "Exactly?"

"I'll take over for a spell, help you with your movements. Guide you."

"Take . . . over. You mean, possess me?"

"Oh, darling, no!" Ava clutched her chest. She released Issa, but the coldness remained, even in the heat of the sun. "I would never do such a thing! How could you even—" She pressed a palm to her cheek. "How dare you—" Instead of anger, her eyes filled with tears, smoke forming at the edges of her figure.

"No, no, I'm sorry." Issa reached for her, managing to snag the loose silk of her sleeve. "I didn't mean that. I just . . . I'm just sensitive . . . about that." Her words felt inadequate, something that Olivia would have understood immediately, aware of Issa's family history and her fear of her powers. Ava probably thought she was naive. "Please don't be offended. I would love your advice. Just not . . . not that."

To her relief, Ava resolidified, brushing away silvery tears.

"Please, Ava," Issa added.

Ava nodded. "Yes, all right, then. You won't make as much progress as Olivia, but I can still be of help."

"Thank you," Issa said. She surprised herself by pulling Ava in for a hug. The ghost's cheek pressed against hers, leaving a tingling numbness.

As everyone filed back inside the soundstage, Issa's spirits felt lifted with Ava by her side.

"Let's try that scene again," the director said, snapping his fingers at Issa to move in front of the camera.

Ava nodded with reassurance as Issa went through the scene, knowing Ireland would call "Cut" before she finished her lines, which he did sure enough.

"Perhaps it's a lighting issue," he said with a sigh, gesturing for the crew.

Issa waited while they adjusted the lamps around her, and Ava approached.

"It's your shoulders," she said. "You're pushing them back too much. It comes off as overconfident."

Issa couldn't respond under the spotlight with everyone watching her, but she made a confounded expression, pretending to stretch her facial muscles. She was supposed to be a star, and this was a leading role.

"Your character is weak and docile," Ava said.

Issa scoffed.

"Think of it this way," Ava continued, draping an arm about Issa. "Exaggerating her weakness here will show the audience how much she's grown. And you need to build goodwill with this director. Once you prove that you'll listen to his direction, obtuse as it is, you'll be able to push your own ideas down the line, when it matters."

Issa nodded, taking in Ava's words. There was no harm in giving her advice a try.

"All right," Ireland called out. "Are we ready now?" He leaned back in his chair, scowling.

"What a patronizing man," Ava whispered. "Don't worry, dear. I'll take care of him."

"Wait," Issa stammered. What did that mean?

But the slate snapped, and the camera whirred. Issa hunched her shoulders, concentrating on saying her lines as pathetically as she could, wondering if she wasn't overdoing it quite a bit, even making her voice waver. When she finished, she was surprised that the director hadn't interrupted.

She even dared to enjoy herself a bit when Ava's wispy form caught her eye, floating around the director. She whispered something in his ear, and he batted her away a few times, but didn't react beyond that. Perhaps Ava didn't have the same effect on him that she did on Goldman. What was she saying to him?

But once they finished filming for the day, Ava had disappeared, and Issa couldn't ask her.

Eventually she became busier than ever, leaving as the sun rose, spending all day on set, and coming back well after dark. Issa never asked Ava to come back, though she was tempted to, and Ava never showed up on her own. She figured Ava was with Olivia, and Issa wasn't sure whether she was resentful, jealous, or relieved.

She didn't even consider staying when she visited MGM on Friday that week to pick up more clothes.

In the living room, Olivia danced around in a flowy kimono robe, sloshing wine about in her glass and not caring when it spilled on the rug. At least it was white wine. Oddly, Ava was nowhere in sight, though her trophy sat on the side table.

"What are we drinking to?" Issa asked, throwing her bag down and going to the bar cart to pour herself a drink. She was desperate to set things right with Olivia, eager to move beyond what she'd overheard between her two friends while also feeling guilty over calling on Ava without Olivia there, even though she knew Olivia did it all the time. But Olivia had sought Ava out with a genuine need to improve her craft, while Issa . . . well, she would be lying if she said she'd called on Ava purely for help and not because she also felt insecure about her friendship with both women.

She was grateful Ava wasn't there and hoped she could talk to Olivia about the growing distance between them, though she also felt childish because perhaps it was all in her head. What if Olivia didn't see it as a problem at all?

"Didn't you read the paper?" Olivia asked. "I'm a real star!" She threw up her hands.

"Where? What paper?"

"There." Olivia pointed while she drank and danced at the same time, and Issa grabbed the newspaper off the couch and skimmed the article about Olivia's latest role and how phenomenal she was.

"Oh my God, Olivia, this is amazing!" Issa squealed. "We have to celebrate!"

"Yes we shall!" Olivia clinked her glass to Issa's. "Let's go to Savoy. I really want steak."

"Absolutely. This is a big occasion," Issa said. She'd hardly seen Olivia eat much of anything since they'd gotten their contracts, only the occasional splash of cream in her coffee.

"I know, but I deserve it, don't I?" Olivia asked. "I mean, I'm in *Variety*. That's got to mean something."

"It absolutely does."

"Go get ready—make yourself pretty," Olivia said. "We might get photographed."

They took a cab to downtown Los Angeles.

Unfortunately, Savoy did not have any free tables.

"Do you have a reservation?" the host asked, standing behind the podium with his hands folded over the pages of an open appointment book.

"No, I didn't think we needed one," Olivia said.

"At Savoy?" he asked, barely concealing his contempt for such country girls. "We're booked months ahead of time."

"We're actresses," Issa blurted for some reason.

The man's smile turned into a cringe. His lips twitched a few times as if he was fighting the urge to make some off-color joke, but in the end he simply nodded. "My apologies."

They walked back out, Olivia stomping her heels once the doors closed behind them. "Darn. I should have known."

"How would you? We hardly go to places like this. Let's go to that noodle restaurant across the street."

Olivia glanced at it with derision, but then her stomach growled. "They better not turn us away."

They didn't. It was a small, family-run business. An older Asian lady led them to the only empty table in the surprisingly packed space, dimly lit except for the wall sconces placed close to the ceiling. The smell of beef broth and jasmine rice and pork dumplings permeated the air, while the chatter of people around them created a low buzz, not too loud or unpleasant.

"This is nice," Issa said. They were overdressed. The other restaurant-goers stared at them as they sat, but Olivia basked in the attention, flicking her long hair down her back.

The old woman kept making eye contact, then quickly looking away. She placed little bowls of appetizers and sides on the table in the middle—pickled radishes, dipping sauces, and sliced fish cake—took their orders, and left.

Issa couldn't help glancing around. People were staring, whispering. They weren't *that* out of place. Most of the faces in the restaurant were Asian.

Olivia still hadn't recovered from being rejected at Savoy. "We should book that restaurant up for weeks and then just not show. See how they like that."

"I don't think it's their fault we didn't know to make reservations. It was an honest mistake."

"You're right, you're always right." As was her habit, Olivia ripped up her napkin to keep her hands busy, and she balled up the little scraps between her fingers. "Still, I doubt Katharine Hepburn gets turned away from restaurants whether or not she remembered to call ahead of time."

"Another level of fame to aspire to," Issa said with a smile, hoping to lift Olivia's spirits.

"At least they have steak here."

Issa nodded. She couldn't think of anything to say to Olivia. Silence wasn't uncommon between them—they'd lived together for years, they didn't always keep up a steady stream of chatter. But that kind of silence was often peaceful, lightened from the burden of making small talk because they knew each other so well. Now she felt pressured to ask something or say something innocuous, some banal comment to fill the air. It wasn't what she was used to feeling around her best friend.

She kept hoping Olivia would speak, but Olivia was too lost in her own indignation, tearing the napkin over and over, then looking up as if expecting Issa to comment on it.

When their food arrived, they rolled up their sleeves so as not to get them dirty, and Issa paused. "Olivia, what happened to your arms?" she asked.

Silver scars marked Olivia's skin in random crosshatches that looked almost artistic, as if they'd been made on purpose.

"Oh, it's nothing." Olivia yanked her sleeves back down.

"It's not—is this . . ." Issa's mind reeled. "Are you still—" She forced herself to ask. "Is Ava making you do that?"

"Ava doesn't *make* me do anything."

"But this is the pain sacrifice you talked about?" Issa's voice had risen, and she took a deep breath. "She offered to 'take over' me the other day. She said you do it all the time. How often?"

"She helps me," Olivia said, avoiding the question. "Please, I don't want to talk about it now." She blinked furiously, her eyes glassy with tears.

Issa fought the urge to keep asking, to keep pushing. She didn't know whether it was dangerous for Olivia and Ava to continue as they had, and maybe she shouldn't worry. After all, Ava had done nothing so far but help them. "All right, then." Issa looked down at her food, but she'd lost her appetite.

The silence was too unbearable.

"How's your movie going?" she asked instead.

Olivia's face practically crumpled. "It's so hard, Issa." She sucked in a breath as if she was holding back a sob. "Everyone is just incredibly unfriendly. The director is horrid. He keeps telling me I'm not doing things right. We did thirty takes on a scene the other day."

"Olivia, I'm so sorry," Issa said. "I didn't know it was that bad."

Olivia blinked back tears. "It's supposed to be a good role. The story is strong, the director is known for good work. It's just . . . it wasn't what I expected. If it weren't for Ava . . ."

Issa's insides twisted. She forced the jealousy away. "I'm glad she's there to help."

"She gives much better feedback than the director. He'll say, 'Be sexier'—but doesn't tell me how. She's the one who shows me how to position my hips or my shoulders a certain way." Olivia posed to demonstrate, and at that moment someone approached their table, a girl a few years younger than them.

"Hi," she said shyly. She wore what looked like a school uniform—a white blouse and a pleated navy skirt. "Are you Olivia Nong?"

Olivia's face grew slack with surprise. "Why yes, I am."

"Oh my goodness." The girl covered her mouth. "I knew it was you. But my friends kept saying it couldn't be. You're so famous, why would you eat here?"

"I love noodle soup," Olivia said with a charming smile, propping her chin on a fist.

"Oh wow." The girl looked back at her friends. "We loved you in *Lost in the Queen's Love.*"

"Really?" Olivia sat up straight. "My friend was in it too. Issa Bui."

"Hi," the girl said politely to Issa who also straightened, but the girl quickly turned back to Olivia. "This is so rude—I know you're just here to eat dinner—but can I have your autograph?"

"Sure!" Olivia beamed. It was the first time, as far as Issa knew, that this had ever happened to Olivia, and Issa was overcome with the fact that she was present to witness it. When the girl didn't move, Olivia reached out her hands. "What would you like me to sign?"

"Oh! Oh, um." She looked around.

"What about this napkin?" Issa suggested, handing hers over.

"Oh, sure, if that's all right," the girl said. She gave it to Olivia, who scribbled something hardly resembling her correct signature. "Thank you so much." The girl bowed as she walked away to rejoin her friends, who giggled and gasped over the signature.

Olivia looked around the restaurant as if she expected everyone else to recognize her and ask for her autograph, but though most people smiled back, they left her alone.

"That was history in the making," Issa said. "You were recognized!"

"I know," Olivia whispered in delight. "This is going to be a wonderful night after all!"

Chapter Thirty-Five

That Saturday, she and Jem managed to squeeze in a late dinner. Their schedules had been so packed that they'd hardly had time to meet. His eyes were rimmed red from late nights working, and as he picked up his hamburger Issa noticed his fingers were stained with ink.

"Sometimes I feel as if I'm writing the same story over and over again," he said when she asked him about his work.

"Is that a complaint?" she teased. Jem never had a bad thing to say about . . . well, anything.

"After my contract is up, I might take some time to work on my own script. I've been thinking about it for years, but I keep putting it off for a quick paycheck." He laughed, his mirth quickly chasing away his serious mood.

"That sounds like a lovely idea." Issa picked listlessly at her salad. "I wish that worked for actors as well."

"Are you struggling with your movie?"

Issa's first instinct was to brush it off, to say that things were going swell. She didn't want to spoil the evening when they didn't have much time together, but it spilled out anyway. "Perhaps I'm just not good enough. I know I can do this, but every time I say a line, I can feel everyone judging me, wondering why I'm in the lead. Especially the other actresses. Which is ironic because I didn't want the part in the first place, and now I just want to do well in it."

"The role is very different from who you are," Jem said. "But perhaps you can use that to your advantage. Channel all the emotions you've never been able to show into your acting."

Issa wasn't sure how to respond. She'd never known how to answer when someone asked her about herself, and she was always at a loss when told to be "who she was." It was as if by mentioning her identity, it ceased to exist, and she had no clue what or who replaced it.

"I can help you, if you'd like," Jem said.

"Like a coach? Would you have time?"

"After I finish this treatment, I can fit it in my schedule. I don't mind reading it again, thoroughly, and perhaps try to decipher what the writer means."

"Oh, that would be lovely." Issa promised to send over a copy, and they made a plan for him to stop by in the morning later that week.

After dinner, they went for a walk along the neighborhood's main street, a five-block stretch lit up with display windows of stores closed for the night, dessert parlors, and a few bars where laughter and music drifted through briefly opened doors. Jem took her hand, and she slipped her fingers between his. It was a moonlit night, and other couples strolled the sidewalk, the women dressed in skirts that hit just below their knees and heels that clicked a beat on the pavement, the men in suits or button-ups.

"Oh, how lovely," Issa said, stopping in front of a storefront with a display of flowers growing out of a typewriter.

"They destroyed an Underwood for that?" Jem groaned.

"Oh my God," another voice interrupted them. A teenage-looking girl had stopped in front of Issa with a shocked expression. "Are you Olivia Nong?"

For a second, Issa's stomach had flipped. She thought the moment had finally come—the moment she was recognized. But now her heart sank.

"No, Olivia's my friend," she said. "I'm Issa Bui."

The girl covered her mouth. "The other one?"

"Um." Issa wasn't sure if that was a compliment, but she decided it would suffice, so she plastered on her best smile. "The . . . other one!" she said as cheerfully as she could manage.

The girl squealed. "I saw you in the queen movie—you were both wonderful." She dug through her purse. "Can I have your autograph?"

"Oh." Issa hadn't expected that, especially not when the girl originally thought she was Olivia. "Um, sure."

"Issa Bui," the girl repeated as she handed over a piece of paper. "Is that your real name?"

"Yes. I don't have a pen."

"Here," Jem said, pulling one out from his pocket. "Wouldn't be a writer if I didn't always have a pen on me."

Issa signed the paper and handed it back to the girl. "Thank you!" she squealed, hugging it to her chest. She dashed off, joining her family. Jem and Issa hesitated before they continued walking because the family kept turning to glance at her. They were Asian, and the parents kept smiling as if Issa were their own daughter and they were very proud of her. Issa felt both encouraged and a little too vulnerable in the moment. She was just one woman, and she could hardly represent them the way they seemed to expect, yet she knew that her face and skin and eyes on the screen meant a lot to many people.

"You're famous," Jem said.

She laughed. "Hardly. She thought I was Olivia."

"She was just as excited to meet you, though. Don't sell yourself short." He slipped an arm around her, and Issa found his warmth comforting, the solidity of his body easy to lean against. "Bask in the glory. You deserve it."

On Sunday morning, Issa visited Auntie Yen in Chinatown for their next lesson. One of the staff answered the door, a woman wearing a traditional Vietnamese áo dài, which Issa rarely saw around the city. The woman greeted Issa with a bow, then gestured to the mirror room where Auntie Yen conducted her conjurings. She hung back in the hallway as if afraid to get too close to the room, but nodded at Issa to let herself in.

Issa rapped gently on the door until her aunt opened it a crack.

"Why'd you knock for? I told Chi to let you in." Auntie Yen stepped aside to let Issa into the room, the air thick with incense smoke.

In the mirror, Bà Ngoại's reflection stared at Issa. A large framed photograph of her sat on an easel in the center of the room so that she appeared the same size as they were.

"Oh, hello, Bà Ngoại," Issa said, bowing with her arms crossed.

Bà Ngoại smiled, but Issa detected a danger lacing it that made the back of her neck tingle. "So you've been learning more about your powers from Yen as well. Good. Soon you can help with the séance requests. It would be good for you to practice, before you take over."

"Take over?" Issa asked. "But you said I had a year. I still have plenty of time."

"Are you a star yet?" Bà Ngoại asked.

Issa pressed her lips together. "We were recognized the other night."

"Time's running out! The Uncles are encroaching on our territory, and we need to strengthen our numbers. You need to be prepared. You need training, proper schooling. None of this dabble-dabble. Yen isn't going to live forever."

Issa and Auntie Yen looked at each other. Feeling ambushed, Issa swallowed against the knot that tightened in her throat. It would not be wise to cry in front of her grandmother, who valued strength and hardness and composure, so Issa willed her eyes to remain dry.

"You didn't mean it, did you?" she asked. "I knew it. All along, you were setting me up to fail. You had no intention of considering any other cousins to take over. You didn't want to help me at all."

"Ungrateful child!" Bà Ngoại spewed. "Who do you think gave your producer money after those actors and writers quit that ridiculous movie about some queen?"

"What? Money?" Issa looked at Yen in confusion, and her aunt's calm face confirmed it was true. "You bribed them to cast us?"

"The production was falling apart," Bà answered for her. "And you were nobodies. You think all it took was replacing two small roles to keep it going? Of course we bribed them."

"We didn't say specifically that it had to be the two of you," Auntie Yen added at Issa's gasp of dismay. "We just said it needed to be someone who . . . fit your descriptions."

Issa didn't know why she was so upset. All along, Yen and Bà had made it clear that their connections would help Issa and Olivia achieve their dreams. But part of her had thought she had done it on her own, a little. Which was ridiculous, because they'd had Ava's help. It was just . . . she'd been good at the role. She had *loved* it. So much so that she'd forgotten she hadn't actually earned it.

"All of that, and you're still not famous yet," Bà went on. "I doubt that will change in the next few months."

"Then what?" Issa asked. "You force me to come back here and take over for Auntie Yen?"

"No one will force you to do anything, Issa," Auntie Yen said, her stoic tone contrasting with Ba's shrill anger. "But you made a promise."

Issa wanted to protest. It made no sense to push her into the position when she didn't want it, when a whole horde of people—the Uncles, for instance—would literally kill to take over. Would it be so bad if Issa ceded control?

She knew bringing up this line of thought would only anger Bà and mark Issa as a traitor, so she tried to change the topic. "Ava grows stronger every time she visits us. So does that mean that if you keep visiting us, you might be able to come back? Really come back, the way Ava does?" Then Bà could take over the business again and stop bothering Issa about it.

"Why would I want to do that?" Bà Ngoại asked. "You think all ghosts aren't happy where they are? Some of us like resting in peace. If only I can do so, knowing my one and only heir would do as she said!"

"I still have time," Issa said.

"But not much," Bà Ngoại said. "Don't forget your promise, Issa."

Being recognized at some obscure restaurant proved to be the start of Olivia's fame. Like she'd predicted, they'd been photographed, so covertly that neither had noticed. The following Monday, the tabloids mentioned Olivia in a very small section featuring stars spotted doing normal things. Issa was in the shot with her and got a casual mention as a "fellow cast member," but the column said Olivia was an upcoming actress to watch for.

Issa tried to be supportive and happy, smiling and hugging Olivia whenever she suddenly released a little burst of joy, which Olivia did frequently the rest of that weekend. It quickly became exhausting. Olivia kept bringing up the tabloid and what it could mean, wondering if she would get better roles now or be paired alongside actual celebrities like Clark Gable. Did Issa think Olivia was attractive enough to star opposite Clark Gable? And would a magazine like *Mademoiselle* ever reach out to do a feature on her?

It didn't help that Ava was always around and just as enthusiastic about Olivia's fame as Olivia was herself, which made Issa feel ashamed. Was she a terrible friend for not being genuinely, absolutely overcome with ecstasy at Olivia's success? Why wasn't she happy every single moment of the day for her own best friend? Why did she feel insecure about herself and her own rise to stardom, or lack thereof? Was she horrible for worrying about her own roles, her own fame, when she should have been simply happy for her friend?

By the end of Sunday, Issa's face hurt from smiling so much, and she felt drained from having to react enthusiastically whenever Olivia wanted to talk about her stardom. She was relieved to return to Warner Bros. to continue work on her film, then guilty because if the roles were reversed, if Issa had been mentioned in the gossip columns, Olivia would be absolutely over the moon on her behalf.

She'd never been happier to see the set of her film, and even more relieved when Jem met her as promised at the studio's restaurant.

"I read the script again," he said.

"Goodness, did you give up the rest of your weekend?" Issa asked.

He grinned. "I live for this, you should know that."

"What did you think?"

"Like I thought, the character is so unlike you. You're quite . . . joyful, from what I can tell. You have a . . . lightness about you. This character has struggled throughout most of her life, and I'm just going to assume that you haven't," Jem continued. "I mean, I'm sure you've had your problems. Everyone has. So that's what I would examine. Dig into all the ways life has wronged you. Play it up. Dredge up the tears when you can." He laughed.

Issa smiled as she considered his advice. Was it true that she'd never truly struggled? Of course, compared to other less fortunate people, perhaps, but she'd faced hardships too. When Ma first left the clan, she'd endured poverty, even if Ma sheltered her from as much of it as possible. In school, other children had picked on her mercilessly, pulling on her braids or poking her or calling her names when the teacher wasn't looking.

Perhaps that was why Olivia excelled more than Issa did at acting. She'd always lived a tough life. She had more experiences to draw from.

"There," he said. "That's a wonderful face. Take note of your facial muscles, and do the same thing on set today."

Issa wasn't sure that would be enough, but it was a start.

"We can continue meeting," Jem added with a sly smile.

"What about your work?"

He shrugged. "I'll consider this research."

"Or I can have Mager hire you as a coach."

He took her hand. "Is it so hard to let me help you?"

Issa's breath hitched. It felt as if someone had poked her hard in the sternum. Did she have a problem letting people help her? Of course. As soon as Jem said it, she knew she did. That's why she struggled to receive Ava's feedback, never liked to mingle in crowds with Olivia, buttering people up for something in return, hoping for a scrap of assistance. Perhaps Ma had ingrained it so deeply in her, the idea that nothing good came for free, that no one owed her anything.

"All right, then," she said. "I suppose I can let you help me this one time."

Jem gave her hand a squeeze. "Good."

Issa took Jem's advice and got through the rest of the rehearsals that week with no cast member glaring at her, and the director actually nodded as she said the lines in a particularly difficult scene. Improvement at last. Even Mager clapped, surprising her one afternoon. He didn't come to the set every day, but often enough that she felt both scrutinized and looked after.

To her immense gratitude, Jem met with her when his schedule allowed it. Sometimes they spent their lunch break together poring over his notes. She had to resist the urge to cringe every time he analyzed one of her scenes, but he was always professional, especially in front of the other crew, who watched them curiously. She'd never have gotten through the next few weeks without him.

The scene that day called for her to sob as her character's lover abandoned her, leaving her to fend for herself, and while Issa had no issues conjuring the tears, she felt it wasn't the right reaction for the character, at least not in that pivotal moment. She remembered Ava's advice about how the character had been shown as weak, at first, and Issa had complied, but only because she wanted to show how her character had grown.

"Let's give it one more take," she told Ireland.

"You were perfect, sweetheart," he said, not looking up from the call list.

"I'm serious," she said firmly. "I want to try something different."

He sighed. "All right, then." It was clear that he thought it would be a waste of his time, but Issa didn't care.

She stepped in front of the camera, and this time, instead of sobbing tears of sorrow, she hardened her facial muscles and expressed a profound rage that she knew existed deep within her. It bubbled up and threatened to spill out, but she kept it in, let it sit under the surface of her skin, showing only in the subtle clenching of her jaw, the flare of her nostrils. She knew she was not a pretty sight, but she cared more about the story than looking beautiful, and when she finished the scene, Ireland stared, riveted. He didn't say anything, but they both knew she'd made the right decision.

When the crew broke for lunch, Issa went back to her dressing room to lie down. Her knees shook. Maybe it was the emotional scene or the act of standing up for herself, even just a little, but she felt exhausted.

She nearly screamed when she opened the door and found Ava at her vanity table.

"What are you doing here?" she whispered, shutting the door.

"I wanted to check in on you," Ava said, tinkering with a jar of powder. "Especially after last time when you needed my help."

"I don't today. Or anymore." Feeling ungrateful, she added, "But thank you for your advice last time. It was very helpful."

Ava dropped the lid of the jar with a clink. "Are you sure, darling? Perhaps I'll join you on set. I'm so bored with Olivia's film—I want to see a lead in action." She gave Issa a wink.

"You're welcome to watch," Issa said. "But I really don't need your help." She wasn't sure why she felt so uneasy all of a sudden.

She ignored the weird feeling in her stomach when it was time to walk back to the set and Ava followed her. The dead star had never been so intrusive before, but Issa figured that was because she was usually so distracted by giving Olivia notes or direction. As Issa stepped into her blocking, Ava kept getting in the way, and Issa had to muster all her acting skills just to pretend that nothing was out of the ordinary.

"Oh, don't hold your mouth like that, darling," Ava said as Issa spoke her lines. "Your nose is all scrunched."

Issa spoke over her and kept going with the scene, but her body flushed with heat. She couldn't stop thinking about all the wrong ways her face moved.

"That doesn't look right at all," Ava said, squinting at the lighting. "This supporting actress is going to outshine you. Want me to smear her lipstick?"

"What? No," Issa said, interrupting the other actress's lines. The woman gave Issa a confused look.

Ava's lips twitched. Had she done that on purpose?

"I'm sorry," Issa said.

"Cut!" the director shouted.

"I'm so sorry," Issa repeated.

"Stop apologizing!" Ava exclaimed with a laugh. "You're the star here. Act like it."

"Let's take it back a few lines," the director said.

Issa took a deep breath. She couldn't remember what that line actually was.

"Issa?" Ireland said.

"I need a moment," she said and hurried off the set.

Outside, Ava grinned at her. "Oh, come along now, that was just a bit of fun."

"Well, not for me, it wasn't," Issa hissed at her, hoping that anyone walking by assumed she was just practicing her lines. "I said I don't need your help."

"Yes, but you clearly still do—"

"No, I don't." Issa sucked in a breath. Perhaps she was still reeling from her conversation with Yen and Bà Ngoại, but her hackles rose, heat flooding her face. "I mean it, Ava. I want to do this on my own. I'm grateful for your earlier advice, but I can manage now."

"You're certain?" Ava asked. She held Issa's gaze, as if hoping to convince her through the intensity of her stare that Issa was actually quite wrong and incompetent. "I could make you great, you know. That's what you called on me for."

"But I didn't call you here today. And, for all we know," Issa continued, "I am already great. Just on my own."

Ava gave a humorless laugh. Her eyes roamed Issa's face in a last once-over. "Fine then," she said. "I guess I'll stay with Olivia from now on. *She's* happy to have me around."

To Issa's immense relief, the ghost left.

In the final week of production, Issa had a very emotional scene. She didn't care what she looked like as long as her face conveyed the emotion the character felt. She sobbed and railed, and when she finished, she felt both exhausted and energized.

Applause erupted in the soundstage. She looked up, wiping her tears, to see the rest of the cast members beaming at her.

"That was jolly good," Larry Mager said, reaching down to pull her from her knees. "I dare say it might even win you an Oscar." He handed her a monogrammed cloth handkerchief.

"Should we do another take?" she asked as she dabbed at her eyes, careful not to ruin any more makeup than she already had.

He laughed. "I think you landed that, but we'll leave it up to Tony."

The rest of the filming went by smoothly, and Issa was almost shocked when it wrapped. She had done it. Her first lead role under her belt. Weeks ago, she had longed for it to be over, but now . . . she couldn't wait for another project just as challenging so that she could show the world what she could accomplish.

Chapter Thirty-Six

As other articles came out about Olivia, more directors requested her for their next film. When Issa moved back to their rooms after her Warner Bros. film wrapped, she gasped upon seeing the state of her former home. It was in complete disarray. Jackets, blankets, pantyhose, and an assortment of items hung over the back of the sofa and the armchair or dripped onto the floor. The only thing that remained pristine among the clutter was Ava's trophy, sitting on the side table as if on a pedestal.

"Goodness, what happened here?" Issa asked.

"The studio will send someone to clean up," Olivia said, as if that answered the question. She sat on the sofa among the mess, throwing several scripts into a pile, and sighing dramatically. "I can't choose. They're all equally bad."

"That can't be true," Issa said, moving aside a coat to sit next to her on the couch. She picked up a script. "*Brunettes Are Best*, ugh. I take that back."

Olivia smiled. "Congratulations on finishing your film!" She threw her arms up and hugged Issa like they hadn't seen each other in ages. "You get to come back, right? Here, pick one of these, and I'll demand that we're in it together."

"I thought you said they were all bad."

"Yes, but so are most of the movies being made nowadays. The scripts just aren't very good anymore, but people still see them, so we might as well be in something that will make us famous. Plus, if you're there, it will be worth it."

"What about Jonathan something-or-other's movie, the one about the two sisters. That sounded promising."

"But they'd have to lease us out to WB, and I simply can't," Olivia said.

"It wasn't so bad," Issa said. "They were actually quite lovely to work for."

"No, darling, MGM is the studio we need to stick with. They're known for making better movies, and we're already here. Going to WB is like a step down."

Issa laughed, but stopped when she realized Olivia was serious. "Who told you that? I've never heard such a thing."

"All the execs say it." Olivia waved a hand. "Anyway, I'm going to tell them that I can't be in anything else unless you're in it as well."

"That would be nice," Issa said. It would bring them close again. Issa reassured herself that they hadn't grown apart. They'd just been busy working on different projects.

"Great, read through those and decide. My brain is about fried."

"Are you shooting any scenes today?" Issa asked, flipping open a script while Olivia went to the kitchen to make tea.

"No, I don't think I even have to be on set anymore. The famous actors only show up when they're needed, so I don't know why I should have to waste my time standing around." The aroma of vanilla filled the air as she poured hot water into a mug. "I don't even want to go to the cast party at the end, they're so dull. We should check out this bar I heard about in downtown. All the stars go there. I can get someone to get us in."

"Sure, I'm not busy," Issa teased.

Olivia touched her own forehead with the back of her hand. "I feel like I'm coming down with something. Do I feel warm to you?" She came back to the couch so Issa could touch her face.

"You don't have a fever," Issa said.

"I haven't been sleeping well," Olivia said. "It's all the work. I'm so exhausted, I can't relax, and then it's back up and at 'em in the morning." She returned to the kitchen, opened a cabinet, and took out a bottle of pills.

"What's that?" Issa asked warily.

"Just a caffeine pill," Olivia said. "Mr. Grenier gave them to me. It helps me be more alert when I can't seem to shake myself awake. Want one?"

"I'm all right, I don't have much going on today."

"That's right—you're so lucky."

"You've met with Mr. Grenier again?"

"He gave me those scripts." Olivia gestured toward the stack. "Wants to discuss my future. Ours—he'll speak to you too. We'll go see him next week."

"Oh, we will?" Issa couldn't keep the irony out of her voice.

If Olivia heard it, she didn't care. "I've got to change."

"I thought you weren't going on set."

Olivia went to her room. "I changed my mind!" she called out.

Issa took advantage of her free time by attending the many classes offered to MGM contracted actors. There were dance lessons, singing coaches, accent classes. After her consultations with Jem, she had a craving for more, knowing she could always improve no matter how many films she acted in. As she was about to sign up for another acting session, Maggie Laken, the actress she'd worked with on *Lost in the Queen's Love*, appeared next to her.

"Oh, you don't want to burn yourself out, do you, hon?" Maggie asked, stopping by Issa's table and seeing her filling out the registration form.

"Hi there," Issa said, surprised and happy to see her. "We should go out for a drink or something," Issa added on impulse. It was too late to take the words back, and she didn't regret them—she did want to spend time with Maggie. For some reason, though, a small bit of guilt rose to the surface as she thought about how Olivia would react. But that was silly because Olivia had Ava . . . and other people, surely. She was so friendly and social that she must have made a hundred other friends on set, something that never came naturally to Issa.

"I'd love that!" Maggie said. "Anyway, come to my dance class with me. You'll have a blast, it's fantastic for keeping your figure, and we can chat afterward about that drink."

"Oh, all right."

"You can always ask for an acting coach," Maggie said. "Or hire one yourself, but from what I heard, you don't need one."

"What have you heard?" Issa asked.

They walked into a classroom with mirrors on the walls, which immediately made Issa jump. She looked about as if Ava might appear out of nowhere, remembering a few seconds later that Ava didn't need a mirror, nor would Ava prefer to follow Issa to a dance lesson when she could watch Olivia film something much more glamorous.

"They're saying your movie is going to be a huge hit," Maggie said.

"Oh, well . . . it was a bit like selling my soul."

Maggie guffawed. She had an explosive, unattractive laugh, nothing like the tinkling bell-like giggles of the other actresses, but it sounded all the more beautiful because she wasn't self-conscious about it.

"Aren't we all?" she asked.

Issa had trouble keeping up with the dance class. The other girls seemed so proficient, the steps memorized to the count of four. She couldn't get the rhythm down and felt as if she had woken up with four extra limbs she couldn't control. By the end of the lesson, she was sweatier than she anticipated, but she hadn't felt so exhilarated in a long time. Maggie hung behind to walk out together.

"Let's grab a bite to eat at the cafeteria," Maggie said. "Then if you don't mind, we can change and head out together."

"I should probably invite Olivia," Issa said to assuage some of the guilt she felt for making plans without her. "She's in the middle of production, so I'm not sure if she'll be up for it." The commissary wasn't that busy since it was only ten in the morning. They were seated right away.

"So tell me what you love so far about all this," Maggie said.

Issa found Maggie delightful, the way she listened as if nothing else mattered, interjecting the occasional *hon*, and *don't you know it* so naturally that Issa wondered if some people were just given a script for life that she never got a copy of. She told her about the film with WB and how different the experience was, and she was just getting around to talking about the next script she might take with Olivia when she spotted Jem walking into the commissary.

"Ooh, is that your beau?" Maggie asked.

"Yes," she admitted with a blush.

"You're quite serious about him, aren't you? I've seen you two together a lot."

"Well, it's just supposed to be a bit of fun," Issa said.

"He seems rather happy to see you," Maggie said as Jem made his way over.

"Hi there," he said, smiling at Issa in a way that made her feel as if he saw no one else but her in the entire restaurant.

"Hello," she said. "This is my friend Maggie."

"I recognize you," Jem said, shaking her hand.

"I know you're lying to flatter me, but I'll take it," Maggie said. She stood up tactfully. "I best run. I'll see you later, darling?" she asked Issa.

Issa waved goodbye while Jem took the vacant seat. "I hope I didn't interrupt your lunch date."

"Oh no, I think she was done, and we're meeting again soon anyway."

Jem folded his hands over the Formica tabletop. "How did the rest of production go? I've heard wonderful things about your performances."

"Really? How?"

"News travels fast in these circles."

"Well, if it's true, it's all thanks to your help." She leaned forward. "I should hire you on retainer for script consultations in the future."

He had unruly black hair. Some flopped onto his forehead, almost over his eyes, and she had a sudden urge to brush it away for him.

"Anytime you need my help," he said, "you just have to call."

"Perhaps you should write me a script," she said.

His expression opened with excitement. "That's a marvelous idea. When is your birthday?"

She laughed. "I was only teasing."

"I wasn't. You'd be the perfect muse."

"As long as it's not a tragedy," she said.

"No." He studied her face with a pleasant seriousness. "You deserve to be in something happy." He grabbed her hand across the table, and the expression on his face was so openly warm, so . . . loving. Something gave way in Issa's chest. She let their fingers intertwine, aware that everyone in the commissary could see them, but not caring. Was this what it was like to fall in love with someone—deeply, madly in love, the kind that erased every other desire or ambition? She imagined telling her mother, could picture her shocked expression, but nothing beyond. Would Ma be happy or angry? But she knew it wasn't her mother she had to worry about. Her grandmother would . . . Well, Issa didn't know what she'd do, but somehow the picture of mirrors exploding came to mind. And Auntie Yen . . . Well, Yen might not be as livid, but Issa didn't want to disappoint her, and she imagined that her aunt would not react pleasantly to . . . love. Or whatever this was.

Still, Issa looked at Jem and wished that her life was different, just a little bit.

Issa let herself in the house, excited from her day and eager to tell Olivia all about the hip places Maggie wanted to show them. Olivia lounged on the sofa with a hand draped over her eyes.

"Say, didn't you say you wanted to go out?" Issa asked Olivia as she put her purse down on the entrance dresser, trying to ignore the mess. "Remember Maggie from that period piece?"

"What?" Olivia asked. She lifted her arm from her face and blinked at Issa in confusion. "What are you talking about?" she practically snapped.

Issa was surprised by the sharp tone. Maybe she had woken Olivia up from a nap. She should have knocked or greeted her gently first. "Are you all right?"

Olivia sucked in a deep breath and covered her eyes with her arm again. "Yes . . . ," she groaned.

Issa sat down as slowly as she could on the edge of the sofa. She was about to place a hand on Olivia's arm, but she was filled with a self-conscious reservation she rarely felt around her best friend. "Didn't you say you wanted to go out more? I thought it'd be fun to visit a bar or club tonight. I ran into Maggie—you know, the actress on *Lost in the Queen's Love*—and she knows of all the popular joints."

Olivia made a sound of annoyance. "I'm in the middle of shooting, I can't go out." She got up so suddenly that she almost pushed Issa off the couch. "Can you not bombard me with these things when I'm just getting home?" She wore a silky kimono, and she flicked the sleeves dramatically as she went to her bedroom.

Issa frowned as she followed Olivia. "What's the matter? Did something happen?"

Olivia sat on the bed and took off her shoes. "No. Nothing. It was a tough day, and I need to work even harder if I want to earn a bigger role."

"Olivia, you're barely getting any sleep just to finish this film. Shouldn't you take a break before you dive into something new?"

"I want to be successful, Issa. You used to want the same."

"What does that mean?" Issa asked. "I still do."

"Then you should understand how important it is. I can't think about anything else right now. I need to focus on my work."

Issa hesitated. She fought several reactions, her chest churning with fiery emotions. Anger at being snapped at, but also concern. She took a deep breath to calm herself. "Do you need any tea, or . . ."

"No, Issa, *please*," Olivia snapped.

Issa was so shocked, she couldn't move for a moment. Olivia had never spoken to her so rudely, not even on their most tiring days.

She stood in the doorway, but Olivia turned to the mirror, running a brush through her hair with jerky motions.

Not wanting to leave things in such a charged state but also unwilling to prolong the tension, Issa went back to her room to get ready. When she emerged, Olivia's door was closed, and she heard shuffling and muttering inside, like Olivia was cleaning. Ava was with her, but Issa caught only disjointed words, like *fame* and *willing*, so perhaps they were strategizing over how Olivia could garner even more success. Bitter resentment left a sour taste in Issa's mouth—apparently, she wasn't good enough to join this meeting.

Issa tried not to replay the incident in her mind, but it kept creeping up as she met Maggie outside, making a noncommittal excuse for Olivia's absence. Olivia had never been so mean to her before. What had happened to put her in such a state?

Maggie took Issa to a bar not far from the lot, and it felt very much like any cast party that she'd attended, except she didn't recognize most of the people and some were too famous to acknowledge. She appreciated the distraction, but she was so distraught by Olivia's attitude that she didn't pay much attention, not even when a lurking presence appeared at her shoulder while she ordered a drink at the bar, standing so close, his chest pressed into her arm.

Issa turned around sharply, but she stopped herself when she looked up at the familiar mustache of Weston Redrick. His expression was difficult to read, but it was clear from his tense muscles and domineering looming that he wasn't happy to see her.

"Enjoy your time on Mager's movie?" he asked.

The bartender called out her drink and slid her glass tumbler across the bar. Issa was grateful for something to do with her hands as she swirled the straw around in the glass.

"I did, actually," she said. "I heard it's going to win some awards." She had no idea, of course, but it was satisfying to see his sneer slowly disintegrate.

"Oh, I'm sure the board is going to choose some low-budget film with a nobody as their lead over Jonathan Graylick's feature and his two glowing stars," Redrick said. He shrugged. "But you never know. Sometimes they feel sorry and throw the little dogs a bone."

His drink was ready as well, and he took a swig, his lips wrapping repulsively around the mouth of the beer bottle as he walked away without giving her time to reply.

Chapter Thirty-Seven

Issa didn't see Olivia for a couple of days after that, whether by design or accident, she couldn't tell. She wanted to tell her about her run-in with Redrick, but after a few days, the resentment died down, and she found herself laughing it off. What a disgusting man. He was probably just goading her, or maybe he'd figured out that they had deliberately invited people to his dumb dinner party. Had he discovered that they'd stolen his trophy? Oh, who cared. What was he going to do about it anyway?

Olivia usually got home after Issa fell asleep, and since she wasn't filming, Issa let herself sleep in until well after Olivia had left for the day. It hadn't exactly been a fight, had it? It felt like it, but the more time passed that neither of them addressed it, the more Issa began to doubt herself. Maybe Olivia hadn't spoken so sharply. Maybe Issa had just been overly sensitive. They were both so tired from working all the time. Perhaps things had simply blown out of proportion.

When she visited Auntie Yen, she wanted to tell her about Olivia, but Yen seemed as distracted as always. There was a time when her aunt would have remarked upon Olivia's absence. Yet Yen didn't ask or even seem to notice. Their lessons were no better than the instructions Issa had received from Bà Ngoại, usually cut short because Yen had to deal with an emergency—some attack on a business or negotiations with the Uncles, which didn't seem to progress in any way and only caused the shadows beneath Yen's eyes to grow darker each time Issa saw her. When Issa asked if she could help, Yen brushed aside her offers.

On Friday morning, Issa was surprised to see Olivia being her cheerful self as she flitted around the kitchen.

"Tea?" Olivia asked, already setting out their mugs.

Tension pulled at the air between them, but Olivia was so astutely ignoring it that Issa wondered if perhaps it was one-sided and she was placing too much weight on things.

"Sure," she said, taking a seat at the dining table.

"You don't have anything to do today, do you?" Olivia asked.

"I was going to go to more lessons."

"Can you skip them?" Olivia was being overly nice, more sweetness lacing her voice than usual. The manipulative tone she usually used on other people. "Mr. Grenier wants to meet."

"Of course. We can't very well turn down a summons from the great Grenier."

"Perfect. We'll just have our tea and get ready to go."

They made the trek across the studio lot toward the executive building, not saying much. Issa couldn't help noting the difference in this walk compared to the first. They'd been so hesitant and nervous before, and now they strode through the backlot with the confidence of people in a hurry who didn't have time for such silly insecurities.

Grenier didn't even make them wait—it must really be important. Issa sat down in front of his desk, feeling like a student in the principal's office about to get in trouble. Were they going to end her contract? Had she been so horrible that they didn't want to lose any more money on her? What about Olivia? She looked just as nervous, wringing her hands together in her lap.

"Did you like any of the scripts?" he boomed across the desk.

Issa fought not to wince.

"I did, I like the one about the two best friends," Olivia said. "I'd like to be in it with Issa, please."

Grenier looked between the two of them. "That's what I asked you here to talk about." His tone had an ominous ring to it, the kind that preceded unwanted news.

Issa stayed quiet.

"But you said we could do a movie together," Olivia said.

"I said if the last one does well, you can," Grenier said. "But we won't know for a few months now."

"That's a bit of trickery, isn't it?" Olivia said, crossing her arms.

Grenier ignored the sullen glare Olivia shot at him. "The good news is, Warner Bros. wants to buy your contract," he said to Issa.

"What?" Issa asked. She'd heard him, but her entire body went numb, knowing what it meant.

Olivia bolted upright. "No, you can't. You simply can't."

"I can," Mr. Grenier said. "And that's why I wanted to talk." He looked down at some papers and picked up a package. "After some negotiating, we decided to lease you out. It's a generous offer, and you'll get a large bonus out of it." He handed the contract to Issa.

The numbers were underlined. "Wow," she breathed. It was more than she had ever hoped to make. "Three hundred a week with a thousand dollar signing."

"What?" Olivia took the contract to see for herself. "But . . . but . . ."

It was more than their original contract with MGM, which meant Issa would make more than Olivia.

"You can't leave," Olivia said. Her eyes welled up. "Where will you live? You can't stay on the lot if you're not contracted here."

"WB will compensate us for your stay," Grenier said.

"I don't want you to go." Olivia grabbed Issa's hand as if afraid she'd make a run for it.

"It's not up to her," Grenier said. "It's up to me."

"Then you can't make her," Olivia said. "I don't want to be in a movie without her. I won't."

Grenier leaned back in his seat and gave Olivia a blank, serious look.

"You're under contract, Olivia," Issa said. "You have to."

"No," Olivia said, tears streaming down her face. "We're supposed to stick together. This is our dream."

"I know, sweetheart." And just like that, Issa's anger from the other day was forgotten. She put an arm around Olivia's shoulder. "It'll be all right. It's just for a little while. Look, it's only three movies, and once they're done, I'll come back to MGM as if I never left. We can always renegotiate once these contracts end."

Olivia gave a soft sob in answer.

"Warner Bros. will send over their details in a few days," Grenier said to Issa over the sounds of Olivia crying. "You can stay in the suite until they sort things out—and you can still—"

Olivia hiccupped loudly.

"—take advantage of the lot, of course," he continued. "You're still one of us until we talk again."

"Until the contract is bought, you mean," Olivia said.

Grenier ignored her. "Congratulations, Issa. You're going to be a huge success, I can feel it."

"He's lying," Olivia said when they got home.

Issa hadn't said anything during their walk back, still trying to decide how she felt about the entire business. It couldn't be as horrible as Olivia made it out to be. Sure, she was disappointed they wouldn't get to be in their next movies together, but Issa hadn't minded her time at WB.

"If you were really going to be a huge success," Olivia continued, "he would do everything to keep you. I don't know who's really pulling the strings here. It must be Redrick. He knows we took the trophy! This is his payback."

"I ran into him the other night," Issa said. "He didn't admit as much, but I think he's responsible for me going to Warner Bros. He knew Mager wanted me on his film."

But Olivia wasn't listening to her, not really. "See? He couldn't stand a bit of rejection, so now he's taking away the one thing I love."

"Olivia," Issa said with a sigh. "What—are you saying you don't think Warner Bros. really wanted me for me?"

"Why would they?" Olivia threw her hands up. "This is a conspiracy."

Issa frowned but was too focused on her hurt to question where Olivia had gotten *that*. "You don't think I'm going to be a success?"

"Not at Warner Bros.!" Olivia shrieked.

Issa stepped back. She had never heard Olivia shriek like that, never seen her so angry. Her color had risen, her cheeks splotchy and red, the muscles hard around her eyes.

"This is not fair! How could you leave me?" Olivia cried. She swung her arms out, knocking Ava's trophy to the ground.

Issa bent to pick it up. Olivia breathed hard, staring down at something Issa couldn't see. She didn't look like herself, her hair a frizzy halo, her jaw clenched, her shoulders drawn up like some humpbacked creature. As her breath returned to normal, her face smoothed into a shocked expression. She looked at Issa and burst into tears.

Issa placed Ava's trophy on the side table and went to hug her. But before she could, Olivia covered her face with her hands and ran, sobbing, to her room.

She wouldn't come out no matter what Issa tried, whispering words of comfort through her door, then begging her to come out. Issa even called on Ava to talk some sense into Olivia, but for the first time, the ghost didn't show up. Or maybe she was already with Olivia on the other side of the door.

Chapter Thirty-Eight

The last time Issa had been at the Warner Bros. lot, she'd known exactly where to go, but a couple of weeks later when she was summoned to the studio, she felt lost. Luckily, Larry Mager met her at the gate.

"The other execs want to meet with you," he said, using a handkerchief to wipe the sweat on his face. It was a gloomy but hot and humid day.

"Am I in trouble?" Issa asked as she followed him across the lot.

"No, no, it's just to discuss your new contract with us, perhaps some scripts and other business."

"What business?"

He waved a hand. "You'll see. Don't worry so much. They're excited to have you. They wouldn't have paid for a lease on you otherwise."

He took her to an empty conference room in a high-rise building. From the fifth floor, they had a lovely view of the rest of the lot as well as Burbank's hills, green landscaping, and charming houses. A secretary brought Issa some hot tea in a paper cup and bowed from the waist like she was some foreign dignitary, a gesture Issa chose to ignore.

After several minutes, two men in stiff suits came in.

"Larry!" the first one said, clapping Mager on the back. He was short and slim, and he held his hand out when he noticed Issa.

"Issa Bui," he said like her name was all one word. "It's wonderful to meet you."

She shook his hand, struggling only a little when he pulled her in for a hug. The other man, who was much taller, nodded at her politely.

"Jordan Garner," the first man said, holding a hand to his chest. "Executive producer. My colleague Henry Bookerman, also an executive producer."

Issa wasn't sure exactly what executive producers did, but she understood that they had a lot of power. "Nice to meet you," she said, remembering that she should probably get in their good graces if she had any hope of getting worthy roles in her next three movies with them. "I must say, I'm incredibly excited to be part of Warner Bros. now."

"Oh, so are we." Garner sat down across the long table, unbuttoning the middle button of his jacket. "We've got some exciting scripts being rewritten right now for you."

"Really?" Was that something they said to all their actresses? She shouldn't read too much into it, though, since Jem said that scripts were rewritten all the time. "I hope they're good roles."

Garner chuckled and looked at Bookerman, who also laughed. Mager gave a few hearty shakes of his shoulders but remained quiet, waiting for the other two men to speak.

"We'll get your scripts to you soon, we promise," Garner said. "But first we want to talk to you about something else."

"Oh?" Issa studied Mager's expression for a hint of what that was, but he remained blank faced.

Garner waited for Bookerman to speak.

"Is it true you've struck up a relationship with Jem Meier?" he asked. His voice was deeper, and he had a much more serious attitude about him, his glasses lending to the effect.

"What?" Issa asked. "He's been helping me with some script . . . reading . . . and, well, yes, we've gone out a few times." She blinked, unsure why this would matter professionally.

"You were seen," Bookerman said, and like they were in some sort of detective movie, he pulled a photograph from the inside pocket of his jacket. It showed Jem with his arm wrapped around her shoulder, his head lowered close to hers. Issa remembered that night, the first time she'd been recognized as they'd walked past a storefront. He had merely been offering her words of encouragement—but anyone looking at the picture would assume they were about to kiss.

"We were sent this photograph by someone who works in the tabloids—a friend," Bookerman went on. "Sometimes, they offer us the opportunity to quiet any rumors we might not want circulating about our stars."

Issa was flattered to be included in this group, even though she hardly felt like a star. "You bribe them to keep photos from being released to the public?"

"Precisely."

"But why would you need to pay for this one?"

The men fell quiet, their faces slates of discomfort as if they couldn't bring themselves to explain the exact reasons Issa was an embarrassment.

"Are you aware, Miss Bui," Bookerman said, which was never the start of a good question, "that interracial marriages are outlawed in our country?"

"Marriage?" Issa tried not to laugh. "But Jem and I are just having fun. We're hardly going to get married." In fact, she had made that clear with Jem when they began their relationship, though she'd rather choke than bring that up.

"But you have an image to protect. And this picture would indicate that you are . . . acting in a way that would be misconstrued as untoward . . . outside the bounds of marriage."

Issa sat back, speechless. "Goodness," she whispered to herself.

"You've created a rather . . . wholesome persona," Garner said, stepping in with a cheerful smile. He lifted his palms up. "It's what the audiences love about you. Your roles, they're all wonderful girls. We want to boost that public image in any way we can."

"Which starts with eliminating instances like this," Bookerman said, tapping the photograph.

Issa didn't know what to say, her teeth grinding together without her realizing it. "It's not interracial," she said eventually.

"What?" Garner asked, twisting his head a bit to turn his ear toward her, a gesture that reminded her of a fifth grade teacher.

"Jem is Filipino," she pointed out.

"He looks Caucasian to me," Bookerman said.

"But he's also—"

"It doesn't matter what he *is*," Garner said. "It's what he *looks* like. As well as you, Issa. I can call you Issa, right?"

"That is my name," Issa said, though she didn't charge it with nearly enough sarcasm.

"Your public image belongs to the studio now, you must recall," Garner continued. "As stipulated in your contract. It represents the studio, as well as the movies you play. It has a large impact on the way audiences view you and whether they're willing to see your films. And you do want them to see your films, Issa, otherwise, well . . . what's the point in making them?"

It was a badly concealed, happily delivered threat.

"I see," Issa said.

"We're so glad that you do," Garner said. "Of course, we understand the impact your career has on your personal life, so we've set you up with some comfortable accommodations. You'll let Mager know if they're to your liking?"

Issa could only nod.

"And not to worry about Mr. Meier," Garner added. "We'll make sure he knows that it was our decision."

"What—what does that mean?" Issa asked.

"We'll have the same discussion with him. He's in the business, he'll understand, though of course his contract doesn't have the same stipulation as yours. He'll no doubt agree with us, however. Unless, that is, you'd rather tell him yourself?"

"I—I don't—" Issa stumbled.

"Not to worry, dear," Mager said, patting the air as if it were her hand, but sitting too far to actually do so. "We'll take care of it."

Issa took in a deep breath, her lungs pushing against the bodice of her dress, unable to form any words. Her Peter Pan collar, a detail on most of the dresses the studios chose for her to amplify her "wholesome persona" as Garner had put it, constricted around her neck, and she sat there, ignoring the two men as they got up and left.

Chapter Thirty-Nine

She seethed all the way back to MGM, where she was supposed to pack up the rest of her things to move into the new apartment Warner Bros. had arranged for her—a fancier and much more spacious apartment, not just a dressing room, in walking distance from the lot. At first, she had wanted to resist—she was used to living in small quarters and didn't require such extravagances, but after the meeting with Garner and Bookerman, she decided she would take whatever she could get from the studio and never look back.

What annoyed her most was that she had never even sought out any sort of romance, had insisted that any relationship she got involved in remain as unserious as possible. She'd always considered herself too busy, too above all that nonsense. The fact that men in her clan never seemed to survive for long—whether romantically or in life—meant that Issa rarely entertained the thought of such frivolity. But she had to admit that Jem . . . Jem was different. She had let herself think, just for a moment, that it was possible . . . for love . . . for anything resembling love . . . to perhaps . . .

Well, it didn't matter, did it? Not when she was under contract.

She should call him. But the idea of it filled her with dread. Later. Once she was settled in her new place, she'd ask him to meet, discuss what to do in person. Surely there was some way they could work around this.

The moment she stepped into the dressing room she'd shared with Olivia, her tension only grew. They hadn't spoken since Olivia's explosive reaction to her contract getting leased. Olivia had holed up in her room whenever Issa was home, or she was out filming or . . . doing whatever else she got up to these days.

So much had changed between them. Olivia's door was closed, so Issa figured she was probably napping or simply signaling she didn't want to be disturbed.

Issa stuffed as many clothes as she could into her weekend bag. She'd have to send for the rest of her things—she'd gotten so many new items from the studio since moving. All lovely, but all similar. Cute, wholesome outfits that made her appear younger. Naive and demure. An obedient little girl. MGM and WB, it was all the same.

Olivia's door opened slowly. Issa stopped in the middle of folding a shirt to stare at it. It was quite eerie, the creak of the hinges, the darkened room beyond.

When Olivia emerged, she wore a striking costume. It must have been from her movie, something historical, though Issa couldn't remember if Olivia was in a period piece. The dress was made of golden fabric, almost like thin, threadbare chainmail, scantily assembled pieces barely hanging on to Olivia, revealing more than what she normally chose to. Matching jewelry adorned her hair and ears, a golden headpiece draping down her back like a veil.

Olivia swayed about in a dance. Perhaps she was practicing for a number in her film. She didn't seem to realize Issa was there.

"Olivia," Issa said, following her to the living room.

"Oh, Issa darling, hi," Olivia said, not missing a beat. "Do you like my outfit?"

"Is it for your film?" Issa asked.

Olivia laughed. "No, there's a costume party tonight. You should come."

"I'm sick of parties."

"Don't you dare say such a thing—that's sacrilegious here."

"Are you really going out like that?"

"Why not? I look sexy, don't I?" Olivia swayed her hips, the bones protruding against the dress. Her eyes had a glazed look to them, but Issa didn't smell alcohol.

"You sure do," Issa said. She thought about saying more, but Olivia continued dancing freely, her arms moving above her head, so Issa went back to packing in her room. When she finished, she found Olivia stretched out on the sofa, fast asleep.

She had to talk to someone about Olivia's behavior.

But when she visited Yen's apartment, her aunt wasn't home. The man who usually acted as some sort of butler answered the door.

"There's been a disturbance," he said haltingly in English. "A store—a fire."

"A fire?" Issa echoed in horror.

"Third one this month," he added.

"Is Yen all right? Should I go find her—where is it?"

He shook his head. "No, no, she did not want you to know. Please, I shouldn't have said. Don't. Please."

Issa nodded. She took pity on the man and left him, too antsy to return home after that.

Instead, she visited Ma. It was the perfect time in the afternoon to catch her. She'd be awake and making something to eat before going to work. Issa took the Red Car out of habit, which she regretted immediately, plagued with the self-conscious sensation that everyone was staring at her. She was used to stares since she looked so different, but recently it happened more frequently than usual. Passengers ahead of her twisted around to look, then whispered to one another.

Issa got off the streetcar early, partly to avoid the staring, and partly because she wanted to visit a nearby bakery and get Ma one of her favorite pork buns.

Holding a box of six pastries, Issa walked the remaining four blocks, a familiar pang hitting her as she went up the steps to her old apartment building. After living in the luxurious accommodations the studio provided, the crumbling bricks stood out to her, the peeling paint on the walls, the dusty corners full of cobwebs, the low ceilings, the dim, flickering lights.

She let herself in with her old key, stopping as Ma rushed out of the hallway to the entrance, still in her floral-print pajamas.

"Ayah, you scared me half to death," Ma said. "Why didn't you say you were coming?"

Issa was used to her mother's rough manner, but it still rankled that Ma wasn't ecstatic to see her after the many weeks apart. "How? Did you get a telephone?"

Ma didn't like to be outsmarted. "What do you want, hah?"

"Gee, Ma, I'm glad to see you too." Issa placed the box of pork buns on the table, about to turn around and go home. "I just wanted to say hi."

Ma took a deep breath. "You're right. I'm sorry—you scared me. It's been a while, how was I supposed to know? I thought maybe something bad happened."

"No." Issa thought about Olivia. But how could she explain that they went behind Ma's back and did exactly what she forbade them from doing? And neither could she express her concerns over Auntie Yen. And what could Ma do with the information, anyhow? "Everything is going fine."

"You sure?"

Issa nodded.

Ma took a seat at the table, and gestured for Issa to do the same, so Issa sat and opened the box. The smell of freshly baked bread and savory meat hit them, and Ma reached in.

"Thank you for bringing these," she said. "You're such a good girl."

"Even though I don't visit often?"

Ma shrugged. "You're busy. You have your own life. Always knew it would happen."

She didn't say it, but Issa wondered if tacked on the end of that was a subtle, *I'm proud of you*. Not that Ma would admit it out loud.

"I'm at a different studio now," Issa said.

Ma waved a hand, a dismissal. She wanted nothing to do with Issa's work. And it was just as well, because Issa didn't know how to explain her meeting with the Warner Bros. executives without having Ma go into conniptions about her dating some man in the same industry anyway. Ma wanted Issa to settle down with a good Catholic Vietnamese man from her church. She was probably secretly waiting for Issa's movie phase to pass so she could introduce Issa to the son of a friend of a friend.

"How are things at the hotel?" Issa asked.

"It's the same. I go in, I do laundry, I leave. Simple."

"Oh. Right." Silence. "And your church?"

At that, Ma smiled. "We're having a bake sale next month. Perhaps you can come to that, hah? Meet someone?"

Issa smiled. "I'd love to," she said truthfully.

"Really?" Ma almost dropped her pork bun. "All right, then, I'll give you a pamphlet."

While she went to her bedroom to grab one, Issa wrote down her new address on a piece of paper, in case Ma ever needed her for anything. She glanced around for the best place to leave it. The apartment seemed the same—the piles of clutter on the counters, the cabinet of junk mail still so full it remained perpetually open, the blankets and throw pillows on the couch. Nothing had changed, as if it didn't matter one way or another whether Issa was there.

She stared down at her address and doubted that Ma would ever need it. But she taped it next to the entrance anyway, just in case.

Chapter Forty

Her new apartment was indeed extravagant. With two bedrooms, it was much bigger than she needed or wanted, but she would never complain, especially when she saw the bathroom, which was probably as big as Ma's entire apartment. A large tub that could fit five dominated one corner, and across from it double sinks, as if she expected to have more company than they'd ever allow her to. She had a large balcony with a round balustrade, and stepping onto it, she felt like a princess in a tower. She imagined someone dashing waiting at the bottom, smiling at the mental image until Jem's face appeared on the charming gentleman in this scenario.

She considered calling him to explain how the studio executives didn't want her to see him. But the idea of it felt too embarrassing to contemplate. She didn't like the idea of him hearing it from the stiff men in suits, either, but she couldn't bring herself to pick up the phone, and the longer she put it off, the harder it became until she forced herself to stop thinking about it altogether.

She spent the week moving her things in, somehow managing to avoid Olivia whenever she went back to MGM to pack.

That weekend, the shrill ring of her telephone woke her. It was Olivia.

"Issa, darling," she said happily into the phone. "I've missed you! I just heard the news, congratulations!"

"What news?" Issa asked.

"Your movie! The one you were in for Warner Bros. *Across Stormy Waters*—it's making major waves. Pun unintended." Olivia laughed. Her voice sounded different, an affected accent lilting her vowels like she was playing a part.

"What sort of major waves? I haven't heard anything."

"Apparently WB was getting nervous about such a controversial film, so they did a soft release on the East Coast, and it's garnering lots of attention. Didn't they tell you anything? Oh darling, let's see each other soon, shall we? I've missed you."

"Sure," Issa said, feeling somewhat vindicated to have Olivia beg for an outing together, although she did actually look forward to it.

"Right now?" Olivia asked. "We'll have a late breakfast. I can come to you."

"That'd be great. I'll get ready."

Issa hung up the phone and got out of bed. Maybe this was all they needed, some time to talk, just the two of them, no movie or work to distract them.

The phone rang again as she came out of the shower.

"I wanted to tell you the news," Larry Mager said.

"About the movie?" she asked. "I heard from Olivia."

He laughed. "Of course, she heard about the nomination first."

"Nomination? She didn't say anything about that—she said it's making waves on the East Coast."

"Oh. Oh, well then I do get to break the news first. You're up for an award."

"An Oscar?"

He laughed so loud, it created static through the phone. "Well no. It's an independent award, known as the Committee of Cinematic Excellence. But it's very much like an Oscar!"

Issa laughed. Winning an Academy Award was a far-fetched dream she knew would never come true. "That's still so exciting."

"The execs want to meet with you again. Shall we say next week?"

"All right, then."

"Great. We'll arrange it. See you then. And good job, dear."

Issa finished getting ready in a hurry, thinking Olivia would arrive soon. But after she'd styled her hair and applied makeup, she sat around and waited for at least thirty minutes, irritation flaring wider and wider as each second passed. She even called the doorman and asked if Olivia was waiting in the lobby, but there was no one that fit her description.

Issa thought about leaving to do something else, to show Olivia that she had important plans and a busy schedule and couldn't afford to wait around for her all day.

An hour after that, she was practically in tears, angry and disappointed, when the phone rang.

"Your friend is here for you, Miss Bui," the doorman announced.

Issa thanked him and hung up, tempted to ditch Olivia completely and never come down. She lingered by the balcony, taking in a deep breath to calm herself while she pretended to enjoy the view of the city. It wasn't like she and Olivia had decided upon a time, so she couldn't be angry at her for being so late. But still, Olivia had said *now*, and it was nearly two hours later.

Several deep breaths helped to calm her nerves, but Issa wanted to stomp and cry every time she thought of Olivia. She would leave her waiting downstairs. She wouldn't come down.

But then what? She'd have to hole up in her apartment until Olivia left. She hadn't gone anywhere in days, except to move her things, and the idea of another minute cooped up by herself was unfathomable. She had to get out of there. She had to see someone, talk to someone who cared about her, really cared. Not Ma, who wasn't interested; not Bà Ngoại, who only wanted other things from her; not Auntie Yen, who was too busy with her own problems. Olivia had always been there for her. She'd been the only one who understood Issa's worries and dreams and all the things that made her *her*. So they had grown apart recently. That's what people did, but it didn't change a thing about their friendship.

When Issa reached the lobby, an apology was already on her lips. But Olivia wasn't sitting by herself, waiting for Issa to show up. She was surrounded by a crowd of people, signing autographs. She looked radiant amid all that attention, her skin glowing, her hair shiny and thick as it flowed down her back, her smile so genuine, so bright.

Issa stood at the edge of the crowd. She'd never been recognized by so many people, had never been adored by such loving fans. People in the building stared at her a lot, but no one had approached her with any amount of reverence. She shouldn't compare herself to Olivia, but she couldn't help it. They had started their careers at the same time, and if anything, Issa had more films under her belt than Olivia had.

Of course, she had always suspected it would be like this. Olivia had always been the more beautiful one. She'd always had a magnetism that drew people to her, attracted attention when Issa got barely a passing glance. So it was only natural that as stars, Olivia would shine brighter.

Issa was about to turn around and go back upstairs, but then Olivia caught her eye. She held up a hand, making heads turn toward Issa.

"That's my friend!" Olivia said in a high singsong voice. "The one who has just been nominated for an *awaaaard*." She drew out the last syllable like she was on a musical set, handed a man his notebook back, and pushed her way through the crowd. She grabbed Issa's elbows, leaning down a little to kiss her on both cheeks. They had never greeted each other that way before. Olivia was putting on quite a show. "Congratulations, darling!" She took Issa's elbow and pulled her toward the door. "We must celebrate now."

She waved at the crowd. Issa looked over her shoulder as people turned to whisper to each other, their eyes on her now instead of Olivia.

"Oh thank goodness you arrived when you did," Olivia said, pulling a pair of sunglasses from her purse.

"You looked to be enjoying yourself," Issa said, her annoyance at Olivia's lateness amplified by the fact that Olivia had barely noticed.

"I have to, otherwise I'd have no fans." Olivia sighed. "What's a good place to eat around here? Should we take a cab to downtown?"

Issa was about to say, *Whatever you'd like to do,* out of habit, but she pressed her lips together to stop herself. "There's a nice café I like to eat at."

"A café? To celebrate? Shouldn't we do something fancier?"

"Come on, it's me we're celebrating," Issa pointed out.

"You're right, darling." Olivia laughed. "I'm just so used to having it my way. You should see our suite now. It's practically covered in gifts—I don't know where to put them all. You should come over and take what you want."

"Gifts for what?" Issa asked.

"Why, for my nomination."

"Your . . . you were nominated as well?"

"Yes." Olivia laughed. "I always told you, you should read the newspapers more often. Don't you subscribe to *Variety*?"

"I do—I did—when I lived with you."

"I'm surprised the studio didn't just get you a subscription."

"It's here," Issa said, gesturing to the café. It had a winding staircase covered in vines, lending the place a whimsical and fairy tale–like atmosphere.

"Oh, how lovely!"

"This is your celebration, too, then," Issa said as they were seated. "Are you also up for an award from the Committee of Cinematic Excellence?"

"Well, no . . ."

"I admit, I'd never heard of the organization," Issa said. "It's no Oscar." She paused, trying not to show any sign that she was upset. "Are you up for an Oscar?"

"Yes! Isn't that insane?" Olivia laughed beautifully. "Whoever thought it was possible?"

Issa forced herself to smile. It was easy, now that she'd taken so many acting classes. "Congratulations, Olivia!"

"Nonsense, I came to congratulate you," Olivia said. "But if you must insist, we can go out this weekend to celebrate. Have you been to the Green Room yet?"

"No—what's that?"

"It's quite the rage. It's exclusive to actors and actresses. If you're not recognized, you won't get in."

"Oh, then maybe we should try something less—"

"Darling!" Olivia flicked her white napkin out and placed it on her lap. "You're going to have to get used to your fame and enjoy it. They'll surely let you in, and if they don't, you'll be with me. I've been there loads of times."

Issa's energy left her, deflating like an unknotted balloon. Why did she think going out with Olivia would be fun and rejuvenating? Why had she deluded herself thinking they would go back to the way they used to be?

She stared at Olivia, noting all the little changes—the more expensive clothing; the makeup, which Olivia had always been good at applying, that now looked even more professional and flawless; the hair, the glorious, shiny strands like a black river down her back. Her posture had improved as well, her spine straight, shoulders back, and neck elongated. Issa had never noticed how much Olivia used to slouch until now. How much life used to weigh her down. Did it still weigh Issa down? Did Issa slouch like that? Surely a director would have told her by now, but then again, none of her roles had ever been for elegant, well-to-do women, had they?

Her ears filled with a distracting buzzing, her mind fuzzy while Olivia chatted on and on about what she was up to, barely touching her salad, and Issa nodding while she ate, grateful, actually, that Olivia filled the silence so she wouldn't have to think of something to say. If Olivia noticed, she didn't show it, happier than Issa had seen her in a long time.

As they walked back to Issa's apartment, she looked forward to being back inside her little cave. She planned to change into her most comfortable nightgown and lay on the floor and perhaps have a nice glass of wine and a good cry.

"So we'll meet this Saturday night?" Olivia asked. "Why don't you come to the lot, and we'll take a taxi from there?"

"All right, then," Issa said, exhausted and sleepy from the large meal. "I'm looking forward to it."

Olivia blew her a kiss.

"Give Ava my regards," Issa added as her friend turned to leave.

Olivia looked briefly surprised. "Oh, I certainly shall."

Chapter Forty-One

She wanted to talk to Jem. Knew she should have called him days ago. But at this point, the execs would have met with him, and he was probably wondering why she hadn't gotten in touch with him first, and the idea of it only made her sink further into despair. Besides, what if they were seen? Would the studio cancel her contract? She couldn't risk it.

That Saturday night, she got dressed in one of her skimpier outfits. She telephoned Olivia to say she was on her way, but it kept ringing and ringing. Perhaps Olivia hadn't remembered their plans. Maybe Issa should stay home and play it safe.

But if she was being honest with herself, she had looked forward to going out all week. Dancing would be good for both her body and soul, and who knew, maybe she'd meet some new friends while she was out. Not just connections for furthering her career, but friends who might enjoy her company.

Feeling a little anxious that Olivia might have ditched her for someone or something better, she took a taxi to the MGM lot and walked through the studio to the dressing rooms. The lights were on. Issa knocked, but no one opened the door. She still had her key, so ignoring the feeling that she was breaking in, she unlocked the door.

She stopped, her hand frozen on the knob. The place was a disaster, even worse than the last time she was there. It looked like someone had ransacked it searching for valuables—the kitchen drawers were open, the counters cluttered with dishes, some with food still crusted on them. There were clothes all over the floor and sofa. A lingering odor permeated the air, subtle but undistinguishable, like it had already fused into the walls. Not quite rancid, but reminding Issa of mold and rot. What was it?

"Olivia?"

Something stirred on the sofa, making Issa jump. A hand emerged from the layers of clothes.

As Issa got closer to the sofa, she realized Olivia was sleeping there, black strands of her hair appearing randomly from beneath the fabric, an arm flung over the side. "Olivia." Issa bent down and tried to shake her. Beneath the clothes, something hard and sharp jutted out. Issa pulled off a shirt and a scarf, discovering an Oscar trophy. Ava's. Wrapped around it was a bony arm. Olivia's.

Olivia was sleeping with Ava's trophy.

Issa wasn't sure what to think. Did Olivia want an Oscar that badly?

Olivia's hand stirred again, reaching up to pull off the dress covering her face. She blinked out at Issa in confusion.

"Ava?" she asked.

"What?" Issa said. "No, it's me."

When Olivia continued to blink hazily at her, Issa pointed at her chest.

"It's Issa." Was Olivia drunk? Or on drugs? It wouldn't be the first time Issa had heard of actresses resorting to such a thing to get through the grueling work hours and the parties practically mandated after. "Olivia, are you all right? Are you on something? Do you need a doctor?"

"No, God, why?" Olivia groaned and hugged the trophy to herself.

"Because you're . . . not . . ." Issa didn't know how to describe the state Olivia was in. "Where is Ava?" she asked instead. "I haven't seen her in a while." Then, feeling stupid because she was the medium between the two of them, she looked at the mirror. "Ava?" The familiar smell of incense hit her nostrils, but Ava didn't appear. "Have you seen her lately?"

Olivia sat upright. "I'm up," she said.

Issa sat next to her. "Are you all right?"

"Yes, why do you ask?"

"You were sleeping under a pile of clothes."

"Oh, that." Olivia flicked aside a blouse. "I was trying them on and got tired."

Issa glanced around the little house. "How long have you been trying them on?"

Olivia shrugged. "You know how it is. You think something looks nice, then as soon as you step out of your bedroom, you notice how ghastly your knees look."

It was odd, this change. Olivia had always been so neat and fastidious, so careful not to step on anyone's toes or leave anything out of place for fear of offending anyone whose graces she depended upon.

Olivia gave a big yawn and leaned back, blinking like she might fall asleep again. "What are you doing here?"

Issa's disappointment tasted like chalk. "We had plans to go out tonight. Some club you said was incredibly exclusive."

"Oh right, right. I forgot."

"We don't have to go," Issa said.

"Of course I want to go." Olivia stood up. "Give me ten minutes." But she swayed, holding a hand up to her forehead, and sat back down.

"It's fine, Olivia," Issa said, though she could barely keep the exasperation out of her voice. She would go home and change out of her uncomfortable dress and brew some tea instead.

Olivia smoothed her palm down her face and breathed heavily. Heart melting, Issa scooted closer to her on the couch, ignoring the piles of clothes in her way.

"Really, it's all right," Issa said, taking Olivia's free hand.

"Oh, it's so silly," Olivia said, almost nonsensically. "What's the point of me?"

"What?" Issa wasn't sure she'd heard correctly. "What do you mean?"

"I mean, what's the point of me?" Olivia repeated. "I'm so useless. No one loves me. No one cares about me at all. My own parents—" Her voice ended on a sob.

Issa wrapped an arm around Olivia's shoulders. She had never heard Olivia talk like that. Her shoulders heaved, and she sucked in gasping breaths like she couldn't get enough air.

"What's brought this on?" Issa asked. "Was it your uncle? Did he come by asking for money again?"

"He can't get through the gate," Olivia said. "But he's sent a few messages."

"I'm sorry, Olivia. What are you going to do?"

"I don't know." Olivia's face tensed with worry, then crumpled as tears fell down her cheeks. Issa barely understood her next words. "He was the only one who cared about me."

"That's not true, Olivia, I care about you," Issa said. "Of course people love you. Ma cares about you, and Auntie Yen does too. They're always asking about you."

Olivia only sobbed, and Issa didn't know what else to say, her chest twisting with anguish as she could only sit there being useless.

"I care about you," Issa repeated. She wasn't sure, however, that Olivia heard her above the sound of her own sobbing.

Chapter Forty-Two

Issa spent the night at Olivia's, sleeping in her old bedroom, which felt cold and foreign. Despite her weariness, she tossed and turned, her night filled with dark dreams she couldn't remember, and she woke up in a shivering sweat. Finally, she gave up and went into the kitchen to make tea, surprised to find Olivia already up and about, tidying the mess in the living room.

Olivia smiled. "Make me a cup, will you?"

Issa pulled out two mugs and prepared the hot water while she watched Olivia drape dresses over her arm and carry them into her room.

When the tea was ready, Olivia came back out and joined Issa at the table.

"Olivia," Issa said, unable to stop thinking about last night. "Are you . . . feeling all right?"

"What do you mean?" Olivia asked, widening her eyes in cheerful innocence.

But Issa knew Olivia. She knew when she was acting and when she wasn't. "I can ask Auntie Yen to speak to your uncle," she said.

"No." Olivia shut her down. "It's fine. He's harmless, really. What could he possibly do? He'll go away once he realizes I'm not going to pay him." But her eyes shifted, and it was clear she didn't truly believe her own words.

"I care about you, you know," Issa said softly.

Olivia's face flashed with panic, which she covered up with a smile. "Of course I do, silly." She laughed. "I care about you too. We're best friends. I was thinking," she added quickly, "for your next movie—our next movie—we should fight to be in it together. We can ask WB to lend you back. Isn't it time to renegotiate your contract? It's been, what, four movies?"

"Only one," Issa said with a chuckle. "And that was under a different leasing contract."

Olivia waved a hand. "Studios do it all the time. You just need to take a stance. Be firm." Olivia's eyes were red, dark shadows underneath. Yet despite how less-than-perfect she appeared, Issa recognized a lucidity in her eyes that seemed to have been missing the last few times Issa had seen her.

"I'll ask Mager about it," Issa said, though it was unlikely WB would return her to MGM after paying so much for her lease before they'd even made anything. But she didn't want to ruin Olivia's happy mood.

"I'll talk to the director," Olivia said. "We'll make it happen, you and me. We'll be together again." She reached across the table and took Issa's hand, and Issa smiled, her heart warmed. All the insecurities she felt about Olivia's friendship disappeared, at least for that moment. They would always be close, even if they drifted apart now and then, lived their own lives and worked toward their own ambitions. Bonds like theirs were unbreakable, and Issa had nothing to worry about.

She called Larry Mager to tell him about the film Olivia had suggested, and was summoned to the studio for a meeting to discuss it later in the week.

"We've got something great," one of the suits told her—she couldn't keep their names straight anymore. They all blended together, white middle-aged men who seemed more knowledgeable about what was good for her than she was. The movie they told her about had nothing to do with the one Olivia mentioned.

"We've got a strong actor for you to play against," one man said. "Richard Jenner. You'll look great together. Of course, there will be no romance, explicitly. Just implied. I'm sure you'll agree."

She sat there, only half listening, knowing there was no point in discussing it.

"But what about Olivia?" she asked.

"Perhaps after this one," one of the men said placatingly. "If you make a profit, we'll let you decide whatever you want to do next. Even if it means lending you back to MGM."

"Olivia and I were really hoping to be in the same movie together again," she insisted. "We thought since both our movies were so successful, we'd have more of a say."

The men gave each other looks.

Mager leaned forward. "I think you'll find this is for the best."

She tried arguing some more, but there was no hope for it. They'd already decided, and she couldn't turn the role down, not without breaking her contract.

Issa dreaded having to go back to MGM to deliver the news to Olivia.

When she got to the suite, Olivia was on her way out. "I'm just stopping home to get my lipstick," she said, holding up the tube of red. "They don't have my shade on the set, and those other ones make my teeth look ghastly. What are you doing here?"

"I was hoping we could have lunch," Issa said.

"Perhaps after?" Olivia hurried down the path, and Issa fell into step with her. "Or you could come with me on set." Olivia took Issa's arm and looped it through her elbow, the way she had done a hundred times before. "It will be like old times. We shan't be too long. I saw the call sheet, and we only have enough light for one more scene."

"Oh, certainly," Issa said. "If you don't mind me tagging along."

"I'm inviting you, silly. I can't wait for you to see how much I've improved."

"I can guess. Oscar nomination and all." Issa nudged Olivia playfully.

A wave of nostalgia hit her as they hopped on the trackless trolley to get to New England Street on Lot Two.

Olivia's movie was a contemporary piece, so she didn't have to get into a complicated costume or put on a ton of makeup. Issa hung back from the spotlight, remembering the days when she had a small role, filling the time by watching the other actors at their scenes.

Issa couldn't help but notice the change in Olivia, and she tried not to show her awe. Olivia was more confident—she had always had a natural sophistication, but now she lacked that self-conscious, almost apologetic way of existing. Instead, she made demands of the makeup artists and gave orders to the producers. She glanced at Issa now and then with a conspiratorial expression, and then it was her moment in front of the camera.

Issa hugged herself, smiling when Olivia faced her, but an unease made her skin tingle as she observed the scene. There was something different about Olivia's acting. The way Olivia threw her head back, held her chin high, her lips pursed. Something more . . . affected. Not quite old-fashioned, but dramatic. Her mannerisms had more flair, more . . . Well, Issa couldn't quite put her finger on it.

Perhaps Olivia had picked up this new method from a fellow actress—or perhaps it was a result of so many notes from Ava.

That was it. Ava's generation had had a different style, and that's what Olivia reminded Issa of. Ava had coached Olivia after all, gave her tons of notes and advice. And the director didn't seem to mind, so there must not have been anything wrong with it.

"How was I?" Olivia asked after she finished for the day. She didn't bother wiping her makeup off or stopping to change as they took the trolley back to Lot One.

"You were wonderful," Issa said truthfully. Olivia had done the scene in just a few takes. "You've gotten very good. You've always been good, I mean, but now you're star material."

"Oh, hush," Olivia said, but she beamed at Issa while they walked to the commissary. It was hard not to bask under the light of such bright happiness.

Once they were seated, Issa remembered why she had wanted to see Olivia today, and her stomach twisted with nervousness. She wasn't hungry and ordered a tea.

"I have to tell you something," Issa said before she lost her nerve. Why was she so scared? It wasn't like Olivia was in charge of her career.

Olivia's salad arrived, and Issa stressed over whether she should wait until Olivia finished eating first, or even wait until they were alone. But Olivia looked up expectantly.

"What is it?" she asked.

Issa pressed her lips together.

"Come on, you can tell me," Olivia said, picking up a fork. She smiled a genuine smile that crinkled the corners of her eyes.

Issa twisted her napkin in her lap, not wanting to ruin Olivia's good mood. But the longer she put it off, the harder it would be. She took a deep breath and came out with it. "My next movie is with an actor named Richard Jenner. They're saying they can't lend me back to MGM until I prove myself. If this movie does well, then they'll consider it."

For a second, she thought she had spoken so fast that Olivia simply didn't understand. Olivia sat there, her face frozen, clutching her fork until her knuckles grew bone white.

"Did you tell them how important it was to you?" Olivia asked quietly. Her voice was like steel, something Issa had never heard before. It almost didn't sound like her, so calm and cold and scary.

"Yes, certainly," Issa said, though she couldn't remember doing such a thing. The old men told her what to do. She had just sat there, docile, agreeing to whatever they commanded, grateful that she was getting work at all.

"But you didn't fight, did you?" Olivia continued as if reading her mind. "You didn't argue. You never do. You just agreed, didn't you?"

Issa's blood rushed hot and cold, and her mouth opened, but she couldn't think of a word to say. Her fingers started to shake. Olivia's face looked tense—not ugly, never ugly—but a meanness was present that made her almost unrecognizable.

"Olivia," Issa started to say.

"Does our friendship not matter to you?" Olivia asked.

"What—how can you say that—"

"You're not willing to stand up for yourself, I can see that. But for *us*. You couldn't even do that for *us*? I'm so sick of you," Olivia hissed.

Issa's mouth fell open. Her ears started to ring, a high-pitched sound that made the rest of the restaurant seem distant, time standing still.

"You're pathetic," Olivia continued. "Get out of my sight."

"Olivia," Issa said again.

"Get out!" Olivia shrieked.

Everyone in the commissary turned to look at them. Issa stood up, anger mixing with fear, her blood churning at a low boil.

"We'll talk about this later," Issa said.

Olivia held her head high and ignored her.

Issa didn't know where to go after that. Home was the reasonable solution, but the idea of returning to her empty apartment set her teeth on edge. Instead, she walked back to their dressing room, not sure what she planned to do there but hurrying as if she had a purpose. She clenched and unclenched her fists as she walked.

Who did Olivia think she was, talking to Issa like that, as if Issa were a nobody? Olivia was no better than her—just because she'd had better roles so far and had gotten more famous didn't mean Issa deserved to be treated like that. They were supposed to be *friends*.

She stood in the middle of the living room, breathing hard, sweating from the brisk pace. She wasn't sure what to do.

Her reflection caught her eye. The big mirror on the wall showed her in the wide-collared dress the studio had picked out for her, her hair black and shiny as it curled about her shoulders.

She stepped up to her own image. "Ava," she demanded. "Ava, where are you?" She remained alone in the reflection. "What's happening with Olivia?" she asked anyway. "What went wrong?" Still, the dead actress didn't show up. Perhaps she'd gotten what she wanted out of them, and that was it. But she hadn't even said goodbye, which hurt more than Issa expected.

She knew she should leave—probably for good. After that argument with Olivia, what was the point in trying to restore their friendship? She almost choked on a sob, coughed instead, and then couldn't stop. Still coughing, she made a hasty cup of tea in the kitchen and brought it back to the living room, where she scalded her throat to get it down.

A moment later, the front door opened, and Olivia stormed in. Issa placed her mug carefully on the side table where Ava's trophy usually sat, though it wasn't there at the moment.

"I told you to leave!" Olivia shouted as soon as she saw Issa.

Issa still couldn't quite believe Olivia's reaction. This was not how you treated a friend.

"What's the matter with you?" Issa demanded. "Why are you acting like this?"

"I'm acting like this because you're getting on my nerves!" Olivia shrieked.

Issa stepped back. "Olivia."

"Stop saying my name!" Olivia turned, searching for something to throw, except she had just cleaned the place, so there was nothing at hand. Instead, she shoved the coffee table. But it was too low and stable to fall over.

Issa moved toward the door. "Fine, I'm leaving. Just like you want."

"Want?" Olivia was on a roll now, her tantrum at full capacity. "When have you ever cared what I want?" She picked up a couch cushion and threw it at the mirror, where it bounced back onto the floor without doing any damage. "It's always been about you! Your life, your dreams!"

"That's not true!" Issa shouted back. "You're the one who wanted this more than I did."

"Don't pin this on me!" Olivia threw another cushion to the floor and kicked it with her strappy-sandaled foot. "You wanted it just as much. But I did all the work. I talked to all the right people, I gave up my own sweat and blood! All so you could piggyback off my success. You're just jealous that I'm prettier and more popular than you are."

It hurt. Even more because it was true.

So without another word, Issa opened the door and left. Behind her, something thunked and fell, glass shattering. Issa hoped it was the large mirror, hoped it would send Olivia into a spiral of bad luck.

Chapter Forty-Three

Issa couldn't concentrate for days after that. Luckily, production wouldn't start on her next film for weeks.

Frustrated with all areas of her life, she longed for a place that had nothing to do with acting. The most obvious choice was to visit Ma, who never wanted to listen to anything having to do with her job. But by the time she made up her mind to go one day, it was too late. Ma would be at work.

Issa went to Auntie Yen's instead.

As soon as she got to the Red Car station, a girl at the stop whispered to her friend, and then they both ran up to her.

"Excuse me, are you Olivia Nong?" one of them asked.

Issa let out a sigh. "No," she said shortly.

"But you look so familiar."

"I'm Issa Bui, the other one."

"Oh! Please, sign this for us." It was a notebook with a picture of Olivia glued on the front.

"I'm not signing Olivia's picture," Issa said. She knew she was being rude.

The girls flipped the book open to a blank page. "Here you go."

Issa signed it, forcing herself to act glad for the attention. This was what she wanted, wasn't it? To be famous and recognized. To mean something to someone. As more people arrived, they gathered around her, whispering to each other.

"It's Issa Bui," she heard someone say. It was the first time she was recognized as herself, though perhaps it didn't count because the person probably overheard her correcting the first girls.

The streetcar came and went, and she stayed there signing autographs. It would have been a wonderful moment, but she was still smarting over her argument with Olivia and she simply wanted to be somewhere else, somewhere safe and quiet. So when a taxi drove by, she waved frantically for it to stop, handed the napkin she was signing back to her admirer, and got in the back.

"Oh thank God," she said. "Please take me to Chinatown."

The driver peered at her in the rearview mirror, but luckily didn't say anything. She put on her sunglasses just to be safe and stared out the window. How did other stars do it? Did they enjoy the attention? Shouldn't she enjoy it? What was it all for, if she didn't?

Her aunt's building was a welcome sight, but as she went up the steps, the hairs on the back of her neck rose. Something was wrong, a disturbance in the atmosphere.

The front door was slightly open and the hallways were empty, but an unease lingered.

She climbed the stairs, where a hushed quiet permeated the air. The apartment door was slightly ajar as well, the low buzz of conversation drifting outside.

Issa eased it open, not wanting to barge in and surprise anyone. No one noticed. It was mayhem inside. People hurried about, carrying rags dripping pinkish liquid. Watered blood, it looked like. She heard suppressed groans, and that was what was most disturbing. It was all so subdued. No one shouted or screamed, they only muttered to each other in calm response to the chaos that reigned.

Issa searched the faces for her aunt. The rags seemed to be coming from down the hall, where she knew Auntie Yen's room was. No one noticed as she went to the end and slipped through the door.

Auntie Yen's room was quiet, but a woman sitting by the bed bolted up as soon as Issa closed the door.

"Who are you?" she demanded.

Issa held up her hands. "I'm Issa, Yen's niece."

From the bed, a hand moved up. "Let her be."

The woman looked Issa up and down. She'd probably heard all about Issa, the girl who didn't want to take responsibility for her part in the clan.

"Leave us," Auntie Yen said. Her bed was canopied, and the curtain was pulled back, but it still covered Issa's view of her face.

The woman glared at Issa as she left the room. Issa waited before stepping closer to Auntie Yen's bed. She gasped and covered her mouth at the sight of her aunt, whose forehead was covered in bandages. Blood seeped through the layers.

"What happened?" Issa asked.

"Attack," Auntie Yen said. Her voice was hoarse.

"Was it the Uncles?"

"Yes." Auntie Yen's face was swollen and red, inflamed. "They've been carrying on for a few months, hitting smaller businesses. But yesterday, they got the big liquor shop on Fifth Street. Can't afford to lose that one, so we tried to stop it." She took a deep breath, as if talking pained her.

"Oh, Auntie Yen, I'm so sorry. Is there anything I can do?"

Auntie Yen gave a humorless laugh. "No, sweet. What can you do that I can't do?"

Issa wanted to take her hand but was afraid to hurt her.

"Why are you here?" Auntie Yen asked. "Something the matter?"

Issa shook her head. Her fight with Olivia seemed small in comparison to Auntie Yen's problems.

"It's been a long time since our lessons," Auntie Yen said. She closed her eyes, too drained to continue.

Issa patted her as gently as she could on her shoulder. She sat for a while, wishing she could do more but knowing that she had nothing to offer her aunt. Yen eventually drifted off into a deep sleep, her breathing ragged.

⯐

Back in her apartment, Issa set up a mirror and a cup of rice, plunking some incense sticks into the grains. She put her grandmother's picture against the reflection, lit the incense, and waited for smoke to float over the image.

"Bà Ngoại?" she asked.

To her immense relief, Bà Ngoại stirred almost instantly. Issa grinned, so happy to see someone—anyone—who remotely cared about her, tears filled her eyes.

"Hi," she said.

"What's the matter?" Bà Ngoại asked, her usual gruffness softened a bit. "Something happen?"

Issa pressed her lips together to keep them from quivering, but then the story burst out of her. "Olivia has been acting so odd. She got so angry at me, and it wasn't my fault, and everything feels horrible."

Bà Ngoại listened with a calm expression as Issa described their interactions, going into detail about the last conversation.

"Wait, wait," Bà Ngoại said, stopping her. "She said she poured her own sweat and blood into it?"

"It's just an expression," Issa said, dabbing at her eyes.

"But she did use blood," Bà Ngoại said.

"The connection wasn't very strong," Issa reminded her. "So you said it was okay."

Bà Ngoại nodded. She looked thoughtful. "How is Ava lately? I haven't seen much of her here."

"Neither have I. I tried calling for her the other day, but she didn't show up."

"She ignored a summons from you?"

"Well, I didn't do all the ritualistic stuff, I just called her. It always worked before."

"Hmm." For the first time Issa could remember, Bà Ngoại had a worried look on her face.

"What's the matter?" Issa asked. "Did I do something wrong?"

Bà Ngoại looked up as if remembering where she was. "No. You haven't. I . . . I need to look into this."

"Oh." Issa hadn't finished venting about Olivia, but she did feel slightly better. Still, she wished Bà Ngoại could stay longer and keep talking.

"In the meantime," Bà Ngoại continued, "you should stay with Auntie Yen."

"What? Why?"

"It's safer for you there."

"Safer? Did you hear about the Uncles' attack?"

"Yes, I heard. You're right." Bà Ngoại chewed on this. "Go stay with your ma, then. She's better than nothing."

"Bà Ngoại." Goose bumps rose on Issa's arms. "What's happening? Should I be scared?"

"Nothing to be concerned about yet. But trust me, please."

Bà Ngoại spoke with a finality that Issa found too frightening to even consider arguing.

"I'll go stay with Ma," Issa said.

"Call on me again once you're over there," Bà Ngoại said. "I should have more information then." Her picture went still, and the incense snuffed itself out even though there was plenty more to burn.

Chapter Forty-Four

If Bà Ngoại, the gangster matriarch who wasn't afraid of anything, told Issa to go stay with her mother, then Issa wasn't going to dawdle about it. She packed her bags in a hurry and hailed a cab to Culver City.

When she arrived, the apartment was empty—Ma must have been at work—but the air felt staler than usual, as if no one had been home for much longer. Or perhaps that was Issa's loneliness interjecting itself, flitting from one so-called home to another.

Everything in her bedroom remained untouched except for the sheets, which had a pristine, ironed look about them as if Ma still washed them weekly even though no one slept there. Issa's heart broke just a little as she ran her hands along the bedspread, trying not to read too much into it. Every time she thought her mother did something out of love and affection, she was proven wrong. They were what they were—old rituals her mother did because that was what one did. Still, she lay face down on the covers for several minutes, breathing in the familiar scent of her mom's favorite detergent, a hint of lavender and a suggestion of spring.

Then she pulled herself together and went to the kitchen. The cupboards remained as bare as before, despite the money Issa gave her mother every month. She made herself a cup of tea before returning to her room, where she set out the conjuring mirror and incense along with her grandmother's picture.

Bà Ngoại appeared and didn't waste time on pleasantries. "She's a demon," she said as soon as her image could move.

"What?" Issa asked, though she'd heard correctly.

"Ava. She's not a spirit. She's not dead. She never died, Issa. That's why her death wasn't reported in the news. Everyone assumed she did but—"

"Then why is she in that realm? What is she then, if she's not a ghost?"

"She's a demon," Bà Ngoại repeated. "She gave up her spirit willingly, when she was still alive. She must have made a deal with a dark one, and once that deal was over and her wish fulfilled, her spirit was banished to this realm."

"What sort of deal? What's a 'dark one'?"

"Ayah, you think I know everything? Some evil entity—perhaps the devil himself, for all we know. She probably made a deal to become a star, in exchange for her soul. The things people do to become famous! This is what I've been telling you—"

"Bà Ngoại, please."

"She would have been banished here once the deal was done. It's not natural. In fact, I hear it can be quite painful—stuck here where you don't belong. They're not real souls. Ava is . . . something else."

"She always said it was tougher for her to be dead than the other spirits, but I thought that was just . . . loneliness."

"That's why she was so willing to help the two of you—she must have had some sort of plan from the beginning. And now, with constant contact with the human world as well as the sacrifice of mortal blood, she's grown stronger."

This did not sound good. "But Ava isn't evil. She's always been good to us."

"For what reason? Because she wanted something. Needed something from you."

Issa shook her head. "I mean, she got her trophy, that's not such a terrible thing, right?"

"Issa, Issa," Bà Ngoại said, speaking with the slow patience one uses with a toddler. "What is it about the word *demon* do you not understand? Nothing good will come of this. We need to banish her."

"Fine, but . . . maybe we can talk to her first?"

"Ayah, I should have trained you from the start. There's no time. Quick, we need drained tea leaves, and a picture of her, and a strand of hair from the mortal who has been sacrificing their life for her."

"I have the tea leaves," Issa said, holding up her cup. "But I don't have a picture of her. And mortal—what mortal? No one has been . . ." She trailed off. "What do you mean, sacrificing her life? Is Olivia—but Olivia . . ."

"What?" Bà Ngoại asked.

"Is Olivia going to die?" Issa asked.

"Once that bond is established, it's hard to break."

Issa felt completely out of her depth. "How strong? It's not too late, is it?"

Bà Ngoại shook her head. "Issa, I do not know. This happens so rarely—perhaps once a century, or I would not have let Olivia give her blood like that."

Issa's breath was hard and fast. "What's going to happen to her? Is that why she's been so mean lately?"

"I don't know."

"Bà Ngoại. Just tell me. Whatever it is, I can deal with it."

"I really don't know, Issa. I wouldn't hide things from you."

"You hid this!"

"Not deliberately! And don't talk to me like that."

"I'm sorry." Issa bowed her head. "I'm just . . . she hasn't been herself. I'm worried."

"I need to find out what the demon wants," Bà Ngoại said. "What she intends to do. But if my suspicions are correct, Ava plans to take over Olivia's body."

"What? How? Like . . . possess her? Forever? What will happen to Olivia?"

"Olivia's soul cannot escape. It will be trapped inside with her, as if imprisoned, for eternity. But let's not wait to find out. We must banish the demon immediately."

"All right," Issa said. "I'm sure I can find Olivia's hair somewhere here." Issa scrambled to the closet to look through the clothes. They both had dark hair, but Olivia's had always been longer, growing to her waist, whereas Issa preferred a shorter shoulder-length style.

"Here," Issa said, going back to the mirror. She held up a long strand of black hair. "Now what?"

"Finish your tea," Bà Ngoại said. Her movements were starting to flicker, so Issa lit more incense and gulped down the rest of the cup, the scalding liquid searing her throat. "Now rip up Ava's picture and put it in with the tea leaves."

Issa looked all over the floor in her panic before she remembered that she didn't have one. "Can't I use something else?"

"You don't have a picture of her?" Bà Ngoại looked heavenward. "A poster or advertisement? Surely she's been in magazines."

"Yes, yes, I can look."

Bà Ngoại's photo stilled for a moment, and then she gasped. "I can't stay long, Issa."

"Tell me what to do."

"Once you have her photograph, rip it up, put it in with the cup with used tea leaves—one you drank from—along with the hair from the mortal sacrifice."

"I wish you would stop calling Olivia that," Issa said. It implied that Olivia was beyond saving.

Bà Ngoại ignored her. "Set it all on fire. Burn it until everything is ashes. Leave nothing behind."

Issa nodded. "I'll remember."

"Good." Bà Ngoại's movements came to a complete stop, except for her mouth. "Do it soon, Issa. The longer she stays, the stronger the bond."

Issa nodded, already getting up from the floor. "I'm going now."

Issa scoured their junk drawer for any old magazines that might feature movies or stars or gossip columns, but she found nothing.

Stuffing her keys in her pocket with some spare change, she ran down to the street to a newspaper stand on the corner, but it was hopeless. Why would they have anything on a silent film star from so long ago? Her best bet might be the library where she would have to discreetly rip out a page from an archive, though the idea pained her. But the library was closed. It would have to wait until morning.

On her walk back home, she couldn't shake a prickly sensation on her neck, as if someone watched her. This wasn't uncommon, as Bà Ngoại had often had her men trail Issa for protection, or to pass notes, or just to keep an eye on her. But she didn't see anyone familiar and hurried to Ma's place.

She couldn't sleep, unable to stop blaming herself. If she hadn't wanted stardom so bad, they wouldn't be in this situation. If she had offered her own blood instead, Olivia wouldn't have had to. Issa was the one with the shaman powers. She should have carried the burden, but she let Olivia take it, and now . . . What if she lost Olivia? What did Ava plan to do with her?

At the same time, she wondered if Bà Ngoại was being a tad dramatic. What if Ava had nothing but good intentions? Why couldn't they speak to the spirit—demon—first? What if Bà Ngoại was wrong, and Ava was simply misunderstood?

But even as she argued with herself, she knew that she was being willfully obtuse, suppressing the thoughts like she had in the past whenever her family and its unique powers came up. She was avoiding the truth the way she had avoided being a shaman, and the consequences were coming around to bite her. This was her problem to fix. Her friend to save.

In the morning, she rushed to the Central Library in downtown Los Angeles, finding the large building intimidating with its many floors and stacks. She was humbled but relieved that no one recognized her. The staff seemed perplexed by her questions, as if she were speaking a different language, directing her to several wrong departments before an archivist finally brought out boxes of old magazines for her to dig through.

She spent hours flipping through pages of gossip columns but couldn't find anything with a photo of Ava in it, not even an old advertisement or poster. The staff were little help, dismissive of her requests and slow until, finally, the older gentleman who'd deigned to help her brought three full carts of boxes for her to go through. She curled her body over the desk. Her eyes burned, and her vision swam from studying each face in every photograph.

She had no luck with the pictures, but what she did come across was an article in *Moving Pictures Records* about the dangers of hiring foreign actresses, mentioning Ava by name. It was an outdated source, full of fearmongering terms like *outsiders* and *infiltration*, and the writer of the article seemed to view movies as powerful agents of destruction with actors able to subconsciously affect audiences' minds like some hypnotist. Issa dismissed it as ridiculous, justified when she uncovered a response in the editorials a few issues later that came to Ava Lin Rang's defense.

This is why she left the business, Issa read. *Because of accusations like these. She deserved better roles. She was contracted for a feature film to be released next year, but she quit because of these boorish rumors, and it's a shame, because she was so talented.* Apparently Ava had gone overseas to do some research on her next part, only to decide to retire from the movie industry entirely, and never appear in the public eye again.

⊷

Issa wasn't sure how it happened—perhaps she dozed off, or perhaps she was so focused on Ava that she went into a trance state without meaning to, but she looked up from her magazine with sudden clarity. Her mind felt sharp and alert, as if she'd gulped down several cups of coffee, and her vision appeared richer, the colors deep, the whites glowing in blinding spots.

And she wasn't in the library. She wasn't anywhere she recognized, but it looked like a small house full of clutter and children. Two toddlers a few years apart sat playing under the kitchen table while an older girl, about ten, stirred a pot on the stove. Smoke wafted from the oven as an infant in another room started crying.

"Ava!" the girl called out. "Ava, where are you?"

Ava came running in a second later—only eight or nine years old, but recognizable with her high cheekbones and the fact that she clunked around in heels too large for her feet, wearing a scarf around her hair, as if she'd been pretending to be a queen.

As Ava approached, the older girl slapped her. The sound of it silenced the crying in the other room. Only the sizzling on the stove remained.

Ava covered her face, eyes blinking with confused tears.

"I told you to tend to the baby!" The other girl's scoldings ended in a high-pitched tone as the scene went white . . .

The two girls were older now, in their teens, standing in line at the Lion Building on the MGM lot.

"I'm going to get it," Ava told the other girl, who must have been her sister.

"Don't get your hopes up. We're only here because you won't shut up about it."

Ava glared at her, jaw tense. In the next vision, however, she walked away from the studio, shoulders slumped. Instead of sadness, her expression was twisted with rage.

What followed next was a whirlwind of images that moved so fast, Issa could barely keep up. Ava meeting with a man in a suit at dinner, then being shown to some basement speakeasy. Ava drinking from a ceramic teacup and lighting incense, the smoke swirling so thick, it obscured her face, and when it cleared, she was on the silver screen, beautiful and glowing and magnetic to behold. Ava emerging from a car and immediately surrounded by adoring fans. Ava smiling and happy and radiant, and then—

That slap, as if out of nowhere. Ava covering her face with a hand, but she wasn't a little girl anymore, and it wasn't her sister who had hurt her. The figure who struck her was obscured, as if made of smoke, and then Ava pushed past the plume. As the dark cloud cleared, something in her expression sharpened, and her eyes met Issa's.

Issa startled, tried to calm herself. This was just a vision, and Ava couldn't really see her.

But then Ava came toward her, moving with long, fast strides, and Issa stepped back with a scream—

Her head jerked off the table, back in the library. She looked around, afraid someone had seen her, heard her cry out in her sleep.

But there was no one. The crinkle of a magazine, wrinkled, uncurling from where she'd squished it with her face, caught her attention. There it was, as if Issa had conjured it. A tiny picture of Ava. The photo was round and small, as if meant for a locket, in a side note of a larger article.

Issa gently tore at the page, glancing over her shoulders, before ripping it clean off. It sounded like thunder to her ears. She stuffed the page into her purse, still looking around, but no one paid her any attention. Then she put everything back into the boxes as neatly as she could, told the librarian behind the desk she was finished, and left.

As she exited the building, someone practically slammed into her, almost sending them both down the concrete steps.

"I beg your pa—" she started to say, but the man gripped her purse, and she hung on tightly, unwilling to lose the precious picture of Ava. "Let go—help!" She searched around for a policeman or security guard, but spotted only a wrinkly-dressed man who looked quickly away, not wanting to get involved in the altercation.

"I know you've got money," her assailant said, his familiar voice making her stop.

"Uncle?" she asked. She had never learned Olivia's uncle's name, only knew him by his pockmarked skin and signature stale, sour scent, which lingered in her memory from the two times she had ever met him.

"That stingy bitch won't give me a penny," he said. "You tell her she owes me." He released her so suddenly that Issa stumbled.

Had he been following her?

"You don't deserve a thing," she snapped. "And you leave her alone."

He spat at her feet. "You're both the same." He called her several ugly names, his voice growing louder as Issa walked away, gritting her teeth. She wished Bà Ngoại had taught her how to put a curse on a person after all. But there were more important things to attend to, like banishing a demon.

When she got back to Ma's apartment, Ma had already gone to work. Issa's muscles felt both stiff and mushy from hunching over a desk the whole day, and her shoulders protested as she sat on the floor to begin the ritual. She didn't need Bà Ngoại there, but she conjured her for moral support.

"You have it?" Bà Ngoại asked.

Issa dug through her purse, panicking for a slight second that she'd lost the image or had imagined it altogether, but her fingers closed around the scrap of paper and she pulled it out to show her grandmother.

"Good, good," Bà Ngoại said. "And your tea leaves?"

Issa drained her mug, burning her tongue in the process. She showed her grandmother the dregs.

"All right, now rip up the picture," Bà Ngoại instructed.

The image was so small that Issa could only manage to rip it twice, poking at the pieces to sop up the remaining drops of her tea and tangling Olivia's hair into a clump.

"How am I supposed to light it on fire if everything's wet?" Issa asked, striking a match.

"Magic, that's how, what kind of shaman are you?" Bà Ngoại said.

"Not a well-trained one."

"Whose fault is that?" Bà Ngoại shouted.

Issa dropped the match into the mug. Of course it sizzled out right away. She struck several at once, and the tea leaves and paper caught on fire.

"Now, banish the spirit," Bà Ngoại said.

"Um . . . I thought that's what we were doing."

"Say the words, silly girl. You need to command the demon from your life."

"From Olivia's too."

"Yes, yes, say it."

Feeling silly, Issa took in a deep breath. "Demon," she said.

"Name her."

Issa pressed her lips together. "Demon, Ava Lin Rang, I banish you. From my life, and Olivia Nong's."

Bà Ngoại pursed her lips. "It didn't rhyme, but it's a good start for a banishment."

"That's it?"

"Repeat it four times."

"Why four?"

"Four is the number for death."

"No it's not—"

"Ayah, must you question everything I say? In Chinese, it closely resembles death. Yes, yes, I know we're not Chinese, but there's a close correlation—never mind, just do as I say!"

"All right," Issa said, unable to keep the exasperation out of her voice. "Demon, Ava Lin Rang, I banish you. From my life, and Olivia Nong's." The mug with the tea leaves and Ava's picture remained inflamed, like Issa had prepared a cup of fire instead of tea. "Demon, Ava Lin Rang, I banish you. From my life, and Olivia Nong's." The flames grew higher. "Demon, Ava Lin Rang—"

The door burst open. Issa hadn't realized how dark it had gotten—she hadn't bothered to turn on the lights in her haste to start the ritual, and the fire had been sufficient lighting. Now her vision was spotty as she turned, barely registering who was there. At first, she thought it was Ma, and her natural instinct was to cover up any signs of magic.

But it wasn't Ma.

It was Olivia.

She looked livid. Her complexion was red, her lips pulled back. Dressed in flowy robes, she stepped slowly into the room, her eyes hard, her face tense.

"How dare you," she growled, and her voice sounded raspy and oddly echoey, as if two people spoke at once.

"Quick!" Bà Ngoại shouted at Issa. "Finish the ritual. Say the words!"

The fire in the teacup was diminishing. "Demon, Ava Lin R-rang," Issa stammered.

But Olivia screamed. It was a bloodcurdling, hair-raising scream that sent Issa skittering back on the floor. Olivia didn't stop screaming, her mouth stretching back, creating indents in the flesh of her face, as she stomped into the room. She kicked the propped-up mirror aside, sending it shattering against the wall, and Bà Ngoại's voice cut off. Olivia picked up the picture of Bà Ngoại and banged it against the bed frame until the glass broke. She pulled out the photograph, cutting her fingers in the process. Blood dripped onto the carpet as she shredded the flimsy piece of paper, letting pieces of Bà Ngoại's face scatter to the floor. Then she raised her foot and stomped down on the teacup. The clink of ceramic breaking sounded absurdly anticlimactic against such rage.

Then there was nothing but the sounds of their breathing. The darkness was stifling, and Issa couldn't find enough air. She cowered away from Olivia, curling into a ball against the bed, arms wrapped around her knees to protect herself.

Olivia whirled on her. In the dark, the only thing Issa could see of her friend were her eyes reflecting a small bit of light from the streetlights outside the window. They looked completely black, as if the whites pooled with ink.

"O-Olivia," Issa whispered, but she couldn't tell if Olivia was in there.

And then Olivia gave a low laugh in that same echoing, overlapping voice. "How dare you," she repeated, but this time, there was a wicked humor to it. She wasn't angry anymore. Issa was no threat to her.

And with that, she turned around and disappeared through the doorway.

Chapter Forty-Five

Smoke swirled in the hallway mirror. Bà Ngoại must have been trying to return, but nothing happened—the reflection remained cloudy. It had always been difficult for her to manifest on her own so shortly after a conjuring.

There had to be another photograph of Bà Ngoại somewhere in the apartment. Issa opened all the drawers and looked through the closets but found none. Nor were there any in the junk drawer. She left the mess atop the kitchen table, too distraught to do much else.

Ma's room.

The door loomed in her vision. She hadn't gone in there since she was a little girl, not even when Ma was home. She'd never had a reason to, so it hadn't seemed weird until this moment.

It was late, Ma shouldn't be home for hours. Issa turned the knob and walked in. It felt like stepping into a hotel room, as if no one lived there, everything was organized and sparse. A single bed, perfectly made. A chest of drawers on one end. Any mirror or reflective surface removed long ago. No pictures, no decorations.

Issa felt only a moment of guilt and betrayal before she rushed forward and pulled out the drawers. Ma's clothes were so neatly folded that Issa didn't want to touch them, but she didn't have much to rifle through anyway. The closet was the same: a few dresses hung up on the rod, some coats she wore every winter, a few worn shoes on the floor. But no secret boxes of things. No hidden treasures under the bed or stored in the corners.

She would have to go to Auntie Yen's house. Of course Auntie Yen would have plenty of photographs of Bà Ngoại, conjuring her to visit often. Issa would take several in case she needed them in the future . . . If there was a future.

What a ridiculous thought. Of course there was a future. This was a minor setback. She could still fix things.

As she took a cab to Chinatown, she finally had a moment to collect her thoughts. She couldn't shake her need for urgency, sitting in traffic its own form of torture.

Ava was some sort of demon. Issa hadn't believed Bà Ngoại at first, but that echo in Olivia's voice—the second person who spoke was Ava. And Issa hadn't seen Ava for quite some time, had tried to conjure her with no success. Ava and Olivia . . . must be together. They'd been inseparable since the moment Olivia had offered the spirit her blood. Issa had rarely seen Ava without Olivia, except that one night when Ava had tried to grab Issa and the few times Issa had called on Ava.

As the taxi turned onto Auntie Yen's street, Issa noticed a different quality in the atmosphere. The street looked brighter than it should have, and now Issa saw why. A fire. The building. Smoke everywhere, flames waving from the window and climbing high into the sky, and people out in the streets yelling and pointing at the tragedy. Her aunt's home was charred.

"Stop, stop," Issa said to the driver. She handed over some bills for the fare, not counting how much, and got out of the car. Fire trucks blocked the road, the sirens muted but the red flashing lights adding to the panicked mayhem of the scene. Men in thick, heavy uniforms sprayed water at the building with their hoses.

"My aunt," Issa shouted at one of them. "My aunt lives there."

The fireman gestured at a group of people gathered around an ambulance. "Everyone was evacuated," he said.

Issa thanked him and ran over to the ambulance, where medics assisted several people. She recognized some of them as her aunt's workers, but she didn't see Yen's face among them.

A woman waved at her. "Issa, Issa," she called. Issa didn't know her name, but she often answered Yen's door.

"Where is she?" Issa asked. "Is she okay?"

"She's over there," the woman said, pointing.

Auntie Yen was helping a family—a man and woman and their young son—wiping the tears off the boy's face with a handkerchief.

Issa ran over to her. "Auntie Yen! My God, what happened?"

Auntie Yen's face showed brief surprise and relief. "Issa, you're here. I thought . . . never mind—"

"Are you all right?"

"I'm fine. I got out in time." Auntie Yen's face hardened. "I never thought they would stoop this low."

"I'm just glad you're all right." Issa hugged her aunt, who stiffened for a moment before wrapping her arms around Issa.

"All right? Nothing about this is all right. Half our business was in this building. The rental income, the meeting places, the séance rooms."

"I know, I know. I'll help." Issa held Auntie Yen's elbows. "I have money from my movies. I'll do what I can." Though why? A small voice told her that this could be it. Perhaps they could just let it go, the control, the territory, the life. Without the business, the gang would disperse, and Issa wouldn't have to inherit a single thing. No responsibilities she didn't want. No money, either, but who cared? She made her own money now. She could take care of them all.

But then something cracked in the blaze behind them—a wooden beam, causing the roof to cave in. Around them, the others screamed. Auntie Yen's workers, along with several families who lived in the building. A woman started sobbing, and a man comforted her with his face contorting to hide his own pain.

Auntie Yen pressed a hand to Issa's cheek. The fire blazed from behind her despite the firefighters' efforts, but it was nothing compared to the warmth that flowed through Issa from her aunt's touch.

"Thank you, my darling," Yen said, and Issa had no more doubt about it. She would do what she could for her family.

❖

Auntie Yen had a number of safe places she might have stayed at, but apparently some of them had been ravaged by the Uncles, and others were too far, too small, or involved crossing dangerous territory, which defeated the purpose. The ones that remained safe she assigned to families who needed them.

Despite the catastrophe that was sure to follow, Issa took Auntie Yen back to Ma's apartment. She hesitated outside the door. The sky had lightened, the sun rising over the tall buildings in the distant downtown skyline, which meant Ma should already be home.

Sure enough, when they let themselves in, the light underneath the bathroom door was on. She must have been getting ready for bed.

"You can stay in my room," Issa said, harboring a secret hope that she could stow Auntie Yen away without Ma noticing.

But Auntie Yen had no such plans. She settled herself into a chair at the table—Ma's chair, in fact, the only one that faced the window. "Issa, let me impose on you for some tea."

Tea? There was no time for tea. Well, fine, there was always time for tea, but she needed to hide Auntie Yen safely inside her room before Ma saw her.

The bathroom door opened, and it was too late.

Ma stepped out amid a cloud of steam, already dressed in her nightgown, her wet hair curling into loose dark ribbons about her shoulders. She stopped abruptly at the sight of them. Issa winced. She hadn't even told Ma she was staying over, much less provided any warning that she'd bring Ma's estranged sister whom she hadn't seen in more than ten years.

For a second, Ma stood there, not saying a word. Her face twitched, as if she couldn't decide how to feel, ranging from anger to sadness to something resembling hope. Or perhaps Issa just really wanted it to be hope.

"Chào em," Yen said, calling Ma *little sister* in an affectionately informal way Issa hadn't expected. In Issa's mind, it implied that Ma was once someone young who needed attention and care in a way that Ma's severe exterior had never shown.

Ma stepped forward. "What are you doing here?" Then she took in Auntie Yen's bedraggled state. Yen was usually immaculately dressed, her clothes professionally ironed, her hair styled to perfection, but now she was covered in dust and soot, smudges staining her face, her hair falling in loose strands. "What happened? Are you all right?" Ma jerked her chin at Issa. "What are you standing there for? Make some tea already."

Issa got busy putting on the kettle and setting out mugs while behind her, she heard Ma get a first aid kit from the bathroom and return to mutter in quick Vietnamese at her sister. Issa barely understood it. She caught simple words here and there, like *years*, and *why*, and then she gave up altogether.

Yen responded in short, clipped answers. She had never talked as much as Ma, only interjecting when needed, or giving commands. It had been the same with their lessons. Issa had often felt like unless she asked the right questions, she'd never learn anything because Auntie Yen didn't volunteer information. Then again, neither had Bà Ngoại, who, while boisterous, dished out little facts upon her whim, the way she had often sent Issa money—sporadically and depending on how generous she felt in the moment.

When the tea was ready, Issa set mugs on the table and took the remaining seat, which happened to be Olivia's. A twist in her heart reminded her of why she'd gone to Auntie Yen's apartment in the first place.

As if reading her mind, Auntie Yen turned to Issa. "It's a good thing you were there. But why did you come?"

"You visited her?" Ma demanded.

Auntie Yen placed a hand on Ma's, which was wrapped around her mug. She didn't say anything, but her touch must have sent whatever message Ma needed to hear, because she sighed and sat back.

"Something's happened," Issa said. "With Olivia." And despite her habit of keeping things hidden, she told them about Ava, and what Bà Ngoại had uncovered.

Ma listened with explosive exclamations of horror, though she stopped herself from interrupting when Auntie Yen hushed her.

"That was the only picture I could find of Ava in the whole archive," Issa said, finishing her story. "And it's destroyed—the ritual wasn't complete. I can keep searching for another one, but it will take me so long. Maybe a different archive . . ."

"Photographs aren't the only thing that give spirits their power," Auntie Yen said. "We should call Ma." She looked at Issa's mom. It always took a few seconds for Issa to remember that their ma meant Bà Ngoại.

"Maybe she can just attack Ava on the other side," Ma said, clenching a fist. "I bet she could take her."

"If Ava is here, in Olivia's body, then her spirit wouldn't be there to attack," Yen said.

"Do you really think so?" Issa asked, her eyes welling with tears, but she knew it was a silly question. Olivia had spoken with both their voices. "What will happen to Olivia? What *has* happened to her?"

"She's in there still," Yen said. "But the longer the demon has possession of her body, the more Ava will push her down, gain stronger control."

"Our Olivia can fight it," Ma said.

"I doubt she even realizes what's happening," Yen said. "You said Ava was your friend."

"She and Olivia got really close," Issa said, looking down at her cooling tea.

"She probably trusted the demon, gave in willingly," Auntie Yen said. "She won't notice her strength depleting until it's too late."

"Then what?" Issa asked.

"I'm not sure. It's been a long time since we've dealt with demonic possession."

"Probably not since I was a baby," Ma said with a nod. "I heard a story of one. From Phi."

"Dead Auntie Phi?" Issa asked.

Ma nodded.

Yen slapped her hand on the table. "Everything is burned and gone. All the pictures of Ma and Phi. We can't even summon them to ask."

Ma looked up sharply.

"What is it, Ma?" Issa asked.

Without saying anything, Ma grabbed her purse from the entrance table and dug inside for her pocketbook. The button barely clung on to the closure around the million notes and cards and receipts stuffed inside. She dug through several folds frantically, and then finally gave up and emptied the contents onto the table until she found what she was looking for. Three small black-and-white photographs.

"You kept us with you?" Auntie Yen asked with a soft smile as she picked up the tiny portraits. They must have been old, because in them, Yen and Phi looked younger, perhaps in their teenage years. Bà Ngoại looked like herself, which seemed apt to Issa, who had always imagined her grandmother born as an old woman.

"Issa, go get your incense," Ma said in answer.

"You knew I had them?" Issa asked.

Ma gave her a look. "You think I can't recognize the smell of a ritual, as if I don't know more about it than you do?"

"Why didn't you say anything?"

"You would have listened, or what?"

Issa held up a hand. "You're right."

Fighting off a hundred other questions she wanted to ask her mom, she went to her room and came back with the objects they needed. Ma had already propped the photographs and a small mirror against her bulging pocketbook. She'd procured little bowls of rice into which Issa pushed the incense sticks.

"All right," Ma said, taking Issa by surprise by lighting the incense as if it meant nothing to her to do this for the first time in decades. "Ma?" she called out.

Ma caught the look on Issa's face. "What?"

"You're going to dabble in magic?" Issa asked. "After all these years of forbidding me to do anything with it?"

"Did it work, hah?" Ma demanded. "Did you listen to me? No, instead you get into even worse trouble. Better that I had taught you to begin with."

"That's what I've been saying all along," Bà Ngoại snapped from her mirror, having appeared while they argued. "Better to teach her the dangers and how to control it, than to have her getting into trouble without any help."

"She had your help," Ma pointed out. "And she still got in trouble."

"How should I have known some dead actress would use them this way? She seemed helpful, and the girls wanted it so bad."

"It's true, Ma," Issa said. "It's not Bà Ngoại's fault."

"I know it's not her fault!" Ma said. "It's your fault. Don't think you're escaping punishment when all this is over. You may be a grown woman, but you're still my daughter. I'll ground you if I have to."

"You should talk about being a filial daughter!" Bà Ngoại yelled. "You wait until I'm dead, and then you deign to speak to me—"

"Em!" Dead Auntie Phi cut her off. Tears sprang to her eyes, but she couldn't shed them in the reflection. "Em, I missed you so much."

Bà Ngoại continued muttering her lecture, but Ma pressed a thumb over the mirror where her mouth was, cutting off whatever insults she'd waited so long to dish at Ma. Ma smiled at her sister.

"How are you, Chị Phi?" she asked. "Long time, hah?"

"You bet! You look skinnier than ever! What's your secret, hah? Guess what—on this side, you can eat whatever you want and never worry. Not that I ever did!" Phi laughed with genuine gaiety while Bà Ngoại glared at Ma.

Auntie Yen leaned forward. "Ma, you can scold Linh later. Right now, there are more urgent things at hand."

Ma waited for another second before taking her thumb off the mirror.

Bà Ngoại's face was tense. If the black-and-white photo could show it, she might have been beet red from anger. Instead, she sucked in air through her teeth. "Yes, a demon is loose!" she shrieked.

"We know," Auntie Yen said calmly. "How do we get rid of it? Issa said the photo was destroyed in the last attempt. We can scour the city for one, but there must be a faster way."

"A sentimental object," Bà Ngoại said.

"The trophy she wanted so bad," Issa said. "Once we got it for her, she became much stronger."

"It must be giving her power. Where is it now?" Bà Ngoại asked.

"In Olivia's dressing room." Issa's heart sank. "I can go get it."

"Nonsense," Auntie Yen said. "The demon knows you're on to her. I'll fetch it."

"But you've just been in a fire," Issa said. "And they won't let you on the MGM lot."

"MGM, wow," Phi said, nodding and smiling at Issa with parental approval. "I'll never get used to it. Look at you, big star."

"Well, I'm actually at Warner Bros.," Issa started to explain.

"Not important, not important," Ma said, slashing a hand through the conversation.

"Issa, you'll have to go get the trophy," Bà Ngoại said. "And destroy it immediately."

"Just break it?" Issa asked.

"Destroy it!" Bà Ngoại repeated louder, as if doing so would make Issa understand. "Make sure no part of it remains intact or can be fixed, put together, or resemble anything close to its original form."

"Oh boy." Issa swiped her hair from her face. "Maybe I can throw it in a wood chipper or something."

"Or burn it," Auntie Yen said.

"Take a hammer with you," Ma said. "And smash it to pieces."

"I'm taking notes," Issa joked.

"Where?" Auntie Phi craned her neck to look out from the mirror. "You really can't remember all that? Simple—steal the trophy and destroy it."

"Right." Issa smiled, feeling for the first time in days that things were going to be okay. Even though her best friend was possessed by a demon, something that was probably her fault, Issa knew that there was nothing she couldn't fix with her aunts', grandmother's, and mom's help.

"Go!" Bà Ngoại shouted at her.

Issa pushed her chair back. The legs scraped noisily on the floor. Ma got up as well, dug through the junk drawer, and handed Issa a hammer.

"Wish me luck," Issa said as she grabbed her purse and hurried out the door.

Bà Ngoại sputtered with annoyance. "Silly girl. What do you need luck for? You're a witch."

Chapter Forty-Six

Issa didn't realize how weary she was until the taxi driver woke her up in front of the MGM lot gate. It was a bright morning, the familiar sight of the studio coming to life sending pangs through her heart, reminders of when she'd first started here with Olivia, both of them so full of hopes and dreams for the future that they had every intention of sharing together. What had gone wrong? Or was this the price they had to pay for getting what they wanted?

Would she undo it, if she could? Give up everything—her acting, the films, the recognition—to have her friend back?

That wouldn't be necessary. It wasn't too late to banish Ava without hurting Olivia, and if she destroyed the trophy now, they could continue with their lives as planned. They could take charge of the trajectories of their futures, make sure this didn't happen again, stick together like they'd meant to from the start.

She walked to the dressing rooms, filled with a tense urgency, waving dismissively at anyone who recognized her or called out her name.

As she rounded the corner of a soundstage, she almost ran into someone—a man holding stacks of paper.

"Jem!" she exclaimed.

She'd almost knocked the papers out of his arms, and he scrambled to keep them from tumbling into a confusing mix. It took him a moment to give her his full attention, and his face registered brief happiness before settling into something more blank. He needed a haircut, the thick locks curling over his forehead. The familiar scent of his sandalwood cologne drew her closer, and for a second, she wanted to pretend that they were back here that night on their first date.

"Issa Bui," he said. "Our rising star."

"Oh, well," Issa stammered. "I'm sorry I never—"

"It's all right." His face had gone steely. Issa flushed hot and cold, wishing she had handled the situation better.

"The studio executives," she started to explain.

He held up a hand. "I understand."

"Do you?"

"Of course." He nodded stiffly and then walked around her.

Issa would have gone after him, except there were more important things at hand, like banishing a demon, so she kept going. Images of the hurt behind his composure made her cringe, but she pushed them away. She needed to focus.

Several people were leaving the dressing rooms, and she had no choice but to go against traffic, weaving around them in a hurry while trying to look calm.

"Issa!" someone shouted. It was Maggie Laken. "Darling, it's been ages."

Issa waved but kept going, ignoring Maggie's hurt look of confusion.

Not expecting her key to still work, Issa tried it anyway and nearly laughed hysterically when the door opened. Inside, a mustiness clung to the walls and furniture, like damp mold.

The trophy wasn't on the side table by the sofa where Ava would sit and caress it like some sort of pet. The space was a mess once again, clothes flung everywhere, the mirror on the wall hanging listlessly to one side. The yellow mug of tea she'd used earlier in the week was still there. Out of habit, she almost picked it up to wash it in the kitchen, but then she remembered she had come here for a reason.

She checked the rooms first to see if Olivia was home. Her bedroom was just as cluttered, clothes piled on the bed and items flung on the floor like someone had ransacked the place, but she wasn't there.

Issa's room was worse, the mirror on the vanity shattered, the drawers hanging open, and the closet door askew. Perhaps Olivia or Ava had smashed about in a rampage. The idea frightened her, the violence of the vision.

Issa shuffled through the clothes on the floor, hoping to find the trophy buried somewhere. But she had an inkling of where it was. She just dreaded going near Olivia's room.

She made herself go back. Olivia had slept with the trophy on the couch, so the chances of her bringing it to bed with her were rather high.

Issa entered Olivia's room and approached the pile of clothes, reaching out a hand and prodding it, feeling for the sharp edges of a small statue or solid base. She felt nothing but clothes.

She took a deep breath. If she could go through with shamanistic rituals to conjure the dead, then surely she could flip through her best friend's things when she wasn't home.

She grabbed a shirt from the top of the pile and flung it aside. Easy enough. Dresses and pants and jackets came next.

And there, beneath a scarf or blanket of some sort, she saw the metal glint of the trophy.

Issa grabbed it. It stuck to something. She yanked.

The pile stirred.

Issa scrambled backward, her back hitting the vanity. The glass jars of creams and perfumes and other cosmetics clattered together.

The pile moved again. Issa's heart thundered as she realized Olivia was sleeping under there.

She breathed quickly, unable to decide what to do. She should run, get out of there before Olivia or Ava or whoever would wake up in that body and get to her first. But if she ran, then what? She would have to come back to steal the trophy. She would have to wait until night and hope that Olivia decided to go out, which may or may not happen.

This could be her only chance.

Issa burst forward, grabbed the trophy, and pulled on it with all her might. She used more strength than she meant to, and because Olivia was still half-asleep the statue came away easily. In fact, Issa lost her grip on it and flung it through the air. It sailed and hit the vanity mirror with a resounding crash, shattering the glass and throwing reflective shards everywhere.

Issa didn't stop to assess the damage. She lunged for the trophy and ran out, aware that behind her, a figure jerked upright. As she bolted from the room, a high-pitched scream followed her.

Luckily, most people in the surrounding little houses had already left for the day. Issa ran, not caring how she looked with a stolen trophy in her hands.

Where to destroy the thing?

She ran past soundstages and, in her panic, around a building that always reminded her of storm-shelter bunkers. A forklift braked a few inches from her.

"Hey, watch it!" the driver shouted. "You can't run there. Only walk on the path."

"What?" Issa was breathing too hard.

The driver pointed at the wide tape on the ground, designating where pedestrians were supposed to walk.

Issa stepped aside as the driver continued mumbling complaints. She thought about throwing the statue under one of the big trucks, letting it grind its gears around the damn thing and watching it disintegrate. But people would surely question why, not to mention that the crew would be angry at her for ruining their equipment. Instead, she kept running.

A figure caught her attention. Olivia, dressed in the silk kimono she usually lounged in at home, running toward her with graceful speed.

Issa caught an expression of malicious delight on her face that didn't look like Olivia at all. It looked like Ava.

Standing there, Issa panicked. She couldn't outrun Olivia. So, without any other options, she raised the trophy over her head and brought it down as hard as she could, crashing the head of the small statue against the black asphalt. The little figure broke off the base, several pieces flying in different directions.

It wasn't a complete destruction like Bà Ngoại had specified, but it was a start.

Olivia stopped moving. She was already so close, just a few feet away, her abrupt halt eerie, as if she'd slammed into a wall. She remained rigid and upright. Issa froze as well, waiting to see what happened next. Had it worked? Had breaking the trophy also broken the connection between Olivia and Ava?

She watched Olivia's face for signs that Ava was gone, for the special light to return to her eyes that would tell her that Olivia, her best friend, was back.

For a moment, Olivia's face revealed nothing. Then she met Issa's eyes. And smiled.

Chapter Forty-Seven

It was not Olivia. It was most definitely Ava.

Issa fell to her knees as the demon approached. Her face showed open malice now, unafraid to expose who she really was underneath. Issa realized what a fool she'd been to not see it, the tension in Olivia's face the last few months, the oddity in her voice and stiffness in her movements.

Her purse fell from her shoulder with a heavy thunk. The hammer. She'd taken it from Ma and stuffed it in her bag in her hurry to leave the apartment.

Issa took it out. Olivia stood only steps away. She raised the hammer and brought it down on the head of the statue. It smashed into several golden pieces.

But it was too late. Olivia kicked at Issa's hand, knocking the hammer into the air. Pain shot up Issa's arm and she wailed, clutching her throbbing fingers.

"Silly girl," Ava said in Olivia's voice, or rather, both their voices. It was an echo of what Bà Ngoại had called Issa, but with an entirely different tone. "You're stupider than you look."

"Please," Issa begged, but she wasn't sure what she was begging for. Her own life? Or Olivia's?

Ava-Olivia reached down as if to grab her by the throat. Issa winced as her face came near. Last night her eyes had been pure black, but the whites had returned. A hint of fire roaring in the depths of her irises. For a second, Issa felt the flames lick at something within her, stirring up a searing pain, like gulping down scalding tea. Ava smelled different, that smoky, sulfurous smell Issa now recognized as the same odor that often lingered in Olivia's dressing room.

A car came around the building and Ava-Olivia hesitated, then grabbed Issa's hand and hauled her to her feet, making it seem as if she was simply helping Issa up.

They both waited for the car to move on so they could continue their . . . whatever it was . . . careful about appearances. They were, after all, both of them, still under contract.

But the car slowed to a stop.

To her surprise, Jem leaned over the passenger seat. "Issa," he said. He wore an imploring expression. "Can we talk?"

Issa glanced at Ava-Olivia, whose eyes hardened.

"We're in the middle of something," Ava-Olivia snapped at him.

"It won't be long," Jem said. He didn't smile, but he had never been one to fall for Olivia's charms the way everyone else had.

Issa studied the demon's face, the cunning in her eyes as she considered what to do next. Cars drove by, other crew members walked about the lot. She couldn't do anything out in the open without revealing too much, exposing herself and ruining what she'd worked so hard for. Because it was clear to Issa what Ava wanted: Her life back. Her fame. Her career—a second chance, which she now had through Olivia.

She let Issa go.

Issa fumbled for the car door and got in as fast as she could. She stared straight ahead, aware that she had managed to escape something perilous merely by luck.

"Go," she whispered to Jem. "Please just go."

Thankfully, he didn't ask any questions and stepped on the gas.

⊷

Her hands wouldn't stop shaking. She had so much trouble opening the jar of sugar that Jem took it from her and poured the white grains into her coffee.

He had driven them out of the studio lot to a nearby diner in a Spanish-style building with green trimmings and red accents painted on the wall, lending the atmosphere a cheerful air that was at odds with the turmoil inside her. She was thankful that it wasn't one of the fancier restaurants most stars liked to go to, even though she doubted she'd be recognized. Having stayed up all night to deal with the demonic situation, her hair was an unruly mess, her face bare of makeup, and her clothes rumpled and dirty. She looked nothing like the exotic beauty they made her out to be in the papers.

Jem didn't remark on it, if he noticed at all, except he did look at her with some concern. "Are you all right?" he asked. "What was going on back there? Did the two of you have a fight?"

Issa needed desperately to tie her hair up. It clung to her sweaty neck and made her itchy, though really her whole body felt like ants crawled all over her skin. She resisted the urge to claw at herself.

"Yes, we had a fight," she said, lacking a better answer.

"What happened?"

Her knee bounced. She glanced over her shoulder, almost screaming when a face appeared in the window, but it was just a woman waving to her friend, who sat waiting at the booth next to them.

Jem's hand rested on top of hers, stilling her fidgeting fingers. Issa took a deep breath.

"What do you know about the actress Ava Lin Rang?" she asked. She wasn't about to tell him everything—she knew how absurd it would sound, but she couldn't keep her mind on anything else, nor did she have much time. Ava was getting stronger. There wasn't much of Olivia left—the Olivia that Issa knew. Sweet, kind, generous, ambitious, yes, but not actually willing to hurt anyone to get what she wanted.

Jem leaned back, letting go of her hand. Issa felt vaguely empty, wishing he would continue comforting her with his touch. She sipped her coffee instead, cringing at its sour aftertaste.

"She used to be in the silents?" he asked.

Issa nodded.

"She was famous for a time, but . . . huh. I don't know what happened to her."

"Have you seen any of her films?" Issa asked.

"No. Why the interest? Are they doing a movie about her?"

That would have been an easy story to tell. But Issa couldn't bring herself to lie, not with so much to keep track of.

"I'm entangled with something," she said. "Involving her."

For a moment, Jem just studied her face. Issa didn't know what to say after that, how to explain the situation she found herself in. She watched the reflection in her coffee instead, the dark surface rippling with lines of light from the ceiling and walls, like a moving picture.

She looked up slowly as something occurred to her. At the same time, Jem spoke.

"They probably still have old reels of her movies in the archive."

She leaned forward. "Are we allowed to watch them?"

"Of course. We do it all the time—the writers—for research, or inspiration."

Issa put her coffee mug down. "Can you show me now?"

Jem gulped down the rest of his drink. "Sure, but do you think it will solve . . . whatever it is you're entangled in?"

Issa got out of the booth. "I have no idea."

Chapter Forty-Eight

Back on the MGM lot, Jem showed her to the bunker where they kept the archives of old films. It was close to the writers' cottages—Issa had passed it so many times not realizing what it was. A separate office building was situated at the front, where a man guarded the desk, noting which film they requested in a thick book before sending his assistant to fetch the reel.

"Can I see something starring Ava Lin Rang?" Issa asked him politely.

"Are you a studio employee?" the old man asked.

She showed him her employee card, but he still eyed her suspiciously.

"Come on, Reggie, you know me," Jem said. He sighed and took a business card out of his wallet. "Stop giving us a hard time. This is Issa Bui—you must have seen her in *Lost in the Queen's Love*. Don't deny it."

The old man snatched Jem's business card and studiously copied the details on it down in his book. Jem gave Issa a conspiratorial look, and she smiled back distractedly.

When the assistant returned with a large round box, Issa was surprised at how heavy it was, refusing Jem's offer to carry it for her.

Once outside, she looked around in case Ava-Olivia was waiting for her, but she didn't see the demon anywhere near. She hugged the large box against her body.

"How are you going to view that thing?" Jem asked. "You don't have a projector, do you? We have one in the writers' room. We usually have to book it in advance, but we can see if it's available now."

Not knowing what else to do, Issa nodded. "Thank you so much for your help, Jem."

He glanced at her as they walked, his expression a revealing and complicated mixture of emotions. Issa didn't have time to dissect it all.

"When this is all over," she said, forcing more cheer into her tone than she felt, "I promise I'll make it up to you."

He looked like he wanted to say something else, but decided against it, smiled, and shook his head. "I should have known better than to get involved with someone so beautiful."

"You think I'm beautiful?" Issa wasn't even fishing for a compliment, she was simply surprised. At the moment, she was aware that she resembled a hardworking peasant girl, which was not an entirely inaccurate way to describe who she really was, or at least, the line of women she came from. It was only through hard work—mostly in the hands of other people—that she resembled anything close to a star.

Jem raised his eyebrows at her. "You're really asking me that?"

"I . . . It's . . . it's nice to hear . . . something nice," she said, choking on a sob.

He took her hand as he led her into a cottage where the writers apparently sequestered themselves when working on a script or rewrite. In the first room, armchairs and tables had been set up with Underwoods, and a solo writer napped by the window. In the second room, a typewriter clacked away from behind a closed door.

They walked down a narrow hallway to a larger area dominated by a bulky projector in the center, with two rows of three chairs on each side in a makeshift theater.

"Good, no one's using it," Jem said. She finally let him take the box, which he set on one of the chairs to open. Inside, a large roll of black film wrapped around a metal canister with square holes cut into it. He adjusted the reel into the projector.

"Do you mind getting the light?" he asked.

Grateful for something to do, Issa clicked off the switch, marveling at how the white wall transformed into a silver screen. She took the seat next to Jem at the front to watch the movie.

As Ava's image appeared on-screen, Issa couldn't help appreciating the actress's talent. The way she knew how to hold her body, the careful display of emotions on her face. The acting style was different in her time, more exaggerated to make up for the lack of speech, which was shown through titles instead.

At the end of the movie, Issa had tears on her face. It wasn't the story that affected her—she had hardly paid attention, and anyway, the storylines were all the same, some love affair between a rich man who abused some poor girl in an attempt to win her affections, changing only slightly and deserving very little of his rewards in the end, while the female character existed solely to develop his arc.

But Ava's acting was phenomenal, and her potential was barely recognized in the movie. Issa cried because Ava was exactly the kind of actress Issa wanted to be—her talents, her looks, her everything. She could have been a true star, just like any of the other actresses Issa and Olivia had been obsessed with, had she been given half a fair chance. She might not have had to resort to whatever it was she'd had to do.

The reel ended. The projector kept whirring until Jem stood to turn it off.

Issa wiped at her tears and took in a deep breath. Her brief moment of rest was over. She had to figure out what to do next.

As Issa got out of the cab in front of her mother's apartment building, she couldn't stop looking over her shoulder. The hairs on the back of her neck stood on end, and that creeping feeling as if she were being watched remained with her as she walked up the steps. But she didn't spot Ava-Olivia anywhere, just a few of their neighbors sitting around and some people who looked like Auntie Yen's staff, hovering around corners as if they were standing guard.

Inside Ma's apartment, the air was full of incense smoke. Mirrors were propped up everywhere—some Issa recognized from her room. The large hallway mirror that Ma usually kept covered was exposed. Ma and Auntie Yen were nowhere in sight.

"Hello?" Issa called, setting the large film reel on the kitchen table. Her arms ached from carrying it so far. "Ma? Auntie Yen?"

"You're back already?" Bà Ngoại's voice sent Issa's heart racing. She peered out from the reflection of her photograph on the kitchen counter, a stick of incense releasing smoke in the air from where it sat in a bowl of rice grains.

"Bà Ngoại," Issa said with relief. "Where are Ma and Auntie Yen?"

"They went to get more supplies, and to see the damage the Uncles wreaked. What do you have there?"

Issa explained about Ava's film reel. "Do you think this would work? As a way to banish her? Instead of a portrait or something, we could use a whole movie." She would have to explain to the archivist at MGM what she did to his precious material, but she would deal with that problem later.

"It will work," Bà Ngoại said.

Issa rubbed her temples, a headache starting to throb along with her pulse.

A moment later, the front door opened, and Ma and Auntie Yen came in, carrying paper bags full of supplies.

"It's no good," Auntie Yen said when she saw Issa. "They've ransacked one of our liquor stores. We only just managed to lose them."

"The Uncles?" Issa asked, her chair scraping on the floor as she got up.

"They'll find us soon," Auntie Yen said. "I have my staff giving them the runaround, but we must go."

"What's that?" Ma asked, gesturing to the box on the kitchen table.

"We're going to use that to banish the demon," Issa explained. "It's one of Ava Lin Rang's more popular films. There must have been a hundred in the archive, so we'll have plenty of images with which to banish her."

"It's somewhat beautiful, isn't it," Auntie Yen said, despite the urgency. She opened the box, and they all admired the large roll within.

"And we are going to burn it," Bà Ngoại said with high-pitched glee.

But Auntie Yen frowned. "It won't be enough," she said to Issa. "You said Ava has reels and reels back at the studio."

"Yes, in the archives," Issa said. "She was in a lot of movies."

"That means someone can use a movie to conjure her again," Yen said.

It took a few seconds for the implication to settle over all of them.

Issa looked at Ma for help, but Ma's face was impassive and unreadable.

"You mean we have to steal all those movies?" Issa asked. "How?"

Yen was already moving toward the door. "No time for that. We'll talk about it on the way."

Chapter Forty-Nine

It was dark and the MGM lot was virtually deserted. Issa watched Auntie Yen's worker drive off, bracing herself for the tough night ahead while simultaneously wishing she could simply go home and return to her normal life.

"She's not going to stay in case we need to get away quickly again?" she asked.

"No, she has other things to do," Auntie Yen said. "Now, hurry, we need to do this before the Uncles catch up to us."

"Do you think they followed us here?"

Yen glanced sideways at her but didn't answer.

Ma ogled the buildings as they walked through the studio lot. Everything was closed, the darkness interrupted by the rare streetlamp casting long shadows over the gray pavement. It wasn't exactly glamorous, and Issa found herself wanting to defend the lot.

"You worked here?" Ma asked, her expression as serious as ever. Issa couldn't tell if she was impressed or horrified.

"I did," Issa said. "Before I moved to the other studio."

"It's so . . . big."

"Well, they are a big company."

"I had no idea." Ma's eyes glistened in the moonlight. "This is quite an accomplishment, isn't it?"

"I suppose so," Issa said. "It took us a long time to get here."

Us. Olivia. Who was no longer *there.*

Ma took Issa's hand. She didn't say anything, couldn't seem to find the right words, but she wrapped her other hand around Issa's as well, sending warmth over her fingers. Issa understood what she couldn't say, and patted Ma's hand with her other.

"That way to the archives," Issa said.

The front office was locked. Why wouldn't it be? It was close to midnight.

But that didn't stop Auntie Yen, who pulled a pin from her hair bun and began working on the knob. Issa looked around, convinced they'd be caught and kicked out, but no one roamed the studio this late.

"Oh my God," she said with relief when Yen pulled the door open.

It was pitch-black inside, and the sound of their breathing echoed off the concrete floors and walls. The smell of something sour hit her nostrils, like vinegar. No one had thought to bring a flashlight, but Ma had the sense to flick a match, which lit their way for a few seconds before it went out and she had to light a new one.

"Save some for the ritual," Auntie Yen said.

Ma nodded and handed the matches to Issa.

Issa had no idea how to find a reel of Ava's—earlier it had been as easy as asking the man at the front desk for it, though now that desk was empty. She went through the low swinging door and looked through the ledger. It was a huge tome, and several more filled the shelves behind the counter. Luckily, they were labeled by years, and she could still remember the date on Ava's trophy.

"It's in Bunker 27," she said, once she located the record.

They went back outside and found the door on the second floor of the storage building. Yen worked her magic once again with her pin.

When they stepped inside, they saw shelves upon shelves stacked with boxes. They followed the labels until they got to the shelf where Ava's movies should have been.

It was empty.

"No," Issa said. "This is it—it can't—they're all gone."

Ma and Auntie Yen stood looking up at the shelf, as if the reels would reappear by magic in the night. Dust swirled in the weak beam of light from the skylight above.

"Ava must have gotten to them first," Auntie Yen said. "After you attempted to banish her, she must have known you'd go after her reels. Maybe she followed you and took the others."

Issa balled her hands into fists. "Then let's go find them."

"Issa," Ma said, in that tone that mothers used when their children were being unreasonable, as if Issa were still five years old.

"What else can we do?" Issa asked, near tears. She was exhausted from lack of sleep. The events of the night weighed down her limbs, the adrenaline fueling her earlier now leaving her drained. She didn't want to go another day like this. Didn't think she had the energy for it.

Ma glanced at Auntie Yen, who nodded.

"We can take her on, if all three of us go together," Auntie Yen said.

Issa hurried away before they changed their minds.

It had gotten even darker outside, or perhaps it was her imagination. A stillness hung in the air, that eerie calm right before something catastrophic happened. The hairs on her arms rose, but she kept going, determined to end this, here and now. As they made their way to the living quarters of the studio lot, their shadows shifted and overlapped each other, like ghosts on a different plane.

Olivia's apartment was dark, the windows unlit. Issa didn't bother approaching quietly, bursting through the door.

Or at least, she tried to. Something blocked it. Boxes similar to the one she had carried earlier. Reels stolen from the archive warehouse.

Issa shouldered her way inside. She reached down to snatch a reel when she heard something. Olivia's laugh. Or rather, Ava's. Their mixed chuckle coming from just the other side of the door sent shivers down her spine.

"I've been waiting for you," that same doubled voice sang. The door slammed shut behind Issa. The lock clicked.

"Issa!" Ma shouted, banging on the door. "Issa, are you all right?"

"I'm fine, Ma!" Issa called back, fingers scrabbling to unlock it. A figure appeared at her side, dressed in flowy chiffon robes. The sleeves and hem trailed down, leaving wisps of fabric in the air like a sort of ghostly ectoplasm or smoky tendrils. Issa drew back.

It was Olivia—her body—but she seemed taller somehow, her figure towering over Issa. Or perhaps it was the shadows behind her, stretched like they were cast by some larger beast.

"Care to join me in a dance?" Ava-Olivia asked as she started twirling. Shadows moved on the wall, playing with the dim glow from the streetlights just outside the windows.

Issa would have run for it, but Ava-Olivia blocked the door, so she stepped back and nearly tripped over the many boxes cluttering the floor. She started for her old bedroom, but Ava-Olivia's shadow seemed to be everywhere at once. Olivia sneered at her. Her eyes looked different. Lost and empty.

"Stop it, Olivia," Issa snapped, hoping her best friend was inside there somewhere.

Ava shrieked in laughter. She grabbed Issa's wrists, her fingers ice cold, and swung her around in an imitation of a dance. Issa tried to break free, but Ava's grip was incredibly strong, and the longer she held on, the colder Issa grew. Her teeth chattered.

She collapsed to the floor when Ava let her go.

"Did you enjoy my movie?" Ava asked. "I could tell you did. I could feel it. Every time somebody cries, I know I stirred something in them. It takes a talented actress to invoke that sort of emotion, you know. But of course, you wouldn't know, would you? You were never half as talented as Olivia. You never made it as a star. You're not even a has-been. Just a failure."

Issa remained where she'd fallen, bracing her weight on her hands. She couldn't move, her limbs so cold, her fingers shaking.

"No wonder Olivia dropped you as soon as she found me," Ava continued.

Issa looked up. Something was different about Ava's voice. It no longer had the echo of Olivia's in it. Olivia was fading for good, and Ava was taking over completely. Even Olivia's face looked more like Ava's, the cheekbones slightly lowered, the chin not so pointed. Ava had always played the innocent, demure role, the roundness in her cheeks lending to her naivete. She really was a good actress. She had, after all, convinced them to trust her.

"Are these all your reels?" Issa asked, gesturing to the boxes littering the living room.

"Every last one. Did you think I'd leave them out there for you to find?"

"What good is hoarding them if having people watch you is what gives you power?"

Ava stopped to consider this. "Once I get rid of you, I'll make sure my movies are never forgotten."

A loud bang reverberated in the air outside, echoing for several seconds after. Issa ducked instinctively.

Even Ava looked mystified. "Was that a gun?" She fixed Issa with a delighted, maniacal grin. "My, my, you are full of chaos, aren't you?"

Issa spared a brief glance out the window. She couldn't see much other than dark sky and streetlights, but she heard her aunt cry out in dismay, followed by shouting. The Uncles must have found them.

"Olivia!" a man called from outside. It sounded like her uncle. "I know you're in there."

Issa squeezed her eyes shut.

"That horrid waste of a man," Ava said, recognizing his voice too. "I wanted to get rid of him, but Olivia refused. And look. He probably brought your uncles here."

For once, Issa agreed with Ava. "What would you have done to get rid of him?"

"What does it matter now? Your aunt will take care of him, or he'll take care of her. This is quite wonderful, actually. All my problems killing themselves off, and you, practically baring your neck in surrender." Ava laughed.

"Don't you think people will notice that Olivia is so different?" Issa asked. She felt so cold, her wrists like ice where Ava had touched her. She stuffed her hands in her pockets, her fingers wrapping automatically around a little paper booklet. Ma's matchsticks.

"Who cares," Ava snapped. "As if she was so distinguished. As if anyone will care about her. No one does. They barely cared about me. Haven't you noticed? Girls like us aren't meant to be remembered. We're to be used and cast off."

Hearing this hurt more because of how true it was. "But we do remember you," Issa protested. "I wanted to be exactly like you. I wanted to learn more from you—about you. The things you achieved. What happened, Ava?" Issa asked to distract Ava, but she was truly curious.

Ava snorted. "What always happens. My time was up."

"Just like that?"

"I made a deal with a demon. I was a star, and that was what I bargained for, and once I got what I wanted, it was over. You're so stupid," she added, as if unable to resist a chance to put Issa down. "You have all this knowledge at your disposal, all this power, yet you refuse to fulfill your true potential. Whereas I . . . I had no one looking out for me. Otherwise, I would have struck a better bargain."

"So it's true, then. You haven't really died. You just gave up your soul for fame?"

"Oh, don't act so superior, sweetheart. It's nothing short of exactly what you and Olivia were doing."

"Yes, but we didn't give up our souls."

"No, you were only willing to bargain with mine." Ava had moved closer. "I suppose I got what I wanted in the end. But it's not enough. I could have done so much better. I was getting more popular, more successful. But a deal is a deal, and I was young when I made it. Luckily for me, you two came around and gave me a second chance. But you were so stubborn, so cowardly. Too scared to go after what you really want. Olivia was more than willing. She offered herself to me, you know. Her blood and pain and heart. Our bond is unbreakable. Even stronger than yours ever was with her."

Issa's face crumpled. It was all true. Issa should have tried harder to stay close to Olivia. Prevent this from happening. "Ava please. Let Olivia go. She doesn't deserve this."

Ava laughed. "Deserve? What did she do to deserve anything? You both think you worked so hard, but the truth is you're just as privileged as the rest of them. You with your powerful grandmother who pulled strings to get you where you are. You don't deserve anything."

Issa shook her head, but she knew Ava wasn't lying. Issa and Olivia had gotten help every step of the way. Was she even good at what she did? She'd always enjoyed acting, but that didn't mean she was truly skilled at it. What if it was the magic in her veins? What if they'd only come so far because Ava had helped them, like she said? Even the role she'd been nominated for—Ava had whispered in the director's ear to convince him to cast Issa. Could it be that all their success was because of the demon? What if they were nothing without Ava?

"That doesn't mean you can take it from us," Issa said.

"I've no use for *you*," Ava said, pointing a sharp-nailed finger at Issa. "You can die now." Her face morphed, the skin growing sallow and grayish, veins darkening underneath.

"Ava, please," Issa begged, falling to her knees. "All right. All right, you don't have any use for me. So take me instead. Let Olivia go." The words came out before she'd really thought them through, but she was desperate. If Ava intended to kill her anyway, then at least Olivia could live. It should have been Issa all along, she should have sacrificed her own blood.

Ava paused. "You? Why would I want you? You're nobody, sweetheart. You don't even know who you are. You've been running from yourself all your life. What would I want with someone like that? And why would I settle for that"—Ava gestured at Issa's body—"when I can have this?" She held out her arms again.

"If that's true, then it would be easy to take me," Issa said. All her life, it had felt like other people were so sure of what they wanted. Even Olivia had always known who she was, who she would become, while Issa constantly felt lost. Maybe this was it then, her true calling. To give herself up so the people she loved could go on.

Ava only laughed. "Honestly, darling, I couldn't care less about you." She pulled herself up dramatically, her eyes darkening, the black irises growing wider until they covered the whites.

Issa didn't wait to find out what the demon intended to do. She pulled out her mother's matchsticks and lit one. Fingers trembling, she was surprised that it caught right away. She flung it at one of the boxes, where it immediately went out.

Ava laughed at Issa's pathetic attempt, but Issa ignored her, already lighting another one. She threw it to the carpet, the fibers catching almost instantly. She lit another one and another one, throwing each down as soon as the little flame came to life.

The demon rounded on her. "What are you doing?" she demanded.

Issa threw her last matchstick at an open box, where the strip of a reel peeked through. "I'm getting rid of you," she said.

Ava threw herself on Issa.

It was like having a bucket of ice flung over her head. Ava wrapped her freezing arms around Issa, and Issa screamed, because where their flesh touched, her skin burned. The demon's shriek joined hers as flames grew higher around them, licking at her robes, sending tendrils of smoke into the air.

Issa pulled Ava away as the walls caught on fire. She didn't care about Ava, but she couldn't stand to see Olivia's body getting hurt.

Ava slashed out, her nails catching on Issa's face. It stung, but Issa didn't have time to worry about the damage as the flames grew higher. The drapes caught fire, and after that, it seemed like the whole dressing room was torched. Issa fell against the sofa, rolling over as Ava lunged for her. Her hip hit the side table where Ava's Oscar had once sat, knocking over a bright-yellow mug, the tea leaves inside curled and dry. They scattered to the floor.

Issa looked up at Ava. "Ava Lin Rang," she said, her voice hoarse from the smoke collecting in the enclosed space. "Go away. Leave us alone."

Ava shrieked.

Someone banged on the door, but it was blocked by burning boxes. Ava threw herself on top of the flames, as if she could use her body to salvage the reels. Issa tried to grab her, but each time she did, the demon hissed and gnashed her teeth. Her skin bubbled, as if it were melting along with the reels. Olivia's lovely face . . . her skin inflamed with pustules, her eyes growing bloodshot.

"Ava Lin Rang," Issa croaked again. "Go away. Leave us alone."

The smell of everything burning made Issa dizzy.

She had to get out of the apartment. They both did. But how?

She heard banging on the door, shouting from the outside.

The window. Issa made her way there and tried to push it open but screamed, snatching her hand back from the searing glass. She looked around for something to smash it with, almost laughing hysterically when she spotted the base of the trophy Ava had wanted so badly. She must have taken it back with her earlier.

With no other choice, Issa grabbed it and smashed it against the pane.

Shards cut her as she tried to pull herself through. She was almost out, the breath of fresh air enough to rejuvenate her.

Ava grabbed her from behind.

"Ma!" Issa screamed. She gripped the windowsill, blood dripping as the glass bit into her hands.

"You jealous bitch!" Ava screamed at her as she pulled Issa back inside. "You couldn't deal with Olivia being more successful than you, so you had to ruin everything for everyone. You had to destroy our chance of happiness!"

"We were happy," Issa gasped, falling back against the wall. Flames grew in all the corners of the apartment, getting close to them. Ava didn't seem to care anymore, letting her body take the damage. It wasn't her body, anyway. "Without you. Before you. Olivia and I were happy."

Ava laughed. And then her laughter turned into sobs. Issa thought she could hear Olivia's sweet voice in there somewhere.

"Olivia," Issa said, taking Olivia's hand. Still ice cold despite the fire. "Olivia, please. Come back. I just want us. The way things were. Who cares about the rest?"

Ava jerked her hand away. She stood tall, her eyes black.

"Ava Lin Rang," Issa sobbed, exhausted. "Leave us alone." She didn't want to fight anymore. It would be so easy to let the fire consume them. What was the point of it all, anyway? What would be left once the ashes were swept clean? Just two girls who were too ambitious for their own good.

"Issa!" Ma called from outside.

Issa blinked. Time stood still. Ava was nothing but a dark figure, a shadow enveloping the light around her, as if she were absorbing the flames. Around her, film reels burned and curled as they melted. One had escaped the onslaught, just beyond a wall of fire. Issa jerked away and kicked it, sending it into the flames.

"Ava Lin Rang!" she shouted as loudly as she could, her throat scratchy from the smoke. "Leave me and my friend alone!"

Ava shrieked. She thrashed around, a shadow monster. It was horrible to watch, the screaming going on and on forever, like watching something small and helpless drowning. But Ava was far from helpless.

Then whatever it was, whatever was left of her, crumpled.

Issa caught Olivia in her arms. Her best friend was limp and so light, it was almost easy to drag her over to the window. But Issa was too weak to pull both of them through. Every time she sucked in a breath, her lungs constricted, and her body racked with coughs so intense that she doubled over and felt completely drained after. The smoke was too thick. She could hardly see or open her eyes without them burning from the dry heat. She would fail, and it seemed only apt, considering everything else she'd done with her life.

Ma's hands. Taking Olivia away. Ma's face, her mouth speaking words Issa couldn't hear. And then Auntie Yen was there, and more of their clan, women reaching forward to pull Issa through the window. Something fell behind her, the ceiling beam, the walls caving in. Their dressing room falling to pieces.

"Olivia?" Issa asked as soon as she could gather enough breath.

"She's fine," Ma said. "She'll be fine."

And that was all Issa cared about.

Chapter Fifty

They blamed everything on the gang war, which had been in the news for so long that they didn't have trouble convincing everyone. Auntie Yen and her clan had time to get away while Issa and Ma stayed behind, caring for Olivia who was still unconscious, until the authorities showed up.

Issa ducked her head, trying not to look at the bodies strewn along the paths around the buildings. Most of them the Uncles who, Issa learned from Ma, had followed them to the studio ready for an attack, led there by Olivia's uncle, just as Ava had predicted. What they hadn't counted on was that Auntie Yen had sent her driver off to round up the other Left Tusks, and so the Uncles unknowingly walked into an ambush. Olivia's uncle had been caught up in the fight, and Issa was relieved for Olivia's sake.

The fire spread to the neighboring buildings, and by the time the firefighters arrived, most of the inhabitants had rushed outside to watch the destruction. They all exclaimed over Issa and Olivia, whose face was covered in severe burns. Issa didn't know if it was damage from the fire or a result of Ava's possession, and couldn't bring herself to think about the permanent scarring. She could only imagine what her own face looked like from the horrified reactions of everyone who looked at her.

They were taken to the hospital, where several police officers questioned her and Ma. Issa told the story Auntie Yen had come up with—Issa and Ma were visiting Olivia when they heard gunshots and fighting outside, and saw the Uncles set fire to the dressing rooms. No, she didn't know why.

The fact that she was a small, demure-looking young Asian woman added to the helplessness they must have perceived in her, because after a few perfunctory questions, they left her alone.

Issa had asked to share a room with Olivia, who remained unconscious, a curtain separating their beds. Ma came in after her own checkup. Because Auntie Yen had kept her safe during the altercation, other than a few minor scrapes, she was unhurt.

"How are you doing?" Ma asked, sitting in the armchair in the corner of the room.

"Fine," Issa said. It felt like a lie, with how tired she was, her body wrung out and inflamed, covered in bandages.

Ma didn't push beyond that, only reaching out to touch her gently on her hand. Neither of them talked, and Issa eventually fell into the deepest sleep she'd had in months.

When she woke, Ma was gone. She pulled back the curtain dividing the room, relieved to see Olivia still in bed. Her face was covered in bandages so that only her eyes and nose were exposed. Issa fought back tears.

Later that day, she asked the nurses for a mirror, which they reluctantly provided for her. When she saw her reflection, she was both dismayed and relieved. She had a dark bruise on one cheek and her skin looked red and scabbed, but she didn't think it would scar, and even if it did, makeup would cover most of it.

Olivia didn't wake up. Even after a week had passed and the doctors proclaimed Issa well enough to go home, her best friend continued sleeping.

"What's wrong with her?" Issa asked when Auntie Yen came to pick her up on her last day at the hospital. "Is she . . . gone?"

Olivia wasn't dead, but Yen knew what Issa was really asking. Instead of answering, she put a hand on Issa's back, a gesture meant to console Issa that didn't work at all.

Issa went to stay with Ma. Her Warner Bros. apartment had never felt like home, and she desperately needed to be with people who cared about her. She spent most of her days at the hospital by Olivia's bedside, willing her friend to open her eyes.

Eventually, she had to call Larry Mager. "I can't do the movie right now," she said. As soon as she said the words, she knew she'd made the right decision. She should have never agreed to it in the first place. She should have chosen Olivia.

"I heard about the fire," he said. "We can delay production for a while. Take the time you need."

She was grateful for the reprieve but couldn't think much beyond the next few days. Though Olivia remained in a coma, the nurses unwrapped her bandages. The scars made little pockmarks on her beautiful face, but over time, they might fade to charming freckles, and there was nothing that makeup couldn't cover. Issa was sure of it. Still, she wept over the damage when she applied the salve the nurses allowed her to help with.

Auntie Yen's building repairs were underway, so she set up shop at a different location, a larger house in Chinatown where Ma and Issa sometimes visited. One day, they conjured Bà Ngoại and Dead Auntie Phi in the new mirror room.

"She's certainly not here," Bà Ngoại said when Issa asked about Olivia. "She's not gone yet. There's still hope."

"Ava said that the bond they shared was unbreakable," Issa said.

"Olivia's blood gave Ava the power she needed to appear at will, without your summons. The amount she must have given . . . no wonder Ava grew so strong."

"But does that mean that Ava still has a hold on her? Could she have dragged her with her, wherever she went?"

"Once you banish the demon, the connection is broken."

"So why isn't Olivia better?"

"I don't know, Issa girl. We just have to wait. Give her time to heal."

"What can I do?" Issa asked. "How can I bring her back?"

"Talk to her," Bà Ngoại said. "She'll hear you."

It couldn't be that simple. "Isn't there a spell I can do, some ritual that will heal her faster?"

Ma took her hand. From Auntie Yen's face, Phi's sympathetic expression, and Bà Ngoại for once looking sad instead of angry or determined, Issa knew what the answer was.

"And what about Ava?" Issa asked. "Can she come back?"

Tense silence followed this.

"You're not thinking of conjuring her again?" Ma asked.

"Of course not. But . . . is she there?"

"Her soul was never meant to be here to begin with," Bà Ngoại said. "When you banished her, she went elsewhere."

"Where?"

"No one knows, Issa," Bà Ngoại said. "Perhaps she's gone for good."

Issa went back to her old apartment one day to pick up the rest of her things, and was just about to leave when the phone rang.

"Oh, you picked up," came Jem Meier's familiar voice. "I've been trying every day. How are you?"

"I'm . . . I'm fine," she said. She wasn't sure if she was, but she had already put him through so much. "How are you?"

"I'm great."

There was an awkward pause.

"I'm so grateful for everything you've done for me," Issa started to say, but he spoke at the same time.

"I know this is a terrible imposition." He paused, then added. "You go ahead."

"No, it's all right. What were you saying?"

"You can say no. You can absolutely say no. I know what you've been through, and I heard about Olivia, so please don't feel like you owe me any favors."

"Jem, please," she said. She owed him a ton of favors. "Anything."

He hesitated. "There's a script I've written. For you."

Issa smiled slowly, enjoying the sensation. "You wrote me a script?" She had only been joking when she'd suggested it so long ago.

"I think it'd be perfect for you. About two . . . friends."

For a moment, Issa's heart stuttered. She didn't want to think about movies right now. It was what had gotten her into this whole mess in the first place. But then her pulse picked up, and her curiosity got the better of her.

She switched the phone to her other ear. "I'd love to read it."

"Really?" Jem's smile was evident in his voice. "That's . . . that's great. But again, you don't have to if you don't want to."

She laughed. "I know."

"I'll have it sent over. Unless . . . can I see you?"

She gripped the phone. "Sure. But I don't have much time."

That was a lie. She had plenty of time. She just didn't want Olivia to wake when she wasn't there.

But when she saw Jem, she was surprised by how much her spirits lifted. They met at a local café where he handed over the script without preamble and they chatted briefly about nothing in particular. Afterward, she had no recollection of what they talked about, but a great weight lifted from her chest, and when his arms wrapped around her in a comforting hug goodbye, she leaned into him and breathed in the scent of his aftershave, and felt as if her soul had been soothed.

When she got to the hospital, the nurse stopped Issa at the desk.

"She doesn't want to see you," the nurse said.

"She's awake?"

"She woke this morning."

Issa was about to rush down the hall. Of course, the one *moment* she decided to take for herself, Olivia woke up.

The nurse put out her arm before Issa could get far. "Darling, I'm sorry, but she asked us not to let you in."

"What do you mean?" Issa's eyes burned, the beginning of an onslaught of tears. "But—I've been seeing her all this time."

"I know, doll." The nurse smiled with sympathy. "But you're not family and . . . she requested specifically to be left alone."

"She asked specifically to not let *me* in? Me?" Issa pointed at her chest. "Are you certain?"

The nurse nodded.

Issa's expression crumpled. She had spent enough time in front of the camera to know that it was not a pretty thing, the flesh of her face folding in unseemly creases, her eyebrows tensing to form wrinkles over her forehead. She knew she shouldn't care—her heart was heavy with the knowledge that Olivia had turned her away, rejected and abandoned her, after all they'd been through—but her hand went up to cover her mouth anyway. She forced the muscles to relax, to smooth out, to spread into a serene and calm smile.

"Oh, sweetheart." The nurse tried to hug Issa, but she shied away.

"Th-thank you," she managed. She swallowed a few times before she could bring herself to ask, "Do you know when she'll be allowed to leave?"

"She seems to be recovering well. Perhaps in the next day or two."

Issa sat on the streetcar, not getting off at the stop to transfer to Auntie Yen's house, instead traveling the routes that she'd so often taken with Olivia—as schoolchildren, as explorers, and finally in pursuit of a dream she was no longer sure of anymore. Issa loved acting, but she'd had to give up so much.

Was she willing to sacrifice more? Because that was what it would entail. Every movie asked for a bigger part of her, a deeper part of her, and it wasn't that she wasn't willing to give it. It was simply that she didn't want to lose anyone else in her life, anyone she cared about.

Thinking of her stardom was easier than analyzing her friendship with Olivia. The wound was too fresh, the scab unformed. Their relationship had been deep, and its destruction felt like part of her soul had been ripped out through her throat.

So she clutched Jem's script instead. For hours, the trolley went back and forth on its route, and Issa sat on the vinyl bench and read. When she laughed at a particularly funny part, a balm spread over her chest, and she finally looked up. The sky had darkened. Only a handful of other passengers remained.

A man smiled at her over the top of his newspaper, his hat shadowing his eyes, but he looked down as soon as she noticed him. He must be one of Auntie Yen's workers, keeping a careful watch on her after the incidents with the Uncles, who, Issa had learned, were no more. Too many of them had died—the powerful ones, anyway—for the gang to continue, and Auntie Yen, though weak, was working to regain control.

When Issa finally finished the script, she hopped down from the Red Car and flagged a cab to Yen's new house. A woman opened the door and led Issa to Yen's office, where she was communing with a few others.

"I'm sorry," Issa said. "I'll come back later."

"No, we were just finishing." Yen nodded at a man, and the others all filed out, leaving Issa alone with her aunt. "What is it? Not more trouble?" There was a twinkle in Yen's eye.

"I think I've had enough trouble to last a lifetime. And beyond," Issa said.

"A wise choice."

Issa held up a script. "I've just read the most marvelous story. It was . . . well, it was written for me. So I suppose I'm biased, but . . . I was wondering."

Yen raised her brows.

"Would you fund it?" Issa blurted out. "I would contribute as well, of course, and I don't know the first thing about producing, but I'm sure I can find the right people. And we can keep the budget low. I can . . . I can make it work . . . with your help."

Yen's mouth opened in surprise. "Fund . . . a movie?"

"Why not?" Issa laughed. "Movies have a lot of power, you know. You could influence thousands of people, generations of young minds. Spread your ideas."

Yen laughed. She picked up a pen from her desk. "You do know your audience."

"In exchange . . . I'll commit to the family. Formally, I mean, just like Bà Ngoại wanted. But I want to make things as legitimate as possible, once I take over. I think producing a movie would be a good start." She would figure the rest out later, but Auntie Yen was here to help her, and she had Ma on her side now.

Yen smiled as she considered the proposal.

"Is that a yes?" Issa asked, breathing quickly.

"How about," Yen said, "we discuss it some more?"

She had a lot of work to do. Issa spent much of her time on the phone, but first she had to talk to Mager to dissolve her contract with Warner Bros. and MGM. In the end, she managed to strike a deal in which both companies would lend her to Auntie Yen's newly formed independent studio, Silver Glass. She talked to several producers and managed to get Maggie Laken on board to play a supporting part, as well as a number of former castmates.

"You're sure you want to ask Eric Goldman to direct?" Jem asked her as they headed to MGM one day. "He's known to be crotchety."

"He helped us so much at first," she said. "He believed in us when no one else did." Granted, with Ava's persuasion, but Issa didn't care to mention that. She would make it up to Goldman however she could.

Goldman spent much too long perusing the script, but when he closed it, he heaved a sigh. "Fine," he said. "But I've got two more films with MGM before I can take this on."

"At the rate you go, you'll be done by next month," Issa said. It was an exaggeration, but Issa needed more time to search for a costar anyway, someone to fill the role of the second friend.

He rubbed his eyes. "This job will kill me one day, I just know it." He grimaced at her, but she saw a trace of a smile behind it. "Yet I wouldn't want to do anything else."

News traveled fast in the industry, so it didn't surprise Issa to learn that Olivia had reneged on her contract with MGM. No one had heard from her directly—not Grenier or Goldman or any of the producers and directors she'd worked with. Since Issa wasn't technically family, the hospital wouldn't give her any information on where Olivia went after she was released. It was as if she'd vanished.

Just like Ava.

Issa put off the casting, stalling for time. She watched screen tests of actresses the producers recommended, and they were wonderful, some of them newcomers, reminding Issa of her earlier days. But they weren't right for the part. Because there was only one person she could picture in the role, and Olivia refused to be found.

"Issa," Jem said to her one night at dinner after a long day of discussing a critical rewrite in the script. "Perhaps it's time to decide on someone new. Aurora Hoa seemed like a good fit, and you would be supporting a new actress."

Issa had liked Aurora, a young woman with cherubic cheeks and a lovely heart-shaped mouth that made her a plausible, adorable younger-sister type. "All right," she said. "I'll call her tomorrow."

But Issa had trouble sleeping, tossing and turning as she pictured Aurora in the role. It didn't seem right to her, but she forced the image to play out, made her mind acquiesce to the decision. Frustrated that she couldn't get any rest, she got up and put on something warm, a winter astrakhan fur coat that was usually too thick for Los Angeles weather but perfect for a midnight stroll.

She had the urge to walk . . . to visit all the places she used to frequent with Olivia, as if retracing the steps of their childhood would help her find her friend. Or at least some sort of answer.

She stopped in front of the theater they'd gone to that first time, sixteen and young and feeling flush from the dollar in her pocket. The moment that had started it all. She went to the ticket window, but it was closed. The last showing had just finished. A crowd exited the doors as she pocketed her wallet and hugged her coat to herself in the abnormally cold night.

And that was when she spotted her. Olivia. Walking out the door in a worn jacket so unlike the posh things she used to wear that Issa didn't recognize her at first. Olivia had cut her hair short as well, the blunt shape hitting just above her chin, making her jaw look more prominent and changing the effect of her face to something harsh and angular. Or perhaps she really had changed in the past few months. Thinner. Sharper.

"Olivia," Issa breathed out. She said it so quietly that she doubted anyone could hear, but Olivia turned her head. She didn't spot Issa right away, so Issa stepped in front of her path. "Olivia."

Her friend stopped. Slowly, her gaze moved upward until it finally met Issa's. For a moment, neither of them said anything. Olivia's jaw clenched, but Issa knew her enough to understand that Olivia wasn't angry. Instead, she was hardening herself to keep from crying.

Without another word, Issa threw her arms around Olivia's shoulders, squeezing the two of them together until neither could breathe.

They went to a nearby café, open at all hours of the night and popular among the night shift of entertainers, musicians, and comedians.

"I missed you," Issa said, warming her hands on a mug of hot chocolate.

Olivia didn't say anything in return, and Issa studied her anxious face. Olivia's lips were pinched, her eyes downcast like she was trying hard not to cry.

"I'm sorry," Olivia choked out eventually.

"What? Why? *I'm* sorry. I'm the one who brought all of . . . that into our lives."

Olivia's lower lip quivered. "I'm the one who wasn't strong enough to fight her."

The *her* hung between them.

"We didn't know we had to fight her," Issa said. "Ava . . ." Olivia flinched, and Issa struggled not to. ". . . was our friend."

Olivia sucked in a breath. She gasped a few times, on the cusp of a sob, and finally managed, "She really was, wasn't she?"

Issa pressed her lips together. Olivia had been so much closer to Ava. The ghost's betrayal likely hurt her so much more. "She helped us. We wouldn't have gotten so far without her."

Olivia's throat bobbed as she swallowed a few times. She'd only ordered a tea, which she ignored, steam floating from the surface like smoke. "I miss her." Olivia finally met Issa's eyes. "I know . . . I know what she did . . . But still. The before. Even if it was fake. For me, it was real."

Issa nodded. Like a movie, a fictional story, Ava's friendship might have been a calculated one, but it had still mattered to the two of them. They were irrevocably changed in its aftermath.

"I've missed both of you," Olivia said.

Issa's smile wavered. "I wasn't there for you. I was so selfish, wanting my own career."

"There's nothing selfish about that. We worked so hard for this." Olivia smiled sadly. "It was both our faults."

"It really was, wasn't it?"

Olivia reached for her hand. Her skin felt soft and papery, the fingers bonier than Issa remembered.

"You saved me," Olivia said, a strange quality in her voice as if she couldn't quite believe it. "You came back."

"Of course I did," Issa said. "Do you think Ava would have left me alone afterward?"

"I suppose not. She would have cleaned you up, like evidence."

"And obviously I cared about you, silly," Issa said. "I can't believe you didn't think I would try everything I could to save you. I banished a whole demon. I spent an entire day in the library."

Olivia smiled. "I guess, I just . . . I still find it hard to believe."

"What?"

"That anyone really cares about me that much. You've always been so . . . selfless. I owe you so much. I think that's why . . . with Ava . . . I knew what she wanted. I could buy her friendship, I knew exactly how. But with you . . . you've never really asked for anything, and I've always felt like such a burden to you and your mom and—"

Issa squeezed her hand. "Olivia—"

"No, listen," Olivia interrupted her. Her breath hitched on a sob. "I knew what Ava wanted. She never tricked me. I struggled at first—you remember—with the acting, and I needed her help, more than just her coaching. At first, all she asked for was blood, along with the pain sacrifice. Dead Auntie Phi taught it to me—please don't blame her. I begged her for it." Olivia held out her arms, covered in silvery scars. "It hurt, but it was worth it, and they healed quickly. I didn't think anything of it. But then Ava insisted that I could do better, that she would help make me a star. She told me that she would take over my body, just for some scenes I struggled with, and I agreed. I didn't think . . . I mean, I didn't know she planned to possess me completely, but perhaps . . . I ignored all the signs. The more blood I gave her, the more she wanted, the stronger it would make her, and the *better* I would feel—on the set and about myself. I had someone, someone who was there just for me. I'd never had that before—and no, please don't feel bad, Issa. You can't be that for me."

"But I should have. I could have stopped all this."

"You're your own person. What I mean is, you've always had your mom. You're the most important person to her. I've never been important to anyone, not in that way. When you were contracted to WB, I felt so alone . . . I didn't know if I could be as successful without you. I think that was when Ava really got into my head. She was so angry—I think she needed to be close to you. Not all the time, but the longer we went away from you, the more blood she'd need."

"Is that why you . . . she . . . you both got so upset when MGM leased me to WB?"

"Yes." Olivia looked down. "I'm sorry. I wish I can say that I wasn't myself, but the truth is, I was so hurt . . . so worried about what I would do without you. And she used it. She would say things . . . how she was always there for me when you weren't. How no one would care for me as much as her. How I wouldn't get anywhere without her help, and she would never ever leave me. None of them were true, but I was so distraught. I let her . . . When she offered to help more and more, to take over, it was almost easy to give in at first. It was comforting, in a way, to let someone else control my life. You don't know what it was like, Issa. Not that you would ever allow yourself to be possessed like that, but Ava . . . She's so confident. She loves herself. I'd never felt that way before, and when she . . . when she was here"—Olivia touched her chest—"it was such a relief to not feel so . . . unwanted. So alone. To not feel like . . . me."

"Olivia," Issa said, but she couldn't form the right words in response to Olivia's vulnerability.

"My own parents didn't want me. They abandoned me. Left me with an uncle who wasn't even a real uncle, just a roommate who got stuck with me."

"I thought your parents died."

"They died after. Isn't that pathetic? They abandoned me, *by choice*. They came to visit a few times, but then they stopped coming, and I learned—my uncle told me they died in a Cadillac accident. So of course I thought it was a car crash." Olivia gave a humorless laugh. "He meant cocaine—it's what they call it sometimes."

Issa bit her lip to keep from crying. "What a horrible man."

"He still took care of me, though."

"No he didn't, Olivia, he abused you."

"He was the only one who cared. That rotten piece of human garbage. The only person willing to take me in. What does that say about me?"

"That the world is full of trash and that you're one of the few beautiful things in it."

Olivia burst into tears.

Issa went around to Olivia's side of the table and wrapped an arm around her. No one else in the café paid them any attention—they were probably used to seeing people in tears over some rejection or another. "Olivia, you mean everything to me. You're—" She was about to say *like a sister*, but that seemed too trivial. They had said it so many times that it didn't mean much anymore, and it wasn't enough. "You're like my soulmate."

Olivia covered her face with her hands.

"I wouldn't be anywhere without you," Issa continued. "I wouldn't be here. I wouldn't . . . *be*. Ma was right, you know, or sort of. We don't have to be stars. It's all right to be nobodies, as long as we're somebodies to someone."

She ran out of words to express what Olivia's friendship really meant to her, and Olivia didn't seem to know what to say, either, so she patted Issa's hand with hers.

"There's still something we need to do," Issa said.

"What?" Olivia asked.

"I think it's better if I show you."

Issa kept the last of Ava's film reels in a box in Auntie Yen's home. It was the safest place she could think of. She and Olivia stared at it, sitting on the floor of the closet in the room Issa sometimes stayed in.

Issa knew what she had to do. Had known the moment she'd returned home after the night of the fire and discovered the box still sitting on Ma's kitchen table, where they'd forgotten about it. She just hadn't been able to do it alone.

Now she reached down and picked it up.

Yen had a backyard behind her new house, which was outfitted with a lovely seating area—used mainly for meeting with her coconspirators—and a firepit dug into the ground. They went out, and Issa tossed the box into the hole, ash from the previous bonfires bursting into the air. Then she stepped back and stood next to Olivia.

Olivia took a deep breath as if she wanted to say something. But she didn't, and Issa didn't offer any words of her own, even though the suggestion hung in the air, unheard. Could they? One last time? Find out why Ava had betrayed them? Had her friendship all been a calculation? Had she cared about them at any point?

But even if they conjured her, Issa wasn't sure Ava would come back. Bà Ngoại had told Issa that Ava was no longer there, in that other realm. She was gone. Maybe not for good, but for now. She was to them, anyway.

It didn't matter anymore, because in the next second, Olivia pulled out a cigarette and lit it. Instead of putting out her match, she tossed it onto the reel. The flame flickered and then snuffed out. Issa was about to light one as well, but then Olivia took her cigarette and tossed that in too. Embers caught on the cardboard, and that was all it took. Soon a blaze roared in the firepit.

Olivia reached for Issa's hand. They stood there like two small girls. Sisters. Watching the silver smoke rise into the air, glistening in the moonlight like slivers of glass.

"Do you still want it?" Issa asked eventually.

Olivia wiped at the tear that had welled out of her eyes. "Want what?"

"The stardom. The fame. You know . . . all of it."

Olivia took her time considering. "Not as much as I want us to remain the same."

"Not exactly the same," Issa pointed out. "Not always. We're going to change . . . that's part of life. Discovering who we are, and rediscovering with each new year . . . or moment . . ." Issa had thought something was wrong with her for not knowing who she was or what she wanted, but now she understood that it wouldn't have mattered. She wouldn't have stayed that person anyway, and she probably wouldn't in the future. She wasn't some character in a movie, immortalized, her story unchanging. She was real, and her future, her life, had no stage direction.

Perhaps that should have frightened her. But Issa wasn't afraid anymore. There was little that scared her now. And there was freedom in the unknown, in the wisdom that she could reinvent herself whenever she chose, to learn and grow how she saw fit. It was frightening and exhilarating and a great relief all at once.

"But still," Olivia said. "Still us."

"Yes. Us first."

"Always."

"Always," Issa agreed.

"Then yes. I do. I still want it all."

"Good." Issa squeezed her hand. Olivia squeezed back. "I'm glad to hear it. Because there's this amazing script. And we're absolutely perfect for it."

Acknowledgments

As usual, this book wouldn't exist without the support of my unicorn-witch-agent Mary C. Moore. My books are always stronger with your guidance. Absolute heartfelt thanks to Adrienne Procaccini for believing in this story from its very beginning, and to Jodi Warshaw for always being so thorough and kind as you work your magic to bring this story to life. To Laura Van der Veer for your wonderful support, and the team at 47North for once again making my dreams come true.

Thank you to Adrian Garza for braving K-Town parking nightmares and getting me through Saturday writing sessions; Kylie Lee Baker for listening to my writing woes and reading a horrendous early draft of this during the busiest month of the year amid your own impending deadlines; Kristen Schmitt for your kind, insightful, and helpful feedback; Gracie Marsden for your fangirl live texting; and Yume Kitasei for your virtual library with its secret passageways.

Most of my research was made possible by authors like Daniel Spoto, whose biographies illuminated my understanding of complicated starlets and their lives. Thanks also to Graham Russell Gao Hodges's biography *Anna May Wong: From Laundryman's Daughter to Hollywood Legend* for bringing to light what it must have been like to be an Asian star during Old Hollywood. I'm eternally grateful to Karina Longworth's podcast *You Must Remember This* for its accessible yet thoroughly researched episodes on the era. The descriptions of the film studios were made possible by the book *M-G-M.: Hollywood's Greatest*

Backlot by Steven Bingen, Stephen X. Sylvester, and Michael Troyan; and *Warner Bros.: Hollywood's Ultimate Backlot* by Steven Bingen.

I love this book, I really do, but I suffered no small amount of anxiety during its drafting and could not have survived without the support of the staff at Huntington Beach Public Library. Thank you thank you to Dina Chavez for that lovely 1950s-themed afternoon tea and giving me the excuse to buy a pillbox hat, Laura Jenkins for our Friday night vent fests, Nick Auricchio for wearing pink on Wednesdays, Amy Crepeau for all the mochi, Jessica Framson for always having the time to chat no matter how busy you are, Melissa Ronning for being around to solve my problems, April Lammers for giving me e-book purchasing power, Marissa Chamberlain for rescuing the 1930s fashion book from the weeds, Christany Edwards for the easy s'mores and jug of boba, Andrea Sward for such lovely encouragement, Lucy Lu for our pirate adventure, and Caroline Yin for always listening to me jabber on about my life. And thank you to all the library staff at HBPL and all the librarians, parents, teachers, and community members everywhere for fighting for everyone's right to access the books they need and saving the world one story at a time.

Thank you to my book club members for our lively discussions every month: Alyse Hendrick, Diane Pavesic, Sharolyn and Jennifer Pendleton, Melissa G., Maggie Ratanapratum, Melanie Bergeland, Laura Steingard, Melissa Koller Nielsen, Claudia Bennett, Naomi Abeywickrama, Marie Murphy, Gloria, Jane, Teresa, Theresa, Marcela Curtiss, Jacquelyn, Cassie, Bonnie, and Elizabeth. To Kitty Rozenstraten for all the vinyls that have transported me back in time through the decades. To the entire Wise Owl Tween Book Club for making me laugh even though you're too young to be reading this.

To Lety Aceves, without whom I would never get anything done. Last but not least, to my husband for all the support and for helping me foster a creative life, and to our little star for making it all worth it. There will never be enough words, so heart heart heart, cartwheel, cake, fireworks, witch hat, mirror, candle, kiss, jazzy huggy hands, tearing, crying, sobbing.

About the Author

Photo © 2022 Franscisco J. Zuniga

Van Hoang's first name is pronounced like the "van" in "minivan." Her last name is pronounced "hah-wawng." The author of *The Monstrous Misses Mai*, Van earned her bachelor's in English at the University of New Mexico and her master's in library information science at San José State University. She was born in Vietnam; grew up in Orange County, California; and now resides in Los Angeles with her husband, kid, and two dogs. For more information, visit www.authorvanhoang.com.